A TERRIBLE Beauty

Nancy Baker

VIKING

VIKING
Published by the Penguin Group
Penguin Books Canada Ltd, 10 Alcorn Avenue, Toronto, Ontario, Canada
M4V 3B2
Penguin Books Ltd, 27 Wrights Lane, London W8 5TZ, England
Viking Penguin, a division of Penguin Books USA Inc., 375 Hudson Street,
New York, New York 10014, U.S.A.
Penguin Books Australia Ltd, Ringwood, Victoria, Australia
Penguin Books (NZ) Ltd, 182–190 Wairau Road, Auckland 10, New
Zealand

Penguin Books Ltd, Registered Offices: Harmondsworth, Middlesex,
England

First published 1996
10 9 8 7 6 5 4 3 2 1

*Publisher's note: This book is a work of fiction. Names, characters, places and
incidents either are the product of the author's imagination or are used fictitiously,
and any resemblance to actual persons living or dead, events or locales is entirely
coincidental.*

Printed and bound in Canada on acid free paper ∞

Canadian Cataloguing in Publication Data

Baker, Nancy, 1959-
  A terrible beauty

ISBN 0-670-86826-4

I. Title.

PS8553.A3844T46 1996   C813'.54   C95-932120-9
PR9199.3.B35T46 1996

For my parents,
who showed me the kingdom
and gave me the keys

Acknowledgements

As usual, inspiration, ideas and support were provided by a number of people who deserve credit. Kim Kofmel's insights and suggestions greatly enriched the book. David Wright endured my whining protestations that I was a writer not an artist and did his best to teach me the basics of oil painting. I hope that he will forgive me for making it look much easier than it really is (and for radically reducing the amount of time it takes oil paint to dry). Bram Djikstra's fascinating book, *Idols of Perversity*, provided the core of the paintings and insight into the emotions behind them. The enthusiasm of my editor, Cynthia Good, helped me to believe in the story from the beginning. Most of the book was written to the sounds of Sarah Mclachlan, whose *Fumbling Towards Ecstasy* provided the best soundtrack I could ever have imagined. Last and never least is my husband, Richard Shallhorn, who went through it all again with his usual humour and love.

A TERRIBLE Beauty

Chapter 1

The letter lay among the others on the hall table for three days. Then the housekeeper moved it to his desk, where it sat for three more, awaiting his return from the sanatorium. When at last he shuffled into his study to sit at his desk, it ended up at the bottom of the pile, under the latest *Journal of Archaic Languages* and more promising missives from colleagues around the world.

Simon Donovan read for a long time, submerging himself in the pleasure denied him by uncompromising doctors and anxious nurses. In the realm of letters and language, in the world of scholarship and theories, there was no room for weak hearts and labouring lungs. Reality only returned when he rose to fetch a text or reference from the bookcases that lined the walls of the study. Then he would hear his joints creak and the harsh inhalation of his breath, very loud in the quiet room. When he reached towards the upper shelves, something in his chest would twitch and throb. The sensation always surprised him. The various betrayals of his body had been a long, slow process that his mind could never seem to remember from one manifestation to the next.

When he set aside the journal, it was to discover darkness waiting beyond the circle of light from his lamp. He leaned back in his chair for a moment, rubbing at his forehead with two fingers. Beyond the window, a thin strip of sky glowed red, caught between the peaks of the roofs across the street and the lowering dusk. He heard voices from the street and the distant toll of the cathedral bell. They will be here soon, he thought. Time to be dressing for dinner and rehearsing his litany of reassurances and platitudes or practising a paternal reprimand in case things got out of hand.

He smiled slightly. Things did tend to get out of hand. They always had, which had no doubt contributed to the amount of time he had spent in his study over the years. Anna had been able to take it all in stride, of course. She could arbitrate disputes with the wisdom of Solomon and both the victor and the vanquished were won over with cookies and kisses. Though, of course, that had been many years ago now. More years than he cared to contemplate had passed since his family had discovered, to their sorrow, that not all things could be cured with cookies and kisses. The magic of such talismans had long been lost to them, lost even before the keeper of them had been.

He thought of his sons, making their way across the city towards him. Peter would be driving. Wife safely absorbed in one of her seemingly endless rounds of social events, children put to bed by the nanny, his eldest would no doubt be here first. Gabriel would hire a cab, as usual. Matthew might as well, unless he had spent his meagre earnings on things far less practical than transportation. If it was one of what he referred to as his "poor periods," he would likely cadge a ride from Gabriel or take the trolley to the nearest stop and walk the rest of the way.

Simon looked back at his desk. From beneath the sober covers of the *Journal of Archaic Languages*, a thin oblong emerged. He reached for it idly, another excuse not to rise from the creaky comfort of his old chair.

The envelope was of heavy ivory paper. There was no return address, only the postmark of a town of which he had never heard. He saw the handwriting on the face and turned the envelope over hastily, aware of a twinge somewhere deeper than his heart. A dollop of crimson wax sealed the envelope, an archaic gesture that did nothing to relieve his sudden anxiety. Pressed deep into the bloody blot was the letter "S" in curving script.

Simon licked his lips, his mouth tasting as dry as dust. He turned the envelope in his hands again and forced himself to consider the handwriting. It had been more than twenty years. More than twenty years since he had expunged every trace of that hand from his files…and his heart. How could he be sure now that he knew it? Most likely, the letter was from some innocuous friend or acquaintance, newly enamoured of an old custom of correspondence.

He looked out the window at the narrow line of red outlining the roofs. His fingers touched the seal. There was still time to be rid of it. If the jumble of torn envelopes in his waste-basket would not do, the fire burning low on the far side of the study would. Burning would be better, certainly. Then, though he might wonder what secret lay inside the envelope, he would never be able to know. Throwing it out, even tearing it up, would make it far too easy to change his mind and succumb to curiosity.

The seal cracked beneath his fingers. The initial step taken, he had no choice but to go on. He lifted the flap of the envelope and drew the single sheet of folded paper out into the light. There was no writing on the outside, though he could see the faint outlines of the ink inside as it bled through the paper. Knowing that he was committing himself irrevocably, he unfolded the letter.

Dear Simon…

It took only a few moments to read it. She had always had an admirable economy about her sentences, he thought absurdly and read the words again. And then a third time, to be certain. Brief fancies flickered through the back of his mind. It was a hoax. She was not serious. But she had always been as serious as she was articulate.

Dear Simon…

Far away, the doorbell tolled. He heard the door open and the murmur of voices. Someone called his name.

He looked up from the letter and saw that the sun had disappeared.

There were footsteps on the stairs and a knock on the door. "Dr. Donovan?" Mrs. O'Brien's voice came, muffled by the thick oak door of his sanctuary. "Dr. Donovan, Mr. Peter is here."

Simon Donovan stared down at the letter in his hand. The words ceased to mean anything, the writing changing from the language he knew to the angular strokes of the ancient tongue with which he had struggled all those years ago. "Sidonie," he said softly, for the first time in twenty years. "Sidonie."

Chapter 2

There was someone knocking on the door.

Matthew Donovan shook his head, emerging from the vision of red rain and dark figures huddling along narrow streets beneath the angular spires of half-seen buildings. He pushed his hair off his forehead and blinked. He heard a voice calling from a long way away.

"Matthew...I know you're in there. Open the damned door!"

He crossed the room without thinking and reached for the doorknob. Once it had been black but now it was mottled with paint of a hundred hues. His fingers added a smear of crimson to the mixture.

Gabriel stood on the narrow landing. "You're not ready. Of course not. I should have known better than to agree to this." He pushed past Matthew into the attic room. "Good God. I assume your tyrant landlord hasn't turned on the heat yet."

"I haven't paid the rent yet either," Matthew replied with a sudden shiver as he shut the door. "Thank you for mentioning it...I had managed to avoid noticing up until now."

"Well, Father's house will be warm and there will be hot food and good wine. So hurry up and change. The cab is downstairs." Gabriel looked around. "I notice the cleaning lady hasn't been in lately either."

Matthew laughed and went to the easel before the window, careful to avoid glancing at the painting propped there. If he looked at it, he would want to finish it now, despite his commitment to dinner with his father. He hurried through the rituals of cleaning his brushes, aware of Gabriel pacing across the room from him. When he was done, he went to the wardrobe on the far wall and opened it carefully. The floor of the room was uneven and the wardrobe tilted at a precarious angle, as if ever on the verge of falling forward and flattening him. For a time, he had contemplated surrendering to the inevitable and pushing it to the floor himself then chopping a hole in the back to allow him to reach his clothes. In the end, he had decided that he could live with the threat in return for more floor space. He had, however, moved his bed to the other side of the room.

"Wash your hands first," Gabriel said as Matthew reached for a clean shirt. "And your face too." His brother had settled onto the bed and was contemplating the painting. Matthew stepped behind the wooden screen that separated the bathing area from the rest of the room and turned on the water. He tried both taps but, as usual, only the cold water worked. That never changed, even when he did pay the rent. He scrubbed at his skin, watching the crimson and black paint stains dissolve.

He glanced up into the spotted mirror nailed above the sink. There was a streak of red across his forehead and smudges of black on one cheek. His hair was tangled and greasy. With a sigh, he bent his head into the chilly stream of water and completed the job. When he emerged, rubbing at his wet hair with a towel, Gabriel was standing in front of the wardrobe, holding up a clean white shirt and his best black jacket. "Put these on. Bring the towel. You can finish your toilette in the cab. And if you are going to forget to shave, you might at least grow a real beard."

Matthew laughed. Gabriel was impeccably dressed with his usual flair; red vest, shirt so white it glowed, jacket of the latest cut. The studs on his collar flashed ruby in the dying sunlight. His hair, the colour of pale, polished pine, was swept back and cut to the precise length that separated cultured sophisticates from bohemian rebels at one extreme and from bourgeois businessmen on the other. "Father doesn't care what I wear," Matthew protested automatically as he pulled off his stained shirt, dropped it on the floor and took the new one from his brother.

"Father does. He has simply stopped mentioning it. However, if you show up in your usual déshabillé, I shall have to listen to Peter complain about it for ten minutes and I find that incredibly tedious. If I am paying for your ride—as I am at this exact moment, I might add—the least you can do is spare me that."

Matthew recovered the wet towel and followed Gabriel to the door. On the way down the creaking stairs, he saw his brother give him a quick backward glance. "I liked the red and black thing, by the way. Nice perspective. Just the sort of thing one of my friends likes, as well. I'll mention it to him."

"Thanks. That assumes I can finish it, now that the creative process has been interrupted."

"Nonsense. You'd interrupt the next *Venus Rising* for a hot meal and you know it. Speaking of friends and paintings, are you sure you won't sell that wooden screen you use to uphold whatever standards of decency you possess? I described it to someone and he was most intrigued."

"I need it," Matthew said. This wasn't the first time Gabriel had asked about buying the screen. His brother never seemed to understand that he could not sell it. It was, after all, the project that resulted in his expulsion from art school six years ago. The assignment had been to replicate the pastoral themes of a group of artists hundreds of years in their graves. While their techniques with soft colours and perspective had intrigued him, the subject matter had been so saccharine he could not resist the urge to embroider it somewhat. In the rush before the school's major art show, no one had looked carefully at the work and it was mounted in a place of honour. Unfortunately, it had been the wife of the school's patron who noticed that the shepherd and nymphs in the background were involved in activities rather less innocent than those favoured by the pastoralists. Matthew thought that he would have gotten away with the fornicating couple and the pissing contest. It was the shepherd and the sheep that had gotten him thrown out of the school.

"Think about it," Gabriel said. "I wouldn't even expect a family discount."

"Considering you are the only member of the family who has ever bought one of my paintings, I think it could more safely be called the 'Gabriel discount,'" Matthew pointed out. The truth was that Gabriel paid far more than Matthew could ever have received from one of the few galleries that took his work. He also doubled the regular prices whenever he sold a piece to one of his friends. The only thing that made it bearable was the knowledge that his brother genuinely liked the paintings he purchased. The one time he had tried to protest, Gabriel had waved his words away. "It is an investment, not an act of charity," he had said, "though if you do not manage to become famous soon, dear brother, I might have to kill you to hasten the process along."

"Have you talked to Father?" Matthew asked, rubbing at his damp hair as they sat in the back of the cab.

"Only for a few moments. He swears that everything is fine, but then, he always does. We will have to corner Mrs. O'Brien and insist on a full accounting. I told the doctors that I would do my best to keep him from situations that might 'stress his constitution,' I believe the phrase was." Gabriel frowned. "I should have cancelled this dinner. Or at least managed to make sure Peter was unable to attend."

"Has he been after Father about retiring again?"

"Of course. The idiot has even contacted the Chancellor. As if forcing Father to give up the thing he loves most could possibly make him better. I suppose we should be thankful that the university knows that as well as we do. And that they have a tradition of keeping professors in their chairs until they die there." Gabriel's voice was light but, when Matthew looked at him, he was staring out the window at the passing street, his hand clenched hard over his gloves. They spoke of other things until the cab arrived outside the townhouse.

Mrs. O'Brien answered the door. "Good evening, dear lady," Gabriel said, managing a bow as he removed his coat. Matthew did not try to duplicate the trick, settling for watching the pink surge beneath the woman's lined cheeks as she bantered with his brother.

"Is Peter here?" he asked at last, knowing the answer before she nodded.

"He is. But your father is not down from changing yet, so dinner will be a few minutes," she assured him.

"Best get the lecture over with then," Gabriel said and preceded him into the drawing room. Their older brother was sitting by the fireplace, a glass of whisky in his hand. "Peter, how are you? How is Catherine? And the children?" Peter stood up on the tide of Gabriel's questions and held out his hand.

"Everyone is well enough. And you, Gabriel?"

"Wonderful. The new play is packing them in, as they

say. We're making outrageous heaps of money, you'll be happy to hear." Gabriel's business involved investing in theatre productions. That was as much as Matthew had ever been able to determine, though he was constantly surprised that it afforded Gabriel as rich a living as appearances suggested. All the theatre people—actors, musicians and stagehands—that Matthew knew were even poorer than he was.

"Matthew. How are you?" Peter asked, his hand extended. Matthew took it and shrugged.

"Fine."

"Good."

As the silence lingered on for a moment more than was comfortable, Matthew looked at his brother. Of all of them, he most resembled Father. Thick dark hair beginning to go grey, heavy brows, blunt jaw, nose surprisingly aquiline in all that broad solidity. The most like Father on the outside, the least on the inside, Matthew amended the thought. Though perhaps not. Perhaps it was only that the language that sang to Peter was that of money and mathematics, while to Simon Donovan it was the song of dead empires and dusty documents. Perhaps we all have our puzzles that possess us, he thought. Father has his ancient civilizations, Peter has the mystery of success and respectability, Gabriel has the lure of pleasure and performance. For himself, he supposed it was the secret of the line and the pigment and the hidden connections between brain and brush that could make those things more real than reality.

They all seemed to hear the step on the stairs at the same time and turned to face the doorway to the hall.

For a moment, all Matthew saw was the smile, the hands extended to them in welcome. Then he noticed the pallor of his father's face, the lines that had added themselves to the fan around his eyes, and the tremor in the outstretched arms. He looked ten years older than his sixty-five years. He's dying, Matthew thought, and dread churned inside him, as it had when Gabriel had first told him that Father was at the sanatorium. Peter had arranged it, promising the best care, the finest physicians. It was necessary, it was safe. He knew that but he also knew that for all the soothing words, the confident promises, the path to the sanatorium often ran only one way. He saw the great iron gates in his mind, closing like heavy, hungry jaws.

Then Peter was shaking Simon's hand and Gabriel was enfolding his father in an extravagant embrace. Released, Simon turned to Matthew. Their greeting was awkward, Matthew suddenly afraid the weight of his arms might break the old man's frail shoulders. "You look well, son. Though I'm not sure what your mother would say if she could see your hair."

"Blame Gabriel," Matthew said with a smile, grateful for the familiar sound of his father's voice and deciding not to try to determine whether the criticism was in jest or not. "He made me dry it in the cab on the way over here. How are you feeling?"

"Much better, much better," Simon answered, but Matthew noticed that he turned away before he could meet his eyes.

"You must take it easy this time, Father," Peter said and Simon laughed.

"Nonsense. I have had a month of ease. Now I need to get back to work. You should have seen the pile of corre-spondence that needs attending…" His voice trailed off. Matthew saw Gabriel's mobile features freeze and Peter's mouth tighten.

"Dinner's ready," Mrs. O'Brien announced from the doorway.

"Another thing I have missed, believe me," Simon said,

his voice steady again. "I have not had a decent meal in a month."

"Do you mean to tell me you have become a gourmand? The man who never raised his nose from a book long enough to notice whether he was eating filet mignon or mutton?" Gabriel asked, taking Simon's arm as they walked towards the dining room. How does he do that? Matthew wondered. Gabriel could make Simon laugh without seeming to try, could offer him support and comfort disguised so cleverly the old man seemed never to notice it at all. When Matthew tried, his every movement seemed awkward and uneasy, his every phrase patronizing. Even Peter's overbearing concern seemed sometimes to serve the purpose better than his own fumbling. He had thought that some of the distance between him and Simon had lessened in the last years, the old memories fading. Yet every time they were together he was reminded of how great the gap still was, how raw the wounds beneath the accumulated anaesthesia of years. He shoved his hands into his pockets discontentedly, ignoring Peter's automatic look of disapproval, and ambled after them into the dining room.

The food was wonderful, especially after his uncertain diet of the last weeks. For all the time he spent in cafés or restaurants, it seemed that eating was never the central purpose. He consumed complimentary bar edibles, finished his friends' half-eaten meals and, when necessity demanded it, ordered whatever item appealed to his taste and wallet. If he was fortunate, Allegra would take him home and they would eat caviar or sweet cinnamon rolls or ices while sprawled in the silken sea of her bed.

Despite the delights of good food and better wine, Matthew sensed a tension that he could not entirely attribute to Simon's illness. There was something distracted about his father's conversation, a worry that he could occasionally glimpse in the lines on his father's fore-head. More than once, he saw him touch the breast of his jacket, just over his heart and then the lines would deepen.

Back in the drawing room, settled over brandies, Peter tried again to persuade Simon to retire. Matthew caught Gabriel's glance and saw his brother roll his eyes. If Peter would not be quiet, Gabriel would want to leave soon, Matthew thought, and if he went, Matthew would have to go as well, or miss his ride. He did not want to leave yet, wanted a few more moments to feel the heat of the fire against his skin and the warm burn of the fine liquor in his stomach.

"You are what?" Peter's surprised voice drew his attention back to the conversation.

"An old...student...of mine has invited me to visit. I might go."

"Where does this student live?"

"North. I will take the train."

"Father, you cannot just—"

"You are always after me to rest, to take life more slowly. I cannot imagine anything more leisurely than a train journey north and a quiet visit," Simon countered but there was something about the heartiness in his voice that rang false.

"And if you suffer another attack?" Peter demanded.

"There are doctors in the North. It is not a barbarous wilderness."

"Father—"

"Peter, I know what I am doing."

"If you are going, you should not go alone," Gabriel said. "Take Matthew with you." Matthew and Simon's sounds of surprise came at the same time. "Why not? You've no particular reason to stay in town. And think of all those wild landscapes and strange people you can paint. It will be an educational experience for you."

"I do not require a nursemaid. No one is coming with me." Simon stood up and took a step forward. "Now I am tired of arguing with you. I am going to bed." With his next step, his face paled and his hands rose to clutch his chest. Matthew rose quickly, reaching out as his father sagged into his arms. He heard the babble of his brothers' voices as he lowered Simon into the chair and crouched beside him. Simon's breathing was ragged but some colour was returning to his face.

Matthew reached out to put his hands over his father's, as if somehow he could feel the old man's heartbeat through the layers of flesh and bone. He saw panic flare in Simon's eyes and heard the sound of paper crackling. There was something in the breast pocket of the jacket. It was that Simon had been touching all night, not his heart. Whatever had caused his worry and the strange talk of the journey north, it was concealed in that pocket. "What is it, Father?" Simon shook his head. Peter would bluster it from him, Gabriel seduce it away…but Matthew could do neither of those things. "If you show us, then maybe we'll understand why you want to go away," he said and then managed an awkward smile. "If you don't show me, I will insist on going with you…and neither of us would enjoy that very much."

"I am sorry but no," Simon managed. His hands slipped away from his chest and gripped Matthew's. "Trust me." His eyes were desperate, pleading for understanding. For a moment, Matthew felt guilty. Who said the old man was not entitled to his secrets, after all? What right had they to demand that their father live his life the way they expected? Wasn't that why he had left home so many years ago—so that he could live the life he chose?

A hand dipped past his shoulder. Matthew saw his father's eyes widen, his mouth open in protest. Peter drew a folded piece of paper from its place in Simon's pocket.

"Give me that!" Simon said, pulling his hands free from Matthew's grasp and clutching the arms of the chair to push himself to his feet.

"No. This is for your own good and you know it." Peter opened the letter. Simon sank back into the chair and closed his eyes. Matthew saw the shadow of something that might have been relief cross his face and wondered if, despite his protestations, he was relieved to no longer have to bear alone whatever burden the paper represented.

Peter's mouth tightened and his heavy brows drew together. Matthew tried to read his expression. If his brother were a painting, what had the artist intended by those lines? Anger? Bewilderment? Some of each, surely. To his surprise, Peter said nothing, merely handed the letter to Gabriel.

For a moment, Matthew thought he would read it aloud. His mouth even opened as if that was what he intended but then it closed slowly. When he was done, he extended the folded paper to Matthew.

He rose, looking at the letter in his brother's hand. At last, there was nothing to do but reach out and take it. The paper was thick and textured, cross-hatched with fibres that were strangely smooth beneath his fingers. For a moment, his eye saw only pattern: the angular complexities of black on white. Then the words came clear.

Dear Simon,
I know that you must be surprised to receive this letter after so many years. I regret that my departure then was so sudden but I had no choice.

I know that you took what was mine and named it yours. I know what taking it has brought you over these last twenty years. Though many years have passed since the wrong you did me, the time for repayment has come. I must ask that you come and stay with me—you will find the instructions below. It is only face to face that this debt can be settled.

Please do not believe that because so much time has passed, I have forgotten. I remember everything that we accomplished...and what we did. If you do not do as I request, then the rest of the world shall know as well.

I will expect you on the 30th day after the date of this letter.

Sidonie Moreau

Matthew read the letter again and the instructions outlining the journey into the far reaches of the North. He looked at his brothers, then his father. "I don't understand. Who is this woman? What does she want?"

"She wants restitution for a wrong I did her," Simon said slowly, after a long moment. "Or else, perhaps, she wants revenge for it."

"Who is she?" Peter asked.

"She was my research assistant, more than twenty years ago." Matthew saw his father swallow. "She was also the woman with whom I betrayed your mother."

Chapter 3

"It was twenty-two years ago," Simon began, his eyes on the dying fire. "Your mother was expecting. You, Matthew, were ailing, as you had been since your birth. We were still living in that four-room apartment near the university. I was forty-two years old and still nothing more than an associate professor. The dreams I had cherished for so long seemed increasingly unattainable. And what dreams they were. When I had been granted access to the scrolls of Acquita ten years earlier, I had imagined the fame that would come to me with their translation. There would be a full professorship and then chair of the department. Highly acclaimed papers published in the journals. Conferences around the world. Trips to the lands I had studied for so long.

"Yet for ten years the secrets of the scrolls had eluded me. For all those years I dutifully taught classes each day and pursued my studies each night. I left your mother to deal with you and the five flights of stairs to the apartment. She never complained. She kept the household together on my meagre earnings and never once mentioned that I had promised her a life so much better than that. That was what your mother was, the stuff of which she was made. I took it for granted, perhaps even resented it a little. Her stoicism was like an unspoken criticism of me, her essential cheerfulness in the face of crying babies and genteel poverty a reminder that I could not bear those things. For I could not and so escaped into my research.

"Then one day, shortly after the new year, a new student arrived in one of the evening history classes I taught." He gave a short, bitter laugh. "How could I have guessed what her arrival meant? I did not even notice her until the class was almost finished. She was not the kind of woman you noticed immediately. After that first meeting, I recalled only that she had dark hair bound tightly back and wore a shapeless dress of the same hue. Her name was Sidonie Moreau. That detail intrigued me briefly, for Sidonie means 'enchantress' in one of the regional dialects of—" He blinked and stopped, as if recalling that this was not another scholarly lecture. "Well, it hardly matters. I remember that I thought it was an incongruous name for so unassuming a creature. At the fourth lecture she attended, I remembered to ask for her transfer papers. She apologized most profusely for forgetting them and promised that she would bring them to the next class. But she never did.

"She seemed very shy. She rarely spoke in class, yet when she did, her comments were always surprisingly insightful. The first paper she submitted was well reasoned and researched, though some of her conclusions were quite unorthodox. It also became apparent that she had a considerable facility for language, so much so that a plan presented itself to me. The university would not fund a research assistant for me and I could hardly afford to pay one out of my own earnings. If Sidonie could be persuaded to assist me with some of the routine work, that might give me the time I needed to make serious strides with the translations. I do not say I chose this plan easily, for there were some aspects of it that were not perhaps perfectly ethical, but at last I approached her.

"She agreed eagerly and that evening we began. She worked quietly, like a dark wraith in the shadows of the room. The competence she showed in the classroom was continued in the research. For the first time in months, I began to feel equal to the task I had set myself.

"One night, she came to me, arms full of texts and papers. She had discovered something, she said shyly. It was probably nothing, she was probably misguided, but would I look...? She spread out her burden on the desk and began to point out similarities between the scrolls and a series of texts translated earlier from ancient Midothian. At first, nothing she said made sense and then I saw it. It was no great revelation, no mystic key to all the secrets, but it was a way in, a tiny sliver of light from behind a door that had seemed closed forever. I was so excited I did not even notice that her explanation of how she had discovered this made no sense.

"From that moment, things seemed to change. The unhappiness that I had lived with for so long was gone. I felt energized by my work instead of drained by it. I was even happy at home...yet not as happy as I was in my office at the university. I think, in my happiness, I stayed away from home even more. I do not know if you boys remember or if you even noticed. I know your mother did. Even then I could see the shadows in her eyes, though I willed myself to ignore them.

"If it seemed that I looked at the scrolls with new eyes, so too did my vision of Sidonie change. She was not nearly as quiet and diffident as she had at first appeared. She had a quick intelligence and a broad, if odd, range of knowledge. She could speak with vivid certainty about the market of ancient Tyren and yet be uncertain about the current political situation. At the time, this did not strike me as odd, perhaps because I was not always entirely certain about the complexities of modern life myself. She possessed a genuine fascination with the world. Her humour, though rarely displayed, was as keen and refreshing as her intellect.

"She was also not as plain as I had thought. I began to notice that her hair, though held back in a simple braid, shone like ebony. She had only to tilt her head and her features, which I had thought unremarkable, would seem suddenly compelling. Her eyes, which I had believed were black, turned out to be a blue so deep it was like indigo. If she kept her body swathed in severe dresses, it did not matter. The line of her throat, the slender grace of her fingers, the translucent skin of her wrists...all of these were enough to make me certain of the beauty of what those shapeless clothes concealed.

"You must not think that I accepted all these realizations without resistance. There had been other young women in my classes and some had possessed charms that were difficult not to notice. But you must believe that 'notice' was all I had ever done. Indiscretions with students may have happened among my peers, but the penalty for scandal was dismissal and I had never been willing to risk that. And I loved your mother. In all our years of marriage I had never been tempted to break my wedding vows to her. I attributed my attraction to Sidonie to the satisfaction of the work we were doing, to the excitement of discovery.

"That excitement also blinded me to another fact: that it was Sidonie who made most of the breakthroughs. Never blatantly, of course. It was done so that I could choose to ignore it if I wished, as if she feared that if she did too well I might banish her from the project. I knew the truth, in the darkest part of my heart, but ignore it I did, just as I ignored the moments I sat watching her instead of working.

"Then, so suddenly it shocked me, we were done. The scrolls yielded up the last of their secrets and ten years of work was completed. I had been saving a bottle of champagne concealed in the bottom of my desk for all those years, awaiting this moment. That night, everything went to my head. My triumph, the champagne, the blue light in her eyes."

Simon fell silent for a long moment. Peter stared at the fire. Gabriel shifted in his chair. Matthew looked down and discovered he had been tearing mindlessly at a loose thread in his shirt and had ripped a hole in the cuff.

"Those are the excuses I use. The truth is that I knew what I was doing every moment. I betrayed your mother, knowing full well what I did and yet somehow unable to stop myself.

"I dreaded the next class, when I would have to look at Sidonie and conceal what we had done. She never came to class or to my office. Assuming that she felt as torn as I, I did nothing but continue finalizing the paper that would announce our findings. A week passed and she still had not appeared. I swung agonizingly between relief and despair. At last I went to the registrar's office to inquire about her address. There I discovered that no Sidonie Moreau was registered at the university. No one had ever heard of her. In desperate folly, I went to the student gathering places and asked after her. No one knew her there either.

"A week later, I acknowledged that she was gone. The mystery of it maddened me. She had come into my life, helped me to solve...no, I must be honest, solved by herself...the greatest scholastic challenge of my career, shared one night of adulterous passion with me and then vanished. I struggled with that puzzle, worrying at it, until the day came to submit my paper to the field's most prestigious journal.

"I sat at my desk, looking at the title page. By rights, Sidonie's name should appear there. Beneath mine, of course, but that was customary for scholarship. Yet I made no move to set it there. Sidonie was gone. No one had any record that she had ever been here. She had helped me with the work, true, but she had also caused me untold pain. As well, if I put her name there, I would have to explain to Anna who she was.

"So I submitted the paper without her name on it. You know the rest of the tale. Publication caused a sensation in my field. I was offered a full professorship and then the chair. I bought this house. All of my dreams came true, at least for a while.

"I thought Sidonie was gone, as dead to me as if she had never existed. But, as my work should have taught me, nothing ever really dies."

Chapter 4

"This is..." Peter's voice failed for a moment, "outrageous." No one else spoke. Matthew looked at the ragged tear in the cuff of his shirt and wondered with distant curiosity what his brother meant. Which of the various revelations did he consider outrageous? That their father's scholastic achievements were based on a lie? That he had been unfaithful to their mother? That this mysterious woman dared to resurface twenty years later and demand her due? Perhaps uncharitably, Matthew thought the latter.

"What do you suppose she wants?" Gabriel asked carefully. Simon gave a weary shrug.

"Money, perhaps. Perhaps only acknowledgement of what I owe to her. So you see why I must go."

"Not at all. She has done you enough harm already," Peter said. "You should ignore her. Surely she would not dare to do what she has threatened. And if she did, who would believe her? You said yourself that she was never registered at the university. Is there any evidence to support her claim?"

"Perhaps. I destroyed all the notes that she had left but that does not mean she did not retain something I did not know about. I am not prepared to believe that she has no proof. And if she makes the allegations loudly enough, it will not matter whether she has proof. There is nothing that delights this city more than a scandal and very little that the university loves less."

"Good heavens, this all happened twenty years ago," Gabriel said. "Will anyone even care any more?"

"It does not matter," Simon insisted. "Look at what happened to Ronald Schiller." Matthew saw Gabriel's eyes widen. He opened his mouth to inquire about the fate of the unknown Dr. Schiller and caught his brother's worried, warning glance. As he closed his mouth, he remembered the story of a professor dismissed amid suggestions of impropriety, examination scores and sexual favours. The scandal had ended in the professor's suicide.

"This is blackmail," Peter said impatiently. "We should contact someone. The authorities."

"And tell them what, brother? That our father stole this woman's intellectual work and now she wants repayment for it?" Gabriel demanded. "I am sure they will be most sympathetic."

"You will tell no one. Not even Catherine, Peter. This is my problem and I will deal with it. I made a terrible mistake and I have put off payment for it for over twenty years. I should consider myself lucky."

"Did Mother know?" Matthew was surprised to hear himself ask.

"Matthew—" Gabriel began but Simon held up his hand.

"You have a right to know. I never told her, if that is what you mean. Whether she knew or not...who can say? It never happened again. I swear that."

Just as yesterday I would have sworn you were a brilliant scholar and a faithful husband, Matthew thought. Had everything else that had happened in the family stemmed from that one fateful decision? If Simon had resisted Sidonie, would it have been different for their mother? For all of them?

"I must ask that you come and stay with me…" Gabriel quoted from the letter in his hand. "Perhaps she is only lonely, so far away from the city. Perhaps she is still…infatuated with you."

"That seems unlikely," Simon said. "There is nothing to do but go to her and find out what she wants."

"You cannot go," Peter said. "None of the reasons for that have changed. I will write to her and offer her a reasonable sum for her silence."

"Of course," Gabriel said. "Everything is manageable by money. Do you suppose the woman who wrote this letter wants your bribe?"

"What else could she want? She has no doubt fallen on hard times and sees a way to gain an easy fortune. But if you have a better suggestion, please do not keep it to yourself."

"From what Father told us of this woman, and from the tone of this letter, she wants some acknowledgement of her achievement. She wants an apology, preferably an abject one. Surely there is some way to give her credit for the work without making it seem that Father cheated her. If she can be persuaded to say that she wished for anonymity until now, then we can announce her contributions—and make some financial compensation to her as well—without jeopardizing Father. As for the rest of it, that need never be mentioned." Peter frowned and nodded slowly.

"That might work. Now we have only to decide on a sum and an agent to handle the transaction."

"You do not understand," Simon insisted. "You did not know Sidonie. I do not think 'an agent' will fare very well with her. She was not…" his voice faltered, "she was not like other women."

"She was enough like other women for us to be in this situation," Peter snapped. Silence filled the room again. After a long moment, he cleared his throat. "I am sorry. That was unnecessary."

"It was true," Simon said softly. "I know that this must have been a bitter revelation for you. You have all been kinder than I deserve."

It *had* been a bitter revelation, Matthew thought, and one in which he should have taken a perverse pleasure. His father was mortal after all…and just as much a hypocrite as the rest of the world. He could recall the thousand lectures, the myriad denunciations of the life of pleasure, decadence and laziness his father had believed he had chosen. He remembered the terrible battles endured before he had left home for art school, all the accusations voiced and unvoiced. It would be natural to gloat over this pillar of intellectual honesty exposed as a cheat, this champion of moderation and fidelity revealed as an adulterer. Ten years ago, Matthew might have flung these failures back in his father's face with malevolent glee. Five years ago, he would have used a stiletto to inflict the wounds, but inflict them he would have done. He might even have believed that his father's crimes somehow absolved his own. Would they? he wondered automatically. Would everything have been different if I had known about this back then?

But it was too late for all of that. He felt nothing but a strange, sorrowful sympathy for his father. Of his own crimes against his family…nothing had changed. He had lived with the past too long now and it was far too late to alter anything, least of all how he felt about it. He would get no pleasure, no absolution, from watching Simon suffer.

"I'll go," he said, into the silence. "I'll go and find out what she wants, what price has to be paid."

"Matthew—" his father began.

"Gabriel was right. I have nothing to hold me in the

city. Peter has his family. Gabriel has the theatre. There is no reason at all that I can't travel for a while. And there will no doubt be interesting subjects to paint."

"Are you certain that you can do this?" Peter asked. "It might require some...tact...and cleverness."

"And I have never demonstrated either of those things to you, is that it? Don't worry. I can be quite charming when I want to be. Clever, as well."

"Pay him no mind, Matthew. The real question is whether you are certain that you *want* to do this?" Matthew met his father's gaze and nodded.

"I want to do it." For a moment, he thought he saw the shadow of guilty relief in his father's eyes. He looked past Simon to Peter and managed a wry smile. "Though one of you will have to pay for my train ticket."

Chapter 5

"To journeys into the unknown!"
    "To suffering for art!"
    "To brothers who buy train tickets!"
    "To Matthew!"
The toasts dissolved into laughter and the gasped exhalations that followed the gulps of burning liquor. To Matthew it seemed that he could feel the mouthful of absinthe dissolve into his blood, joining the others already there. It made his scalp prickle and the muscles below his ribs seem to melt. He closed his eyes, savouring the sensations because they allowed him to ignore the cold thing that coiled in his gut, twisting whenever he remembered the truth of why he was going north.

He had lied to his friends, inventing a need for solitude and reflection in order to paint and a distant relative with an empty country retreat to supply the setting. He had told the truth about Peter buying the train ticket.

It seemed to have happened so quickly. Only four days had passed since the dinner at his father's house. The letter from Sidonie had been a long time in transit and had sat unattended for a week during Simon's illness. Now the date stipulated for his arrival was only three days away. He thought about the bags waiting packed in his apartment. With blind optimism, he had sacrificed clothing to paints and brushes, a selection of small canvases and the materials for assembling larger ones. After all, this strange woman had even less reason to care about his appearance than his family did and if she tired of seeing him in the same attire every day, well, then perhaps she would decide to drop her demands in order to be rid of him.

The touch of a hand on his arm brought him back to the café, to the voices and music and clatter of glasses. He opened his eyes into Allegra's cool green gaze. "Don't go to sleep," she said softly.

"Sleep?" Andre leaned across the table as he caught the word. The lenses of the glasses slipping down his nose contained reflected candle flames, almost obscuring his eyes. His hair looked like another flame, a shaggy dandelion of ginger. "Nonsense. Matthew is not going to sleep tonight. He can sleep on the train for three days."

"Am I expected to spend the whole night here?" Matthew asked with a smile and a sidelong look at Allegra.

"Why not? You are going to exile in the frozen North. You will be alone among the savages and beasts. In a week, you'll be desperate for a night like this."

"Maybe. But perhaps I will like it in the North. Perhaps I shall enjoy being among savages and beasts."

"Better company than we are, is that it?" Paul put in, punctuating the question with a series of smoke rings from his cigarette.

"I thought we *were* savages and beasts," Jack said, his attention drawn from his customary survey of the other patrons. "The papers say we are. 'Bohemian degenerates and primitives,' isn't that the phrase?"

"Exactly. To ensure that you do not become corrupted by the purity of the North and decide to leave us here in our decadence, we took up a collection and bought you a present." Paul bent to hunt through his leather satchel then presented a clumsily wrapped object with a flourish. "Open it carefully."

Matthew laughed and took the present from his hand. The wrapping did nothing to disguise that the item was a bottle. Other objects of indeterminate shape rattled at the bottom of the paper. He tugged carefully at the wrapping and revealed a bottle of brandy. He stripped away more and uncovered a tube of paint and a small wooden box. "Vermilion," he read from the side of the tube. "My favourite colour." Andre inclined his head in acknowledgement.

"After all, you won't be able to borrow mine when you run out at midnight."

Matthew lifted the wooden box to his ear and shook it experimentally. Something rattled. His friends feigned innocence, suppressing smiles. He set the box on the table and slid open the grooved lid. The box was lined with white silk, so pure it seemed to glow in the candlelight. For a moment, he saw nothing beyond its gleam then noticed the tiny glass vial pushed into one corner. The vial was full of powder, as intensely blue as the silk was white.

He drew a ragged breath and closed the box. He looked up at his friends. Andre was smiling. The lid of Paul's right eye dropped in a wink. Jack lifted his eyebrow. Allegra licked her lips. "Is that...?"

"Yes, it is," Allegra answered in a whisper. "Nethys. The best. From the East."

"But..." He had never sampled it, only heard stories about what the narcotic could do. *It makes you see your dreams...it makes you live them...*

"For when you're lonely," she said, her fingers touching his sleeve again. "You can take it and dream of me."

"Or us, if you'd rather," Jack added, one eyebrow lifted

in a mock leer. "Or anything you like."

It makes you see your dreams. And your nightmares, Matthew wondered with a sudden chill. What about your nightmares?

Then Paul called for another round and he drowned the thought in the sweet fire of the absinthe. The night whirled on in a carousel of music and laughter and alcohol until at last he and Allegra were standing at the doorway, waving goodbye and Andre was making them promise not to sleep.

"I promise," Allegra said, her arm sliding through his, her eyes glittering like the green gems in her ears. "Sleep is not at all part of the plan."

The cobblestones were wet with the rain they had missed, safe in the warmth of the café. Fog turned the lamps into smears of light. Allegra shivered and Matthew put his arm around her shoulders. "I did not think that you were interested in landscapes," she commented.

"I'm sure there are other things to paint, if I become tired of trees."

"Why are you really going away?" she asked after a moment. He looked at her sharply but her eyes were trained on the uneven ground beneath her thin shoes.

"To paint." He felt her shoulders move beneath his arm in a shrug.

"If you insist. I wish you luck then. It might be good for you to get away from the city. It might be good for your art."

"And what is wrong with my art now?" he asked, before he had time to think that perhaps he did not want an answer to that. Not this night, at any rate.

"I think you are very talented, Matthew. You know that. But sometimes…" She paused and he knew she had felt the involuntary stiffening of his arm across her shoulders. "Sometimes I think that you should paint what you need to paint, instead of always painting around it."

"I don't understand."

"Neither do I," she admitted and stopped to put her hand up to his cheek. "I am much too drunk to indulge in artistic criticism tonight. I promised you no sleep and here I am boring you to it. So take me home."

They were at his room before he knew it. He had a moment of disappointment that they had not gone to Allegra's elegant apartment, where there would be food and hot baths and the expanse of her bed. But his bags were in his room and the train left early, she pointed out reasonably, swearing that she did not mind his empty larder, cold water and narrow cot. "You will keep me warm," she whispered as the fur wrap slipped from her shoulders to the floor. "You will make me forget where I am."

The thought flickered hazily through his mind that she did not want to forget where she was, that his poverty and artistic asceticism were as much a lure as his kisses, because she could leave both of them behind and go back to her real world of servants and luxury. Then her dress followed her wrap onto the floor and her motives, or his, did not matter at all.

Much later, she rose from the bed and went to crouch by her purse, searching for cigarettes and a match. Matthew lay watching the line of her back in the moonlight. Gooseflesh crept from the dimples at the start of her hips. She returned to the bed, bringing her wrap to fling over the thin covers. Her skin was chilly against his. Propping himself on his elbow, he watched her light her cigarette. He put his hand on her lower ribs and felt them expand as she inhaled. Smoke flowed into the semi-darkness and he thought absurdly of the protoplasm that mediums claimed issued from their bodies. The thought that the smoke was the incorporeal form of some spirit that possessed her ran ice down his spine.

"When will you be coming home?" she asked, and the mundane question drew him back from his wild thoughts.

"I don't know. Whenever I am done what I am going to do."

"I will miss you."

"You won't. You have other lovers." He knew that it was true. He even knew one or two of them. Paul had slept with her for a time, perhaps still did.

"Of course. But I will still miss you." She drew on the cigarette again and Matthew watched the red tip brighten and glow.

"You'll have forgotten me by the time I return, Allegra," he said, half-believing it was true, half-hoping she would deny it. There was a silence and then she exhaled her strange, protoplasmic soul again.

"I know that I am frivolous and promiscuous," she said after a moment, her voice light. "I know that I live for my own pleasure. The truth is that we are both parasites of a kind. You and the others feed off my wealth and I feed off your glamour, your talent, your rebellion. Yet despite that, I believe that we could be friends. Perhaps that is shallow of me as well."

"I did not realize that my friendship interested you," Matthew said, knowing it was more excuse than apology. Everything that she said was true. They all knew it but, like conspirators in an act of self-delusion, said nothing. Put as baldly as she had done it, the equation lost the rebellious allure with which they had all tried to invest it. Allegra turned to look towards the window and he watched the moonlight slide across her cheek.

"Of course it does. I will not be young and beautiful forever. Neither will you. I expect that I will always be wealthy, but I have no guarantee of that. In time, no one will want to make love to me, no matter what my wealth. The only things that will last are the things you discover at your easel…and perhaps whatever we can find between us that is more than what our bodies do in your bed or mine." She lifted her hand. Her palm pressed against her cheek and for a moment the cigarette's glow was like another eye, red and open where the green ones were closed.

"Allegra," he began, but then her hand lifted again, waving away his words.

"Look what promising to stay awake has done to me. It has made me foolish and sentimental." She twisted to crush the cigarette in the ashtray on the bedside table. Far off in the night, the cathedral bells tolled four times. "What time do you have to leave?"

"Six."

"Only a few hours then. Do you suppose we can do it? Stay awake until dawn?"

"What shall we do? Tell each other stories?" Matthew forced himself to smile, to find the bantering tone that they had always taken with each other. To pretend that her serious words had never been said.

"No. We have talked too much already."

"Will you let me paint you at last? As a parting gift to comfort me during my northern exile?"

"Oh no. Your hand would be unsteady."

"I am insulted. My hand is never unsteady." He reached out and found the canvas of soft skin. "See?" Allegra drew a quick breath and laughed softly.

"We shall see about that, my artist lover. We shall see."

In the end, he slept anyway and woke to a cold, empty room, with Gabriel pounding on his door.

Chapter 6

Matthew glanced from the passing countryside to his sketchbook, his hand moving in rapid strokes. Black lines became trees, a curve suggested the undulation of the edge of a field, quick hatching the shadows of furrows beneath the setting sun. The speed of the train's passage left no time for rendering any one scene accurately, so he settled for capturing broad outlines or small details in a way he hoped would cue his mind when he tried to paint.

He had slept for the first five hours of the trip and awakened to discover that the city was far behind him. The full car into which he had squeezed that morning had lost a third of its passengers. The businessmen seemed to have vanished, leaving the families, the old and those whose appearance, like his own, was less easily classified. For a moment, he had panicked, full of the irrational fear that he might have slept for the entire journey and somehow missed his stop. Then he remembered that the conductor had assured him that when the time came, someone would see that he left the train. For their benefit not his own, he supposed, but the assurance had made him feel less uneasy. He tried to think only of the promise and not of the conductor's curious, considering glance when Matthew had named his destination.

He looked up at the landscape again. Across the sere fields, he could see a line of trees that seemed to run parallel to the track. Autumn had turned their leaves an orange so intense it almost hurt to look at it. It made his fingers itch for paints and palette to re-create that gaudy splendour. The sumacs were red flames along the banks of the tracks. He looked down at his sketches again and, after some consideration, blocked in the darker shapes of pines, like shadows against the brighter deciduous trees. The contrast, and the odd geometric precision of their shapes, intrigued him.

He set down his pen and became aware of the ache in his wrists and arms. He stretched out in his seat, shifting his neck and shoulders to ease the tightness from them. Perhaps his assertion that this trip was to paint was not a complete lie, after all, he thought idly. Then he remembered the letter tucked into his jacket pocket and felt a pang of guilt. The reason for this trip is to save Father, he reminded himself. If you paint nothing for the entire visit, that does not matter.

He took Sidonie Moreau's letter from his pocket and unfolded it over his sketches. He knew it, and the instructions on reaching her house, by heart by now but he found some obscure comfort in rereading it, in studying the black marks of her words on the white page, as if they held some clue to her purpose and personality. "I must ask that you come and stay with me." That sentence always disturbed him. Why "stay"? Why not "visit"? If all she wanted was recognition or restitution, then why would it matter to her how long Simon remained with her? The word hinted at purposes beyond those Peter and Gabriel had discussed. It also suggested that she might not be entirely pleased to see that Matthew had come in his father's stead.

Staring at the letter and remembering the look on his
father's face as he spoke of her, Matthew could not ignore
the uneasiness that lay like a cold weight beneath his ribs.
It was not as simple as Peter believed. His brother thought
that Sidonie Moreau was nothing more than a strange
adventuress turned shrewd and desperate now that whatever allure she possessed was fading. Peter's world
included only two types of women: necessary companions
like Catherine and their mother and untrustworthy
temptresses who might fulfil a man's regrettable physical
needs but should never intrude on the real business of his
life. His brother had made it quite clear in which category
the women of Matthew's acquaintance could be considered. "A pompous idiot," had been Allegra's assessment
after she had met him at a society function. "He didn't
dare cut me, of course. But he didn't dare look at me
either…because he wanted to." Matthew smiled at the
memory. It had given him an uncharitable pleasure to
think of his brother bowing obsequiously over Allegra's
hand—her blood, after all, had been blue for ten generations while theirs was still unseemly academic and mercan-
tile red—never knowing that she was one of his younger
brother's scandalous companions. It had given him even
more satisfaction to know that his brother wanted her and
he had shamefully wished that there was some way to tell
Peter of their relationship. He had never done it, of
course. It would be unfair to Allegra and he had long since
discovered that the best way to maintain peace with his
brother was to allow Peter as little insight into his private
life as possible.

Gabriel might believe that there was more to Sidonie's
summons than greed, but he too seemed convinced that
money and an apology, preferably private, would suffice to
silence her. The greatest sacrifice he thought likely to be
required would be the public acknowledgement of her part

in the translation and he remained convinced it could be done in a way that absolved their father of blame. "It is simply a matter of presentation," he had assured Matthew, "and presentation is my business."

They might be right. There was no point in fearing that they were not. But the letter, the firm black lines, the cold simplicity of the sentences, seemed to hold the promise of motives much deeper than greed or fame, suggesting a need that could be malice, desperation or something less definable.

He folded the letter away and closed his sketchbook, stretching again. He looked out the window, trying to see the passing scenery the way the rest of the passengers did, without the urge to capture each tree and far-away church steeple in ink. He had not been on a train in years. Not since he and his brothers had travelled to Grandmother Donovan's the summer that he was sixteen. Now, as then, the motion of the car, the churn of the wheels beneath him, filled him with a feeling of escape...or perhaps of exile. There was a finality about it, as if the track that now took him north could never take him home again. The sound of the steam engines, the stale, smoky scent of the car, even the slanting light beyond the window seemed to summon up a strange confusion of emotions: curiosity and loneliness, excitement and melancholy.

The train's whistle sounded, announcing their arrival into another tiny station. No one in Matthew's car rose to leave, but after a moment several travellers entered. One man chose the seat across the aisle from him, depositing his heap of battered bags with a grunt. Matthew had a moment of dismay at the loss of his solitude, but the man promptly settled into his seat, closed his eyes, smacked lips half-hidden by a bushy grey beard and went to sleep.

The train moved on, seeming to Matthew to proceed much more quickly than the time within it. The landscape outside the window did not seem to change and he lost his urge to sketch it. He staved off boredom by starting on Jack's latest collection of short stories and, when hunger prompted him, wandering off in search of the dining car. The food was surprisingly good, the wine even better, and he spent more of Gabriel's travelling money than he should have, for it had to last him for two more days. Afternoon drifted into twilight and the train ran on, parallel to the mauve- and crimson-clouded sunset.

When the darkness outside and dim lights of the railway car changed his window from a lens to a mirror, Matthew stretched out on the seat and went to sleep.

He awoke in near darkness. Most of the travellers in the car were asleep, either in their seats or in the tiny cabins for which they had paid an extra fee. Someone snored, the sound trailing off like a sigh. Matthew eased the ache from his shoulders and then rose to move carefully down the car to the men's room.

As he returned, he glanced curiously at each set of seats that he passed. Most were empty. A few held huddled figures indistinguishable by age or gender. The snoring had stopped and a strange silence seemed to fill the car, the soft darkness muffling even the clatter of the wheels. With an involuntary shudder, he settled back into his seat, intending to sleep again.

Ten minutes of shifting and twisting later, he acknowledged that he was no longer tired. He leaned against the window, cupping his hands around his eyes, and peered out. He could see nothing, not even the moon. Disappointed, he sat back and sighed.

"Can't sleep either, eh?" a voice asked quietly. He glanced to his left and saw that the old man across the aisle was awake as well.

"No."

"You'd think I could. Slept much rougher than this in

my time, I have. But my bones are getting old. Seems I don't like much but my own bed these days." The man hunted in his capacious coat and retrieved a small silver flask then tipped it to his lips. After a long swallow, he rubbed the top on the ragged fur trimming of his sleeve and held it across the aisle to Matthew.

He accepted and lifted it to his mouth tentatively. A quick sip was enough to set his throat burning. "Good stuff, eh?" There was laughter in the man's voice. "Make it myself. Got the taste for home-made fifty years ago and can't seem to shake it."

"It's strong," Matthew admitted, returning the flask, acknowledging that it was a much better vintage than had resulted from Andre's attempts to brew cheap liquor. He looked more closely at the man. He had removed his fur-flapped hat to reveal a bird's nest of grey hair. His eyebrows, bushy and startlingly white, met above the bridge of his nose. Beneath them, his eyes were pale blue and narrowed into a perpetual squint, as if held captive by the web of lines around them.

Somewhere down the car, someone snuffled and shifted, the squeak of the seat springs surprisingly loud. The man jerked his head a little, gesturing for Matthew to come over and join him. For a moment, he considered refusing and trying to sleep, or at least feigning it. The odd purpose of his journey and his own reticence, amplified by the feelings stirred by the train, made him want to hold onto his isolation. But, he acknowledged, sleep was unlikely to come, feigning it would be dull and uncomfortable and another sip of that fiery liquor might not be entirely unwelcome. And the man had an interesting face, one that he might one day be able to use.

He shifted over into the seat the man vacated for him. "Will," the man said, his handshake hard and callused.

"Matthew."

"Ever done this trip before? No? Me, I've done it more times than I can count. My boy, he lives down in that last town. Good kid. I go visit him when I can. Always after me to move down there but I've been too long in the old place. Couldn't take to town life now, not after so long."

"Where do you live?"

"Got a little cabin up back of Ghost Lake. What about you?"

"The city."

"City boy, eh? Thought so. Where you headed?"

"Bitter Creek."

"Bitter Creek?" Will took another swig of his liquor and passed it to Matthew. As Matthew drank, he was aware of the narrow eyes watching him. "Ever been?" Matthew shook his head. "Got family or business in those parts?"

"I'm visiting an old student of my father's." That was the story he had decided upon, as it was not exactly a lie.

"Ever been North at all?"

"No. We spent summers at a cottage a few hours from the city when I was young but that's as far as I have gone."

"Not like the South."

"I hope not. I'm a painter. I'm hoping to see something I can't see in the South."

"You'll see that, you can bet. Bitter Creek, eh? Used to trap up that way once, must be going on forty years ago. Young man, I was."

"What is it like?"

"Beautiful," Will said, after a long moment's pause. "Not your soft southern beauty, don't think that. Country there can kill a man faster than you could guess. Snow, avalanche, wild water. And other things."

"Other things?" Matthew echoed, partially because he was curious and partially because this garrulous old man seemed to demand it. It was part of the storytelling ritual; the hints, the reticence, and then the reluctant recitation.

Whatever wild tale he would spin would at least be enter-
taining and perhaps there might even be enough truth in it
that it would give him some clues to the world he was
entering.

"Never saw nothing myself, understand. Not really saw.
But there was a feeling sometimes. You'd be alone in the
forest, walking the trapline, and all of a sudden you'd
know you weren't alone no more."

"Animals?"

"Not animals, though there are those. Bears bigger
than three men standing together. Catamounts you'd
never see till they was tearing out your throat. No, there'd
be something else. Watching you. Nothing you could do
about it but keep walking. Had my rifle out though, I tell
you. No, like I said, I never saw nothing. The only man I
ever met who might have...well, he was half-dead and
half-mad." A swig from the canteen, timed to perfection.
Matthew took the bottle, drank, and returned it. Ritual
complete, Will continued.

"Found him out in the woods one winter, after a big
blizzard. He was all covered in snow. His beard looked like
it was made of ice. When I got a good look under all that
white I saw it was a trapper I knew, big guy named Mike.
He was mostly dead by that point, frozen so it would take
the fires of hell or the breath of an angel to thaw him out.
Wasn't nothing I could do for him but I couldn't leave him
so I set a fire and sat there in the snow with him. After a
while, I see that his lips are moving, just a little. I lean
close as I can and I hear him muttering away. It didn't
make much sense, just some raving on about the ice and
cold as if it were real, as if it were a woman sucking the life
from him. Cold does things to your mind, you know.
Biggest danger of all is that you start to feel warm, so you
sit down, and then you go to sleep, and then you die.
Simple way to go, really, if you can stand the first bit.

"Anyway, after a few minutes of this, he goes quiet again. Next time I looked closely, he was dead. I buried him in the snow beneath a fallen tree—last place to thaw, you see—and when it was spring some of us went back and got him to give him a proper burial. Weren't much else I could do for him."

The old man glanced over at him and laughed. "Disappointed, are you? No proper end to a story? Well, maybe not. But life don't end like stories. So you just take that as a warning, for what it's worth. Be careful in that country, that's all."

In the silence Matthew thought about his father's description of Sidonie Moreau; quiet, scholarly, demure. There seemed to be no possible correspondence between the world Will described and the woman his father had known. The old man's stories are forty years old, he thought. Surely things must have changed. No doubt he exaggerates as well, for effect.

Will yawned suddenly, revealing to the dim light a set of teeth so straight and yellowish that Matthew knew that they were false. "Been nice chatting with you, boy. Always did talk a lot, for a man of my type. Even if I did most of my talking to myself, up there on the line. You be careful, hear me?"

Those words seemed to echo in Matthew's mind as he resumed his seat, as sleep caught up to him again.

He slept through the next two stops. When he woke, Will was gone. A sallow-faced young man sat in his seat, as if no one else had ever sat there at all.

Chapter 7

꧁꧂

"Bitter Creek. All out for Bitter Creek. Bitter Creek." The conductor paused by Matthew's seat. "We're here, sir." Matthew sat up, drawn from his immersion in Jack's book. He snatched a quick glance out the window but saw nothing but trees. The station must be on the other side, he decided, as he assembled his bags. He pulled on his coat and followed the conductor towards the exit.

At the doorway, the man climbed from the train to set down the portable step that would ease his way onto the platform. Except that there was no platform. "This can't be the place." His voice sounded weak, swallowed by the idling chug of the train's engines and the wind in the trees.

"This is Bitter Creek, sir."

"But there's nothing here. No station, no town."

"No, sir. There was a platform here, thirty years ago, but it's gone now. Are you sure this was where you thought you were going?" There was a mixture of impatience and sympathy in the man's voice. Matthew put his hand to his pocket to retrieve Sidonie Moreau's letter, then let it drop. He knew by heart what the letter said. This was the place, this thin line of weed-strewn gravel on the side of the

44

track. He took a deep breath and stepped down from the train. "Is someone meeting you?" the conductor asked. He nodded.

"When does the next train pass?"

"We do the southbound run in three days. About noon." The man picked up the step and blew one loud blast on his whistle as he swung back aboard the train. "Good luck, sir." Then the door closed and the train engine huffed back into life. Matthew stepped hastily back as it began to move. He watched it go, swallowed with frightening speed by the trees.

Slowly, he set down his bags and looked around. On either side of the track, the pines presented an unbroken line of green. Above the trees, he could see the grey bulk of mountains, half-shrouded in cloud. He had caught glimpses of them through the windows of the train but the forest had blocked so much of the view for the last few hours that he had barely bothered to look at all. He had long since satisfied any urge he had to draw a seemingly unending series of trees.

He crossed the track to get a clearer view of the land to his left and saw another range of mountains, these far closer. Putting his hands over his eyes and squinting against the pale afternoon sun he could see the snow on their peaks and the rough granite of their buttresses. He heard Will's quiet voice: "not your soft southern beauty." Not that, he thought, definitely not that. But beautiful all the same, a wild beauty that tugged at his heart. Landscape painting had never been one of his stronger interests, despite his brave words to his friends and family, but now that seemed only to have been because he had never seen this landscape.

He crossed back to the huddle of his bags, which looked forlorn and alien in this natural world. He was grateful that he had indulged in one extravagance before he left—an old military greatcoat gleaned from a used-goods shop. Despite its age and history, it was solidly made and warm, if somewhat ragged at cuffs and collar. As the wind slipped down from the trees to rush along the track, he stuffed his hands into his pockets and suppressed a shiver.

Someone would meet him, the letter had promised. Surely that person knew the train's schedule and would not leave him standing here for long. It would be hard for Sidonie Moreau to obtain restitution from someone who died of exposure beside the railway track. Unless, of course, it was not restitution that interested her but revenge. In that case, this might suit her purposes admirably.

You will hardly die of exposure in two days, Matthew told himself severely. If no one comes for you, you will simply wait for the next train. Besides, he thought, looking around again, this wilderness cannot be deserted, otherwise why would there be a stop here at all? There must be trappers, like Will, out there in the woods. Perhaps there is a town over one of the hills. Even if Sidonie Moreau planned to abandon you here, surely someone else will come along.

He selected one of his suitcases, stood it on one end beside the track and sat down. Retrieving his fingerless gloves from his pockets and his sketchbook from his satchel, he set to work on a study of the mountains beyond the trees. When his fingers grew numb and his concentration scattered, he paced along the tracks and then by the line of the forest. It was not as impenetrable as it at first appeared. He found the beginnings of what appeared to be trails, though he did not dare take more than a step or two along them. Even at that, the forest seemed to swallow him up inside its green stillness and he was relieved to return to the reassuring artificiality of the track and the warmth of the dull sun. He saw no trace of a creek, despite the name.

He checked his pocket watch again. The thin wands of the hands had managed to make only ten minutes disappear since his last consultation. He kicked at the gravel of the track idly, thinking about what he would do if darkness fell and he was still alone. The forest would provide some protection from the wind, he supposed, though what else might seek shelter in its branches disturbed him. Bears and catamounts, Will had told him. He hoped again that the old man had been exaggerating. Still, he had matches in his pocket and there was no shortage of wood. If necessary, he could light a fire beside the track and wait out the night there. He could don some of the clothing in his suitcase, if need be...

Something crunched on the gravel behind him and he spun around, half-expecting to confront one of the creatures from Will's tales. Instead, a man rode towards him, two more horses trailing behind on leads. Ten feet away, he pulled his mount to a halt.

Matthew looked up at him, torn between wariness and relief. The man wore a heavy hide jacket with fur, richly brown, at throat and cuffs. A black felt fedora was pulled low on his forehead. The tanned face it shadowed was seamed with lines at the eyes and mouth but there was an odd agelessness about it, as he could be anything from an old forty to a young sixty. The hair that lay across his collar was the colour of old bone.

"Donovan?"

"Yes."

"You're too young," the man said after a moment.

"My name is Matthew Donovan. My father, Simon, was too ill to come." For a long moment, the man stared at him, his expression unreadable.

"Get on then." He jerked his head towards the small

black horse waiting passively behind him.

"My things…"

"I'll take care of them." The man dismounted in an easy swing and lifted Matthew's suitcase to the back of the pack horse, roping it on with practised skill despite the awkward shape.

"I'm sorry, I had no idea we would be travelling on horseback," he felt compelled to say then wished he hadn't, for his voice sounded thin and strained in the silence. The man simply shrugged and hefted up the other case onto the pony's back. It snorted in disgust but did not move. The satchel was fastened to the back of the black's saddle.

The man was back on his mount before Matthew could move, leaving him to scramble awkwardly onto the black under the other's watchful eyes. Matthew could not remember the last time he had ridden: not since his adolescence surely. It took a moment or two to settle the heavy coat around him and when he looked up, the man wheeled his roan closer and tossed the black's reins back over the horse's head. Matthew snatched at them and managed to gain some semblance of control before the roan moved away down the track, the pack horse trailing behind it. He noticed for the first time the rifle slung across the man's back.

As they entered the trail, he finally thought to ask the man's name. "Joseph," came the reply. No surname—nor any suggestion that more conversation would be welcome.

Despite the roughness of the trail—or perhaps because of it and the slow pace it required—he found his body remembering the mechanics of riding. The black was a steady creature, seemingly content to follow the pack horse without complaint. On even stretches, he experimented with heels and reins, and though it laid back its ears in half-hearted protest, the beast stopped or broke into a reluctant jog as he requested. Perhaps this journey

would not be so bad after all, he thought, though he was
under no illusions about the aches he was likely to suffer
after it.

The track they followed led steadily up and then much
more sharply downward. After an hour, the trees began to
thin and they emerged into a meadow. The grass had died
and there was no trace of green remaining, only a dull dun
hue. The far side of the valley was already in shadow and
the sun, burning in the hazy sky, hung just over the top of
the distant mountains.

The trail took them across the meadow, through sparse
stands of trees and finally along the bank of a river. The
water level was low, just a thin film of silver racing over a
layer of rocks. It was not such an inhospitable place,
Matthew thought. In summer, it must be quite peaceful
and even now was possessed of a strange, desolate beauty.
Throughout their passage, he half-expected to round a
bend or emerge from the trees and find a cabin waiting for
them. But the ground began to slope inexorably up again
and he called a question to Joseph's back. "How far is it?"

The man looked back, for almost the first time since
the journey had begun. "Some ways yet." Irritated, he
almost asked again, demanding some more specific answer,
but the remoteness in Joseph's voice made him hold his
tongue. Keeping quiet was not a particular hardship for
him for he was accustomed to solitude. Keeping quiet
when he had a thousand unanswered questions was not as
easy, to be sure, but it could be done.

They had passed into the shadow of the mountain and
its chill seemed like a taste of what night must be. Surely
they would reach Sidonie's home before then, he reasoned,
and irrationally held to that thought until they reached the
edge of the forest that blanketed the ridge ahead of them.
A few yards into the trees, Joseph turned onto a barely visible side trail that ended in a tiny clearing. "We camp

here," he said and Matthew thought he caught the faintest twitch of the man's lips in a smile.

"Fine," he forced himself to say, as if it was his own preferred habit to sleep on the ground in the most distant forest he could find. After all, it could not be much more uncomfortable than some of the beds in which he had found himself over the years. He eased himself from the black, wincing involuntarily at the twinge in his thighs.

After following Joseph's lead in removing the saddle and bridle, he was surprised when the man left all three mounts untethered. "Won't they wander off?"

"My horse doesn't wander. If he doesn't, the others won't."

His offers to help shrugged aside, Matthew found the most comfortable spot he could on the ground, grateful again for the thick coat, and watched as Joseph gathered wood and started a fire. Two bundles emerged from his pack, and, upon opening his, Matthew discovered cold meat from some large fowl and two thick slices of bread. Joseph passed his canteen that contained, unlike Will's, only water.

They ate in silence, then Joseph tossed him a blanket and proceeded to give every indication of bedding down to sleep. Matthew checked his watch. It was only eight o'clock. He could not imagine lying awake, listening for sounds that he could not attribute to the fire or the horses. "Is it safe here?" he asked.

"Safe as any place."

"I met a man on the train who said he used to trap around here. He said there are bears and catamounts."

"Got those," Joseph acknowledged. "Wolves too."

"He said there were other things." Matthew saw the man's grey eyes rise swiftly and study him for a long moment.

"Those too."

"Do you work for Sidonie Moreau?"

"Sometimes."

"What is she like?" The question might be impertinent but he could not help but ask it, especially as all he risked was Joseph's refusal to talk and that seemed inevitable anyway. His answer was a noncommittal shrug. "My father knew her, twenty years ago," Matthew persisted. "He told me a little about her. Was she born here?"

"No."

"How long have you known her?"

"Can't say. Most of my life."

"Then you knew her when she was young. Has she changed much?"

There was a long silence. Joseph stared at the fire. "Not much," he said at last. "She knows this is our land, even if the government says she owns it. She pays good money for work we do. She takes nothing without asking. We got no complaint of her."

That was the most he had spoken since he had emerged from the forest. Matthew pressed on. "We? Is there a town near here?"

"My people's places. We live out here." Matthew envisaged an entire village as taciturn as Joseph and hid a smile. Garrulousness was not a northern trait then, despite Will. He did not imagine that Joseph talked to himself. "Early start tomorrow. Best rest now."

That was dismissal, there was no doubt about that. Matthew resigned himself to attempting to sleep, assuring himself rather desperately that if Joseph did not fear bears, catamounts and wolves, there was no need for him to do so.

To his surprise, his next clear thought was that it was morning and his back hurt.

Chapter 8

The clouds sealed the sky the next day, covering the mountains and threatening rain. Despite Joseph's prediction that it would hold until they reached their destination, by late afternoon it had begun. The light, chilly drizzle made Matthew grateful that they rode in the relative shelter of the trees. He had no idea where they were going, only that he thought that they were riding west. What landmarks there might be were swathed in cloud and there was nothing to see above him but branches and rain.

The grey began to blend into black and the shadows between the trees darkened into impenetrability. He sat on the horse, his shoulders hunched against the steady drip of the rain. His fingers were nearly numb on the reins. Joseph's tan coat seemed the only light thing in the forest and he kept his eyes on it. The man never turned around; that tawny rectangle, bisected by the black line of the rifle, was the strongest impression Matthew had of him. Idly, he considered asking how much farther they had to go but decided he could not bear to hear the standard answer—"some ways yet"—again.

At last, the trees thinned and released them onto a stretch of meadow. Matthew saw something gleaming and wiped the rain from his eyes. In the deepening gloom, he could not discern the details of the landscape ahead but there was no doubt that the glow was a lighted window. He sagged in the saddle, relieved that he would not have to spend the night in sodden misery on the muddy ground. Suddenly, he did not care in the least about the reason for Sidonie Moreau's invitation. If she wanted revenge, at least he would be warm and dry when she took it.

Then something else caught his eye, a glimmer of light where there should have been nothing but darkness. He peered ahead again, squinting against the rain. The glimmer resolved into a dim reflection of light on water. The house was on the other side of a river, he thought at first, then saw that the water was too wide for that. A lake then, with the house on the other side. Yet Joseph was leading them straight forward, not angling left or right as would be necessary if they were to go around the lake. Perhaps the path runs right beside the water, Matthew told himself, to still the sudden sick churning in his stomach. The trail slanted slightly to their right and he felt a surge of relief. The change brought more of the scene ahead into clear view and the relief faded. The light did not have its source in the cheerful windows, as he had at first assumed, but in a lamp set at the end of a wooden dock. As he absorbed this fact, they topped a small rise and he saw the dock's twin not more than thirty feet away from them. No light burned there, but a small boat rocked on the choppy water.

An island. The house was on an island. He thought the terrible words, or said them aloud, for Joseph gave him a sharp backward glance. Matthew had not thought it was possible to be colder than he was, or more miserable. Now the chill in his fingers and his skin was nothing compared with the icy dread in his heart. He sat frozen on the black's back as Joseph unloaded his bags and twitched the canvas cover off the row-boat. The horse stirred restlessly under him, as if disturbed by his failure to follow the expected ritual.

Joseph finished stowing his bags and straightened. "Come on."

"Why not wait till morning?"

"In this? The lady said to have you there tonight. I got places to go. Come on." When Matthew did not move, Joseph stalked up to stand at the black's head. "It's the only way across. We got no choice in this. Either of us." Behind the hard truth of the words was the first trace of feeling Matthew had heard from him. Not anger, or disdain, as he might have expected, but sympathy.

He took a deep breath and forced himself to dismount onto legs gone rubbery with riding and tension. He said nothing—there was nothing he could say—as he followed Joseph onto the dock. The boat moved in its moorings, knocked against the dock by the waves. His bags were dark with rain. He took another breath and stepped into the boat.

His body remembered, as it had remembered how to ride. Somewhere beneath his panic and the twisting of his gut, his body knew how to find its balance and settle him onto the seat. The boat shuddered as Joseph boarded. Matthew closed his eyes and clenched his fingers around the edge of the wooden seat. The darkness behind his lids was too much, summoning the memory of the black water closing over his head, and he opened his eyes again.

Joseph rowed with practised ease, despite the rough water. Matthew could not see their destination, only the line of the shore as it receded. He focused his gaze on the dock and the horses waiting, heads bent beneath the miserable rain, and swallowed the sickness in his throat. The memories receded a little, sinking back down to the deep

reaches of his mind to which he had banished them. He
was not meant to drown, he told himself, with as much
conviction as he could summon. If he was meant to drown,
it would have happened twelve years ago.

After an interminable time, it was over. They reached
the far dock and he scrambled gratefully onto its steady
haven. Joseph tossed out his bags and began to turn the
boat around. "Go up the path there," was his last
instruction.

"Goodbye. Thank you." Joseph lifted one hand from
the oars in a brief salute then returned all his attention to
the boat. Matthew stood on the dock for a moment,
watching the little craft heave against the waves, then he
collected his bags and hurried up the flagstone path
through the bushes above the dock.

The path widened into a terrace and then he was at the
front door, a massive wooden slab banded in riveted metal.
There was a lamp above it and an iron door knocker in the
shape of a rose in its centre. He dropped one bag, pushed
his sopping hair back from his forehead and reached for
the knocker. Before he could touch it, the door swung
inward.

For a moment, he could see nothing but a slender form
silhouetted against the light. "Hello," he said. "My name
is Matthew Donovan. I am Simon's son."

"Where is your father?"

"He was not well enough to make the journey. I came
instead." The dark dazzle resolved into a woman. In the
dim light, he caught only the impression of black hair
pulled back from a narrow face, dark eyes and a column of
sombre, shapeless clothing. Exactly as his father had said.

Exactly as his father had said...

"Who are you?" The words were out before his tired
mind could grasp the obvious answer.

"Please come in," she said, as if he had not spoken. "I

would not want you to come all this way only to drown on the doorstep." Grateful, not caring that she had not answered his question, he stepped inside the foyer, to stand dripping onto the polished wood floor.

"Where is your mother?"

"My mother…is not well either." She closed the great door and turned to look at him. "I am sorry the weather was so unpleasant. You must be tired. I will show you to your room and you can change. There will be hot food in the dining room if you are hungry."

She stooped to retrieve one of his bags, lifting it easily as she passed him. He snatched up his other luggage and followed. He had a brief impression of a great empty room, lit by the large stone hearth on one wall, then she was leading him up the broad wooden staircase to the right of the foyer. At the top, lamps illuminated a shadowy landing. To his right, a long hallway disappeared into darkness. "Most of the house is empty," she said, as if she had caught his curious glance down the corridor.

"How long have you lived here?"

The black shoulders shifted in a gesture as noncommittal as Joseph's had been. "Some time now. Ah, here is your room. I apologize that there is no washroom attached but there is a full bath two doors down. Yes, there is running water," she finished, answering the question he had been too polite to ask.

She opened the door and stepped aside to let him precede her into the room. A fire blazed in the hearth, sending flickers of light across walls panelled in polished wood. The far end of the room seemed to extend in an angled hexagon from the square lines of the house. Heavy curtains of faded burgundy velvet covered the windows there, shutting out the dreary night. Two wing-backed chairs were set before the fire. A canopied bed, its heavy brocade curtains drawn, was flanked by armoires of polished wood.

The air held an edge of chill and smelt subtly of pine, as if the windows had been left open to banish the last traces of disuse and dust. He dropped his bags and put his numb hands towards the flames.

"I hope you will be comfortable. Please feel free to bathe—the water is hot. Come downstairs whenever you're ready."

The words, as polite and impersonal as the practised greetings of a hotel clerk, made him turn around. She stood at the door, one hand drawing it closed. "Wait. You haven't told me your name."

"Sidonie," she said with a smile. "My name is Sidonie."

Chapter 9

❧❧❧

The lamp in the bath was out of oil but whatever device heated the water worked well enough. Matthew lay in the candlelit gloom and let the heat seep into his chilly, aching body. Fine impression he had made, he thought, dripping on the carpets, his hair in his eyes. It was just as well the elder Sidonie had not answered the door. Though perhaps his bedraggled state might have made her feel sorry for him.

He thought about the young woman who had been waiting for him. To his surprise, he had a hard time visualizing her face. Long practice in school, studios and sketching on the street had made him skilled at reconstructing features, finding the essence of a face in a few quick moments. It was true that he had been shocked by his initial, irrational conclusion that it was the same woman his father had known, and then he had been preoccupied with becoming warm and dry. Still, he should be able to do better than a blurry mental image of black clothes and severe hair. An unassuming creature, his father had called her. At first, he corrected himself and remembered the strange tone in Simon's voice as he described her again, as he had

come to see her. There had been no doubt of the current
of fascination and warmth running beneath the otherwise
dispassionate recital. Whatever had happened in the end,
Sidonie Moreau still had a hold on his father more trou-
bling than guilt over infidelity or stolen credit.

The thought disturbed him. He hauled himself stiffly
from the embrace of the water and wrapped himself in the
towel he found hanging on the rack beside the tub. He ran
his hands through his damp hair then over his jaw, rough
with two days' worth of beard. He should shave, he
thought, hearing Gabriel's disapproving voice in his head.
For once, his brother was right. It was important to all of
them that he make a good impression. He looked around
for a mirror and was surprised to find none. Even a hunt
through the drawers of the chest beneath the sink yielded
nothing. Perhaps it was just as well—in the dim light he
would no doubt have cut his throat.

Ten minutes later, as presentable as a change of clothes
could make him, he ventured from his room. For a
moment, he lingered outside his door, looking down into
dark reaches of the hallway. How long had this place been
here? he wondered. If Sidonie Moreau had bought it, or
inherited it, surely she had no need of the meagre
Donovan fortune. Isolation might make it an undesirable
home but it had no doubt made it a very expensive one to
build. The wooden floors, the panelled walls and the solid
furniture all had the look of quality and expert craftsman-
ship. The cost of bringing stone, wood and manpower in
from the railroad must have been staggering.

He started down the stairway, looking out across the
expanse of a Great Hall, such as were common in ancient
castles. The vaulted ceiling rose two stories, vanishing into
shadows. The walls, ivory-hued plaster crossed by heavy
beams, were brightened with tapestries and the floors
warmed by thick carpets. Two chairs and a settee seemed

to huddle around the huge hearth. Two great banks of windows at one end reflected the cavernous space back on itself. He stood in the centre of the room for a moment. He could hear nothing except the crackle of the fire and, distantly, the patter of the rain on the terrace.

"Hello?" His voice echoed back at him, tentative and thin.

"Over here." He turned and saw the young Sidonie standing in an open doorway. "Please come into the dining room. Are you hungry?"

"Ravenous," he admitted and she gave a quiet laugh.

"I suppose that Joseph's trail rations are less than satisfying."

"What there was was quite good, actually. It is only that he didn't believe in eating very often. In fact, he ate even less frequently than he spoke."

"He is somewhat taciturn."

"He is. Though that's useful in a servant, I suppose." Matthew stepped past her into the dining room.

"He is not a servant. But it's a useful virtue just the same." He heard her laugh again. "I know. It is rather imposing, isn't it? Especially for one." Matthew nodded, aware that he had been staring at the long, gleaming table that surely sat more people than he knew. A place was set near one end, before a candelabra.

"One?" he repeated, her final words sinking in at last.

"I dined earlier."

"You will at least sit with me, won't you?"

"If you wish," she said and took the seat across from him. Covered silver serving trays opened to reveal steaming vegetables and several thick slices of roast. The aroma alone made him delirious and he almost forgot the necessity of good impressions. When he looked up after several intoxicating mouthfuls, Sidonie was watching him. He managed a weak smile of apology and consumed the rest, along with the rich red wine she poured, with more grace.

"I hope that your room is adequate," she said, after a few moments.

"It's beautiful. Though I couldn't find a mirror. Otherwise, do believe I would have had enough couth to shave."

"There are no mirrors in this house. It is a phobia of," the pause was so brief he thought that he imagined it, "my mother's."

"I didn't bring one. I was afraid it would break on the journey."

"You might be able to buy one in the village."

"Joseph's village?"

She nodded. "I'll ask him or Helen, the girl who comes to clean."

"Joseph said your mother owns this land," he ventured, moving his dinner plate to make room for the iced cake that ended the meal. He glanced up to catch her nod.

"My family inherited it many years ago when the original owner died. There is coffee in the carafe, if you wish some." He did and the hot, sweet liquid tasted of home and the life he had left behind in the city. It seemed as if that world was many miles and many years behind him. Disturbed by the thought, he sat back and looked at the young Sidonie again, determined this time to make her real, to solidify her in his mind.

Beneath the crescent of her hairline, her face tapered at her temples, flared briefly into cheekbones and then narrowed sharply to the chin. Her brows were as black as her hair and slightly arched. He could not determine the colour of the eyes beneath them, only that they were dark. Her nose was straight, her mouth pale and wider than expected in the thin face. She had the smooth, unlined skin of a young girl, but he did not think she could be more than a few years younger than he was. She was not beautiful. In a crowded café, no one would look at her twice. And yet, there was *something*. He could not identify it, could not even pin down what led him to believe it, yet he knew it was there, subtle and intriguing. Perhaps this was what his father had felt, with her mother. It was not a reassuring thought.

Her head dipped a little, as if she were embarrassed by his scrutiny. "Sidonie. That's an unusual name." He said the words to say something, anything at all, and then regretted them.

"Unusual for the daughter to be named for her mother, you mean."

"That as well."

"None of your brothers are named for your father?" The inflection made it a question but just barely.

"No. How did you know that I have brothers?"

"Your father spoke of his family, a little."

"Did he?" He could not help the shortness in his tone but she did not seem to notice.

"Why did you come and not one of the others?"

"My eldest brother has a family and a business to manage. My second brother had concerns of his own."

"And you had no business? No family?"

"I live alone. I'm an artist. I had nothing that I could not leave for a while."

"Ah." She smiled then, leaning back in her chair. "The black sheep."

"I am the representative of my father in this matter."

"Don't be offended. I did not suppose they sent you to be rid of you. Or to insult me...us." Her words, softly spoken with an undertone of amusement, made him aware that he had stiffened in his seat. "What sort of artist are you?"

"I'm a painter. I hope to paint while I'm here. If your mother has no objections."

"I cannot think of any. You are more than welcome to whatever inspiration you might find here."

"Thank you. My thanks for the dinner, as well. It was very good."

"I can cook, if it is required of me." Her reply caught him off guard, the words implying that he had in some way doubted her. He did not think his compliment had suggested that but he was tired and losing his concentration. He lost the battle with an impolite yawn as well. Sidonie rose from her chair. "You have had a long day, if I know Joseph. You should sleep."

"I think that would be a good idea," he said. She walked with him to the foot of the stairs. "Will your mother be better tomorrow?"

"I cannot say. I regret that I will be...unavailable...most of the day but I ask you please not to disturb her rest."

"Of course not. Where is her room?"

"Just avoid any locked areas," she said, as if that was an answer. "You can look around if you wish but remember that this is an old house. Many areas are not safe and so have been sealed."

"Of course. Good night, Miss Moreau."

"Good night, Mr. Donovan." We are so polite, Matthew thought with absurd humour as he climbed the stairs. As if my father hadn't done her mother any harm. As if I was here on a holiday, instead of under duress.

When he glanced back from the top of the stairs, she was gone. He stood for a moment, looking out over the empty room. In the heavy silence he heard the clatter of dishes, muffled, as if from a long way away. He found the simple, homey sound strangely reassuring.

In his room, he could hear nothing but the wind. He contemplated drawing the curtains to see what lay outside his window but, full of food and warmth, did not feel inclined to face the darkness. He unpacked those clothes that would wrinkle unforgivably but left the rest in his suitcase, as if that could ensure his imminent departure.

Ensconced in the huge bed, the curtains open to let in the last light of the dying fire, he considered what he had learned and what his course of action should be. If the elder Sidonie was ill, that might explain her sudden return to events that were two decades old. Her condition must be serious, despite her daughter's seeming unconcern. If it was not, surely she would have managed to be there to greet him, especially as she would have believed it was Simon who was arriving. Would the approach of mortality be more likely to make her vengeful or forgiving? He hoped for the latter, of course, but could draw no conclusions until he had met her.

Then there was her daughter. It had never occurred to any of them to suppose that Sidonie Moreau had a family. After all, her surname had not changed. Peter would no doubt consider the presence of an illegitimate daughter vindication of his convictions about Sidonie Moreau's suspect moral nature. Matthew grimaced automatically at the thought and then returned to curious consideration of the questions the situation raised. Who was the young Sidonie's father? And where was he now? Had she lived in this isolated place for her entire life? The odd formality of her manner, the appearance that was an echo of his father's memory of her mother, suggested that she might have. Yet, just as with her appearance, there was a subtle air about her demeanour that suggested that the surface might be misleading.

Whatever she was, he dared not alienate her in case that influenced her mother's decisions about his father. He was quite certain he dared not trust her either, however unprepossessing she might appear.

As he lay back on the cool pillows and felt weariness begin to weight his limbs, he wondered if he should lock his door. He was still wondering when sleep claimed him.

Chapter 10

In the deep hours of the night the rain stopped and even the wind stilled its passage through the valley. The darkened halls of the house were silent. No boards creaked beneath her bare feet. The doorknob turned noiselessly beneath her fingers. She smiled, half-expecting to find it locked. Not that it would have mattered, for there was no room in the house that she could not enter.

The faint glow of the last embers in the fireplace was the only light. That did not matter either; she could see well enough. She felt the soft kiss of the carpets against her soles as she moved to the bed. The heavy bedcurtains had been left drawn and she looked down at the bed's occupant.

She had not counted on this. She had thought that it would be Simon who answered her summons or no one at all. It had never occurred to her that he might send one of his sons. She had not thought he would even tell them the truth. All her plans, from beginning to end, had been based on it being Simon sleeping in that bed. Now all the levers she had thought to use—guilt and honour and the memory of passion—were useless to her.

You could send him home, the watcher thought. Demand some token of atonement from his father and let him go, safe and untouched. There will be another chance, another time. You have nothing but time.

She crouched down beside the bed, a swift slide of darkness blacker than the rest. The sleeper stirred. There was a ragged hitch in his breathing. She froze, still as the silence, and waited. He did not move again, her curious gaze no longer piercing his dreams.

He lay on his side, covers drawn up to keep out the cold. The spill of hair, longer than she remembered as the style of urban men, would have appeared simply black to other eyes, its colour indiscernible in the darkness. She saw old oak, sealskin, the soft brown of cloves. His face was long and narrow, his skin holding the pallor of one more used to night than day. Over the large eyes, delicately veined lids quivered. One hand had slipped out from the cocoon of covers and she could see curious calluses on the well-scrubbed skin. She inhaled, breathing in the subtle scents of oils and turpentine, soap and sweat.

She thought of standing at the window and watching him ride away as her dreams turned to dust and ashes in her mouth.

It did not have to be the end of her plans. If the lures she had counted on were useless, she had others. If they were older, and crueller, well, there was nothing else to be done.

Oh Simon, you should have come, she thought staring at the sleeping face among the pillows. But if you would not, then he will have to do.

If only he were not so terribly, terribly young.

Chapter 11

꧁꧂

When he awoke and drew back the curtains from the window, Matthew was astonished to discover that the sun,
though no more than a pale smudge of light through the
clouds, was already well over the mountains. Sealed in the
darkness of the bedroom, he had risen twice to the surface
of wakefulness and then sunk back into sleep without even
turning over. Now, looking out across the lake, he guessed
that it must be close to noon. A sudden hollow grumble
from his stomach confirmed it even before he retrieved his
watch.

Fifteen minutes later, he descended the stairs, remembering Sidonie's warning that she would be gone for most
of the day. He found himself surprisingly eager to explore
the house, especially without her decidedly disconcerting
presence, but acknowledged that the place he would have
to start was the kitchen. He stood for a moment in the
Great Hall. A fire already blazed in the hearth, providing
some modicum of warmth. The room felt dim and shadowy, despite the windows flanking the foyer and lining the
far wall. It had an air of sadness, as if the builder had imagined bright trappings and cheerful inhabitants to counter-

act the dark grandeur and both had failed to materialize.
Or else, they had existed once and now were gone, leaving
only the ghostly bones to which they were to have given
flesh.

His stomach complained again, banishing his morbid
thoughts. Where would the architect have placed the
kitchen in such a place? Near the dining room seemed a
reasonable guess. At least he knew where that was located.
He crossed to the closed door and pushed it open.

There was a woman standing at the far end of the
room. For a moment, he thought it was the younger
Sidonie, but then he saw her clearly. Her face was broad
and tanned, her cheeks marked faintly with the scars of
childhood illness. Her hair was tucked beneath a red scarf
but several strands had escaped to lie like black threads
against her skin. She wore a faded blue dress beneath a
heavy sweater of bright red wool.

"Good morning." Her head bobbed in reply but she
did not move. She simply stood still at the far end of the
great table, clutching her polishing cloth. He walked
towards her, determined not to waste a chance to discover
more about his strange surroundings and mysterious host-
esses. "You must be Helen. I'm Matthew Donovan." She
nodded again. "You knew that already?"

"Joseph said you come."

"You know Joseph?" he asked, aware of how foolish the
question was but willing to sacrifice sense to keep her
speaking.

"My uncle." Closer to her, he saw she was younger
than he had at first supposed, no older than seventeen.

"Do you work here all the time?"

"My mother does, usually. She been sick, so I come."

"You and your mother must do a good job. Everything
is very clean." Her gaze, which had lifted to the point of
his chest, dropped back to the table.

"Came in all last week to clean," she admitted.

"How often do you usually come?"

"Once a month."

"Miss Moreau does everything the rest of the time?" She gave him a quick look of incomprehension and dread then shrugged.

"Do you want lunch? Joseph said I was to cook for you, if you wanted."

"Thank you but no. I can take care of it...though I suppose I should have breakfast before lunch." The feeble jest elicited no response other than the awkward shift of her weight from one foot to the other. Her desire for him to be gone was palpable. "How do I get to the kitchen?" She pointed to a door along the opposite wall. At the door, he remembered about the mirror. "I need to buy a mirror. Could I get one in the village? Or give you money and you can bring one to me if you're coming back tomorrow?"

"A mirror?" she stammered, giving him another frightened glance.

"Yes. Miss Moreau said it might be possible to get one from the village. There are none here and I need to shave." He ran one hand across his chin.

"I'll ask Joseph," Helen said at last.

"Thank you." Just as the door closed behind him, he saw her hurry from the room. The strangeness of the encounter summoned up some of the unease that daylight had banished. She had seemed calm, if shy, until he mentioned Sidonie. Could she have been cruel to the girl? She did not seem like the sort to beat the servants. Nor did Joseph seem like the sort of man who would tolerate mistreatment of his family. Everything he had so grudgingly said about the elder Sidonie suggested that he respected her. Perhaps that respect did not extend to her daughter.

His stomach grumbled again and he looked around, pushing aside the useless speculations. The kitchen was dominated by a great black iron stove and yet another fire-place. Weak light flowed in through the windows across from him. It was sufficient to allow him to examine the cupboards and find the entrance to the pantry and ice-room that had been build onto the side of the house. There seemed to be a suitable selection of staple food-stuffs, seeming fresh and newly bought.

Busy preparing a breakfast of eggs and bacon, it was not until he stood, plate in hand, that he realized what was unusual about the room. There was no table. No place for servants to eat—or for anyone who did not want to dine at that intimidatingly long table in the other room. He looked around again. The kitchen was clean and neat, except for the disorder he himself had created, but it had no air of warmth or use. It was as formal in its way as the dining room, as if it were only to be used on special occa-sions or for show.

Disconcerted, he went into the dining room, drew all the curtains and sat as close to the light as he could. Unwilling to put his plate on Helen's carefully polished table, he balanced it on his knees as he stared out at the cloud-shrouded mountains. It looked as if rain were immi-nent. If he wanted to explore the outside of the house, he had best do it soon. The thought was surprisingly wel-come. As little as he liked the thought of contemplating the water all around him, the thought of investigating the interior of the house with Helen avoiding him like a timid rabbit was even less appealing.

When he stepped outside, he discovered that the air had lost a little of the chill that had numbed him during the previous day's journey, but not so much that he was not still grateful for coat and gloves. He looked around the terrace. It was composed of granite flagstones, edged and patterned with the shrivelled remains of grass that had thrust its way between the stones. There might once have been a garden along the wall to his right but now it was full of tangled rose bushes that grew high enough to partially obscure the windows. On the far side of the terrace, the land sloped away towards the water and he had a clear view of the lake and mountains.

Matthew walked to the edge of the flagstones and turned to take his first clear look at the house itself. It rose in three stories of grey stone, looking as solid and ancient as one of the mountains. The roof, shingled in dark grey, sloped to heavy eaves that overhung the few small windows of the upper floor. At each end of the house were towers whose roofs topped that of the main structure like turrets. He identified his bedroom on the second floor of the tower to his left, recognizing the curtains he had left open that morning. Moving to his right, he caught a glimpse of shelves of books through one of the windows on the main floor. That was one of the rooms off the Great Hall, he decided, most likely a library. A blur of movement crossed on the windows and he started before realizing it must be Helen, continuing her cleaning. Through the windows to his left, he could see little but the shadowy shapes of furniture.

Two paths led from the terrace. One he recognized as the one he had taken from the dock, so he followed the other. It dipped through pines that screened his view of the house and lake and then emerged onto an expanse of bedrock, the granite forming a natural plateau. From the clear ground, he continued his contemplation of the house.

Straight ahead, another line of tall windows presented themselves and he had a clear view of a large, empty room that ended in another of the tower extensions. Wooden shutters, smoke-coloured paint peeling and patchy, framed each window. Some had been closed, making the house appear as if it was possessed of many sets of eyes, some closed, some winking, some watching him curiously.

Intrigued, Matthew moved closer, the rock beneath his feet sloping up again. Another patch of shrubbery gone wild kept him from getting close enough to be able to peer into the curious space. He found the path again. Past another line of twisted pine trees, several cracked steps took him up onto another terrace.

He turned to consider the empty room again. Where the wall straightened, there was a glass-paned door. Cupping his hands around his eyes, he leaned against it and peered inside. The ceiling of the room was painted in white tinged with the faintest hint of blue. It seemed to soar skyward, though he knew it could be no higher than that of the dining room and kitchen. Complex mouldings circled the room above the line of the windows and he could see the glint of old gilt on them. A ballroom, he thought, just as it occurred to him that the room would make the perfect studio. It was obviously unused and the extravagance of windows meant it would provide enough natural light for him to work.

He tested the door, discovered it locked, and moved to continue his explorations. Beyond the ballroom were two sets of curtained windows, then he was passing the Great Hall again. Though he knew that on the other side of it lay only the dining room and kitchen, he continued along the path, discovering a dusty, unused sunroom beyond them.

The last part of the trail brought him around the south-eastern axis of the house and back to the more travelled path he had followed from the dock. For a moment he stood on the trail, contemplating continuing his survey by considering the dock and lake by daylight. After a moment, he worked his way back towards the front terrace. The house was larger than he had imagined the previous night and he marvelled at the effort, and expense, that must have gone into its creation. The eccentricity of it intrigued him and he wondered who had built such an extravagant mansion in a place so far from the world—and why.

Back in the foyer, he discovered a coat rack fastened rather inelegantly to the one wall. A fur-collared coat hung there. He shrugged off his greatcoat and settled it there as well.

As he stepped into the hall, he considered where his explorations should take him next. Left or right, up or down? At last, he decided to start at his bedchamber and work his way to the room he most wanted to see.

On the second floor, he discovered that most of the rooms, save his bedroom and the bathroom, were locked. Those that opened showed no signs of recent habitation. Mattresses lay rolled on dusty beds and open wardrobes bared their empty hearts. Halfway down the corridor, he passed a staircase leading up and down. At the end of the hallway was another narrow staircase leading only upwards. He climbed it slowly, aware that the air seemed to grow colder with each step he took. It was darker here as well, the only source of light a small window high in the stairwell, and he wished that he had brought a lamp.

When he reached the top, he found himself standing on a small landing, faced with a corridor before him and another hallway leading back towards the front of the house. After a moment, he chose the second. The floor was thick with dust. Helen and her mother obviously did not number cleaning this floor among their duties. Tiny rooms, empty except for the occasional worn wooden bed-frame or forgotten chair, lined the inner side of the hall-way. These were the servants' quarters, he guessed, and shivered at the thought of how cold they must be when winter came.

After a brief survey, he returned to the stairs and ventured down the other corridor. It led across the end of the

Great Hall, he decided, serving as the only connection between the two ends of the house on the upper floors. The passageway was narrow and dark, the thin light from the stairway unable to penetrate its heart. He groped his way along, uncomfortably aware of the cobwebs that shredded beneath his outstretched hands. He remembered Sidonie's warning about the unsafe state of the unused portions of the house and imagined himself plunging through a decayed floorboard onto the polished wooden floor of the hall. It was not a pleasant image and he was relieved when he emerged into a hallway that seemed a twin to the one he had just left. From reflex more than curiosity, he checked the doors and found more empty rooms and abandoned furniture.

He descended the other staircase to the second floor and discovered that all of the rooms there were locked. Remembering the ill woman who lay sleeping somewhere in the house, he gave up his door-rattling and continued down the stairs, emerging into the library.

He lingered there for a while, surveying the shelves. They held a startling diversity of books, many in languages he could not identify. Old leather-bound volumes stood next to newer books bound in cloth. It did not surprise him to see classical plays, histories and commentaries, but he was intrigued by the fact that below them was a shelf of the most recent, and the most controversial, works of fiction. At least if he was required to wait for the elder Sidonie to recover, he would not lack for things to read.

An open archway led into a sitting room. Compared with the spare, deserted nature of the rest of the house, it seemed like a luxurious bower. The couches and chairs looked comfortable and welcoming. On a small table set in the extension was a selection of plants in terracotta pots. In the sunlight, their green leaves and stems looked startlingly lush and vibrant. They were the first signs of life he had seen anywhere in the house and he lingered over them for a moment, running his fingers along a leaf, poking at the damp earth. He knew very little about horticulture but thought, from the decidedly undecorative appearance of most of them, that they must be herbs rather than flowering plants.

An unlit fire had been laid in the small hearth, awaiting a match. Where the sun touched the thick carpet, it glowed in red and amber. More shelves lined the walls, some holding books, others a bewildering array of ornaments. A broken vase, its shattered pieces carefully arranged about the intact base, triggered memories of careful childhood examination of his father's collection of antiquities. A scattering of coins bore a face and lettering he did not recognize. There was a small alabaster unguent jar, ink fading from the zigzag patterns etched into its side. A jointed female figure rested its carved head against the wall, its wooden legs splayed before it. Was it an idol, he wondered, or a child's toy? There were also more plants, some with blossoms furled in tight, secret buds, others whose scent hung subtle and tantalizing in the air.

A small desk was set under one window. Matthew drifted over to it. It showed signs of use—scratches in the wood, an old burn mark—but was bare. With a surreptitious glance towards the door, he reached for the top drawer. It opened with a creak that sounded perilously loud. Inside, there was nothing but a small collection of paper and envelopes. Matthew knew without touching what the feel of them would be, for Sidonie's letter was still in his jacket pocket, over his heart.

He closed the drawer and went back to the hall. Across from the library, a door opened onto a room full of sheet-shrouded furniture and cobwebbed corners. One strange shape intrigued him and he lifted the sheet to discover a gilded harp. When he touched the strings experimentally, a sour, off-key note echoed through the room. He dropped the sheet and moved on. The next room had obviously been shuttered for many years. He saw that one of the windows had been broken, the glass still lying half-hidden in the dust.

Withdrawing, he passed through the door at the far end of the music room. This was the chamber beside the ballroom, he decided, the one with curtains so tightly drawn. As he stepped inside, he realized that it was a gallery designed to demonstrate the artistic taste and investment acumen of the owner. Even in the dim light, he could see that the wall bore only a few works. That they had once held far more was clear from the odd, asymmetrical manner in which those remaining were hung and the patches of darker paint, unfaded by the sun, that patterned the walls like monochrome canvases.

Curious, Matthew pulled back the curtains and turned to consider the paintings that had survived the culling. There were a few landscapes, none that seemed in any way exceptional, two portraits of aristocracy from centuries past and one more contemporary rendering. This last drew his eye and he moved to study it. The brushwork was good and the shading of the face exquisite. After a brief contemplation of the technique, he stepped back to examine the painting itself. It was of a man of the last century, dressed in a high-collared shirt and sharply tailored jacket. A drop of crimson denoted a ruby pin in the black gloss of his silk cravat. He appeared to be in his forties with a thin, vulpine face. There were fierce, bitter lines about his mouth and an edge of madness in the deep-set eyes. Perhaps the artist had only used too much white in them, Matthew thought, then saw again the complex modelling of the light on the throat and decided that the unknown painter must have known precisely what he was doing. He bent closer to see if he could find a signature but saw none.

Who was he? The builder of the house or an ancestor? He looked for some resemblance to Sidonie but saw none, except perhaps for the line of the cheekbone.

With a last glance at the mysterious painting, he pulled the curtains closed again. There was only one room left to consider. Unable to quell the sudden, acquisitive eagerness he felt, he put his hand on the knob of the door to the ballroom. As it turned, he half-expected it to stop, denying him entrance to the place that intrigued him the most. The door opened with a soft sigh. Two steps led down to the vast, empty floor. He had expected marble, without considering how much it would have cost to bring it to this isolated place. Instead, the floor was composed of strips of wood, patterned in shades from whitish pine to darkest mahogany. It was dulled now by dust and neglect but he imagined that it once must have been beautiful.

This was another room Helen and her mother had obviously not spent time cleaning, he decided. Cobwebs shrouded one corner and hung like ghostly banners from the high ceiling. The windows could stand to be scrubbed as well but the light they allowed in was entrancing. Even dulled by cloud, it reached all through the room. The western exposure meant that mornings would be dark, but then he had always been a late riser. He was accustomed to working into the evening, guided by memory, imagination and lamplight.

He took a deep breath as he moved in a slow circle about the room. He must not want this too much. It would distract him from the reason he had come. He might not be here long enough to use it. But he *did* want it. He did not care about the dust and cobwebs, the chill in the air that no doubt could not be dispelled by any fire. All he needed was an easel. He did not have one but somewhere on this island would be the means to construct one.

Right now, he did not even need that. A chair from the

music room and his sketchbook would suffice. He did not give himself time to consider it. A few moments later, he was sketching the view of the lake through the dirty windows, incorporating their imperfections and obstacles to clear vision into the image.

The light moved across the terrace and the hills. The sun turned the clouds to a palette of reds, tinted with edges of orange and hints of purple. Matthew became aware of the numbness in his fingers, the ache in his shoulders and stood up, stretching out his sore muscles. There was a movement along the shore of the lake and he stepped closer to the windows. He squinted at the small figure, wrapped in a heavy coat, and identified the bright red flag of a kerchief. It was Helen on her way back to the village. He watched as she moved away from the water, vanishing at last into the line of trees. She walked quickly and easily, as if there were a trail. Perhaps tomorrow, if the weather cleared, he would see if he could find it and locate the village.

That practical thought sparked a twinge of hunger. He had eaten nothing since the breakfast he had made for himself at noon and now it was nearly dusk. He had seen or heard nothing of either Sidonie all day. "Unavailable," the daughter had said. For the first time, he considered what that might mean. It had the same ambiguity as her mother's letter. Had she gone out? If so, where?

He made a restless circuit of the empty rooms of the lower floor. There was no sound but that of his footsteps. Uneasiness creeping back, he stoked the fire in the great hearth and then climbed to the upper floor.

In his bedchamber, he stood for a moment at the window, uncomfortably aware that the eastern sky was dark and that his reflection was clearer than the far mountains. He drew the curtains and set about laying the fire from the stock of kindling and logs on the hearth. As he worked, he decided that he was far too hungry to wait on Sidonie's return. He would make his dinner in that empty, hollow kitchen and eat it in the echoing loneliness of the dining room. If she did not appear by midnight, then he would see what he could do about the locks on the doors. There had not been a lock in his own home that could keep him out when he was determined to get in. He did not think these were much different.

He crouched by the cold fireplace, hearing the silence of the house and thinking suddenly of Will's tale of the frozen trapper. He found himself holding his breath, certain that he could hear the distant echoes of someone muttering of slow death in the embrace of the mountain winter. It was only the wind in the trees, he told himself, or the settling of the boards and stones of the old house.

He suppressed a shiver and returned his mind to practicalities. He changed from his dusty clothes and went to wash his hands, smudged with pencil and grime. Feeling as presentable as he could without a mirror to gauge his appearance, he returned to his room.

"Here you are." The words seemed to issue from the air. He turned quickly, the sickening chill of fear welling inside him. A shadow shifted and he saw the pale circle of Sidonie Moreau's face hovering, disembodied, in the darkness beyond the fire's light. Another shift and the flickering glow caught the black folds of her dress as she stepped forward. "I am sorry I was unavailable for so long. I hope you had an interesting day. Are you hungry?"

The pleasant words washed over him, as if trying to steady the hammering of his heart. The practical, polite tone of her voice restored his equilibrium. She had not materialized in the shadows like a phantom. It was simply that the sound of her footsteps on the stairs had not penetrated the closed door of the washroom. He let out his breath and managed an inward amusement at his own paranoia. He was hungry—and tired. It was no wonder that his imagination had been inflamed by the strangeness of the house, the oncoming night.

He managed a smile and polite words of his own, then followed her downstairs, aware of the darkness that closed behind the light of her lamp, swallowing the world behind him as they descended.

Chapter 12

❦

"I met your cleaning woman. Or her daughter, at least," Matthew said, looking up from his dinner to where Sidonie sat across from him. Once again, she had said she had eaten earlier but agreed to sit with him while he dined. "I asked her about a mirror and she agreed to ask Joseph. She seemed quite shy. Even frightened."

"She is not used to strangers, I suppose."

"She said she only comes in once a month. It must be hard work to look after a place of this size by yourself."

"It is not so difficult. Most of it is not in use."

"I noticed." He took another sip of wine. "How is your mother?"

"A little improved, I think."

"When might I be able to speak to her?"

"That is up to her."

"The sooner I can meet her, the sooner we can resolve this."

"I did not think you were in a hurry to return to the city. The letter did say that you should be prepared to stay for a while."

"I know." He set down his fork with a clatter that

seemed to echo through the room. "My father is very sorry for what happened. He wants to make amends. That's why I came. But it is difficult to do that without knowing what it is your mother wants from us." There was a question there but if she heard it, she chose to ignore it.

"I am certain it will all be made clear. In the meantime, you should try to enjoy yourself. Did you paint today?"

"I did some pencil studies, but I did find the perfect place to paint, if you will allow me to use the ballroom."

"Of course. Is there anything you need?"

"An easel, a chair. A hammer and nails for framing. I don't suppose those things can be obtained in the village."

"I think there might be an easel upstairs. I believe the original owner's daughter was an amateur artist. There are certainly plenty of chairs. Down by the dock there is a storage shed and workshop. You are welcome to whatever you can find there."

Intrigued by the thought of a glimpse into the rest of the house, he persuaded her to begin the hunt immediately. Lamp in hand, she led him up the stairs to the bedroom wing opposite his own. "Here, I think," she said, pausing in front of the door and handing him the lamp to hold while she took a ring of keys from her pocket. There were fewer keys than locked doors, Matthew noticed. Each key must open more than one door.

The door swung inward and the scent of dust and stale air swept out. Sidonie took the lamp and lifted it into the darkness. "Yes, this is it." He followed as she threaded her way through the bulky obstacles of covered furniture. At the back of the room, he saw the tell-tale shapes of canvases propped against the wall. Irresistibly drawn, he had crouched beside them before he knew it, turning them into the light of the lamp Sidonie had set on a dusty table. Some of the canvas and wood had weakened with rot and mildew, he saw, but much was certainly salvageable. He felt a pang of guilt at the thought; he was planning his own use of the canvas before he even considered the art that already covered it.

He tilted the one he held out of the shadows and examined it. It was a still-life, competent but uncomplicated. The paint was thin and cracking, as if the artist had feared to use enough pigment to give the picture any substance. Through the cracks, he could see the faint lines of her original sketches. It seemed like a practice work, executed without any conviction or interest. The next was stronger: a landscape of the dock and the mountains beyond.

As he turned the third painting, he heard Sidonie speak but her words were lost. It was not quite a portrait, he thought, for there was something too exaggerated about it for that. A woman sat in a chair, white hands neatly in her lap, feet placed precisely together. A loose black dress covered her from throat to ankles. The artist in him noticed that the drapery of the dress was clumsily executed. A smear of red in her lap caught his attention and he saw that the little hands held a knife edged with blood. The woman's face, slightly bent, was surrounded by a flow of ebony hair that merged into the darkness of her dress. Black eyes were turned up, looking out of the canvas, and the thin red lips were curved in a smile. She looked malevolent and self-satisfied.

The lines of perspective were not right, the throat was awkwardly done and the face did not seem altogether human, but one thing was certain nonetheless. The woman in the painting looked remarkably like Sidonie.

A shadow moved across the canvas and Matthew started. Sidonie shifted to let the light fall on it again, studying it over his shoulder. "I found the easel," she said after a long moment.

"This painting..."

"Looks like me. I had forgotten about it." There was a

long pause. She stooped to look at it more carefully, her hand falling on his shoulder. His muscles tensed involuntarily and the hand lifted. "That was my grandmother."

"But..."

"It's a long story. I will tell you, if you wish, but not here. Bring anything you think might be of use to you and we'll find somewhere more comfortable." Matthew hunted through the rest of the canvases, selecting those in the best condition on the chance that he might be able to reuse them, and followed her from the room. The unsettling portrait he took with the rest, sandwiched between two innocuous, amateurish landscapes.

He thought that she would choose the sitting room but it was to the two chairs in front of the great hearth that she led him. He stacked the scavenged canvases against the wall as Sidonie set two more logs on the fire.

"The man who built this house," she began, "was possessed of great wealth and considerable eccentricity. I suppose that is easily apparent. He was sole heir to his father's fortune, which even in this time would be substantial. His own oddities did not prevent him from being a canny businessman and increasing that fortune. He married late in life and had one child, a daughter. He disliked and distrusted most people but was loyal and protective of those few he loved.

"As he grew older, he became increasingly convinced that the world was a terrible and dangerous place. Gradually, he began to cut his ties to it. He sold his businesses, he sold his great mansion in the city and the grand summer house by the shore. He believed that his only hope of happiness, and his family's sole guarantee of safety, was to build himself a fortress far away from the world."

"This house," Matthew supplied and she nodded. "How did he manage it? The cost must have been incredible."

"More than he expected. It took three years to build

the house. A railway spur was cut through the mountains to the north to bring goods from the main line. From the end of the track, they were carried on wagons over the last ridge and down to the lake. A bridge was built to the island. When the work was finished, he had the track that joined the main line torn up and the bridge destroyed. He and his reluctant wife and daughter arrived here in the summer and none of them ever left again.

"It was a great curiosity at the time, of course. His peers in society thought he had gone mad. They waited for invitations to see this folly of his but none were ever received. He never appeared in the city again. He had lost so much of his fortune in the building of the house that he was no longer one of the richest men in the country, though he was still very wealthy. After a few years, most people had forgotten about him or believed him dead.

"But his great refuge turned out to be an illusion. His wife died of pneumonia the second year that she spent in the house. So he invited someone else to join him in his exile; the woman who had once been his lover. They were kindred spirits of a type, both withdrawn from humanity in their own ways. The isolation and austerity of the place suited her. His daughter, who was now in late adolescence, could do nothing. That winter, she passed away as well.

"The recluse lived another five years before the madness that had been waiting in the wings all his life overtook him and he drowned himself in the lake. He left the house and all of his fortune that remained to his lover."

"Your grandmother," Matthew guessed. Sidonie nodded. He leaned forward, staring into the fire for a moment. The story had a fantastical feel, enhanced by the quiet, empty darkness of the hall surrounding them. He suspected there was a good deal more to the tale than she had told, though whether it was by deliberate omission or simple ignorance he could not tell. He glanced automatically at the ominous portrait hidden among the other paintings propped against the wall. "The daughter must have hated her. How did she die?"

"Constance? She contracted a wasting disease, I believe."

"What was your grandmother's name?" he asked, looking over at her. The wings of the chair shadowed her face and he could see little but the curve of one cheek and the gleam of an eye.

"Sidonie," she answered after a moment.

"I might have guessed. Did she stay here after the old man's death?"

"Yes. She travelled a great deal but she always returned here."

"Your mother did the same?" He saw her nod. "The man who built the house—was he your grandfather?" She shrugged. Though it seemed a careless gesture, he knew that it meant the subject would not be discussed, no matter how he asked. Nor would any question that pertained to her own parentage, he suspected. "I saw a portrait in the gallery. Is that him?" She nodded. "What happened to the rest of the paintings there?"

"They were sold or donated to museums. You are not missing any masterpieces, I assure you, though there was a rather fine Desjardins and an unusual Giardello."

"You had a Giardello?" he echoed and saw the flash of her teeth as she smiled.

"Yes. That one went to a museum. It seemed a shame for it to languish here, seen only by the crows and the squirrels." She was right, though he was not certain that he could have brought himself to surrender a Giardello. He thought of the few paintings that remained, hanging forgotten and unseen in the gallery.

"Aren't you lonely here?" he asked.

Her face turned away into the shadow. "Sometimes." It was a voice he had not heard before, not the calm, detached tone she usually used but one that was brittle, full of icy edges and sorrows.

"You should do what your mother did," he said without thinking. The double-edged meaning of the words struck him but he went on. "There is an entire world beyond this valley. You should see it. You are too young to be immured here."

The laugh from the shadows of her chair chilled him. "I am somewhat older than you might think. But I thank you for your concern."

"It is only that I know what it is to be forced to choose between what you need and what others want of you. Honouring your mother does not mean sacrificing your life for hers."

"There is no danger of that." She shifted in the chair and her face re-emerged into the light, expressionless and composed. "Is that how you honour your father? In the breach rather than the observance?" Matthew stiffened, remembering the old arguments, the old wounds inflicted and received.

"I live the way I choose to live," he answered after a moment, his voice as formal as her features. "My father does not necessarily approve of everything I do but he has had no choice but to accept it."

"How do you live?" The question confused him for a moment. It must have shown on his face for she smiled a little, her expression softening. "It is true that sometimes I miss the world. So tell me about yours."

He did, as the fire burned low and the hours of the night moved on. He told her about his cold room, with its skylight that caught the light better than any place he had ever lived. He told her about the cafés and bars, about Jack and Andre and Paul (but not Allegra, though why he was not sure). He told her about the way the hours would flow by beneath his brush, about the pleasure of seeing his paintings on a gallery wall and the pain of noticing all their flaws in the same moment. He told her about Gabriel, and Peter, and Simon.

When at last he yawned and looked at his watch, it was nearly one in the morning. "I must apologize. I didn't mean to ramble on so. I am usually less tedious than that," he said.

"I asked. It was not tedious at all. But it is late and we should save some conversation for tomorrow."

"It will be your turn to tell me the story of your life." She laughed. It was not the sound that had chilled him earlier, but there was something beneath its youth and amusement, an undercurrent of ironic darkness that confused him.

"I will be away again tomorrow until the evening," she told him, handing him the lamp for his journey into the dark hallway of the second floor.

"Where do you go? Where can there be to go around here?" She smiled and shook her head.

"Ask me again tomorrow night."

"Will you tell me then?"

"Perhaps. Ask and see."

"Will your mother…?"

"Tomorrow night, Mr. Donovan."

"All right. Tomorrow night—Sidonie."

At the top of the stairs, he looked back into the hall. Despite the darkness, he could see a figure crouched beside the fire. A white oblong moved and tilted in the flickering light. He turned away quickly, guilty and unnerved at once, so that he would not see Sidonie contemplating the picture of the ancestor whose name she carried.

Chapter 13

The door to the ballroom closed behind him with a slow creak. Matthew stood in the dark gallery for a moment. The light from his lamp touched the remaining paintings into shadowy, half-visible life.

He looked at them, squinting into the gloomy depths of the room. They were no clearer to him than his purpose here, he thought. Sidonie continued to vanish during the day, reappearing at twilight to cook his dinner and sit across the table as he ate it. Despite their conversations, it seemed that he knew little more about her than he had at the start. Of her mother, there was no sign. He wondered if the daughter spent her days in her mother's locked rooms. That supposition made some sense but left nagging questions unanswered. Was there another kitchen within one of those closed rooms? He had paced the quiet hallways more than once and never heard a single sound or caught any scent of cooking.

Helen, who had returned to repeat her cleaning rituals, was no more forthcoming than she had been on their first encounter. She had also forgotten, or neglected, to inquire about the mirror.

He passed the hours working in the ballroom, unwilling to waste the chance offered. Most of the labour was preparatory: assembly and preparing the larger canvases he had brought down, stripping some of those painted by the dead daughter of the house's builder. He made some progress on a smaller painting based on the images of his train journey. His sketches had proved an adequate prompt to memory and, as his work was usually not strictly representational, his imagination supplied whatever else he required.

But now, that painting completed, he was struggling with the next, his fingers refusing to translate what his mind saw, perhaps because his mind's vision was not yet clear enough. Whatever the cause, there was no point in continuing to work. He was far more likely to waste his paints than to achieve an artistic breakthrough. He left the problem behind him in the ballroom with a feeling of relief.

Abandoning the gallery, he wandered into the hall and stood there for a moment considering his options. He had not seen Sidonie since dinner and he was not certain that he was in the mood for another of her elliptical conversations. Those always seemed to raise more questions than they answered and left him feeling both fascinated and frustrated. Perhaps it would be best to simply select a book from the library and retreat to his room. One of the scandalous contemporary novels he had seen there might be just the thing to distract him from the mingled boredom and uneasiness he felt.

The faint glow of a lamp limned the door to the sitting room and another burned on one of the library tables. The fire was nothing but embers. With a guilty glance at the sitting-room door, he stepped carefully towards the shelves, pausing to set his lamp beside the other. Something moved at the edge of his vision and the involuntary leap of his heart froze him in place.

"I apologize for startling you," Sidonie said softly. Matthew saw her clearly then, settled in the chair by the dying fire. Her face seemed very white in the darkness. He remembered the night she had seemed to materialize from the shadows of his room and thought that for all her apologies she seemed to make a habit of it. He decided that pointing that fact out to her might not be prudent.

"I should have looked more closely," he said. "I thought the room was empty." Chagrin at having been caught attempting to avoid her company made the words more abrupt than he had intended. If she was offended by his tone, no trace of it showed on the pale canvas of her face.

"Have you finished your work for the evening?" she asked politely.

"Yes. It is rather harder than I expected to paint landscapes from memory. I need something more concrete." He moved to scan the shelf for the book that had drawn him into this awkward trap in the first place. "Perhaps you would sit for me."

"I do not think that would be a good idea." He glanced at her and caught the edges of an enigmatic smile. "Look at the legacy my grandmother left when she agreed to such a thing."

"I am a better artist than Constance was."

"I am certain that you are," she replied with a laugh. "But the true question is whether I would be a better subject than my grandmother."

"I would promise not to require you to pose with a knife."

"Would you? I am afraid that I still must decline." He turned his attention back to the books and after a moment she asked: "What are you looking for?"

"I thought I saw that book by Richardson," he admitted reluctantly, annoyed at his own embarrassment. "The one that was banned several years ago."

"Oh yes, I remember the one. It is there somewhere." She rose and came to stand beside him, considering the selection. After a moment, she plucked a crimson-covered book from the shelves and handed it to him. "It is interesting enough…though the author seems to believe that this age invented licentiousness and that he has broken some new ground unimagined by artists over the last three thousand years."

"Every age does that, I suppose. No one likes to think that ancients were as sophisticated about such things as we are. Or as human," Matthew said with a smile. "The painting that got me tossed out of art school was nothing compared to the wall frescoes at Deridian. I understand you are required to have a certificate of moral rectitude, or a great deal of money, to get a glimpse of those." He looked from the book in his hands to the other volumes that filled the shelves. "Have you read all of these books?"

"Most of them."

"Even those in other languages?"

She nodded and seemed amused by his surprise. "All it takes to learn a new language is time and I have plenty of that."

"My father said that your mother had a great facility with language. Perhaps you inherited it."

"Perhaps."

"What are you reading now?" he asked, noticing the book in her hands and wondering how she could possibly read at all in such dim light. She lifted the book and turned the cover into the lamplight. "*The Siren's Song*," he read aloud. "By Lucien De Nunques."

"He was a poet." Matthew had never heard of him, though he supposed Jack and Paul had. They might even have quoted him, for all Matthew knew. Many of Jack and Paul's conversations devolved into drunken orgies of quotations from increasingly obscure writers. Matthew had long since learned when to stop listening. Sidonie seemed to take his silence for interest.

"I'll know the riddle's answer before long
The truth that lives inside the siren's song
And while my heart waits on its final beat
I drift and dream of kisses sharp and sweet,"

she quoted, without a glance at the pages. Matthew suspected that it was not very good poetry but the final image was oddly compelling. In her quiet voice, he thought he heard an undercurrent of something that might either have been promise or warning.

He looked at her, prepared to make some meaningless, polite comment, and for a moment their eyes met. He was suddenly and acutely aware how close her body was to his. He had the dizzying sensation of falling into the dark depths of her eyes, swallowed up by their hungry, sensual light. That light seemed to shimmer off the arch of her cheekbones, the curve of her half-parted lips and he wondered how he could ever have thought that she was not beautiful.

The blue light in her eyes... His father's voice echoed in his ears and stalled the hand that he had lifted, leaving it hovering an inch from the edge of her jaw. Sidonie tilted her head, as if to brush her cheek against the offered caress. He felt his body lean forward, his head bend towards hers.

Her eyes closed.

Matthew blinked. She was standing several feet away from him, the book of poetry held tightly against her breast. "I think that I should say good night now." The words seemed to hang in the air for a moment, then she was gone, vanishing into the hall. He leaned back against the bookshelf and took a deep breath.

He must have imagined it, that strange light in her eyes, that exquisitely erotic aura that had seemed to envelop her for a moment. He remembered Simon's descriptions of her mother's subtle, mutable attraction. *He* was not attracted. He was almost certain of that. The flirtatious air that sometimes edged their conversation was born of boredom and isolation. What had just happened, whatever it had been, was bred of the same thing.

He was a novelty to her. She was young and female and his only real human contact. It would be unusual, under the circumstances, if their interactions were not charged with a certain tension.

Whatever the cause, they were not required to act on it. Acting on it would only complicate an already complex situation, he told himself sternly. Sidonie appeared to feel the same way. It would be best, for everyone concerned, if they both forgot the whole thing.

That sensible conclusion reached, he straightened. He had taken a step away from the shelves before he remembered the book in his hands.

The author seems to believe that this age invented licentiousness...

Hastily, he pushed it onto the shelf and snatched instead the oldest, most innocuous volume he could find. It might prove less interesting, he thought, but would be infinitely less dangerous.

Chapter 14

Matthew sat on the steps at the top of the dock, staring at the calm lake and the landscape beyond.

Two days of rain had kept him hemmed in in the house. It was a relief to be outside, to breathe the sharp air and feel the sun, surprisingly warm, on his face. There was a brightness in the air that seemed to defy the darkness of the house and the mysteries it held.

He looked down at the sketchbook lying open in his lap. The page was full of images of Sidonie, drawn from memory. They were only quick studies but recognizable. He had caught the odd tilt of her eyes, the line of her nose and mouth. Yet there was something wrong about them. Her flesh was realistically rendered but still it seemed a mask. It did not match the bone structure he could feel lurking beneath it. It is only because you were relying on memory, he told himself, trying not to remember the difficulty he had initially had fixing her image in his mind or the transformation that had momentarily dazzled him the night before.

There was no hint of that bewildering beauty in his sketches, yet he could not quite forget it and its strangeness added to the unease he felt. Even considered rationally, without the overlay of disquiet, his situation was disturbing. He was almost certainly trapped here, unless he could beg or buy the assistance of Joseph or someone from the village to take him to the railway. The other man's careful respect for the woman who owned the island made that unlikely. If pushed, he supposed that he might be able to follow the trail on foot. He might even make it without falling prey to any of the myriad dangers Will had outlined and Joseph confirmed.

That plan presupposed, of course, that he could get across the lake.

He looked at the row-boat resting on the shore, tipped over to protect it from the rain. There was a boat at each dock, he noticed, making it theoretically possible to reach—or leave—the island at any time. The lake was considerably calmer than it had been the night of his first crossing. It would be no great thing to right the row-boat, push it into the water, and row himself to the mainland.

It would be no great thing at all...save for the fact that until four nights ago he had not been in a boat in more than ten years. He had not gone swimming or had water beneath him except to cross a bridge. Even then he was careful never to look down, afraid of what he might see in the dark glitter of the water. Afraid of what his mind might conjure from the depths of his guilty memories.

If you cannot do it now, a voice inside him whispered, how will you know if you can ever do it? If you cannot do it, you are truly trapped here.

Matthew looked down at the sketches in his lap. He could feel what little control over the situation he had held slipping away. Nothing had gone as planned. He had not seen the elder Sidonie Moreau. All his queries and questions about her motives were met with evasions and shrugs. He could feel a trap waiting, a coil of black hair

and veiled beauty that had ensnared his father, but could
not seem to stop himself from drifting towards it. Even
line and form seemed beyond his control, he thought, running one finger along the line of a cheekbone that was not
quite right.

He closed his sketchbook, stuffed it into a capacious
pocket and stepped down to the row-boat. One heave and
it turned over, another and it was riding on the gentle
waves that licked the shore. He was in it, fumbling with
the oars, before he could change his mind.

It was not as bad as he had feared. He kept his gaze
moving between the house and the far dock, to prevent
himself from looking into the water. The boat was easily
controllable in the calm water but the requirements of
rowing and steering kept his body and mind well occupied.
Memories shifted and swelled in the back of his mind but
did not surface. Still, he was grateful to reach the dock and
scramble onto its wooden solidity. He crouched there for a
moment, wiping the chill sweat from his forehead, before
he tied the boat and rose.

He had proved it could be done but had to admit that
he was in no hurry to repeat the experience. Now that he
was on shore, he should take the opportunity to locate
Joseph's village. Once there, he could buy a mirror and
continue his attempts, so far fruitless, to obtain more
information about the Moreaus.

He could see the track clearly, heading to the left, and
set off along it. Fifteen minutes later, the lake had vanished
behind the trees and he was walking beside a creek. The
trail passed through meadow and forest, angling west
towards the end of the valley. Matthew forced himself not
to be distracted from his consideration of the path; he did
not want to risk becoming lost through inattention.

After an hour, he saw a thin line of smoke rising above
the far trees. Relief sped his pace and moments later he

rounded a curve in the path and saw the first cabins, heard the first call of children's voices and the barking of dogs.

The village occupied a broad clearing that was bordered on one side by the river. There seemed no arrangement to the settlement except for a rough, muddy track that appeared to form a main street. In the field to his right, a herd of horses grazed. He saw a young man standing in their midst, watching him.

The warm weather seemed to have drawn the inhabitants of the village outside, just as it had him. By the river, he could see a small group of children playing, several large dogs leaping among them. The porches of the first houses he passed were empty, but he could see figures lounging farther along the street. He headed down the main track, gambling that if there was any sort of store or trading post in this place it would be there.

Three houses down the road, a woman was standing on her porch, shaking out a blanket. He saw the curious surprise in her eyes as he passed and gave her a polite smile and nod. Two little boys came pelting around the corner of the next cabin and slid to a halt in the mud in front of him. Before he could say anything, they had recovered their balance and run on, shouting in a language he could not understand.

He should not be surprised at their reaction, he told himself. He did not think Sidonie Moreau received many visitors. Strangers were unlikely to simply wander out of the woods. Still, he felt a combination of embarrassment and vulnerability as he walked, aware of curtains twitching in windows and silent stares from the people he saw.

At last, at the centre of the village, he recognized a face. Helen sat on a porch with a group of women. She was watching him with that strange mixture of shyness and dread that he had come to expect. He forced himself to walk up to the edge of the porch and smile. "Good morning." Her reply was a mumble and a dip of her head.

He looked at the other women on the porch. Two were old, seemingly older than anyone he had ever seen. Kerchiefs covered their heads and their bodies were swathed in layers of sweaters and long skirts. Their faces were landscapes of folds and shadows, wrinkles fanning out from black eyes and narrow mouths. They regarded him with frank curiosity.

The other women sitting on the porch were a good deal younger. One gave him a look of matronly disdain and returned her attention to the sewing in her lap. The other flicked back a length of long, brown hair and smiled.

"My name is Matthew Donovan. I'm staying at the house on the lake." The smiling woman leaned over to her two older neighbours and said something he could not understand. Two black pairs of eyes moved over him again, two covered heads nodded. Matthew looked at Helen, whose gaze slid away again. "It was such a beautiful day I thought I would see if I could find the village."

One of the old women spoke imperiously and Helen muttered back. He supposed that she was translating. He watched the woman as she listened. Her face was fascinating, full of lines and shadows, animated by the dark liveliness of her eyes. He put his hand on his sketchbook. "Would it be permissible for me to sketch you? All of you?" Helen translated that even more reluctantly.

There was a moment of discussion among the women. Matthew guessed that the sewing matron was opposed, the smiling woman in favour and the two older women had the final decision. The old woman looked at him again and spoke. "Mother Norit says to show her your sketches and she will decide," Helen told him.

Under normal circumstances, Matthew considered his sketchbook private, to be shared only with those he trusted most. In its own fashion, it was his diary. What would this old woman, who had no doubt lived in this village or one like it all her life, think of his studies of the city, of his friends, of his models? But if he wanted to include her in its pages, he had no choice, that was clear.

Reluctantly, he handed it to Helen, who passed it to the matriarchs. He saw the pages flip, caught glimpses of sketches as they turned. Once or twice they paused and stared for a long time or looked up to study him. At last, the book was closed and handed back to Helen with another instruction. "Mother Norit says it will be all right, but, if you do a good job, you must leave one with her."

"That's fair." He unfastened his coat and sat on the porch, nearly at Helen's feet. The angle was not perfect— he was looking up at the women who sat on wooden chairs—but the light was good and the composition interesting. Aware of their eyes on him, he began to work. "Will you tell me their names?" he asked Helen.

"This is Hannah," she said after a moment, gesturing to the matron. The woman frowned and looked down at her work. "Beside Mother Norit is Mother Rachel. At the end is Rebeke." Matthew caught their nods as he glanced up from the page.

Under his pencil, they began to take shape: Hannah's profile with its stern mouth and hawk nose, Mother Norit smoking a carved pipe, Mother Rachel's bony hands moving across the dark furs in her lap, Rebeke's booted ankle emerging from her long skirt as she crossed her legs.

Mother Rachel's voice and Rebeke's echoing laughter brought him back to awareness. He glanced at Helen for a translation but the girl only blushed and looked away. He suspected a joke had been made at his expense.

"She's too shy," a voice said and he looked up to see Rebeke leaning forward to look at him. She smiled again, eyes narrowed in amusement, sliding her fingers through the curtain of hair that had fallen over her shoulder.

"Will you tell me then?" She spoke to Mother Rachel, who laughed and put one hand over her mouth.

"She says it's up to me to decide."

"Will you?" He started a small sketch to the side of the page to capture her new position, her elbows on her knees, her chin resting on her hands as she looked at him. His pencil outlined the generous curve of her mouth, the laugh lines bracketing it, the slightly crooked nose, the dark brows.

"I think…yes." Her eyes flashed towards Helen and her smile turned to a grin. "Mother Rachel says that the old one has good taste in men. She says she might have to go to the city and get one for herself someday."

Matthew kept his eyes on the sketchbook to hide his astonishment. After a moment, he found a reply and looked up. "Tell Mother Rachel that though the city is full of young men who appreciate older women, I do not think any of them would be good enough for her."

Rebeke translated and the women dissolved into laughter. Even Hannah's lips quirked. "If they like older women in the city, maybe I'll go there instead," Rebeke said.

"I do not think any of them would be good enough for you, either." His answer, translated, evoked another round of chuckles and a wide, slow smile from Rebeke. "Did you know that the older Miss Moreau is ill?" He saw her eyes shift to Mother Norit, the amusement fading from them. Rebeke shook her head. "Do they ever come here?" She shook her head again and retreated into translations.

Matthew turned the page and began another sketch. When he looked up again, he caught Mother Norit's gaze. To his surprise, the humour there was gone, replaced by sympathy and sorrow. As he worked, he tried twice more to ask questions about the Moreaus but received only shrugs and noncommittal responses. At last, he gave up and put all his concentration into his work.

When he was done, he rose and handed the sketchbook to Mother Norit. She considered the two sketches and showed them to the others. At last, she smiled and pointed to the second one. When he nodded, she tore it from the book and set it in her lap. "Thank you very much." As he retrieved his sketchbook and stepped down from the porch, he remembered the main reason for his trip and looked at Helen. "Did you have a chance to find a mirror?" She shook her head in confusion. Matthew heard Mother Norit's sharp voice then Helen's reply. A brief argument ensued, composed mostly of the older woman's commands and the younger's silence, then Helen got up and went into the cabin. As she re-emerged, Matthew heard a voice behind him.

"What're you doing here?" He turned to see Joseph striding towards him, frown well in place.

"I came for a walk."

"She know you're here?"

"I have no idea. Does it matter?" He kept his voice calm and deliberate as he put his sketchbook into his pocket. He saw Joseph glance towards the porch and its row of women. Mother Norit spoke and Helen took a step forward, something clasped in her hands. Joseph protested and the girl froze. Mother Norit put her pipe in her mouth and closed her eyes. Rebeke gestured to Helen and she stepped to the edge of the porch and stretched out her hands. Matthew saw that she held an ancient, spotted mirror.

"From Mother Norit." He glanced at the old woman and saw the glint of one half-open eye. He remembered the money tucked into his pocket then decided that to offer it would insult her. He took the mirror and bowed slightly.

"Thank you, Mother." The only acknowledgement was a ring of smoke escaping from the pipe. He turned to

Joseph. "I'll be heading back now." When he moved to pass him, the other man fell in step.

"Come on back any time," a voice behind him called and he turned to see Rebeke leaning on the porch post. He waved and let Joseph walk him to the edge of the village.

"What were you doing?" Joseph asked.

"The ladies were kind enough to let me sketch them." He caught the other man's surprised half-glance backward. "I asked about a mirror so that I could shave."

"Maybe you should give that back to me."

"Why? Does Mother Norit need it?" He felt a twinge of guilt. The village was not a place wealthy in material possessions. Perhaps he had misinterpreted the old woman's gesture. After a moment, Joseph shook his head slowly.

"No. If she gave it, she gave it. But she don't like mirrors." After he sorted out the pronouns, Matthew nodded.

"She mentioned that...but said I should inquire in the village. So now I have." They walked in silence for a moment.

"Why'd you draw my grandmother?"

"Mother Norit?" He nodded and Matthew thought for a moment before answering. "Because she has an interesting face." Joseph snorted. "They all do. I wasn't mocking them. I left one of the sketches—you can see for yourself. Besides," he concluded, unable to resist, "they have excellent taste." Joseph made another sound of disbelief and squinted up at the sky.

"Be dark soon. I'll take you back."

"No. I can find my way by myself," Matthew insisted. He needed to think about what had happened in the village, sift through the few clues he had received, and for that he required solitude. Joseph shrugged and walked a few yards farther with him to the curve in the path.

"Go straight back. Be dark soon and she'll be waiting."
For some reason, the farewell sounded like a warning.

Matthew walked quickly, letting his eyes find the landmarks he had memorized on the initial journey while his
mind drifted. While considerably better humoured than
Joseph, the women had been no more forthcoming about
the Moreaus. None displayed the fear that he sometimes
saw in Helen's eyes, but there had been that disturbing
pity in Mother Norit's. He was quite certain that they, like
Joseph, knew things they would not say.

Mother Rachel's reference to "the old one" was also a
mystery. It must refer to the elder Sidonie, though he
would have guessed that she must be many years younger
than Mother Rachel. The assumption that he was in some
fashion *involved* with the unseen Miss Moreau was also
puzzling. Had she had lovers here in the past? Had her
daughter? Given his age, wouldn't they have assumed he
was the daughter's suitor, not the mother's? The older
Sidonie must be in her early forties, while the younger
could be no more than twenty-two, despite her odd remark
the other night. She could be no older than her mother
had been when she had enrolled in his father's class.

He stopped suddenly, appalled at his own blindness. All
the questions he had asked himself about the elder
Sidonie's motives and the younger Sidonie's origins led
inexorably to one conclusion. That conclusion led
inevitably to one more hard question: did the younger
Sidonie know? If she did, then everything that had happened, especially last night, took on a decidedly sinister
meaning. If she did not, then she was being used in a manner that could only cause her—and perhaps all of them—a
great deal of pain.

He ran the rest of the way to the dock.

Chapter 15

Sidonie could tell that he was not in the house. Nevertheless, she slowly eased open the secret door that led from her chamber and slid out into the darkened room. The long years of solitude had made her careless and now that the house was no longer empty she had to force herself to revert to her old caution.

She went through the gallery and opened the door to the ballroom. A canvas, covered by a cloth, was propped on the easel; others lay along one wall. They had looked exactly the same when she had checked the room the previous night. She noticed that the terrace showed no signs of rainfall. The weather must have improved and he had gone out to paint, she decided. She looked squarely at the sunset, a thin line of red outlining the far mountains, and was pleased at how little it distressed her. It amused her to set herself these tests, to see if her nature had changed. Over the years it had—but she did not delude herself that the changes were anything but the natural consequences of age.

She lit the fire in the great hearth and then wandered into the kitchen, considering what she might make for

dinner. Cooking had begun as another test, and as a sur-
vival skill, but she had grown to savour it as a luxury on
those rare occasions when it was required of her. She
could take no satisfaction from the food itself, of course,
but she loved the other sensations it afforded her: the
heady scent of spices, the texture of dough between her
hands, the contrast of colours on a plate.

She checked the pantry and ice-room and discovered a
pheasant hanging there. Joseph had been by with a token
from his hunting. She would have to remember to thank
him for that. The bird would be better in a day or two, she
decided, and selected the makings of another dish.

As she worked, automatically listening for the sound of
the door, she thought about Matthew Donovan. She did
not think he could be put off much longer. She would have
to tell him the truth soon. Certainly before she made any
more slips like the one last night. Even once the truth was
out, she would have to avoid that trap. Seduction would be
easy but it would never bring her what she needed.

She should never have let the charade go on this long.
It was only a fluke that she had not revealed the truth from
the beginning. Expecting Simon, she had appeared as he
would remember her. Once the first mistake had been
made, it had been easier to continue with the charade.

That is a lie, she scolded herself. It was only easier
because you are a coward. You are afraid of the inevitable
trials ahead. You are afraid that it will all go wrong and
end as all the others have. There was a part of her that was
even afraid of what she would see in his eyes when she told
him the truth. The revelation surprised her. She had lived
with what she was for a long time, seen it reflected in lust
and terror in more eyes than she could count. One more
pair should not matter.

It was that damned painting, she told herself. She had
never liked it. She never thought of herself as looking like

that. Though, of course, it was quite possible that she did.

As she bent to slip the food into the oven, she heard the door open. She closed the oven door and leaned against it for a moment, feeling the heat seep into her body from ribs to thighs. She listened to the footsteps pause in the centre of the hall then move towards the stairs. She waited until the sound of feet faded then left the kitchen and went into her sitting room. Coward, she told herself again as she went through the rituals of lighting the fire and lamps.

A few minutes later, Matthew appeared in the doorway. He had changed his clothes, she guessed, donning the black jacket he wore every night. His face held a hard, closed look that suggested that the masque was almost at an end. "Good evening," she said pleasantly, regretting, however cravenly, that pleasantness would no doubt soon be banished. He nodded in greeting and sat in the chair opposite hers. "Did you go to shore?"

"Yes."

"You should be sure to be back before it gets dark. It is easy to get lost at night in the woods. You must be careful." The warning earned her a response somewhere between a shrug and a nod. "Did you see anything interesting?"

"Yes. I went to the village."

"Oh." A knot tightened in her chest. She had not thought to forbid it, doubting he would go and knowing that she could not prevent him, at least while the sun shone. Something had obviously happened there, despite the fact that most of the villagers spoke only their own tongue and upheld the unspoken pact as their parents had.

"I met a fascinating group of women who let me sketch them. One of them, Mother Norit, even gave me a mirror." She relaxed a little then. Mother Norit was a wise woman; she would know that mirrors could be avoided. "You have them well trained."

"Trained? I hardly have anyone trained. Do you suppose I could 'train' Mother Norit?"

"They never talk about you."

"They are private people. They assume I do not gossip about them either."

"Still, it's surprising what you can discover by what people don't say, the questions they won't answer."

"What have you discovered?"

"Everyone says 'she,' not 'they.' No one knows your mother is ill. No one seems concerned, not even you. It's very confusing, and quite convenient, that you both have the same name." He leaned forward in his chair. "Sidonie, I want to resolve this. Whatever it takes, I...my family... want to settle it. There is no need for all this deception. Isn't it time that you told me what is really going on here?"

She rose and walked to the window. She could not see the darkness without, only that within. She put her hands to the back of her throat and began to unfasten her hair from its tight braid. "My name is Sidonie Moreau. Twenty years ago, I was your father's student and his lover. He put his name on my words. Those words gave him everything he possesses today. He owes all of it to me. And now I am calling in that debt." She said the words without turning, watching his reflection in the window.

"Twenty years..." His voice trailed off and there was silence. Outside, the wind began to rise. She could hear the scrape of dead leaves on the terrace. He did not believe her, she realized. He thought that she was mad. "Where is your mother?"

"In the grave."

"I thought so." She saw him stand up and take an awkward step towards her. Stay back, she thought involuntarily, wanting to delay the moment, wanting him to learn the truth from her and not from a window that reflected all the things in the room except one. "I understand how bitter you must be about what my father did," he began. She heard in his tone the careful, uneasy gentleness of someone dealing with a lunatic who may or may not be harmless. "He cheated your mother, I know that. What hardships she suffered afterwards because of...what happened...I can only guess. But I can understand how you might believe you had to put yourself in her place to obtain her justice. My father, my family, is willing to make amends. Please just tell me what you want."

The words, the promise, tore at her and her answer found its way out in an anguished cry. "I want..." The memory of another promise closed her throat. She put her hand to her mouth to hold the words inside. "I am not what you think," she managed at last.

"I know who you are," he said, his voice strained as if it were being stretched between anger and sympathy. "You are the daughter of my father's lover. You are my sister."

She heard the strange sound she made, the sound of choked laughter turned bitter and raw. It gave her the strength to close her eyes and strip away the glamour she had worn since the night he had arrived, to destroy the illusion that lay on her bones like a mask that did not quite fit. "I am not your sister," she said softly. "I am sister to nothing that has not died and rotted a thousand times over. If you want to know who I am, then look."

She turned and stepped into the light of the fire, the glow of the lamps. His eyes widened, his face paling. The chair at his back slowed his automatic retreat but he fumbled past it. The stone mantel stopped him. "This is what I truly am. I have lived for two thousand years. As a child, I spoke the language your father struggled so earnestly to understand. I came to him so that I could hear it once again, to share some breath of the life I had lost so long ago." She stopped to stem the unexpected pain the words caused and forced herself to remember her goal and the levers she needed to use to obtain it. "But he betrayed me. Someone must pay for that. It seems it will be you."

His hand swept the air, hunting for the poker leaning on the hearth. She stopped her advance. "What do you want?" he managed, as his fingers closed over the metal.

"What did my letter ask?"

"That my father come and stay with you." There was bewilderment under the fear in his eyes and something else, something remote and measuring that she had never seen in all the eyes, in all the years.

"Then that is what I want. Since he did not come himself then it is you who must stay here until I say that you may go. You may do what you wish, as long as you do not leave. No harm will come to you."

"Is that all?"

"One other thing only. Every night I will ask you one question. You are free to answer any way you wish—but I still must ask it."

"What is the question?"

Sidonie looked at him, willing her voice to remain steady, to forget the raw cry that still lay smothered in her throat. "Will you give me your blood to drink, even though you die of it?"

"No!" The answer came quickly, full of instinctive revulsion. It cut, though she had known it was inevitable, even though she knew that a thousand other denials might join it before the end.

"There. That is it then." She sat down again, leaning back in the chair. Matthew remained where he was, the poker raised, half in threat and half as if he had forgotten that he held it.

"Why do you want my blood?"

"Because that is how I live. That is what I am."

"A vampire."

"Yes." The look on his face, disbelieving and frightened and calculating all at the same time, made her want to laugh. But there was no humour in their situation, none at all. "Even if I tell you not to bother, you will undoubtedly try foolish things like fleeing or seeking to kill me with stakes and crosses. I am not bothered by crosses and I do not sleep so lightly that you could surprise me with a stake. If you try to leave, I will hunt you down. There is no shelter you could reach before the sun set. Even if you managed to escape, I would expose your father to scandal, the greatest I can create. He is old and unwell—who knows what such disgrace might do to him?"

"I would expose *you.*"

"Who would believe you? I have proof of my claims. How would you prove yours? The world does not believe in vampires. They will think that you are mad. There are rules to this game that we are playing—they are what protect you. If you attack me, they no longer apply. Is that clear?"

"Not at all. But I take the warning." He seemed to remember the poker in his hand and dropped it. It fell on the stone with a clatter. He stepped behind his chair, moving towards the door.

"You may go, if you want. I said that you might do as you wish, that no harm would come to you. I meant it."

"Why should I believe you now, when everything else you have said was a lie?" His back was against the bookshelves, as if he feared she would leap upon him and rip out his throat if he presented her with the opportunity. She watched with sad amusement.

"I did not lie to you. I simply let you believe your own conclusions."

"And this is the truth? Or in two nights will you turn into something even more..." His voice trailed off.

"Horrible? Monstrous?" she supplied, surprised to find

that the words had a more bitter taste than she had remembered. "I assure you, this is as terrible as it will get." She saw him begin to edge into the doorway. He would not run from her but could not help the slow creep of his retreat. She felt a surge of confused emotion: sympathy, impatience and irrational disappointment. "Go on," she said sharply, suddenly aching to be alone. "Go away."

His silhouette slipped into the doorway and was gone. She heard his feet on the stairs, the distant thud of his door closing. For a moment, she even imagined she could hear the click of the lock turning.

Sidonie looked at the fire. It had not gone badly, she supposed. In the past, it had gone much worse. A wave of absurd, painful humour swept her and she bit her lip against another harsh laugh. It did not matter how it had begun. It would end badly, perhaps for both of them. Certainly, very certainly, for him.

Chapter 16

Matthew leaned his back against the door and took a slow, ragged breath. Locking the door had been useless, he was sure, but he could not help himself. He could no more have refused to lock the door than he could have remained in the sitting room.

He crossed the room, twitched open the heavy curtains and stared out the window. For the first time, the moon was visible through the clouds. Its light touched the lake but did not penetrate the darkness beneath him. He thought about his exploration of the island. Two stories below him was an overgrown garden of thorny brush and the granite bedrock of the island. If he did not dare to risk the stairs and the chance of discovery, he might manage to jump, or climb down, unhurt. From there he could row across the lake.

Then what would he do? Run to the village? But they knew what Sidonie was. They had made some kind of pact with her, that was clear. They would not interfere in her business, no matter what that business might be. If he fled into the woods, he might find the path back to the railway. He might elude pursuit, catch the train and return to the city. He might tell the truth to anyone who would listen.

But who would believe him? It would be easy to discredit him, to denounce him as a penniless bohemian, an eccentric artist, or a madman deluded by drugs and drink. Sidonie would wrap her mask of quiet civility about her, tell the tale of the wrongs done her imaginary mother, and destroy his father's reputation and his own. If she claimed to have proof, he had no doubt that she possessed it. No doubt she had proof of her mythical mother's existence as well. After two thousand years—his mind stumbled over the words for a moment—she would be clever and thorough. Or she might dispense with such subtle vengeance and simply kill them both.

If he ran and did *not* escape? Then he would certainly die.

Matthew closed the curtains. He was not prepared to die yet. He went to the fireplace, body reacting automatically to the chill in the room. Building the blaze, he recognized another motivation—the ancient, primitive instinct of man to use the flames as shelter from the darkness, as protection from the monsters of the night. Would fire preserve him?

He thought about what he knew about vampires, which was no more than a jumble of folklore and penny-dreadful fiction. They had no souls, so did not appear in mirrors. That much seemed true, as did the story that they must sleep safe from the sun during the day. He had never seen Sidonie in daylight. She had said that crosses did not trouble her but implied that a stake through her heart would kill her. Would fire? If he burned the house to the ground would that destroy her? It seemed a reasonable supposition but fraught with uncertainty. Much of the building was stone. If she slept in some protected area, it might not be destroyed. If he burned the house and she survived, she would certainly kill him when she rose.

What did she want? If it was merely his blood, his life, why hadn't she taken it the first night? Why the deception and the repeated assurances of his safety? "You must stay with me until I say that you may go." Those words suggested that he might escape from this unscathed but her words could be as subtly deceptive as everything else she did. What if she never allowed him to leave?

Someone will look for me, he told himself. Father will be expecting news. Gabriel and Peter must remember the instructions from the letter. There must be records of land ownership even here. They will be able to trace her. They will find me, if I can stay alive long enough.

At the thought of his family, he felt a wave of bitter laughter rise in his throat. He had thought that he was so clever to have finally realized the truth. He had believed that she was his half-sister. He had agonized over whether she had known all along or whether she was an innocent pawn in her mother's game. He had been prepared to try to accept her.

He had almost kissed her… His laughter turned into a shudder.

A knock on the door jerked him away from the fire. He heard her voice. "I am leaving your dinner outside the door. In case you should be hungry." The calm, reasonable words made him want to laugh. There was a long silence. He did not move. After a moment he thought he heard a faint footstep, then there was no sound but the crackle of the fire.

He waited ten minutes before he carefully opened the door. The hallway was dark and quiet. A tray with a covered plate and a bottle of wine sat on the floor. He brought it into the room and locked the door again.

The food was good, the wine even better. He sat on the floor, his back against the chair, and devoured the meal, vaguely surprised that he still had an appetite. He drained the bottle of glass after glass of rich, red comfort. It looked like blood, he thought with a laugh, and drank it anyway.

The last glass almost gone, he closed his eyes and

leaned his head against the arm of the chair. He felt tired and empty. His thoughts drifted, sliding away from practicalities and speculations. The scene unfolded again, distanced as if it were one of Gabriel's theatrical spectacles. Sidonie, her black hair loosened, turning into the light...

When she had turned around and shown him her true face, he had been too stunned to think, but his artist's unconscious had ruthlessly examined her new aspect, branding it into his mind. The dark wave of her hair, so black it was almost blue, like ink or oil or the deepest depths of the sea. The skin impossibly smooth, honey poured over flesh, aglow with its own light. The indigo eyes, almost as dark as the hair, flecked with gold about the pupils, like lapis lazuli. The way she moved, each gesture like a brushstroke of surpassing smoothness, like the flow of unbroken lines.

There was no mistaking her for human. The arch of her cheekbones was too extravagant, the narrowing of her jaw too precipitous. Her mouth was so wide it would have seemed reptilian save for the lushness of her lips. There was a stark, predatory beauty to the triangular face, like the impassive, alien elegance of a mantis.

His fingers itched to capture every detail of it. Yet even as his hands twitched towards his sketchbook, his mind flinched away from the thing that lay beneath all that serpentine grace. His aesthetic sense could not help but see terrible, inhuman beauty; the rest of his mind knew there was only terror. Everything about her spoke of death. The beautiful bones of her face were those of a skull; the strange eyes as cold as stones; the smile that of an animal, bright fangs and waiting hunger.

He drained the last glass of wine in a sudden, desperate gulp. Perhaps if he drowned in alcohol, he might discover in the morning that this had all been a mad drunken dream.

Chapter 17

It took him most of the day to pick the locks of all the
sealed rooms. He was slipping, he thought. Granted, he
had not started until noon, when he finally awoke with a
hangover, but ten years ago he could have accomplished
the task in half the time. Of course, ten years ago the
worst that he faced was another lecture from his father or
the annoyance of the friend whose room he was invading.
Now, his fate might be considerably more unpleasant.

You have no choice, he told himself, looking around
the last of the bedrooms. No matter what she said, you
have no choice but to do this.

He had found any number of fascinating things in the
locked rooms. In one, he discovered a wardrobe full of
clothes: evening suits, heavy, fur-collared coats, embroi-
dered vests, rough cotton shirts. Curious, he had tried on
one of the jackets and discovered that it fit him passably
well. The cut had gone out of fashion a hundred years earlier but the fabric was still in good condition. Reluctantly,
he put it away again. However tired he was of his own
meagre wardrobe, it would hardly be discreet to supple-
ment from a supply he should not have known existed.

In other rooms, he found old furniture, dust-covered lamps and statuary, boxes of yellowing newspapers and correspondence, several paintings of considerable quality, and more than one box of jewellery. He identified rooms he believed belonged to the builder's wife and daughter, but who might have inhabited the others remained a mystery.

He did not find Sidonie.

He locked the doors behind him when he could but there were several that stayed stubbornly open, waiting to betray him. As dusk fell, he went to the ballroom and found himself going through the motions of creativity, knowing he was ruining the painting he had started but unable to stop himself. However badly he did it, painting was something that he understood.

Some time after sunset, he heard the sound of a footstep on the floor of the gallery. He did not turn around, delaying the moment that would confirm that the previous night had been more than a terrible dream. "Good evening." Her voice was the same, quiet and even slightly shy. It seemed an awful jest that the sound of it held no horror, only pleasant memories of food, conversation and connection.

He put down his brush, turned towards the door and knew it had not been a dream. The false Sidonie was gone, her demure black dresses abandoned in favour of a velvet gown of lush cobalt blue. Her unbound hair was longer than he had thought, brushed out into a sweep of midnight that fell past her breasts. She moved forward, as if to step down into the ballroom.

"Don't…" he said without thinking. She paused, one slippered foot on the step.

"May I come in?"

"Do I have a choice?"

"Of course."

"Then please don't. I prefer to work in privacy," he added automatically, as if she were any other woman and he feared he had insulted her. The foot lifted and vanished back beneath her dress.

"I understand. I won't come in without your permission...ever," she said and smiled with her lips closed. Matthew forced himself not to study her mouth, searching for some sign of the fangs that lurked there. "I suppose this means that you no longer wish me to pose for you."

"No." She was jesting, he thought, trying to put him at ease. A wave of anger that she believed he could be so easily placated surged inside him. "It would be too much like staring at the sun." He meant to say something more vicious, less ambiguous, but there was some part of him that would not let him lie about his art.

He saw her eyes flicker sideways to the place where the dead Constance's canvases stood. "Ah well," she said after a moment. "Perhaps it is for the best. I don't think I have been well served by artists."

"Then let me go."

"You forget, I am not interested in your paint, but your blood." The smile came back again, as if she had not just been speaking of his death. "Are you hungry? Would you like dinner?"

"You are going to make me dinner?"

"Why not? I enjoy cooking and you need to eat. If I were planning to poison you, I would have done so already, I assure you."

"What about you? Are you hungry?" He wanted to call the words back as soon as he had said them, but the challenge had been given and now he could not back down. He met her gaze as steadily as he could.

"Terribly," she said, her voice gone strange and dry. "But you are perfectly safe. I will dine later."

He had no choice but to trust her, at least this far. "I

would like dinner. Thank you." With a slight nod, she vanished from the doorway. He let out his breath and felt his pulse slow down. He looked back at the painting on the easel but the flames of its autumn trees did not have the power to blot her blue-black image from his mind.

Cursing softly, he removed the canvas from the easel and leaned it against the wall to dry. Tomorrow he would scrape the paint away and try again. Wearily, he settled himself onto the floor beside it and retrieved his sketchbook, flipping through the pages in search of inspiration.

The pictures of the false Sidonie caught his attention. He stared at them for a moment, seeing clearly now why they had not satisfied him. The eyes were wrong, and the mouth, and the thrust of the cheekbones. He had been drawing human flesh over inhuman bone and it hung there uneasily. If he stripped the lies away, the lines should go thus...and thus...

Sidonie's voice from the doorway dragged him from the angry black lines of the sketch. He closed the book with a twinge of guilt and followed her to the dining room.

Everything looked as it had for the last five nights. There was a single place set, candles on the table and sideboards, a decanter of wine beside the crystal goblet. Everything seemed the same and yet everything that mattered had changed. Sidonie sat across from him, the slim stem of a wine glass turning between her fingers. An inch of white wine moved within the crystal like a tiny citrine sea.

Matthew ate silently, the pale flesh of the fish parting beneath his knife. He remembered the rooms he had been unable to lock and wondered if she knew of his explorations. She showed no signs of anger but that might be yet another deception designed to lull him into unwariness. When he glanced up, he saw her take a delicate sip of the wine. "I didn't know vampires drank wine." It was the second time he had said the word out loud; it still sounded strange, fantastical.

"We can take small doses, if we choose. It does not have much taste for us. Very little does."

"I'm surprised that you bothered to learn to cook then."

"It is a useful skill to have, especially for a woman who must make her way alone in the world. Food has sensual delights beyond taste...but it is a waste to indulge in them if there is no one there to eat your creations."

"If it has no taste, why are you drinking?"

"To make you feel at ease," she admitted. Matthew looked up in surprise and caught her rueful smile. "I gather it has not worked."

"No. I suppose that I should thank you for being concerned...though I hope you will forgive me if I don't."

She shrugged in acceptance. "I am out of practice. It has been a long time since I have appeared to a stranger as I truly am."

"How long?" he asked, partly from genuine curiosity, partly to induce her to continue to speak. If he hoped to survive, he needed to learn all he could about her. It was also a great deal more difficult to sit with her in silence than in conversation.

"A long time."

"Did you appear this way to the builder of the house?" She nodded. "So he knew what you were all along."

"From the beginning. Our relationship started a decade before he began to build this house. Christian was a very unhappy man. He always had been. We shared similar interests. Our loneliness was complementary, you might say. Or, to be less charitable about it, we had complementary needs. I needed blood and he needed a reason to despise himself. After his wife died, he invited me to join him here."

"Did you kill his daughter?" Matthew asked bluntly and saw something move across the smooth, alien planes of her face.

"Yes," she said after a moment. "I did not intend to but I did. She was ill and weaker than I had thought."

"Did he know?"

"He suspected. He never asked. I never told." She took another sip of the wine. Matthew poured himself another glass, suspecting he should not drink any more and certain that he would.

"So you murdered your lover's child and he never asked. He let you live with him for another five years and then left you his entire fortune. How convenient for you." He expected some reaction from her, either anger at his presumption or pain at the brutality of the words. She simply turned the wine glass in her fingers and met his gaze with serious eyes.

"Christian was already losing his battle for sanity at that point. He loathed himself for a thousand imagined crimes. His relationship with me and the murder of Constance were just two more. He saw himself as the serpent in his own Eden. He had brought evil to the sanctuary he had built to escape it. The death of his wife proved that. He did not want me to go because I was a daily reminder of his own corruption. And, of course, a reason why he did not need to renounce it. I was his way to cherish both his sin and his victimhood. 'My evil angel,' he used to call me. I did not leave because I needed a refuge from the world and the promise of a home and a fortune that would one day be mine. And he had no one else to care for him. In the last months, he rarely ate or left his bed."

"Did he really drown?" he asked carefully, aware of the distance that had entered her voice and shadowed her eyes. She was not telling the story to him as much as remembering it for herself and if he disturbed the spell that bound her she might refuse to answer or begin to lie. She shook her head slowly.

"No. He wanted me to kill him. The final punishment, he said. He offered his throat one last time and I..." She blinked once and the dreaminess faded from her eyes. "I put his body in the lake and arranged for William, Joseph's great-grandfather, to find it. By that time, no one could have told how he had died. Not that anyone ever bothered to ask."

He caught the clue, the important key in the story and debated whether to pursue it. It might be best to wait but he needed to know. If he had to spend hours or days pondering it he might go mad. "Did you drink his blood all those years?" She nodded. "Then it is not inevitably fatal."

"No. That is the truth, Matthew. It also kills. I also kill. That is the truth as well. If you say yes, I make no promises which it will be."

"I am not planning to say yes," he said pointedly and she set down the glass with which she had been toying.

"If you are finished your dinner," she began, her voice businesslike and brisk, "I think that you should go to the sitting room. There is paper in the desk. You should write to your family and tell them you are safe and will be staying here for a while."

Matthew's own glass rang dully against the polished wood as he put it down with more force than he had intended. The thought of writing polite, empty lies—and of cutting off one of his few chances of rescue—made his stomach churn uneasily. "And if I would prefer not to?"

"Would you have your father and brothers worry about you unnecessarily? Worry so much that they feel compelled to risk their own safety by coming to find you?" Sidonie asked, as she stood with the dirty dishes in her hands. The contrast between the simple, domestic action and the threat implicit in her voice sent ice along his spine.

"Are you saying that they would be in danger?"

"I am saying that this is dangerous country. It would be so much simpler for everyone if you wrote the letter." He sighed and surrendered, knowing that she was right. His father would be expecting to hear from him soon. If he failed to contact them, they would come seeking him and then the very thing he wanted might mean their deaths.

"I assume you will read it first," he said sullenly, rising from the chair.

"I think that might be wise."

In the sitting room, the fire was lit and the oil-lamp on the desk glowed. Matthew sat down and opened the drawer that he knew contained the supply of writing paper. A pen lay in an ebony holder beside the lamp. He looked from the white page on the dark wood to the window in front of him but found no answers there, only his reflection. After a few moments, he began to write.

Dear Father... I have reached Miss Moreau's house safely... it is very beautiful here... she has asked me to stay... confident everything can be resolved... The phrases had the sound of a dutiful but reluctant child writing to an elderly relative. He saw that but could not help it. Simon had received very few letters from him so perhaps he would not notice how odd this one sounded. He scrawled his signature on the bottom and set down the pen, looking back to the dark mirror of the window.

"Thank you." The voice was at his shoulder and he jerked around in his chair to see Sidonie standing behind him. She held out her hand. When he turned to retrieve the letter, he confirmed that he could not see her reflection in the window. There was only his own pale face and the dim outline of the mantel on the far side of the room.

"It must be disconcerting not to be able to see your reflection," he said. "It is certainly disconcerting for me."

"I am accustomed to it now," she replied absently,

scanning the letter before handing it back to him. "This will do nicely. Thank you."

"You're welcome," he answered, but she seemed oblivious to the sarcasm in his voice. He addressed the letter, sealed it and turned back to see Sidonie sliding into her chair by the fire with a grace that appeared boneless. "If you cannot see your reflection, how do you do it? That changing trick?"

"I think about how I wish others to see me and it happens. It is more a matter of illusion than actual transformation. It is almost as if your eye is deluded into making assumptions about who and what I am and then looking no further. Some things I cannot change, of course. I would have to dye my hair to change its colour. A good portion of the illusion is created by clothing. My body is the same under the clothes I wore last night and the dress I wear now—but you might look at it differently."

"Is this what you really look like?" Matthew asked quickly, uneasily aware that he would prefer not to consider how her body might look at all.

"I think so. You must remember that I have not seen myself in two thousand years so I cannot be certain. My appearance has changed a great deal since the last time I saw my reflection." She paused, her brows drawing together thoughtfully. "I have looked like this far longer than I wore my mortal face, yet that is the only face that I remember. I suppose that sometimes I forget I do not look like that any more."

"What did you look like then?" he asked, intrigued despite his misgivings.

"I was somewhat shorter. My hair was black but thicker, coarser. It would curl when it rained. My face..." Her fingers rose and drifted across her cheekbone. Her voice had taken on that dreamy distance he had noted earlier. "My face was rounder. Someone used to tease me by

calling me Moon Face, because my face was so round…"
She blinked twice and her hand slipped back down to her
lap. "It is hard to recall. It was very long ago."

"Why did you change?"

"I am not certain. I only know that all those of my kind
come to resemble each other over time, no matter what
our origins. As for the conscious changes, I do it to suit the
times or a part that I must play. To be invisible and pass
for mortal. For instance, I thought that my appearance
twenty years ago would be unlikely to create problems."
The smile she gave him was half-amused, half-mocking. "I
was wrong about that."

A terrible suspicion blossomed suddenly in Matthew's
mind. Even as he tried to push it aside, he knew that it had
been in back of his mind all day, like a poisonous flower
waiting to bloom. It was wrong, he was wrong, he told
himself savagely. It was not possible. No matter what
crimes and betrayals had occurred, it was not possible.

He turned away from Sidonie and stared at the letter
lying on the desk. He could not ask her the question to
which he desperately needed the answer. If he asked, she
would know his guilty, secret doubts and that was unendurable. Even if he asked her, he could never trust her
answers, not when he would have given into her hands
such a potent weapon with which to torment him.

He swallowed hard and then stood. "I think that I will
find a book in the library and retire, if that is permitted."

"Of course it is permitted," she said, with a touch of
weariness in her voice. "You may do as you wish."

"Thank you. Good night." He was at the door to the
library before her voice caught him and held him there,
staring away from her.

"Matthew, will you give me your blood to drink,
though you die of it?"

"No." He shook his head.

"Good night," she said, and, released, he fled through
the dim room, snatching a handful of books from the
shelves as he went. He prayed that they would hold his
attention long enough to silence, at least for tonight, her
terrible question and his own haunted thoughts.

Chapter 18

He woke with a start to find himself thrashing in sweat-soaked sheets. His stomach heaved and twisted. Matthew staggered to his feet and across the room. He tugged futilely at the door for a moment before realizing it was locked. Fumbling it open, he stumbled down the hall.

He was sick in the darkness, hunched over the toilet. At last he leaned back against the wall, his arms wrapped around his ribs. He had thought the night-terrors and the sickness were long over. He thought he had purged them from his life long ago. He had started to drink in late adolescence, to make himself sleep and give himself a reason for the sickness he would feel anyway. Other excesses had followed: drugs, sex, nights in which he never slept, days he did not remember. When at last he had emerged from that haze, hauling himself back from the abyss before the sirens of oblivion could break his talent on their rocks as they had broken that of thousands before him, the nightmares were gone.

Ice pressed around him...cold seeped deep into his limbs...a drop of blood fell with a whisper... He shuddered and hauled himself to his feet, leaning heavily on the sink. His groping hand found the faucet and he plunged first hands then head beneath the chilly water. Mind somewhat cleared, he moved carefully back into the hallway. It was very dark, here in the centre of the house. At the end of the hall, he could see a faint glow from where the fire in the great hearth must still burn. He padded instinctively towards the light, unwilling to return to his cold, silent room.

From the top of the stairs, he could see that the Hall was empty. In the dying fire, a log broke and sparks flared for a moment. He heard the creak of the front door and stepped back automatically. From the shadows, he saw a slender figure slip into the hall. It was Sidonie. She had changed from her velvet dress into masculine garb and her hair was bound back again. *I will dine later*... She had been hunting, though what prey she might find in the wilderness he did not want to guess. Halfway to the door of the library, she stopped. Matthew saw her look back over her shoulder, her gaze directed at the place he stood. The firelight touched the side of her face, the shadows and light revealing with cruel clarity the skull beneath the golden skin.

After a long moment, she turned away and vanished beyond the fire's glow. He exhaled and backed down the hallway, feeling for the door to his room. Safely inside, the lock turned once more, he lit the lamps and read until sleep claimed him again hours later.

When he wandered into the kitchen at noon, somewhat improved by a bath and a shave, he discovered Helen sitting in the corner, cleaning a pheasant. After one startled glance, she bent her head and tore at the feathers with furious concentration. "Good morning," he said pleasantly, despite the sudden rage that swept him. He stoked the wood stove and put the heavy iron kettle on top to boil. "How is everyone today? Mother Norit? Joseph?"

"They are fine."

"That's good. I assume they have all recovered from the amusement the other day." He watched her fingers clench around the dead bird's throat. "It was amusing, surely. Allowing me to sketch, making jests...as if I were a guest here." He found a cup and a box of tea in the cupboards. "You know what she is, don't you. You all know." She gave a quick, convulsive nod. "I am going to die here. She is going to kill me. But I don't imagine that matters to you at all."

She did not answer, did not even look up, and Matthew felt a moment of sympathy. Whatever bargains her elders had made with Sidonie, they were hardly her fault. It was the others he was really angry with; Joseph, the old women with their ribald jokes and gifts, Rebeke with her flirtatious smile. No wonder the girl had seemed so terrified of Sidonie, even of him. He knew that she was not to blame, but that did not stop him from being furious, a fury fed partly by his embarrassment at the memory of his own ignorant pleasure in that afternoon.

"What else do you do here? Besides clean and pluck pheasants?" The questions elicited nothing but a look of blank bewilderment. "Do you do laundry?" After a moment, she nodded. Matthew returned to his room, gathered up his worn shirts, stripped the sheets from the bed and stalked back into the kitchen to dump them on the floor at her feet. "Can you bring them back tomorrow?" She nodded again. He had reasons beyond petty revenge, he told himself. The more time he spent with the girl, or someone from the village, the more chance he might have to learn about Sidonie. He might even be able to sway someone to help him. All sensible reasons and yet they did not ameliorate the bitter pleasure he got from the childish gesture of flinging his dirty clothing at her betraying feet.

The kettle whistled, demanding his attention. By the time he had prepared his tea and some semblance of luncheon, Helen had finished with the pheasant and vanished

with the laundry. With a sigh, he went to sit down in the
empty dining room. As he ate, he thought about his futile
search the day before. He had established that Sidonie did
not sleep in any of the locked rooms. It was possible that
one of those rooms concealed a hidden closet or chamber
but he was in no mood to pick the locks again today. He
had not yet seen an entrance to either a cellar or attic. It
was logical that a house this size would possess one or the
other. A cellar seemed unlikely, for the house was built on
rock, but an attic was probable. He sighed, acknowledging
that the entrance was likely to be in one of the upstairs
rooms he had surveyed in his cursory search.

Where else could she lie? Was it possible that it was
not in the house at all? His exploration of the island had
been far from thorough. There could be a crypt or cave
hidden somewhere, especially at the northern end. He
glanced outside the window. It was not raining, though the
sky was a uniform grey from horizon to horizon. This
might be his best chance.

Two hours later, cold and muddy, he returned to the
house, forced to admit that if Sidonie had a resting place
outside the house, he was unable to find it. He indulged in
another long bath, reckoning he was owed the comfort
and hot water. Another cup of tea warming his hands, he
went into the ballroom to consider the damage he had
done to his painting the night before.

It was unsalvageable, as he suspected. He spent some
time surveying his sketches and made several half-hearted
dabbings on the next canvas before he was forced to
acknowledge that the landscapes that had delighted him
two days earlier left him bored and unsatisfied now. There
was something waiting inside him, growing somewhere in
the back of his head. It happened this way on occasion.
The painting would shape itself in the darkest part of his
mind and then slide along his nerves, fitting itself into his

fingers as if they were a glove it wore to make its vision clear. He would paint madly, as if possessed, until the bones of the thing were on the canvas. Craft and intelligence would not resurface until then, when they were free to set about the tasks of evaluation and refinement.

He stared at the canvas with its aborted lines and clumsy shapings. There was something in there, something that owed nothing to the mountains and trees he had thought he was sketching. If he allowed his mind to slip out of focus, he could see a downward line that looked like the fall of an icicle from a roof. The trees he had shaped became columns of twisted light rising to meet it.

Everything white except for the blood…the ice pressed around him…cold seeping deep…

His hand moved, turning the tops of the mountains into a vaulted ceiling pierced by jagged ice. His brush found the lines of a Great Hall of frost and shadow. He bent closer, his eyes following his fingers rather than guiding them.

I am not going to paint this, he told himself over and over. It is just a sketch, nothing more. When I am done, I will find the old lines beneath these and cover the canvas with burning autumn leaves and rich brown earth and the green solidity of pines.

He stopped when the light had faded and he would need lamps to continue his work. With a sense of dislocation, he saw that he had already laid down the base coat of paint, the first tone of white touched with blue.

He draped the cloth cover over the canvas carefully and wiped his hands on a rag. Shifting his shoulders to ease the aches from his back, he walked back to the Hall. Now that they were no longer possessed, his hands were cold. As he crouched by the hearth and settled logs onto the smouldering, splintered remains of their predecessors, he wondered if Sidonie had risen. The thought made his throat tighten, something beneath his ribs clench and twist.

He had his answer a few moments later when she descended the stairs from the west wing. He felt brief disbelieving shock at her appearance. It froze him in place, as if, like the mythical Medusa, she had the power to turn men to stone. Part of him still thought that she should look as she had the first night. Even the portion of his mind that knew the truth seemed somehow to underestimate the extent of the change—he was never prepared for how truly alien and dangerous she was. There was a bundle of cloth in her arms.

She threw it at his feet as he rose. With dismay, he recognized the clothes he had discovered the day before. "I thought that perhaps some of these might fit you. What a convenient surprise it was to find the door already open," she said. For a moment, his mind went blank, unable to summon any response. "I warned you. I told you not to attempt to find me. I thought you might be intelligent enough to obey me. I should have known better."

"What did you expect me to do?" he demanded. "Simply lie down and die because you say so?"

"I expect you to be reasonable."

"I *am* being reasonable! If I surrendered without a struggle, that would be unreasonable. If that does not suit you, then kill me right now." He felt a tight, vicious smile stretch his lips. "You can't, can you? Whatever I do, if you kill me now, you don't get what you want."

Sidonie looked at him for a moment, blue-gold eyes unreadable. Her own smile was slow and lazy, a coiling snake. This time she did not attempt to conceal the sharp glitter of her delicate fangs. She stepped across the scattered clothing to stand in front of him, her body inches from his. Matthew willed himself not to move or look away. "Very true. Of course, if I did kill you, I might be sorry. But you, you would still be dead." Her hand lifted and hovered an inch from his face, as if she would touch his cheek with the backs of her fingers. He could not help it; his head jerked away from the threatened contact, eyes closing involuntarily. He heard her soft, sad laugh. "Go on and change. The red brocade vest and black jacket might suit you."

Her voice sounded very far away. When he opened his eyes she had moved back to stand by the chair. "That's all?" he asked, surprised that she had abandoned her advantage, and the argument, so quickly.

"What else is there to say? You will continue to disregard my advice and there is nothing I can do to stop you. If you push me too far and I decide to kill you, there is nothing you can do to stop me." She smiled, lips closed this time, as if that might disguise the brutal equation she related. To his surprise, Matthew found that harsh summation of the truth comforting. To know where he stood lent him some measure of control in the midst of the ambiguity of his situation.

She was right about the vest and jacket, he decided, squinting to consider himself in the tiny oval of Mother Norit's mirror set on the dresser on the other side of his room. He might almost pass for one of Gabriel's set, at least from a distance. Was it possible to turn this to his advantage? he wondered. If his appearance mattered to Sidonie, he could easily let it degenerate. Could he disgust her into letting him go? It seemed a far-fetched idea, though certainly no more far-fetched than some of the other plots he had contemplated. Still, the central premise seemed unlikely. What Sidonie wanted from him lay inside him…it was implausible that the outside would concern her over much.

Shuddering automatically at the thought, he ran his hands over his hair, buttoned the shirt to his throat and went downstairs.

Chapter 19

Tonight the dress was black and the wine was red. He watched Sidonie lift the glass to her lips, saw the subtle convulsion of her throat as she swallowed. His own throat tightened.

She set the goblet down and leaned back in her chair, one hand drifting up to idly stroke the necklace around her neck. It was gold, shaped like a collar of thorns. Blue beads were scattered among the barbs, like cobalt blood. Matthew could see the shadows on her skin, spikes of darker gold across the arch of her collar-bones. He wondered if she could feel the sting of those points, like tiny stakes against her flesh.

She caught his open stare and he looked away, taking a quick gulp of his wine. The liquid tasted warm and heavy with a sweet aftertaste. A question occurred and he asked it quickly to cover his discomfort under her scrutiny. "Do you prefer red wine to white?"

"Because of the colour?" she asked, catching the line of his thought. "No. It only *looks* like blood." She gave him a slight smile. "There is a stock of wine in the room behind the pantry. You might have a look if you are interested in selecting for yourself. It all tastes the same to me, after all."

"I am hardly a connoisseur myself," Matthew admitted. "I drink whatever's cheap or whatever someone else is buying. Unless that happens to be my brother Gabriel, they can't usually afford anything better than I can."

"You are fond of Gabriel, aren't you?" The question surprised him. For a moment he looked at her, considering her motives. "No, better not to tell me, I suppose," she said softly into the silence. "I might use it against you somehow. I might do him harm."

"Would you do that?"

"I would like to say no…but it would be a lie. I am old and desperate. I might do anything."

"What is it that you want?" he asked, disturbed and exasperated in turn by her cryptic comments.

"I want you to give me your blood to drink, even though you die of it."

"I won't do that."

Sidonie shrugged her shoulders slightly and the thorns about her throat shifted. "That is that done for tonight, then." As if it could ever be forgotten, Matthew thought. As if going through the ritual early would make the rest of the evening bearable.

To his surprise, it did. Knowing the question was asked and his refusal given seemed to drain some of the tension from the room. It was almost possible, for a while, to forget what she was, to listen to her voice and imagine only the quiet woman he had begun to like. Then he would look at the narrow inhuman face and shudder back to reality, feeling a vague sense of uneasy disgust at his willingness to forget it.

When he asked her why she had come to the city twenty years earlier, she said only, "Come into the sitting room and I will tell you." So, despite his resolution to leave her company as soon as possible, he ended up in the firelit room again. She led him to the shelves and pointed to the shards of pottery, the scattering of ancient coins.

"I carried a jug with a pattern just like that one to and from the well every day. The coins bear the image of the god I worshipped with my family in the temple."

"You have kept those things for all these years?" he asked, touching the nearest coin with one finger. She shook her head.

"I took nothing of my old life into my new one. I barely even took my name. During the centuries, I have lost almost everything that I possessed more times than I can count. I obtained these things with Christian's money from a dealer in antiquities. I bought them so that I would have some way to remember."

She lifted one of the pot shards and held it cupped in her hand. One finger traced the black pattern dimly visible in the clay. Matthew could not see her expression behind the veil of hair that had fallen over her face. "I read of your father in one of the journals to which I subscribed. I knew that he had access to the Acquita scrolls. I had not heard anyone speak in my native tongue in two thousand years. Those scrolls, and artefacts like these, are all that is left of what I knew. New cities were built, century upon century, over the one in which I was born. I needed…" Her voice died away for a moment and she set the shard back on the shelf. Thin fingers pushed back her hair and she looked at him. "I needed to go home, whatever way I could."

There was bleakness in her voice and sorrow seemed to weigh upon the unlined face. He told himself that he was imagining it, that he was seeing human emotions on a face that was not human, that this seeming vulnerability was likely nothing more than an attempt to manipulate him into surrendering what she wanted. But he found he could ask none of the accusatory questions her story stirred.

Sidonie stepped away from the shelves and went to her

customary chair. She took the heather-coloured shawl draped across its back and wrapped it over her shoulders, as if she could in some fashion feel the cold. "I had never really been taught to read," she said as she sat. "When I changed, I could recognize only a few words in my own language. I had only learned those to impress...someone. But I have learned a great deal in the intervening years. That, and the little I had been taught, was enough to allow me to translate the scrolls."

"Yet you let my father think he had done it."

"I had no interest in scholastic glory. I only wanted to touch the world I had lost. Your father is a brilliant man; he would have found the answer for himself eventually."

"You never cared about the attribution at all, did you? It was only a ploy to bring me here."

"It was a ploy to bring your father here," she corrected. "And whether or not it mattered to me does not justify what Simon did. He stole my intellectual work. If I were not a vampire, that might matter very greatly to me."

Matthew leaned against the mantel, aware of the heat of the fire on the backs of his legs. He did not want to sit down, for it implied an ease he was not feeling. There were questions still unanswered. He was not sure he had the nerve to ask them. Sidonie volunteered nothing and the moment's rage he felt at her for forcing him to this drew the words from his throat. "Why did you seduce him?"

"Did I?" Her voice sounded soft and mocking. "Is that what he said?"

"My father was too much of a gentleman to blame you."

"But now that you have seen me, it is obvious to you that I must be at fault." She shrugged off the shawl and stroked her hands across the tangle of gold at her throat. Matthew was aware of the stretch of amber skin beneath it, of the way the black dress seemed to hover on the very edge of her shoulders, as if it might slip off at any moment. He remembered the bewitching glow in her eyes the night in the library. The heat of the fire was suddenly too much. He stepped away, behind the empty chair. He leaned on the back and focused on the anger her accusation roused.

"Are you accusing my father of seducing you?" he asked, forgetting that once he might have taken perverse delight in the revelation of his father's hypocrisy.

"Must someone be to blame?" Sidonie countered. "Is it only seducer or seduced? When you make love to a woman, which are you?"

"This has nothing to do with me." She smiled, as if his vehemence amused her, and he felt a surge of confused rage and desperation. It felt like a terrible invasion for her to speak of his private life, reminding him of what he would lose forever if he died here.

"Very well," she said at last. "I will tell you the truth— you may disbelieve me if you please. It was not my intention to become involved with your father. It happened. Your father wanted me, for whatever reasons he may have had. I was homesick for the world I had lost, I was happy to have touched some small part of it again. I was lonely."

And hungry? Were you hungry? He heard the words, distant and distorted, and for a moment thought that he had said them aloud. But he hadn't, couldn't, not without risking the black water he could feel waiting to close over him.

"I suppose we should be grateful that you left." The words seemed safe, ones that could be said without any ripple in the dark tide moving beneath him.

"It seemed simpler. These things become messy and end badly." Her lips twisted in a wry smile. "Whether they involve vampires or not." Matthew thought of the few times he had become involved with women tied to husbands or lovers and had to admit that she was right. "There, now you know the truth. You may believe it as you wish. You are free to blame whichever one of us you please."

An automatic retort shaped itself on his tongue: it is not my father who wants to kill me. He swallowed it down and straightened. "I believe that I will do some work before it gets too late."

"There are more lamps in the kitchen, if you should need them," Sidonie replied, her voice as cool as his. When he glanced back from the doorway, she had picked up the book on the table by her chair and begun to read.

He needed more lamps and more surfaces to hold them. He carried in chairs from the abandoned rooms and resolved to find some higher stands the next day. There had to be something he could use amid the clutter of the locked rooms. For a moment, he contemplated asking Sidonie for the keys, then abandoned the thought. He would pick the locks and leave the doors open.

He pulled the cloth from the canvas. The bones of the painting were starkly visible, despite the sketchiness of his drawing and the monotone base wash. For a long moment, he stood looking at it. Images flickered through his mind: the ice-blue whiteness of his nightmare, the slash of blue-bleeding gold across Sidonie's throat, the contrast between lucent honey-toned flesh and black velvet. He blinked and forced himself to focus. There was enough light to work on the background, he decided, especially the expanse of white at the base of the painting. He shrugged off the jacket and vest, despite the chill, and rolled up the sleeves of his shirt.

There was comfort in the rituals of preparation, the assembling of palette and brushes, colours and thinner. He worked for a long time, sitting on a chair close to the canvas, working the thick white paint onto the canvas. He considered each detail of technique thoroughly. With his mind full of the challenges of painting, there was no room for thoughts of anything else.

At last, he heard a faint knock on the closed door of the ballroom. He straightened, aware suddenly of the strain in his shoulders and the dry ache in his eyes. He covered the painting and went to open the door. Sidonie stood there, dressed in boots, male clothing and a long, loose coat. "I thought perhaps you had gone to sleep in there," she said, with a trace of apology. "It is very late."

Matthew started to deny it then yawned instead. "Where are you going?"

"I have things to do."

"You are going hunting."

"Yes, if you want me to be blunt. I am going hunting. Shall I tell you what I hunt?"

"All right."

"Deer, rabbits, whatever I can find." When her brows drew together in a frown, he knew that he had not hidden his instinctive revulsion. "If that disturbs you, you have only to say the word and I will stay here."

"And dine closer to home?" he finished for her. "No. I never cared much for deer and rabbits anyway." That cleared the lines from her forehead.

"Go to bed, Matthew. If you keep this up, you will begin to copy my hours and sleep all day. Then when would you search for my resting place?" For a moment, he thought that their earlier argument had resurfaced, but her tone was unwounding, a jest rather than mockery.

"If you insist," he said with a reluctant smile. She turned away then looked back over her shoulder.

"Good night. Pleasant dreams."

He felt the smile fade from his face. He shut the door and leaned his forehead against it. He was tired. He could feel the weariness dragging at his limbs, weighing down his eyelids. Perhaps it would be enough. It was too much to hope that his dreams would be pleasant. He had to trust that he was too tired to dream at all.

Chapter 20

Arael Arel Dabria Dara Farris Gabriel Geron Hamal Hariel Javan Kadi Lailah Michael Miri Neria Orel Pariel Raphael...

The crabbed script rippled and distorted. Matthew blinked and rubbed his eyes, dry with dust. He turned the crackling pages of the diary carefully, letting his gaze drift across the patterns of faded ink, searching for some semblance of sense amid all the madness.

I hear my walls, my beautiful hard walls of sweet stone. They are saying my name...

He had found the diary in the bedchamber that paralleled his own. He had planned to paint, to take advantage of the early afternoon light, but found himself unable to either continue with the palace of ice or ignore it. He stood in front of the canvas for a long time. He could sense shapes within the painting waiting to be uncovered and was not certain that he wished to do so—or that he had a choice.

But there were things he could choose to do. He remembered Sidonie's words about his search for her resting place. He had not exhausted the possibilities for that yet. Taking a lamp, in spite of the daylight, he ventured back up the stairs.

His exploration was more leisurely this time. He no longer checked his watch constantly, fearful that the dusty air of the rooms would entrap him and allow night to fall without his knowledge. Sidonie knew that he would do this. She might kill him for disobeying her…but she meant to kill him anyway, so what had he to lose?

As before, he found nothing of value and a thousand things of interest. After knocking on walls and considering cobwebbed ceilings, he allowed his attention to be distracted by the strange treasures he found in each room. He read a series of letters to the doomed Constance from a friend in the city, who bemoaned her absence from the glittering balls and amusements. In one chamber, he found a selection of cufflinks scattered across the floor. Gold, silver, studded with diamonds and rubies, they all bore the initials "AS." He wondered to whom they had belonged but found no other clues. The shirts hanging like still ghosts in that wardrobe were particularly fine, however, so he added one or two to the collection of booty he carried with him.

At last, he found the room that must have been the master's chamber. He had dismissed it on his first search as it did not appear to have been opened for decades. A thick layer of dust covered the floor and furniture, including the elaborately carved bed that dominated the room. Matthew stifled a sneeze as he stepped into the sea of dust. Christian must have slept here; strange, mad Christian who had built this fabulous prison for himself and sentenced his family to die in it with him. Sidonie had denied any responsibility for his madness but he wondered just the same. How could anyone be with her without drifting into insanity? Her very existence seemed to threaten all order and reason.

He reached out and touched one of the bedposts. His

fingers came away smeared with dust. He moved closer and considered the patterns carved into the wood. Beneath the layer of gauzy grey, he could see the roses wrapped around the post. He ran his finger along the curving shapes and felt a sudden sting of pain. He drew his hand back and discovered a drop of blood on his finger. The artist had not omitted the thorns. They waited like teeth beneath the shroud of dust. He thought of the golden thorns wrapped around Sidonie's slender golden throat and a chill slipped down his spine.

He lifted the lamp and looked around again. An elusive trace of disease and corruption seemed to underlie the scent of decay and disuse so familiar from the other rooms. Christian had died in that bed, he remembered from Sidonie's story. He had wasted into madness within these walls and then offered up his throat to the evil angel he had brought here.

Matthew turned away, suddenly eager to be gone. Something buried beneath the dust on the bedside table caught his eye and he paused. He lifted the book and shook the dust from it. The pages fell open to the tracery of faded ink.

I watch the sun slide across the floor and wish it would hurry hurry so that she might come again…

It was Christian's journal. Matthew snapped it shut, pulled away from the puff of dust that rose about his face, and hurried from the room, the book in his hand. He closed the door behind him and took a deep breath. The cool air of the hallway tasted sweet after the stale, ancient closeness of the sickroom, the deathroom.

He leaned against the wall for a moment. His mouth tasted like dust. It seemed as if he had been searching for hours, the long-sealed rooms devouring the moments as if hungry for any scrap of time allowed them. He had a mad vision of the house growing around him, adding chamber upon chamber so that he could never hope to discover them all. With a shiver, he pushed himself away from the wall and hurried downstairs.

Matthew turned the pages slowly. From the entries, he guessed that it began some time after the completion of the house. There was little of interest at the beginning. Often there were only endless lists of materials or costs relating to the construction. Many of them were repeated more than once, as if they were spells required to keep the stones together, the roof intact. Gradually, the tone of the lists began to change. They no longer itemized stone and dollars, but rather less concrete things: a recitation of the names of the angels, a litany of wrongs done and sins committed.

Constance's death rated only a brief sentence, then it too joined the incantation, another black mark against its reciter's soul. Paragraphs, when they appeared, became incoherent. Punctuation vanished, turning sentences into nothing more than lists of words. Matthew was forced to admit that much of what Sidonie had told him appeared to be true. Christian hated himself with an almost egotistical loathing. He was also completely mad.

She is coming again which thing will she be there are two masks she wears and I never know never know which one it will be to open the door but I hope oh I hope it is the angel the evil angel with her mouth as wide as the night sky...

It was the other one this time the nurse the mother of mercy the one who brings the food that spoils in my rotten mouth the one who carries away the wastes that my foul body expels the one who washes the filth from my corrupt skin

She had told the truth about that as well, it seemed. She had cared for the sick and dying man. He remembered his mother's decline. Even at the beginning, he had hated to visit her in her room, to see her thin, wasted face and smell the sweet, mocking scent of her sickness. There had been nurses to wipe the sweat from her skin, to hold her hand when she tossed and muttered in the night. At the end, they—a nameless, faceless they that he always saw only as interchangeable figures dressed in white—had taken her away to the sanatorium. All that had emerged from there was a telegram to say that she was dead.

> *She has said she will return and I must cling to that I must believe in that to make me wait is torment to make me wait is hell but where I am but hell and so I will have to wait wait wait for her to come back and shed her*
> *silk*
> *feathers*
> *furs*
> *scales*
> *skin*
>
> *my snake queen my wolf love my mantis wife my evil angel with the wings of a raven and I hear her step in the hallway the sweet creak of my sweet wood the wood that loves me loves me and she is coming back to me with her drowned eyes her black web of hair her amber skin and her mouth her burning mouth her ice teeth and there are torments so exquisite that you cannot help but pray for them not to end never ever to end and I am damned beyond all hope of redemption and only my evil angel will embrace me with her*
> *arms*
> *fingers*
> *thighs*
> *mouth*
> *Her wide and hungry mouth*

Matthew closed the book. Dust wafted into the air, motes dancing in the last rays of sunlight. He did not see them, saw only a man huddled in that thorny bed, scribbling with gnarled hands, his grey hair a greasy tangle about his shadowed face. He heard the scratch of the quill pen and then the faint sound of the footstep. The man looked up, eyes gleaming hungrily, their whites startling bright. His tongue, a fleshy worm, crept across his lips. Matthew shook the vision from his head, standing up to pace across the room.

He stopped in front of the concealed canvas then twitched away the cloth. He knew what was waiting there to fill the space in the centre of the painting. He saw the sweep of raven wings, as black as the ice was white. He caught up his sketchbook and crouched in front of the easel. His fingers found a pencil and began to work on a preliminary study. He had drawn these lines before, he knew them, had seen them buried beneath lies and brought them to life several pages earlier.

At the second knock on the door, he blinked and looked around. The light was almost gone. He squinted at the sketch in his hand. The wings were like an archway over the slender, black-clad figure beneath them. Its hands were pressed together, a gesture both reverent and predatory. The triangle of the face was sketched only faintly but he knew what would go there. He could see the odd arch of the cheekbones and the sweep of the long upper lip.

Her wide and hungry mouth…

The knock came again. He slammed the sketchbook closed and went to answer it. Sidonie stood in the gallery, dressed in sombre cinnamon velvet. She was an incongruous angel, he thought absurdly. The word always summoned for him a pale palette: white flesh, frost hair, eyes of silver grey or arctic blue. Despite the changes that her nature had wrought beneath her skin there was something of the eastern desert about her still, banked within her honey-hued flesh and the black fall of her hair.

She wore another extravagant necklace. This one was composed of great chunks of amber, smooth but irregularly shaped, that lay like droplets on her skin. From the centre of the necklace hung one piece larger than the rest. Within the golden resin, he could see the dark shape of a trapped insect.

She gave him her close-mouthed smile. "Would you care for dinner?"

"Yes. Thank you." He shut the door carefully behind him. Her smile deepened and he saw her gaze drop to his feet. He glanced down and noticed that the cuffs of his pants were covered with dust. He braced himself automatically for her anger.

"Will you give me your blood to drink, though you die of it?" she asked softly.

"No," he answered, unsure whether to be annoyed or amused that she seemed to think his ready acquiescence to dinner might translate into any other surrender. To his surprise, she shrugged and said nothing more, not even as they sat in the quiet dining room and she watched him eat.

"I met a man on the train," Matthew began carefully, thinking of Will's story, "who said that he used to trap in this area many years ago. He told me a strange story about a man he found near death in the woods, raving about the ice sucking the life from him. Was he perhaps an acquaintance of yours?"

"It might have been, I suppose. It might also have been the delirium of a dying man. The cold does strange things to the mortal mind."

"His name was Mike."

Her shoulders lifted in a shrug. "I am sorry. I do not always ask their names." The casual words felt like an icy wind scraping at the back of his neck. He set down his glass and looked at her. The light from the candles flickered across her face, leaving shadows to conceal her eyes as she considered the patterns her fingers traced in the wood of the table.

"How many people have you murdered?" He expected anger from her at the question and the words he used to ask it. She looked up and one side of her mouth quirked.

"In two thousand years? Surely you do not suppose that I have kept count?"

"All right. How many in the last year?"

After a moment, she said: "Four."

"Only four?" he echoed, disbelieving. She laughed and rose, leaning forward to collect his abandoned dishes.

"Does that disappoint you? I am sorry but it was only four. I will not speak for the deer population, however."

"If it was only four, if deer will do, then why am I here?" She paused at the doorway to the kitchen and looked back at him.

"Fate?"

"I do not believe in fate," Matthew said, thinking of his nightmares, his half-articulated fears. He knew that it was more than fate that he feared and denied. Was retribution fate—or justice? He caught the edge of Sidonie's curious glance before she turned away.

"Neither do I," he heard her say as the door closed behind her. He sat in the empty room for a long moment then bent to blow out the candles. In the darkness, he considered what he should do. He could barricade himself in the ballroom for the evening, reading more of Christian's mad ravings. He could find some other, less disturbing, book to amuse him and retire to his room.

Matthew rose and went into the kitchen. It was empty. He found the door to the library and passed through it to pause at the entrance to the sitting room. Sidonie was standing at the table in the window, her fingers moving over the herbs and plants set there. He noticed that one or two of them had opened into bloom with tiny white flowers that exuded an unexpectedly potent sweetness. She worked with intense concentration, plucking away dead leaves, patting the damp earth of the pots. It was an activity as incongruous with her nature as her appearance was with Christian's vision of her as an angel.

"This is basil," she said after a moment, her fingers brushing one broad leaf. "Here is coriander and chives and mint. It is hard to keep them growing through the cold months of the winter so I must watch them carefully."

"Why do you bother? You cannot taste them anyway, or so you said."

"You can," she said. "And they are all that I have left of the sun."

"Do you miss it? Do you even remember it, after so long?"

"I do not know. I think so...but it might only be my dreams that I recall, not the truth." She glanced at him briefly then bent her head to the herb garden again. He noticed that she had only answered his second question. Then he recalled what had drawn him there, the question spurred by her final words as she left the dining room.

"You said that you do not believe in fate. What do you believe? Or after two millennia, is there anything in which to believe at all?"

"God or the Devil, you mean?" He nodded. She looked down at the dried leaf crumbling in her hands. "I try not to believe in things beyond myself. I worshipped gods when I was mortal and they did not protect me. And yet..."

"Yet?"

"You could argue that the old tales are true and that my lack of reflection signals a lack of a soul. In order for me to fail to have one, souls must exist. If the soul does, then perhaps a creator for it exists as well. So you see," her hands stopped moving for a moment, "it is often just as difficult to refuse to believe in something as it is to trust in it."

"The old tales also say that vampires are demons, servants of the Devil."

"I have never met the Devil." Her smooth features tightened for a moment, a clouding so brief he thought that he might have imagined it. "Or at least he never claimed to be the only one. I have known evil—but not all of it came from my kind." For a moment, neither spoke. "What about you?" Sidonie asked at last.

"I was the one who spent all my time in church contemplating the stained-glass windows and statues and not listening at all to the sermons. I suppose that means that all I really believe in is art. Though perhaps I should have paid closer attention," he added. "Then I would know how to pray."

Sidonie pinched a dead bloom from one of the plants. The movement of her thin fingers against the green made him think of a stick-legged mantis moving in the leaves. "Others have prayed," she said softly. "It has never made any difference."

Chapter 21

❧

When Matthew awoke the next morning, he knew that he would have to escape.

His sleep had been wracked with nightmares. His mind was full of confused memories of lying beneath a blanket of dust, the sound of footsteps echoing as they drew near, the shadow of great black wings falling across his face. The rest of the details were blurred, but he knew that they would emerge in his paintings, whether he wished them to or not. That was part of why he had to go. If he stayed, eventually he would fear his art as much as he feared his dreams. If he stayed, the cold corruption of her would turn his fingers to stone.

He would have to act quickly, he thought, as he sat in the dining room, his palms pressed against the warm porcelain of the coffee cup. There was snow on the high peaks of the mountains already and he did not know how long it might be before it claimed the valley as well. There was no strategic advantage to waiting. Once Sidonie knew he was gone she would come after him, whether he left tonight or any other. His only hope was that the head start he could gain in a day's travel would allow him to reach the railway line before she could catch him.

He knew that there would be a price to pay for his escape. She might act on her threat to expose his father. There was nothing he could do about that. He would simply have to deal with it when it happened. After all, Simon surely did not value his reputation over a son's life—even that of the "black sheep" son.

Of course, it might not matter in the end. He might die on the way to the railway.

Matthew put down the cup with a clatter that seemed to echo in the empty room. If he was going to go, it might as well be now. It was early morning still, giving him almost the whole of the day in which to travel. If he stayed another night, Sidonie might somehow read his intention and act to stop him.

It took just a few moments to prepare. He took only his satchel, packed with extra clothes against the cold, his sketchbook and a selection of food from the kitchen. He rowed quickly across the lake, fearing at any moment Joseph or Helen might appear from the woods. He did not know if they would take any steps to stop him but would prefer that he did not have to find out. Both boats were now at the mainland dock but he knew that would not delay her for long. During his exploration of the island he had seen a spare boat and a canoe in the storage shed. He knew now that he should have destroyed them, but was equally certain that he dared not go back.

After a few moments of uneasy contemplation, cursing himself for having been too miserable with rain and cold on his arrival to pay proper attention to the route, he found what he believed was the right path. He was fairly certain that the railway lay to the east of the valley; as long as he kept moving in that direction he was sure to come upon it eventually. He started up the trail at a brisk walk.

An hour later, he had to stop, resting on a fallen log at

the side of the trail. He was sweating beneath his heavy coat and there was a sharp pain in his side. His throat felt dry. He had no water, having been unable to find a canteen or flask in the kitchen. The mountains had seemed filled with water on his first passage through them but now he had not seen a stream since he had begun his walk.

He would never make the railway at this rate. He walked twice this far in the city without a second thought. Without money, he often had no choice but to walk wherever he wished to go. But there, he travelled on streets and parks of mown grass, not on rough trails that seemed always to go uphill. He had reckoned without the altitude as well.

So it is harder than you anticipated, he thought to himself in disgust. What do you propose to do? Go back? That was what she counted on, no doubt, assuming that her prey would not have the stamina to endure the journey and would flee back to the dubious safety of her waiting web.

The thought goaded him to his feet again. He set a slower pace this time and it was two hours until he was forced to make another stop. By dusk, he had no idea where he was, beyond the fact that the sunset at his back meant that he was still moving east. With the fall of night, all the thoughts that he had successfully suppressed during the day returned. He remembered Will's stories of natural predators and Joseph's casual acknowledgement of them. He had no weapons and did not think that he even dared to light a fire, not with pursuit likely.

He kept moving as long as there was light. The night came without moonrise, and, when he tripped over an upthrust root for the third time, he knew that he had to stop. After some consideration, he decided that he felt marginally safer in the thin line of trees that edged an open clearing than he did in either the deep forest or the open ground. His back against a tree, his coat wrapped tightly around him, he ate a portion of his food and tried to determine whether it was better to surrender to defenceless sleep or stay awake all night and risk weariness slowing his pace the next day.

He did not even realize that he had fallen asleep until he awoke with a shudder. For a moment, he did not know where he was, thought he was dreaming the black-and-silver dappled landscape that surrounded him. The moon had risen, full and bright, and he could see the shadowy shapes of the trees arching overhead. He sighed, aware of how much his body ached, and leaned his head back against the tree trunk.

A howl rose. Another echoed it. The sound seemed to shiver down his spine. It was utterly wild, beautiful and pitiless. He sat frozen for a long moment. The sound came again, much closer this time. It drove him to his feet in panic. What did one do when tracked by wolves? he wondered. Run? Stay still? Climb a tree? Pray?

When the first wolf broke from the trees at the far side of the clearing, he ran.

The night seemed to explode with sound: the triumphant chorus of howls, the leaves crunching beneath his feet, the laboured gasps of his breath. He ran blindly, his arms held up against the branches that lashed at him. He almost hit a tree, swerving at the last moment so that only his shoulder slammed into the trunk. Off-balance, he stumbled over a fallen branch and pitched forward onto his hands and knees in the leaves. Something moved in the brush beside him. He saw the moonlight catch the twin fires of eyes and heard the heavy, wet sound of panting.

Terror spurred him to his feet again and he plunged forward into a small clearing. He staggered to a stop, aware of the shapes moving through the dead grass ahead of him. Four wolves, their fur gleaming silver in the moonlight, paced across the open space before him. He saw the red flags of their tongues as they panted, the glow of their eyes as they watched him. He looked behind him and saw two more emerge from the forest to crouch on their haunches. The dark slashes of their mouths seemed to smile.

He took a step into a clearing and heard a soft growl. The wolves had settled into the grass. He swallowed hard, clutched his satchel across his chest and took another step forward.

The largest of them, a great, heavy-shouldered beast, rose and snarled. Matthew froze. He heard a tentative cry from behind him. The gleaming gazes shifted to stare past him. He turned slowly and saw a dark shape detach itself from the trees and step into the moonlight.

She was dressed for hunting. The fur at the collar and cuffs of her coat shone in the moonlight with the same silver sheen as that of the wolves. Her hair was bound back, providing no shadows to hide the alien architecture of her face. He could read no expression, not even anger, there.

"Matthew." Her voice was no more revealing than her face. He said nothing, could think of nothing to say that would make any difference to what was about to happen. She walked to his side and he forced himself to meet her gaze. For a moment, the tilt of her head let the moonlight touch her eyes and he was surprised to see nothing more than weary resignation in them. "It is a long walk back," she said at last. "We should begin."

Matthew stood still. The wolves rose from their positions and watched him. He sighed and shouldered his satchel. "How did you find me?"

"The wolves were not averse to a hunt," she said, gesturing for him to precede her towards the forest. The wolf pack moved around them, guiding them towards the path. "They are somewhat disappointed in being denied a kill so

I would not advise that you run again."

He thought about how long it had taken him to reach this point—and how little time it had taken her. Distant memories of childhood tales returned, the distorted traces her kind had left in mankind's history. Did she have the power of transformation? Had one of the wolves running him to ground been her? He decided that he had little to lose by asking. When he did, she said shortly: "Hardly. I had to do it in this body, which is fortunately much stronger than yours." Her tone made it clear she had no interest in further discussion.

In the trees, he could not see well enough to follow the path. Sidonie took his hand in her cold one and led him. Somewhere in the dark journey she asked him the question and he refused her. She said nothing else. When they emerged into the moonlight again, the wolves were gone. He pulled his hand from the chilly grip of her fingers. She looked at him for a moment, then motioned with elaborate courtesy for him to take the lead again.

He trudged on wearily, his feet aching. It was not possible to reach the house before dawn, he was certain. If they could not, then she would have to leave him or risk exposing herself to the sun. All he had to do was delay long enough...

He stopped moving and then sat down at the side of the path. He did not have to feign his painful breathing or the ache in his side. She stood over him for a moment and then crouched beside him. "If you do not keep walking," she said softly, "then I will have to carry you the rest of the way back." He almost laughed. He had half a head and a considerable number of pounds on her. Then he recalled that she had travelled a distance that had taken him all day in no more than a few hours.

"It took me all day to walk that far," he protested. "I cannot walk all the way back by dawn." He saw her shrug and then her fingers closed over his arm. The touch stirred a shudder and he was on his feet before he had time to think. "I'll walk."

Despite the impossibility of it, they reached the house before dawn. Every time that he stumbled, Sidonie pulled him ruthlessly to his feet. Every time that his pace slackened, she took his hand and dragged him in her wake. He had no choice but to keep moving despite his blistered feet and leaden limbs.

At last, he stumbled into the house and collapsed onto the stairs. Sidonie's voice reached him from very far away. "If you ever do that again, I will call the wolves and hunt you down—and none of us will be disappointed. Is that clear?" He managed to nod his heavy head but did not bother to look at her.

When something touched his ankle, he opened his eyes. She was kneeling on the floor, unfastening his boots. As he began to protest, she tugged off the first one. Even in the dim light, he could see the blood that covered his foot. His sharp breath echoed hers. "Go upstairs," she said, her voice tight. "I will bring you something for the blisters and the pain."

"I can manage," he said, reaching for the railing to pull himself to his feet, angered by her show of sympathy and concern and aware of the uneasy undercurrent of emotion he could feel beneath it.

Climbing the stairs hurt more than he had imagined possible. At the top, he almost gave up and crawled down the hall to the bathroom, but the stubborn core of him refused to do that where she might see. When his shaking fingers managed to light the lamp, he discovered that his feet were not as bad as he had feared. Though both of the blisters on his heels had broken, only one was bleeding.

As he washed the wounded areas, he heard a knock on the door. The door was locked but he did not move to open it. "Matthew?"

"I am fine. Go away."

"I am leaving what medical supplies I have outside the door. Do not be foolish about this." Do not contaminate your blood, he thought. That is what she really meant. Do not die of anything besides her will. He said nothing and, after a moment, heard the creak of the floorboards as she moved away.

On a tray outside the door he found bandages, an unidentifiable ointment and a bottle of brandy. He treated his injured feet and limped back into the bedroom to contemplate the bottle of brandy. It was, he supposed, a medical supply in its own way. It would certainly do to numb the pain and bring him sleep.

In the silence, the coming dawn sealed outside by the heavy curtains, he poured a glass and lifted it in a silent, mocking toast to the darkness that surrounded him.

Chapter 22

He was too drunk to paint. He always knew when he reached that point, some sense too powerful to be seduced by the alcohol always stopping him before he drew the wrong line, mixed the wrong colour. He looked at the bottle of wine on the table beside him. It was almost empty.

She never should have told you to help yourself, Matthew thought bitterly. Unless she hoped all along that it would weaken you so much you would give in to her in a fit of drunken confusion. Tomorrow night he would not make the same mistake, he resolved, conveniently forgetting that he had made that resolution five nights in a row already.

He went through the rituals of cleaning up with clumsy precision and then sat on the chair and considered the new painting.

He had finished the ice palace with its dark angel three days ag, or was it two? He was losing track. It was propped carefully against the far wall to dry, image turned inward. After it was completed, he had tried once again to return to his abandoned landscape. It had not worked. This time, what he had intended to be a tall, slender tree turned into something else. He took another sip of wine and squinted at the half-completed painting.

The background was black cut with red and the faintest trace of purple. To the right of the centre line was the only real image on the canvas. The tree had become a woman's figure wrapped tightly in a shroud. He had done nothing but the first layer of paint and the draperies were only sketched in, as was the faintest suggestion of a face with the stark lines of a skull. Several strokes of yellow marked where the necklace would surround the figure's throat, the spikes of its thorny splendour tipped in red.

He looked past the canvas to the model he had assembled. One of the top-floor rooms had yielded a dressmaker's dummy, another the thin cloth he had wound about it. It was not the equivalent of a live model, he acknowledged, but would suffice for the hard, technical work of shadowing the drapery of the shroud. He pushed himself awkwardly to his feet and went to the headless figure, automatically adjusting a misaligned fold that caught his eye. The fabric was so old he thought it might tear as he touched it. It must once have been white but now was the colour of ivory. Use or age had seemed to thin it as well, giving it a translucence that would have offered no concealment for any real model who wore it. As it was, all that it revealed was the deep rift down the centre of the dummy's torso and a figure that ended at the hips. If he wanted the painting to have the details of the female form, he would have to do them from memory or imagination.

The thought made him laugh as he stooped to dim the lamps he had carefully positioned on tables and plant stands about the figure. It was fortunate that he had a good memory, a better imagination…else he might be forced to ask Sidonie to pose for him after all. Though no doubt she would care no more for this portrait than the one the doomed Constance had done.

He had a sudden vision of Sidonie, wrapped like the ancient dead in the gossamer fabric, the strange glow of her skin visible through the shroud, the skull of his painting superimposed over her face. The thought stirred a sick excitement, dread and fascination combined. He took a deep breath. I am drunk, he told himself earnestly. I am drunk and it is not Sidonie in the painting. Not in this or any other.

He moved to douse the remaining lamps. In the beginning, he had been uneasy painting at night in the ballroom. The blaze of lights through the wide windows must be visible throughout the valley. That knowledge made him feel vulnerable and exposed until he remembered that the true monster in this wilderness was inside the house with him. Now he never glanced at the darkness outside the glass, unconcerned by what might move within it.

Matthew closed the door to the ballroom behind him and went to stand for a moment in the dark, empty Hall. He could see a fall of light on the floor outside Sidonie's sitting room. She seemed to spend most of her time there, at least while he was still on the lower floor. Some of the sounds he heard in the night suggested she moved about the house when she believed he was asleep. He had no doubt that she knew about the rooms he had plundered to assemble his workroom but she never mentioned it. Though he had never again encountered her at it, he knew that she went out for several hours every night, hunting the creatures that kept her alive.

He wondered at that. No tale he had ever heard of vampires allowed that possibility. If she could sustain herself on the blood of animals, what need had she for his? But every night she asked him the question he could only answer one way. Sometimes she asked it while he ate the food she prepared for him, her voice as casual as if she were inquiring how he liked the fish or pheasant.

Sometimes she materialized at the door of the ballroom. Once he had gone straight to bed from painting and she had stood outside his door and asked him.

Best to get it over with, he thought, so that he could spend the rest of the night in whatever peace he could find. He went to the door of the sitting room. Sidonie was at the desk writing. With her head bent, the fall of her hair obscuring her face, she looked mortal. When he said her name, she turned towards him and the humanity vanished.

"That's it for me," he said. "I'm to bed. No, I won't give you my blood to drink." She half-rose from her chair, lines that would never mark her skin momentarily creasing it in puzzlement and concern. That's set her back, he thought with a sudden giddy sense of triumph.

"Matthew..."

"No. That's it. No. Good night." He spun away from her, caught his balance and made himself walk slowly across the Hall, as if he were not afraid that she might come after him. He made it to the stairs unmolested, then up to the second floor. At the railing, he turned and looked back. The lit doorway was empty. He grinned, executed an extravagant bow to the invisible audience and went to his room.

Once there, the sense of triumph faded. He sat in the semi-darkness before the ashes of the dead fire, wishing he had brought another bottle of wine from the pantry. He was deluding himself if he believed his tiny victories—the open rooms, the refusal to allow her to evade the blunt facts of what she was, even the paintings—meant anything. Even the quest for her resting place, which he continued only in the most haphazard fashion, was doomed to failure. Even if he found her, he was not certain he could carry out the required execution. All his actions were nothing more than the petty rebellions of a schoolboy, gestures of defiance to the brutal, relentless authority of reality.

He would never go home. He could deny her every
night until he was an old man like his father but she would
never let him go. After the debacle of his botched escape,
he knew that fleeing would be suicide not salvation. He
would grow old and die in this barren place. He would
turn pale and wasted within these cold walls. He would
never sit in a café, or laugh with friends, or heat the space
between his thin sheets with the friction of his body
against another. He would paint a thousand pictures that
no one would ever see until one day he would stare at the
canvas and nothing would come, nothing at all.

He closed his eyes and leaned his head back against the
chair. In the city, he had valued his isolation. He believed
that he was a solitary person, both by nature and as the
result of lessons, hard learned, in the risks that too much
trust in him could bring. He did not mind the flights of
stairs to his garret room because it meant fewer people
troubled him. He would go a day or two without seeing
another human face and he would revel in it. Now it was
clear to him how profoundly he misunderstood himself.
He treasured his solitude because he could end it whenever he chose. He could enjoy hours of seclusion because
outside his windows the city waited. Now that he found
himself in the greatest seclusion of all, he could not bear
it. He had endured it because he had not known how terrifying he found it. He had deluded himself that the ballroom was his sanctum and that its solitude gave him
shelter. If that were true, he should be there now. He
should sleep there and eat there and never set foot beyond
the boundaries that Sidonie had promised not to breach.

He did not do so not simply because those things
would be inconvenient and difficult. He did not do so
because he could not bear to give up contact with another,
even if that other was his captor. He needed those hours
in the dining room, the conversations in the sitting room.

He needed her deceptive voice and her monstrous, beautiful face.

That was how she would win him in the end, he thought despairingly. That was his weakness. He needed her because he could not bear to be alone. The realization sent a shudder through him.

Wine, he needed wine. If he went to sleep even partially sober, he would drown in terrible dreams. He had thought the nightmares were the worst but he had been wrong. Once or twice he had woken, aroused and aching, from dreams he could barely recall—but what he recalled was enough. If it took all the wine in the house to keep those dreams at bay, then he would drain the store dry.

He had staggered to his feet before it registered that to obtain the wine he would have to go back down the stairs and past the beckoning lure of the light from her room.

Then he remembered the nethys.

He found his satchel and scrabbled in its depths for the little box his friends had given him. When he opened it, the vial fell out into his hand. Even in the dim light, it seemed to possess a rich, dark glow. It was a deep cobalt blue that vibrated in his vision, the blue of the stones in Sidonie's necklace of thorns, of her gold-shot eyes.

It makes you see your dreams... He did not want to see the things that shattered his sleep. He did not need a drug to see them, he had only to close his eyes. Yet perhaps it was controllable. Perhaps he could resolve to dream of his old life and the drug would take him there. To the smoky haze of a bar, to the comfort of friends, to the warm sway of a body in his arms as the music sighed around them. Surely that was what they meant by dreams. There would be no market for a drug that showed you only the things you dreaded.

He lit the lamp on the dresser and retrieved Mother Norit's mirror. It would do to arrange the lines of indigo powder. With shaking hands, he tapped the drug out onto the speckled surface. He had heard of other ways for the drug to enter the bloodstream, ways that promised even greater pleasures, but he had no needle and doubted he could have used it if he had. Inhaling the powder would have to suffice.

He slid to his knees by the hearth and set the mirror on the low table beside the chair. With great care, aware of his drunken awkwardness, he bent over, inhaling the powder through first one nostril then the other. Rubbing his nose with the back of his hand, he sat back and waited for the dreams to come.

Nothing happened. There was no euphoria. The world did not retreat, leaving him cocooned in a bubble of blissful fantasy. There was not even the lurid manifestations of his fears that he had dreaded. After a moment, he started to laugh. Paul and the others had been cheated, sold some worthless powder instead of the fabled nethys. It would have to be the wine after all.

He groped for the edge of the chair and hauled himself to his feet, collecting the lamp to guide him on the expedition through the dark house. He moved as quietly as he could, stepping carefully down the stairs into the Hall. The square of light from the sitting room had not dimmed and he watched it carefully as he began to walk towards the dining room.

Someone said his name. He stopped, eyes fixed on the light. He could not see anyone. Sidonie's silhouette did not appear in the doorway.

It came again, a whispering sigh of a voice that seemed familiar, just beyond the range of memory. It had not come from the sitting room, but from the great closed door behind him.

Joseph, or someone else from the village, must be standing outside the door calling him. He turned and stepped into the foyer. He heard it again, garbled but still undeniably his name. The bolt on the door slid noiselessly back and then he was out into the cold night air. He lifted the lamp and peered about the moonlit terrace.

"Matthew... Matthew..."

There was more than one voice, though they blended so closely they seemed to sound a single note. At the sound, a terrible longing filled him. In the simple syllables, he could hear yearning and joy, laughter and the sweet, subtle sounds of pleasure. The night suddenly seemed very bright. Each leaf, each rock was limned in silver. He set down the lamp and walked towards the path to the dock.

Here, here, he thought each time he stumbled around a curve in the pathway, it's here. The promise drew him on, hands outstretched against the overgrown branches that tried to hold him back. Each time he heard his name, he was certain that he knew who spoke but the knowledge seemed to dissolve before he could focus on it.

The trees vanished and he was standing at the top of the dock. The lake was glazed with a burning blue blackness, as if lit from its deepest part, miles below the surface. At the sound of his feet on the wooden steps, he felt a distant throb of fear but the blue soothed it, cooled away its heat.

He stopped at the end of the dock. "Matthew... Matthew...come down...come down..." He looked down into the water beyond his feet. The darkness beneath the surface parted in great waves, like curtains pulling back from a stage. He could see straight down to the bottom. There was a canoe there, resting on the rocks as if waiting for him to step into it.

"Come down..." The voices echoed and repeated, strands of sound separating themselves. He could hear the voice of an old man, cracked and dry. One was a sibilant, seductive sigh, the voice from his dreams, that wrapped his heart in honey and velvet. The last was that of a young boy.

"Come down…" The first two voices faded away. A face shimmered into the light beneath the water. Matthew felt something crack inside him and then the pain was a river pouring through him, scouring his heart as it sought a way out. His mouth moved on a name that he had not said aloud in over a decade.

"I've been waiting for you," the face said, and the water parted, lifting the canoe to the surface. "Get in."

Matthew knew then that the torrent inside him would drown him, stopping up his mouth with salt tears, submerging him in the cold truth he had so long denied. It could not be avoided any longer. This was why he had come to the cold, barren wilderness, to a prison circled with water. Not to die from a vampire's kiss but in the embrace of the truth, the debt he had run from for so long. The rightness, the inevitability of it took away any need for decision.

"Yes," he said softly, "yes."

He stepped forward.

Chapter 23

The rock was as large as her hand, a rough, reassuring weight in her palm. Once a round node, it had been cut in half to expose the nest of crystal in its heart. Sidonie's fingers stroked the polished surface, an old gesture of unconscious pleasure.

She stared at the window, not seeing the room's reflection in the glass.

It was not going badly, she told herself again. This was only to be expected. She had seen it before. That knowledge did not seem to make it easier to watch it happening again, to watch the dark crescents beneath Matthew's eyes deepening, to watch his face grow pallid and thin. She suspected that he did not eat except for the meals she prepared for him. She knew that he drank far too much. He had grown careless with his appearance, his hair turning lank and unclean, the rough beginnings of beard going unshaven.

Each night, he locked himself in the ballroom and painted. Or, at least, she presumed he did. She had only the scent of turpentine that lingered on his hands and clothing on which to base the supposition. She had not broken her promise not to go into the ballroom, though more than once she had stood at the door, contemplating the mysterious shapes and shadows inside during the hours after he had finally gone to bed. All of his completed paintings were placed facing the wall and she had no idea at all what inspiration he found to cover their canvases. The strange assembly of tables, chairs and the dressmaker's dummy seemed to form circle after circle surrounding his easel, as if somehow such clutter could protect him.

He retired later each night, until she could almost believe his hours had come to echo hers, as she had prophesied. He told her that he still rose in the early afternoon, to catch the natural light. It was as if he were afraid to sleep, even during those hours when she was helpless and he was safe from her.

It had happened despite her best intentions. She had tried very hard not to frighten him more than necessary, though she knew she could have reduced him to gibbering terror if she chose. She had made no move to seduce him, though she could have done that too, despite the undercurrent of fear, even revulsion, that she sensed when he looked at her. Blood won by either of those methods would do her no good; experience had shown her that.

Do you know that blood won by any other methods will be any different? a mocking voice asked. How do you know that you could drink the blood of God himself and have it make any difference?

Her fingers clenched the paperweight in her hand. She had to proceed as if it were possible. She had to choose the path as best she could. She had purged the last traces of mortal blood from her, feeding only on animals for months. She used none of her preternatural powers against Matthew, except for the night of his failed escape. She would have to trust that such measures would be enough.

She heard something and felt her spine stiffen. There was no sound but that of a log shifting in the fire. Yet she had heard it, a dull thump, like the closing of a great door. Setting down the paperweight, she walked out into the hall. Nothing moved...but something had. She went to the foyer and pulled open the heavy door.

A lamp was sitting on the flagstones of the terrace. Sidonie looked around but there was no sign of Matthew. Why would he have come outside? And once out, why would he have abandoned the lamp? Faint moonlight gleamed from behind the shredded clouds and though for her it flooded the terrace with light it was not enough for a mortal to use.

Had he made another escape attempt, despite the harsh lessons of the last one? If so, it must be born of alcoholic optimism and not reason. It was insanity to try to escape at night and he knew it. She felt a resigned annoyance. She would have to find him and bring him back before he did himself some damage.

She went down the path, wondering if he had had time to leave the island. If he had, she would have to retrieve the canoe she had stowed in the storage shed. She was not in the mood for a swim and hardly dressed for a chase. With luck, this attempt would cure him of the urge to flee and she would not be required to lock him in his room from now on.

Rounding the final bend in the path, she stopped abruptly. The spill of moonlight revealed the figure standing on the end of the dock, staring down into the water. He made no move towards the boat resting on the shore. She let out her breath. It was no more than claustrophobia and unhappiness then, she thought, stepping back into the shadows of the trees. She would watch to make sure that it did not turn into escape but he need never know that she did so.

Then he stepped off the dock.

For a moment, she was frozen. She heard the splash of the water as it embraced him. There was no outcry, no sound of struggle and shock as might be expected from the touch of water as cold as the lake must be. Not the escape she had expected, she realized, but the most final escape of all.

She was at the end of the dock in a heartbeat, plunging into the water without regard for the weight of her velvet dress. The lake was bitterly cold even to her inhuman flesh. She opened her eyes and peered into the black depths. There was only the dimmest touch of moonlight here but it was enough for her to see the white glow of his shirt below her as he sank, unmoving, towards the unseen bottom of the lake.

She dove down and snatched at his arm, her fingers closing over the fabric of his shirt. It was enough. She hauled him upward and broke the surface a moment before her grip brought his head clear of the water. She had time to notice that he was not breathing, then she concentrated on pulling them both onto the dock. It took her immortal strength to manage it but at last she crouched beside his prone body, slapping her hand against his back.

Careful, she thought distantly, or you will break his ribs. She knew that mortals had ways of saving each other from these fates and cursed herself for never having bothered to learn them. If he was dying, she might be able to save him...but only by giving him her own curse. Dead or undead, it meant that she had failed. If he died, then she had killed him, as surely as if she had drained his blood.

At last, his body convulsed and coughs racked it. She bent over him, pushing back the sodden strands of his hair with awkward hands. His eyes were open but he did not seem to see her. When she said his name, his gaze seemed to clear a little but he did nothing but curl away from her, shivering.

She had to get him back to the house before the cold accomplished what the water had not. Awkward in her dripping dress, she lifted him into her arms and carried him back up the trail. He did not resist her, for that much she was grateful. He did not help either, as if his disassociation could abrogate their contact.

His room was dark and cold. She set his limp body in the chair and crouched beside the fire to bring it to life. When the blaze roared, she turned back to him. He had wrapped his arms around his shaking chest and some semblance of life had returned to his eyes. His hair was plastered to his head and throat. Sidonie pushed the wet tangles of her own hair from her face, aware that her dress was dripping on the carpet. She shifted to kneel beside the chair. "Matthew?" He blinked, as if clearing water from his eyes, and looked at her.

"Sidonie?" It was a choked whisper, disbelieving and bewildered.

"Yes. You fell in the lake." The twist of his mouth denied the lie. She ignored it and bent to unfasten his shoes.

"I was going to drown." The words had an accusatory tone, though whether he blamed her for his death or his failure to achieve it she could not tell.

"You didn't," she countered. "Now, we must get these wet clothes off you, before you catch your death."

She identified the strange sound he made as a laugh. "I have already caught my death...or it has caught me." It was true, she admitted, but ignored it nonetheless. She struggled with the buttons of his shirt. When her hands touched him, he shuddered away from her. She sat back on her heels, shaken by the depths of his loathing and by the unexpected pain it caused her.

"I am sorry if my touch disgusts you," she said as steadily as she could. "I regret that there is so much blood on my hands. But I only want to help."

Something flickered across his face, some emotion she could not read. It was a break in the blankness but she mistrusted it, aware that whatever had driven him to the water had not left him. He shifted in the chair, straightening slowly, hands dropping away from their protective crossing of his chest. Sidonie reached out hesitantly, uncertain whether the gesture meant acceptance or not.

He caught her fingers in his and held her hands still, palms up to the firelight. "Your hands..." He gazed down at them. "All the people who must have died by these hands." His gaze lifted and he stared at her face unflinchingly. She felt the look, the weight of it on her skin and all the way through to her bones. "And that mouth..." His fingers rose to trace the line of her lips. "Killed by that murderous mouth."

"Yes." The whisper seemed terribly loud in the silence.

"Oh God, your mouth..." Then he leaned forward and kissed her with sudden, shocking ferocity. His mouth tasted like wine and something darker, more elusive. The weight of him coming off the chair tumbled them to the floor in a tangle of wet cloth. She heard the sound of glass breaking but could not tell if it was real or imaginary. She felt the blood roaring in her head. She was not sure if it was hers or his. This should not be happening, she thought dimly, but knew that she did not want it to stop. Resolve and restraint dissolved in a rush of desire that swamped sense with blind need. The hunger opened like a great wound inside her.

When she resurfaced, they were sprawled on the carpet, his body beneath hers. His hands were clenched in the wet snarl of her hair. To her shock, when he released her mouth, it was to drag her head against his throat. His skin was chilly beneath her lips but she could feel the liquid heat beneath it, throbbing through his body. For a moment, she could think of nothing but plunging into that waiting fire and burning away all her hunger, all her aching loneliness.

This is wrong...this is wrong... Some semblance of reason penetrated the dark thrall of her appetites. She thrust against his embrace and broke free, shifting back to kneel over him. Matthew opened his eyes but she could read nothing in them. "Go on," he whispered and pulled his collar away from his throat. The pulse beat there, fluttering beneath the skin as if the blood longed to be free. She licked her lips and swallowed the wet hunger gathering in her mouth.

"Matthew..."

His gaze shifted sideways and she followed it. The shattered remains of Mother Norit's mirror lay against the hearth. She remembered the sound of breaking glass. His hand darted out and caught up one of the shards. She reached for him, suddenly certain that he would cut his throat, like a terrible sacrificial offering, but he evaded her grasp and put the jagged glass against his wrist instead. He did not even wince as the edge parted his skin. "Go on." He lifted his wrist to her. The cut was not deep, just a thin line of blood. She could smell it, rich and hot, more compelling than the most precious spice, the most exotic incense. "Go on."

Her hand moved of its own will, curving around his and drawing his wrist to her mouth. The blood exploded on her tongue. Far away she heard her moan, then the catch of his breath as her teeth slid into his flesh.

If she had taken more than a swallow, she would have been lost. She dragged her mouth from his skin before the blood could swamp her, drown her in pleasure so long denied. Gripping his wrist with both hands, she held it against her breast, where she could not see the blood between her fingers. "Why?" she asked, her voice sounding thin and lost. His eyes flickered open again. "Why are you doing this?"

"Does it matter?"

"Yes."

He frowned, as if the answer required concentration. "I am too long overdue," he said at last. "It is time to die."

It was not surrender, Sidonie realized with bitter clarity. It was suicide. She knew then that it would not work. She could drain him dry, but in the end he would be a lifeless husk and nothing would have changed. The hunger roared that it did not matter, that all that existed in the world was this moment, this vessel of blood beneath her. She pushed it away, furious, sick, aroused, then thrust his hand from her as well.

"Dying I could get from anyone." She stood up and stepped away from him, fighting the trembling in her knees. His eyes followed her, blank and bewildered. "I am going to get you some tea. I expect you to be in bed when I get back."

"But…"

"If you disobey me, I will not kill you, no matter how much you beg me for it. I will chain you, I will imprison you, but I will keep you alive. Do you understand me?" For one wild moment she wanted to strike him, to impress on him the depth of her terror and resolution. But she dared not. If she touched him, she would want him, would want his body and his blood and this time she would not be able to stop herself no matter what the consequences. Matthew sat up unsteadily, glancing in visibly growing distress from his bleeding wrist to her face. "Do you understand me?" He swallowed and nodded, eyes on the red line tracing its way across his skin.

In the kitchen, Sidonie struggled to ignore the thousand mad fears that flickered through her mind. She should not have left him alone, he would use the mirror fragments with true intent, he would lock the door against her and take his own life. Yet something in his final horrified glance at her suggested that whatever strange madness had overtaken him was fading. She did not believe he truly wanted to die. Mortals clung to life with great ferocity. Indeed, it sometimes seemed that was the only mortal instinct that vampires retained. What was her life, after all, but two thousand years of refusing to die?

It was the wine, she told herself, remembering the taste of it in his mouth. The memory brought the hunger back in a wave. She snatched the kettle from the stove, poured the hot water into a cup and with savage deliberation swallowed it. It hurt, though it could not scald her, but it washed away the taste of his blood and his kiss.

When she climbed the stairs again, tea in hand, ruined dress exchanged for another, she found him barricaded behind the uncertain shelter of the bedcurtains, fast asleep.

Chapter 24

❧

His dreams had been terrible. Matthew lay in the darkness, remembering with appalling vividness the face that had summoned him off the dock, the sensation of the icy water closing over his head, the feel of Sidonie's body in his arms. Perhaps that was how nethys worked after all; it gave your dreams a visceral power so strong you believed that you had lived them.

Or perhaps he *had* lived them. The thought was so dreadful that it sent him staggering to his feet to drag back the heavy curtains. He turned and surveyed the room in the thin sunlight. There was no trace of the shattered mirror by the hearth. He took a deep breath in relief then noticed the tiny vial resting on the bedside table. Even from the window he could see that it was empty. He swore, crossing the room to snatch it up, to shake it, to be sure.

He had taken the drug, that was all that was certain. It was possible that all the rest was nothing but a hallucination. Yet if that were true, then Mother Norit's mirror should be sitting on the dresser and it was not. If it had all been drug-induced madness then there should not be a cut on his wrist. He ran his finger along the thin scab and felt a twinge of remembered pain. With a sense of fearful fascination, he lifted his arm to peer at the wound, searching for the traces of Sidonie's teeth. There were two tiny marks on either side of the cut.

His stomach turned sickeningly and something rose in his gorge. He made it to the washroom in time to be ill. He felt feverish, shivering in the chilly air despite the sweat that slicked his skin. Crawling back into bed, he cursed it all; his father, his friends, the drug, Sidonie, himself. Most of all himself. He had bungled suicide just as badly as he had bungled escape. Worst of all he had bungled it twice, he thought bitterly just before he fell back into a delirious sleep. Perhaps he would have to settle for the ignominy of a dose of fatal pneumonia instead.

When he woke hours later, he had to go through it again; the doubts, the confirmation, the nausea. The next time, only the nausea remained. By the time he heard the knock on the door, he knew that, whether he wished it or not, he was not going to die of a convenient illness.

"Go away," he said to the closed door. It opened a little.

"Matthew?"

"Go away."

"Are you all right?" The door moved another inch. The gleam of lamplight slid into the darkness of the room.

"Fine. Fabulous. Never better. Go away."

"Are you ill?"

"No." The band of light widened. "Don't come in. I don't want to see you." Some part of his mind acknowledged that he sounded petulant but he did not care.

"Then close your eyes," came the sharp reply and the door opened. Sidonie stood in the entrance, lamp in one hand, tray balanced in the other. He looked away but not before he felt the customary hammer blow of her otherworldly appearance. "I am coming in to light the fire and leave your dinner. If you do not want to see me, close your eyes."

For a moment, he contemplated doing as she suggested but in the end knew it was too childish to be considered, even in his current state. He shrugged and lay back in the bed, settling for careful contemplation of the dark patterns of the canopy above his head. He heard the dull thump of logs in the grate, then the scratch of a match. Firelight touched the faded, voluptuous roses in the cloth above him.

Sidonie set the tray down on the dresser and came to sit on the edge of the bed. As the mattress bent beneath her weight, Matthew glanced at her. She was wearing a white shirt and dark pants, a man's jacket over them. It was hard to look at her, at the inhuman but perversely elegant arch of her cheekbones, the narrow line of her jaw, the dark unreadable eyes, the wide pale mouth. That mouth, dear God, he had *kissed* that mouth, had held it against his throat. The unbidden thought stirred the memory of shameful, horrifying pleasure. He had kissed that murderous mouth and *enjoyed* it. He looked away before his expression could betray him.

He felt the weight of her cool palm against his forehead. "I am no expert on mortal medicine but I would guess that you are not going to die," she said.

"Not of pneumonia, at any rate." The hand withdrew and there was a long silence.

"Will you give me your blood to drink, even though you die of it?"

"No." He said the word automatically, without hesitation. At the edge of his vision, he saw her shrug and then felt her weight lift from the bed.

"Good night, Matthew." The door closed behind her. He lay still for a long time, wondering what she would do if he refused to ever rise again. Refused to eat, refused to care.

He heard her voice: I will chain you, I will imprison you, but I will keep you alive. In that battle of wills he knew that she would win. He would be betrayed by his weaknesses, his inability to withstand boredom and loneliness.

He still felt the pull of the seductive cerulean depths of the lake. Hallucination or not, that final step from the dock had been waiting for him for a long time. He had kept it at bay with liquor and drugs, with sex and sensation. When he lost his taste for excess, he thought that his art, his life would be strong enough to keep him anchored to the shore. Perhaps if he had stayed in the city it would have been. When the end that was due him was denied, he had courted another, throwing himself into the embrace of his executioner. He had done both of those things under the spell of the nethys—he did not think he could do either of them without it.

Yet whether or not he would succumb to the lure of the lake or of bloody submission to Sidonie, he knew he could not lie here and waste away. With a sigh, he pushed aside the covers and climbed shivering back into life.

An hour later, he ventured down to the kitchen. He did not see Sidonie. There was no light from her sitting room. He retrieved a bottle of wine and went to the ballroom. In the blaze of lamps, the first careful sips of wine warming him, he began to work.

Beneath his brushes, the ashen figure defined itself. When he stepped back to look, he found the changes both satisfying and disturbing. The painting had lost some of its reserve, gained a certain charged edge that pleased him aesthetically. The shrouded figure was no longer an ominous cipher. His brushstrokes had brought out the body beneath the winding sheets and turned the face from anonymous starkness to angular beauty. There was red on the lush mouth now, echoing the bloody necklace.

For a moment, he was seized by the urge to take his

widest brush or one of his knives and blot out the figure with the thickest, darkest paint he could concoct. He took a deep breath. The painting was what it was. If it was not what it had been when he began, that did not matter. The figure was not representational, not an image of any living woman. Nor any unliving woman, he told himself fiercely. If it is an expression of horror, of fear of death and of its lure, then that is only to be expected. It was only what would be natural for any artist in his situation.

Matthew took a small sip of wine, a toast to seal the resolution, and then returned to his task. Creating the folds and shadows of the shroud was careful, detailed work. It kept him close to the canvas, focusing on one line at a time. There was no ambiguity about it, no need to wonder what or why or who. He made it last as long as he could.

He finished the painting that night, unable to stop working even when his back began to hurt and his shoulders tighten. When he was done, he covered it again and downed two glasses of wine in quick succession. He took the bottle back to his room.

That became the rhythm of his nights. He rose later and later. He stayed away from the dining room and Sidonie left his dinner outside the ballroom. He wondered if one day she would make him fend for himself but she never did. He saw Helen only once, as she was preparing to return to the village, but several times he found offerings of clean clothing outside his door. Once, a new mirror sat on the top of the stack. He avoided Sidonie as much as possible. To his surprise, it turned out to be easier than he had imagined. She would knock on the door of the ballroom and, when he cracked it open an inch or two, would ask the question. He denied her each time. Each time she went away. He did not know where she went or what she did.

It snowed, blanketing the valley in white. The lake

turned grey and choppy. Matthew did not go outside, even when the sunset lining the icy trees with red had him reaching for his sketchbook. If he left the house, he knew he would end up at the dock.

He started another painting. This time, he made no pretence at contemplating a landscape. There was an image waiting at the bottom of his brain, coiled and potent. When he stood in front of the canvas, it came and he let it. His brush moved, sketching in a sinuous curve that looked like hair moving under water. He saw the colours as he worked: a thousand shades of blue, a spark of red, a lonely touch of gold, a drowning whimper of white. This time he did not even pretend he did not know what he was painting. He knew that the paint would transform itself into a murderous siren rising from a blackly blue abyss.

He would need more blue pigment when he was done. "The first colour of shadow" one of his texts in art college had called it. The colour he had shunned in favour of the bright heat of red, as if his unconscious mind had known that one day the shadows would overwhelm him.

He drank every night, to still the dreams that came anyway. He woke several times a night, heart pounding, sick and shaking. Some of the dreams were horrifying, some erotic, some a hideous combination of both. He dreaded them all.

Then one night he went to the pantry to select his vintage for the evening and discovered that it was locked.

He found Sidonie reading in her sitting room, curled in her chair with a casualness he had never seen in her before. He stalked to the centre of the room. She looked up. "Where is the key to the pantry?"

"Why? Are you planning to cook?"

"I would like some wine." She marked the place in her book and set it down, straightening in her chair.

"So that you can get drunk and throw yourself in the lake again? I am not interested in ruining another dress rescuing you."

"It wasn't the wine that made me do that. I took a drug called nethys. I have no more of it so you have nothing to fear."

"You drink too much."

"What else do you expect me to do? How else do you expect me to endure this?" He clenched his fists, furious at her composure and his own helplessness. He had never even imagined striking a woman before but for a lunatic moment he wanted to hit her. If he did, would it push her to kill him?

"I have done my best to make this bearable," she said after a long moment, her voice soft. "I do not know what else I can do."

"Let me go."

"I cannot."

"Then let me drink!" The shout seemed to echo in the small room. Her gaze dropped away from him and he saw her fingers twist in her lap. He took a slow breath to calm himself. "It is the only way I can live with the things I know, the things I've seen. Please, Sidonie."

"Why did you say it was time for you to die?"

"I was hallucinating. Does it matter?" He turned the question back on her to deflect her, but it summoned up a startlingly vivid memory of the last time he had said those words with the hard floor beneath his back and the seductive weight of her body against his.

"Yes," she said, just as she had that night.

"It is none of your business."

"It is if you wish me to consider your request."

"That is extortion," Matthew muttered and saw the corner of her mouth lift.

"Refuse then," she said and reached for her book. He

walked to the desk and stood there, staring at his reflection in the window. His face was thin, his eyes shadowed, his hair wild. A drunk, he thought in dismay. I look like a drunk or an addict. He contemplated trying to sleep without the haze of alcohol and his heart twisted in pain. His hands gripped the back of the chair in front of him.

"Why else was I sent here?" he said at last, softly. She was silent, as if she had not heard him.

"I did not think that modern man believed in fate," she said. Matthew closed his eyes and swallowed a laugh. She thought she had an answer, maybe now she would relent. He heard the rustle of her dress as she rose. "But you do not...you told me that." He could hear the puzzlement in her voice and knew that she had not been deceived. "You cannot mean that you believe your father knows what I am?"

Her voice sounded muffled, as if he were underwater. He struggled to find an answer. "No. Yes. I don't know. Doesn't he?"

"If he did, would he send you here?" The question seemed to hang in the air for a long time. "Oh, Matthew, you must not think that. Simon never knew, I swear to you." The pity in her voice felt like a weight crushing the air from his lungs.

"That hardly seems possible."

"It is the truth."

"He was your lover."

"One night only. I never let him see the truth. I never drank his blood." Her voice came nearer, until he could feel her at his shoulder. "He did not send you here to die. Why would you even imagine such a thing?"

He felt trapped, by her questions, by the heat of her at his back. He turned away, stepping blindly towards the door to the library, its darkness promising silence and peace. She caught his arm. "Tell me."

"Let me go. You said I was free." He tried to pull away, knowing that he could not, that her immortal strength could hold him there until the mountains turned to dust around them. To his surprise, her fingers fell away.

"Why did you go to the lake? What did you see in it that made you want to die?" He stepped towards the door, feeling as if he were walking through mud. "What is it that gives you so much pain?"

He was at the door. He was almost free. If he passed through it, he could go back to his isolation. He could learn to endure it without the alcohol. Or perhaps he could buy home-made liquor in the village. He could bear it. Brittle laughter scraped at his throat. He would bear it until the day he cut his throat or walked into the lake or the teeth of the wolves. Until the day that loneliness and despair opened the door that had always been waiting for him.

And if he told her? Would anything change? Would she let him drown himself in the alcoholic oblivion that would only delay the end, not alter it?

There was only one reason to tell; he wanted her to know. He supposed that he should tell someone before he died. Confession was said to be good for the soul.

"I heard voices calling me," he began hesitantly. "I heard Christian. I heard your voice, all seaweed and silk and…" The words caught in his throat.

"Is that who you saw in the lake?" she asked gently. "Christian? Me?"

"No. I saw Raphael."

"Raphael?"

"My brother. My brother who drowned."

Chapter 25

Sidonie took a careful step backwards. She had two thousand years of practice at reading the secret clues to the mortal heart but she needed none of them to see the misery that enveloped him. Curious as she was, she knew she could exert no further pressure on him. All she could do was allow him the chance to make his choice whether or not to finish what he had begun.

He stayed at the door for a moment, staring into the library. At last, he stepped away and walked over to the fireplace. He did not look at her but crouched down by the hearth. As he poked at the fire, Sidonie moved quietly to sit on the ottoman by her chair.

She had never heard of Raphael. She had investigated Simon's life before she had set the plan in motion but had discovered only that his wife was dead, his three sons grown. She knew that his wife had been pregnant with a fourth child during their time together but she had assumed that there had been a miscarriage or a stillborn child.

After worrying one fire-eaten log into sparks and splinters, Matthew set down the poker. "I was five when Raphael was born. Peter, Gabriel, Matthew and Raphael…

I suppose I should be grateful that my father's biblical bent at least restricted itself to somewhat common names. I might have ended up Ephraim or Nehemiah instead of Matthew. I have been told I was a sickly child. I had one illness after another, until I was almost five, when I suppose that something in my body decided it was well enough to survive after all. So then I was healthy but rather badly spoilt. I was accustomed to being cared for and cosseted. I could no longer expect Gabriel and Peter not to hit me because I was sick...not that it had ever really stopped them before.

"I had no interest at all in having a younger brother usurp my place as the baby of the family. I resolved to hate him. But it was impossible to hate Raphael, not once he had stopped being an infant. He was persistent and fearless, curious and quick. He rarely cried and his smile could stop your heart. Peter and Gabriel, of course, believed that they were far too old to pay any attention to me and they paid even less to Raphael. Since they would not have us, I suppose that it was natural that we would play together. Much to my surprise, I discovered that I liked being his older brother. It was a new experience for me. For the first time in my life, I was the one who was admired and followed, rather than being the admirer, the follower. I would complain when he would toddle after me but secretly I enjoyed it."

He picked up the poker, stabbed once at the embers, and set it down again. Sidonie watched his profile, trying to read the words he was not saying in the angle of his mouth, the drawing together of his brows.

"But as I grew older, I became aware of the fear at the heart of that enjoyment. I knew that I would fall, just as Peter and Gabriel had fallen before me. I had worshipped them both in my time, though as each year passed it seemed we grew farther apart. Peter and I had nothing in common and Gabriel had his own struggles. I knew from experience that one day Raphael would climb higher than I could or run faster or do his sums more quickly and then I would no longer be Saint Matthew, the hero, the adored. I would just be one more fallen idol. I would just be another older brother, exasperating and infuriating and mortal. And a part of me still resented him for the injuries that older children claim: he was allowed to stay up later than I far sooner, he was allowed to cross the street alone, he was absolved of guilt because of his age. All the petty complaints Peter and Gabriel had made of me while I had been the youngest.

"So we went on, loving and hating each other as families do. Father became successful," his voice faltered for a moment but he did not look at her, "and we began to spend summers at a cottage north of the city. It was the most beautiful place I had ever seen. I would take my sketchbook and pastels or charcoal and wander the area, drawing everything that caught my eye. I had known for years that I loved to draw but it was at the cottage that I really began to test what I could do. I even sold one or two of my childish landscapes at a country fair held in the nearby town.

"Then came the summer that I was fifteen and Raphael was ten. It had not been as easy a time as previous years. Peter stayed in the city to work. Gabriel would have preferred to stay there as well, though not for love of work. I was more interested in my art or in creeping over to the next cottage to see if I could catch a glimpse of the neighbour's daughter in her bathing costume—in the name of that art, of course. I did not want to play with Raphael as we had before. The pastimes we had once shared seemed like childish diversions to me.

"One night, several weeks after we had arrived, our parents left us alone while they visited with neighbours. Gabriel disappeared in search of his own adventures. Raphael began to badger me to take the canoe out on the lake. The moon was full that night, the water as smooth as glass. I had no interest in going and I said so. He was relentless. He begged and cajoled and whined. When that did not work, he accused me of being a coward. Then he said if I did not go then I must be a queer-boy."

He stopped and took a breath. Sidonie saw him glance at her for the first time, then he looked at the fire again. "He didn't know about Gabriel, of course. He was much too young. I did. It didn't matter to me. I loved Gabriel. But I did not want to be like him. I was fairly certain that I was not…but everyone knew what kind of men artists were supposed to be. I went out on the lake with Raphael to prove I was not a coward. To prove I was a man. To remain his older brother for one more day.

"At first, I was glad that he had forced me to go. It was a beautiful night. Even the water seemed warm and welcoming. We paddled along the shore until we were out of sight of the cottage, in a small bay that held only one home whose owners were still in the city. On the far side of the bay was a great tree that hung out over the water. The children had tied a rope to one of the branches. They would scramble up the tilted trunk, stand on one branch, seize the rope and swing out over the water, competing to see who could let go at the highest point of the swing and leap the farthest, make the biggest splash.

"Raphael insisted that we go to the swing. In the moonlight, I could see the rope dangling above the water. I was preparing to paddle past when Raphael said: 'I bet I can jump from the canoe and grab that rope.' If I had been sensible, I would have kept paddling. But I was not. I said, without thinking: 'No, you can't.' There were no words Raphael loved better. Anything denied him was something he had to have. Now the world could be ending around us and Raphael would be trying to reach that rope. 'Yes, I can,' he said. 'I can and you can't.' I said that I had no interest in grabbing a rope but it was too late. If I did not do it, he would only call me a coward until I did.

"It terrifies me now, the things we risked without a thought back then. This was not the worst of them, or so I believed at the time. It was bad enough though. I knew that even as we manoeuvred the canoe beneath the rope. Raphael made the rules: the jumper had to stand on the edges of the canoe, leap out to grab the rope and then climb it into the tree. The other was responsible for controlling the canoe.

"As I jumped, I knew I would not make it. I fell into the water to the sounds of Raphael's laughter and then struggled back into the canoe. I settled into my place and Raphael climbed onto the gunnels. I kept the canoe as steady as I could while he readied himself for the attempt."

Sidonie saw his eyes close and his jaw clench. "The next thing I knew the water was closing over my head. It was no longer warm or welcoming. It was cold and black and I knew that I was going to die. I thrashed about in the darkness, not even sure which way led to the surface. Then I was in the air again, choking and spitting, my eyes tightly closed. When I opened them, the canoe was overturned before me. Raphael was gone.

"I dove for him again and again. Finally, I climbed out of the water and ran through the woods back to the cottage to find my parents. It took until dusk the next day to find Raphael's body. No one ever blamed me, except that first night when my mother in her maddened sorrow screamed all the things I knew: that it was my fault, that I should have known better, that I should have taken care of him.

"My mother died a year later. There was a long name for the disease that killed her but we all knew the real reason was grief. Peter and Gabriel left home. Simon and I fought about everything or nothing, it did not matter, because neither of us ever acknowledged what wrongs really lay between us. I discovered the anaesthetic of alcohol and drugs and waking in strange beds. Finally, Father gave me money to go to art school and survive as best I could. I suppose that he was glad to be rid of me, that he was relieved to no longer have to see the face of the son who had cost him his youngest child and his wife.

"As the years went by, we all grew older and found some measure of peace with ourselves and with each other. But we have never forgotten. Not Father, not I."

The phrase seemed like punctuation, like the coda of a sad movement of music. He did not cry, though his voice sounded raw and painful. He had not cried, she thought, since the moment they took his brother's body from the lake. Sidonie felt a strange sensation in her own throat, the unfamiliar ache of sorrow swallowed.

She knew that the central truth was still unspoken. He had rendered the event in vivid colours but left untouched the dark canvas at its heart. He was waiting for her to offer up the hollow and empty lies of consolation. She could feel the words, easy and seductive, like little betrayals.

"You killed him," she said softly. His head jerked as if she had struck him but he did not look at her.

"I knew...I knew that he would make it. He would reach the rope. I was tired and wet and angry at being manipulated into failing. I knew that he would succeed and in that moment everything would change forever. Just as he crouched to jump, I swung the canoe sideways. He fell back and hit the edge. It must have been enough to knock the wind from him and tip the canoe. I only meant for him to fall, to fail."

"But you killed him."

"Yes. I killed him. I murdered my little brother." In the silence, a log broke and cracked in the fireplace, the sound of falling timber, burning buildings.

"I absolve you," she said at last. He looked up then,

disbelief in his eyes and in the choked sound that was half-laugh, half-sob.

"You absolve me?"

"Who else could? Your family, who needed the lie of your innocence as much as you did? A thin-blooded priest of a god you profess not to acknowledge? I have been a murderess for two millennia." She leaned forward and reached out to put her hands on his shoulders. "With these murderous hands, with this murderous mouth," she pressed her lips against his forehead, "I absolve you."

She sat back slowly and opened her eyes. He was staring at her, face blank, as if all expression had been leached from it. Then something cracked behind his eyes and his mouth twisted. She had the brief glimpse of tears on his lashes before he hunched forward and buried his face against her lap.

It was her turn to stare, looking down in astonishment as his arms went around her waist and the first sobs shook him. Tentatively, she lifted her hand and rested it on his shoulder. She could feel the bone and muscle move, but to her dim surprise the pulse of his blood stirred nothing but a distant echo of hunger in her. Her palm slid across his back.

It seemed to her that they stayed that way for a long time, as he wept out the black water of twelve years of guilt and sorrow. She felt her mouth remember the soothing sounds of consolation, her hands rediscover the lost language of comfort. For the moment, the blood on them did not seem to matter.

At last, she felt his muscles tense, his head move beneath her hand as she stroked his hair. His arms dropped away. He sat back and put the heels of hands against his eyes. "I am sorry, I..." he began in a shaky voice. He took his hands away but did not look at her. "I think that I should go."

She nodded, aware of her own withdrawal into stiff-backed reserve that seemed too thin a shell to disguise how shaken she was. She watched him climb awkwardly to his feet and start for the door then remembered that she had not yet asked him the question. For a moment, she rebelled. It seemed a cruelty to both of them. It made a brutal mockery of everything that had just happened by revealing the truth—that he had no business seeking solace from his executioner and she had no business offering it to her victim. But she had no choice in the matter.

"Matthew." He turned back to look at her. "Will you give me your blood to—"

"Sidonie, please," he interrupted. "Not that. Not tonight."

"I have no choice. Will you give me your blood to drink, even though you die of it?"

"Sidonie…" She heard the pleading in his voice and knew with guilty triumph that it was not only himself he wanted to spare. If she pressed him now, when he was in her debt…

"Answer what is in your heart," she said at last. "Tonight changes nothing."

"No."

She sighed, troubled to discover that she was relieved rather than disappointed. "Perhaps you will join me for dinner tomorrow night."

"Yes," he said. "I would like that."

She watched him disappear into the hall. After a moment, she put her fingers against her mouth. They tasted of tears, salt and sweet at once. It was so much like blood and yet so different. She had not wept in two thousand years but her body retained some shadow-memory of the process. There was a strange ache in her throat and behind her eyes. She closed them and waited for the great, yearning emptiness that had opened beneath her heart to seal itself again.

Chapter 26

The snow stayed. The lake froze. Matthew walked down to the dock and stood there for a long time, looking at the solid expanse of ice. Images stirred in the back of his mind: a strange blue glow, a contorted face pressed against the ice. He shivered but it was reflex only. He looked beyond the lake, squinting as he studied the patterns of black and white created by the snow-covered trees. They would make an interesting starting point for his next painting, he decided. He wondered what the view would be like from the ballroom.

He turned and tramped back up the path. Helen's footsteps and his own had worn a narrow passage through the heavy snow. He assumed Sidonie used it as well during her nightly hunts, though more than once he had seen lonely footprints in the clean snow, leading off in other directions from the house.

As he walked across the terrace, he glanced upwards. Icicles hung from the eaves like diamond daggers. Snow covered the roof and clung to the rough stone of the walls. The walls might keep the snow out but they did nothing about the cold, it seemed. Only Sidonie's sitting room and the kitchen seemed to hold any heat. The ballroom with its walls of windows was so chilly he often wore his coat while he worked. He contemplated moving his easel and paints to some warmer locale but could not bring himself to give up the light...and his one sanctuary.

He settled for lighting lamps even in the daytime, along with the fireplace, and accepting the ancient braziers that Sidonie offered which allowed him to create a space where his fingers did not turn completely clumsy with cold.

The cold made the unused recesses of the house even less inviting. He had not searched any of the rooms since his initial attempts. He knew that he should. He still had not found the place where Sidonie slept, though he had begun to suspect that it must be in a chamber with more than one hidden entrance. The weather made a convenient excuse, he acknowledged. It relieved him of the necessity of facing a choice he did not want to have to make. Discovering her secret would not in itself give him any power over her. He could only force her to free him if he were willing to use that secret to destroy her.

He did not know if he could hammer a stake into her heart. He did not want to find out for certain that he could not.

Back inside the house, he went to the kitchen to make a pot of tea, warmth for both stomach and hands while he worked. Waiting for the water to boil, he made a cursory examination of the pantry. Sidonie had said nothing, had simply taken to leaving it unlocked again. He customarily drank one glass of wine with dinner. Since the night, two weeks earlier, that he had told her of Raphael's death, he rarely drank alone.

There seemed to be very little left on the shelves, he noticed with a frown. With persistent questioning, he had obtained the admission that there was a town five days'

journey to the north-east and it was from there that
Sidonie obtained food Joseph and her herb garden could
not supply. He knew that she had paid Joseph to journey
there once since his arrival. Had she made arrangements
for him to do so again? Perhaps she has not bothered, a
voice whispered in his mind. Perhaps she does not plan to
require mortal food much longer.

The kettle's whistle drew him away from the empty
shelves and dangerous thoughts. He kept the speculations
at bay with tea and concentration, focusing only on the
preliminary sketches for the winter scene he had decided
to attempt.

Sidonie appeared soon after dusk fell, standing in the
open door of the ballroom. Her greeting had become the
signal for him to leave his paints, if he desired, and return
to his room. Satisfied with his progress but not unhappy to
let it wait another day, he headed up the stairs.

In his chamber, he lit the fire to take away the worst of
the day's chill, washed the paint from his hands and
changed. He had plundered the wardrobes of the empty
rooms, collecting anything that caught his fancy. It was as
much out of practicality as vanity, he admitted, considering his reflection in the new mirror. The task of keeping
out the cold necessitated the wearing of not only one of
his own shirts, but a vest twenty years out of fashion and a
jacket that the dandies of his father's youth might have
envied. If there were frays and moth holes in a few of the
older pieces, well, they still served their purpose and there
was no one to whom it mattered.

Sidonie was stoking the Hall's great hearth when he
ventured back downstairs. She rose, brushing the ash from
her hands. Her dress was almost the same colour, a smoky
grey velvet that had an odd iridescence in the flickering
light. A necklace of silver and opals looked as if it had been
poured over her collar-bones, dripping in pearly circles

between her breasts.

"That is a beautiful piece," he commented, wondering why it seemed familiar. She had not worn it before, indeed, he had never seen her wear the same piece of jewellery twice.

"Thank you. It is a Betrano. It is not precisely suited to my colouring, but at the time I recall that the fashions ran to powdered wigs and painted skin." Matthew looked at the necklace again and knew why he had recognized it. The name she so casually dismissed was one of the most famous in art. He had been sculptor, goldsmith and designer to the wealthiest royal courts in the world two centuries earlier. The "arbiter of elegance" they had called him. He had studied the artist's working sketches at art school. The metal and gemstones about Sidonie's throat would be worth a king's ransom.

"Betrano...did you know him?" She shrugged and the opals ran with blue and red fire in the lamplight.

"I met him once. A singularly unpleasant little man."

"He was a genius," Matthew protested and she smiled.

"That is true. But he was still an unpleasant little man. Not all geniuses are as pleasant as you."

"I am not a genius."

"Aren't you? Well, as you never let me see your paintings to prove otherwise, you shall have to forgive me if I think the best of you."

"If I was a genius, would you let me go?" He saw her smile fade as she glanced away.

"No," she said after a moment. Matthew felt a bitter pleasure, followed by a twinge of guilt at having distressed her. Even if her answer had been yes, it would have made no difference. He was not a genius.

"Did Betrano design the necklace for you?" he asked into the silence. She nodded. "Did he know..."

"What I am? It is possible that he knew that I was *some-*

thing. Something not quite human. Perhaps that is why I found him so unpleasant. This necklace has been a curse, in its fashion. I had to leave the country soon after it was made."

"Why?"

"There was some unrest. The count who had commissioned it for me had died..." He caught the glance she slanted at him. "...Yes, I killed him. Betrano was suspicious. It has been hard to retain possession of it all these years. I try not to become attached to things. It is too likely that I will lose them."

"You have enough of them. Certainly enough antiquities. And jewellery."

"Most of that has been obtained in the last century, since I came to live here. Some of it Christian bought for me."

"That necklace of thorns?" Matthew guessed and she nodded.

"Oh yes. He liked to see me wear that one."

"Do you mean that he made you wear it? That is hard to believe. I cannot imagine anyone who could make you do what was against your will."

"Can't you?" she asked, then put her hand to the necklace, as if half-expecting to feel another one beneath her fingers. "I owed Christian for taking me in, for the promise of this place as my sanctuary. If the price was to wear thorns of gold and to be his evil angel...well, perhaps both of those things were only appropriate."

"You still wear the necklace," he said and she smiled sadly.

"Perhaps it is still appropriate." Matthew was silent, remembering the paintings that lined the ballroom, their blank backs facing outward.

"Why do you stay here, all alone?" he asked, to distract himself from those images. "Why not live in the city?

With your wealth, you could live like..." He paused, thinking of Allegra.

"Like a queen?" she finished for him. "Hardly. But I do leave here, once in a while. The last time was ten years ago, though not in your city. I went farther south that time. I rented a townhouse in the best part of town. I bought the gowns you have seen me wear and jewels to match. I went to the opera and the theatre. I hosted a salon for poets and artists. I took lovers and discarded them as quickly as I changed dresses. When the season was over I left. Four men and two women were dead. Should I do that again? Should I come to the city and appear in the cafés and bars you have told me of? Would I do well, do you think? Would your friends come to my parties? Would they come to my bed?"

Matthew wanted to look away from her, to ignore the soft, seductive drawl of her voice. He imagined her suddenly in one of Allegra's black silk dresses, the curves of her arms and back bare, the necklace of thorns around her throat. He imagined Paul dancing with her, Jack making her laugh. They would go to her parties, no doubt about it. They would go to her bed. He imagined Andre's face, bloodless but ecstatic in death. "Why do you do this?" he demanded angrily.

"Do what?"

"Make me remember that you are a monster." He flung the words at her. In the firelight, he thought he saw her face pale. She blinked.

"You are right. It would suit my purposes better if you forgot that," she said. "Shall I make you?"

"No." He closed his eyes for a moment, so that he could think. The imaginary Sidonie reappeared behind his lids and he opened them again. "I know you can do that. I don't know why you haven't done it, but I thank you for that. But please...promise me that, whatever happens, you will not hurt my family or my friends."

The muscles in her narrow jaw seemed to clench and then loosen. "I should not…but I promise. I am sorry that I upset you. It is only that," she paused and he saw the edges of a reluctant smile on her lips, "you provoke me."

Then let me go, he almost said then realized that the words might well fall under the category of provocation. He had the promise that he wanted, if he could trust her to keep it. For that, he owed her something. "I am sorry for that then," he said and saw in her eyes that she recognized the temptation he had resisted.

"There. Apologies have been given and accepted. Do you suppose that we can make it through your dinner without any further provocation?"

"I will do my best if you will."

"Agreed."

The peace lasted through dinner, though Matthew had to restrain himself from inquiring about the food supplies, for fear of what she might hear in his voice. When she appeared at the door of the ballroom, coat flung over her dress, and invited him to walk with her on the frozen lake, he accepted.

The night air was chilly but, without wind, held no bite. The moon hung bright and silver in the cloudless sky, looking like one of the gems in her necklace. The snow-covered lake seemed to reflect it back, another circle of silver-white. As Matthew stepped from the dock, he felt a brief flutter of distant panic, the primal fear that the ice would open beneath his feet and the lake swallow him. He overrode it and fell into step with Sidonie.

They walked in silence for a time. His mind turned to the one question he had never asked her. It seemed as suitable a time as any to broach it. "How did you become a vampire?" Her silence made him think for a moment that he had made a mistake, that he had provoked her again.

"To create a vampire is a deliberate act," she said slowly. "Merely being bitten does not suffice. There must be a sharing of blood. Whether we are creatures of God or the Devil, we were designed so that we could not simply overrun the world with our appetites but must choose those who would join our numbers. Certainly we must give more thought to our reproduction than mortals do. We make others like ourselves out of love and the desire for companionship."

She paused and glanced at him. "That is the theory, of course. In reality, my kind reproduces from love and from hate, from loneliness and from lust for power. Never from carelessness, however. No matter the reason, it is always a deliberate act.

"I was seventeen when I was changed. I was nothing important in my world, simply the daughter of a moderately successful merchant, the fourth of six children. I had no wealth, no beauty, no great charm. I was somewhat clever, perhaps too much so for a woman of my time, but that is all. If things had been different, I would have lived out my life as everyone else did: loved by some, ignored by others, finding my life's joys or sorrows in my small portion of the world.

"All these facts did not matter to me, of course. It was the only life I had, the only life I could imagine, and I loved it. I was very happy in my portion of the world, no matter how small it was. I had been wed two months earlier to the son of one of my father's business associates. I had known him since childhood and we had always known we were to marry one day. We had chased each other through the streets and played the adolescent games of flirtation and retreat. It was he who used to call me 'Moon Face,' he whom I struggled to impress with my scant scholarly learning. If we were more like brother and sister when we first wed, well, that changed soon enough."

Matthew noticed that she was staring down at the snow as she walked, as if her night-vision were not enough to allow her to find her way with ease. "One day, I went into the hills above the town to gather herbs. My husband had travelled to a nearby town with his father and I was planning a special meal for his return. It was a mistake for me to go alone but I was not yet accustomed to living in the house of my husband's family, not all of whom were as kind to me as he was, and I craved a few hours of solitude.

"I had been in those hills many times with my mother and sisters. I thought that I knew them. But I did not. I took a wrong turn and soon every hill, every scrub of brush looked the same. Night fell and I became afraid, of everything from thieves to the ghosts that were said to roam the hills. Either of those things might have been preferable to what I found. Or what found me.

"As the moon rose, I heard hoof beats on the hard ground. I saw a man riding towards me. He did not look like a thief. He looked like a god. I thought that he would save me. I crept from my hiding place behind the rocks and flung myself on his mercy."

A misstep on the rough snow threw her briefly off-balance. Matthew moved without thinking, holding out his arm to her as if it was a fine afternoon on the city board-walk and he any polite gentleman, she any well-bred young woman. She looked at him, her face unreadable, for a long moment, as if waiting for him to retract the gesture. When he did not move, she slipped her bare hand into the crook of his arm. They walked on and she resumed her tale. "Any other time, he might have simply drained my blood and left my body for the vultures. But he was angry. He believed he had been cheated by a merchant in town. When I asked him to take me home to the house of my husband, he saw his chance for revenge. That is what he told me but I know that it was only an excuse. He preyed upon me because he is a predator—but he was cruel and subtle in it because that is all that gives him pleasure.

"He took me up on his horse with great courtliness. Honey was not as sweet as his words. I thought that angels could not have faces as kind and beautiful as his. I barely even noticed that the path he took did not lead back to town. When I did, it was far too late for any to hear my screams.

"There were ruins in the hills. Everyone avoided them as they were rumoured to be haunted. He carried me to the long-looted tombs in the valley behind them. There, amid the scattered bones, he took me for the first time.

"He kept me alive for three nights, draining enough blood that I was too weak to crawl from the tomb while he slept but not enough that I would die. At first he gave me pleasure as well as pain, but, in the end, he found pleasure too bland a dish. While he slept, I prayed to my gods to let me die. But I did not have the courage—or the honesty— to simply strike my head against the rocks until I sustained some fatal wound. Despite it all, you see, I did not really want to die. I wanted to escape from the pain and from him but I did not want to die. At last, on the fourth night, he cut his wrist and made me swallow his blood. Then he put his mouth against my throat for the last time."

Matthew saw her hand creep up as if to touch her neck. Her fingers settled on the cold silver necklace instead. "He thought that I would go home, as most new vampires blindly do. There, I would feed on my family and the other townspeople until some blunder destroyed me. He thought that it was a fitting revenge, a wicked jest. Just another bit of mischief to mark his passage through the world. So he left me there in the tomb and went on his way.

"When I awoke later that night, it was to terrible pain racking my body. I twisted in the darkness, scattering the

broken bones of the dead in my anguish, screaming sound-
lessly with my raw, bleeding throat. I thought that I was
dying—I did not know that I was already dead. Finally I
managed to crawl out into the moonlight. My murderer,
my creator, believed that he had taken all the blood from
my body. He did not know that there was still one reser-
voir left inside me. It was not to nourish me but another."

Matthew caught his breath and felt her fingers tighten
on his arm. She kept her gaze trained on the snow. "Yes, I
was carrying a child. I did not even know it until my undead
body finally forced out the bloody lump of life it could not
endure. I looked at it in the moonlight and knew what it
was. And knew the most terrible hunger I had ever felt.

"In that moment, I went mad. I still do not know much
of what I did that night, or the nights that followed. I am
grateful for that. I forgot my name, my home, everything I
had ever known. For the next decades, the ruins truly were
haunted. I lived on rats and lizards and stolen sheep and
the few mortals foolish enough to venture into my world.

"In time, my valley held no life with blood enough to
support me. I moved on to find one that could. Eventually,
in one of the caves in which I sought shelter, I discovered a
hermit, a holy man who worshipped the dead son of the
new god. He gave me back my sanity—though if he had
known what I would do with it perhaps he would have
regretted it."

There was a long silence. Matthew waited for the tale
to resume, but she said nothing. "Did you ever meet him
again? The vampire who created you?" he asked at last.

"Oh yes. We lived together for many years, centuries
ago."

"Didn't you hate him?"

"Of course. But the ties of blood are stronger than hate.
They are stronger than love. It does not matter which I
feel for him. I am bound to him as he is bound to me."

"I am sorry. I did not mean to ask anything that would distress you."

"You have nothing for which to apologize. It does not distress me. It all happened a very, very long time ago." Her voice was calm but Matthew saw the slight tilt of her head as she looked away from him. He was accustomed to honesty from her, or evasions that seemed to mean one thing to him and another to her. He did not think he had ever heard her lie before.

He stopped, struggling to ignore the sudden surge of sympathy that swept him. "I'm afraid I am not as immune to the cold as you are," he said awkwardly, clutching at an excuse to put some distance between them. She nodded.

"We'll go back then."

Halfway to the shore, he heard her say his name and knew the words that would follow.

"No," he said without looking at her. "No."

Chapter 27

As the days and nights passed, it seemed to Matthew that the only calendar of his life was the backs of the canvases lined up in the ballroom. The pantry was full again and Sidonie had even agreed to order some of the painting supplies of which he was running low. A tentative hope began to bloom somewhere in his heart, the belief that he might live to see the spring.

Even the house no longer seemed as cold. He painted during the afternoon, when the sun would warm the ballroom. At night, he read in the library or talked with Sidonie in her sitting room.

There were hours in which he did not think of dying. Some of those were even spent in Sidonie's presence. He no longer felt the shock of her inhumanity each time he saw her. It had become no more than a tremor, which would fade for long periods, only to flare up again when the light would emphasize the alien bones of her face or she would move with the fluid grace no mortal woman could duplicate.

Despite those moments, he found that there were times when he enjoyed her company. At ease, she could be

persuaded to tell him some of the tales she had accumulated in the long span of her life. None of them were as
shocking and sorrowful as that of her transformation. He
suspected that she edited them somewhat, though she did
not spare him the truth of her crimes. She proved an
accomplished storyteller, her tales full of wit and wry
humour, often informed by a wisdom hard won over two
thousand years. He found himself breaking his private resolution not to reveal any more of his own life more times
than he held to it.

It was easy to forget the stakes, it seemed, when they
sat before the warmth of the fire or walked in the moonlight across the frozen lake. Easy to forget until that
moment when she would say his name and he knew the
question that was to come. He rarely let her ask it now,
unless she caught him off guard. She seemed to accept his
repeated refusals without emotion, though once or twice
he thought he had caught a flash of pain in her eyes. But it
might only have been a trick of the firelight.

One day, he rose earlier than usual and went down to
the ballroom. He was restless, suspended between paintings and beginning to suspect that the fire of creativity
that had burned in him since his arrival was about to sput-
ter and die. It was not a prospect that cheered him, not
only because he knew that he was doing the best work of
his life, but because he did not know how he would survive
if he could not divert himself with the act of painting. You
could take up drinking again, Matthew told himself, idly
thumbing through his sketchbook. But perhaps not, considering what happened last time.

Abandoning the sketches, he walked to the window and
contemplated the now-familiar lines of the mountains. A
patch of darkness on the ice caught his attention and he
lifted a hand to shade his eyes, squinting at the figure
there. It sharpened into a man, well bundled in furs. It was

Joseph. He had not seen the man since his trip to the village, what seemed like a lifetime ago. He knew Joseph came to the house—they ate the rabbits and fish Sidonie bought from him—but he generally arrived early in the morning, before Matthew was awake.

Impulsively, he headed for the door, abandoning his work with guilty relief. Tugging on coat, gloves and scarf, he left the house, breaking a new trail down to the dock.

When he reached Joseph, the man looked up at him. He held a wooden rod, bearing a thin line, suspended over a hole in the ice. His moustache and beard were edged in frost but the fur-lined, hooded coat he wore looked warm. He stared at Matthew for a moment, then slipped one hand into his pocket. It re-emerged clutching a skin bag. Joseph tipped it to his lips, swallowed and then held it out.

Matthew took a step forward and accepted the offering. The liquid inside was warm and sharp, with an aftertaste that made his eyes water. The heat of it seemed to settle in his chest and radiate through his bones. He handed the bag back. "Thanks." Joseph nodded then rose, tipping over the wooden crate on which he sat so that it would accommodate two, just barely. He sat down again without speaking.

Matthew settled onto the narrow edge of the crate. The silence lingered for a moment. "I haven't seen you in a while," he said at last. "How are you?"

Joseph shrugged. "Been worse."

"Thank you for the food. It must be hard, catching enough for yourself and for me."

The shrug came again. "She pays. A good winter, this one. Lots of game, lots of fish." For the first time Matthew thought about what it would be like in the village in winter. The cabins did not seem well insulated, though they might be warmer than the great stone heap of the house. If the nearest town was five days away, along trails that might be uncertain at best, there would be very little margin for error in calculating the requirements of the winter.

"What do you do during a bad winter?"

"Hunt farther. Eat less." Matthew thought he caught the shadow of a smile on the man's white-rimmed lips. "No one starves, not here. Other places, yes. Not here."

"Why not?"

"She," his head jerked in the direction of the house, "don't let it happen." Matthew looked at him. Joseph was contemplating the water lapping at the hole in the ice.

"Do you mean that Sidonie helps you?"

"If bad times come, she don't let us starve. She helps with the hunt. She gives money for food in town." It was only logical, Matthew thought. She relied on the village's discretion and assistance. It would only be sensible to seal their loyalty by aiding them. What else did she buy that way? he wondered.

"Does she," he began delicately, "feed in the village?" Joseph's line jerked. The man fought it for a moment then pulled the rod back sharply. A silver-sided fish flipped thrashing onto the ice. Joseph leaned down, tapped it once on the head with the end of the pole and it lay still.

"Dinner tonight, if you want it," he said and began to reattach the lure, a home-made device cobbled from a twisted fork and unidentifiable metal objects polished to a bright shine. Matthew sighed. He was not likely to get an answer to his question but perhaps that was answer enough. The line slid back into the water. In the silence, he thought that he could hear the distant pines stirring in the faint breeze. "Sometimes," Joseph said, so unexpectedly Matthew started in surprise. "Sometimes, if an old one is a long, hard time dying, their kin will take them up to the house. Others go, sometimes. Young men. Old men. Women."

"What happens to them?"

"Those that come back don't say."

"And your people...you...allow this?" Matthew asked, horrified at the image of an endless procession of victims making their way up the path to the house. He had not seen any, it was true, but perhaps they had been told to stay away.

"Can't stop them. Their choice."

"And that absolves you? That makes it right?"

"Their choice," Joseph repeated. "She don't ask. She never has. Some people...some people been waiting for the wolves all their lives. Reckon it's an easier way to go than that."

"That relieves me greatly. She's going to kill me. You know that." Joseph gave another maddening, eloquent shrug. "I don't suppose you would help me escape." He shook his head. Matthew looked at the grey, brooding lines of the house, his hands clenched in his pockets. "When do you go to town to pick up my paints?"

"Next week, I reckon," Joseph said.

"If you will not take me, would you at least take a letter for my father?" Joseph shook his head again. "Just so that he will know that I am still alive?" He caught the disapproving twitch of the man's moustache. Joseph had carried the three letters he had written at Sidonie's behest, each as blandly reassuring as the first. He had even brought one or two replies. "I do not suppose that it would do any good to offer you money or safety. I suppose that would insult us both. But you should know that when she kills me, you will be responsible. You will be an accessory to my murder. Can you live with that?" Matthew asked, then laughed, bitterly aware of how pointless both his plea and outrage were. "Of course you can. You must have done so a hundred times." Joseph jiggled the rod and said nothing. "Well?"

"Had to be said," he said at last. "But once is all I'll

hear it, understand? I'm sorry. I like you. But her business is her business. That's the deal. That's always been the deal."

"You made a deal with a monster."

"Don't know about monsters. You ain't dead yet, are you?" Matthew looked at him sharply, startled by the words. There was an implication behind them and behind the bland expression on Joseph's face.

"Do you mean that no one has ever lasted this long before?" he asked carefully.

"Don't know about that. She don't have guests much. Don't know where they go, when they go. But no one ever stayed long as you."

"Did you ever take anyone back to the train? To the town?"

"No," Joseph admitted slowly. "But she can. If she wants to." He passed the wineskin and Matthew took another drink, longer this time. "Be careful, boy. Don't want her saying I turned you back into a drunk."

"Back into...?" Matthew began in bewilderment. "Damn. Helen, I suppose."

"She talks. She's young."

"You can hardly blame me, can you?" Joseph gave a snort and shook his head.

"No." The fishing line shook and after a moment another fish joined the first. "Want to try?" Matthew shrugged then smiled when he realized how much like Joseph the gesture had been. He took the rod and waited while the other man set the lure. It made a soft splash as it entered the water. "Just wiggle it about a bit."

They sat in silence for a while. Matthew kept the rod moving, shifting his feet. His toes had begun to grow numb. "How are Mother Norit and the others?" he asked.

"Well enough. Come to town and find out."

"I don't think so. Everyone knows."

"Nobody cares," Joseph corrected, as Matthew felt the rod jerk in his hands. The next moments were occupied with the task of retrieving the fish from the water. Matthew decided not to try to duplicate Joseph's killing technique and handed the rod back. "Be the midwinter festival in two weeks. Good party. Come if you want."

"If I am still alive, you mean."

"If you want," Joseph repeated. Matthew stood up, stomping on the ice to restore the feeling to his feet. "Take your fish." Joseph speared the creature through the gills with a stick and held it out. "Ever fixed one?" Matthew shook his head. Joseph's teeth flashed for a moment. "She knows how."

"I'll let her do it then. Thank you."

He expected the shrug this time but not the serious gaze that met his. "Wolf isn't a monster. It's just a wolf. It can't help it. That's just its nature."

"That might be true. But does knowing that give any consolation to the deer?"

"Don't know," Joseph admitted. "Maybe."

Matthew shook his head and, fish held gingerly on its stick, walked back to the house. When he reached the ball-room and looked out the window, Joseph was still there. For a moment, he almost waved then saw that the man's back was to him. He dropped his hand.

Chapter 28

❧

"Is that what he really looked like?" Matthew asked, lifting the lamp to let the light fall full on the portrait of Christian. The white paint in the mad eyes gleamed.

"Yes," Sidonie said after a moment. He glanced sideways and saw that she was staring at the painting, her expression remote and unreadable. At last, she blinked and turned away, her gaze moving across the room. "How strange. I walk through this room every night and still have forgotten how empty it looks."

"You could have kept the Giardello," Matthew said as he looked around the shadowy gallery. The odd positions of the few paintings that remained made the empty spaces around them more apparent. The movement of the lamplight across the landscape on the far side of the room caught his eye and he took a step towards it.

"You could hang your paintings, if you wished," she said.

He stopped, thinking of the canvases propped against the wall beyond the ballroom door. Was this what his dreams of artistic renown had come to? An exhibition attended only by passing beasts? And by his murderess.

"I do not think so," he said and felt his amusement fade. "Of course, once I am dead, you can do whatever you choose." He took a certain petty pleasure in his bluntness but kept his eyes on the landscape. It was as unexceptional as he remembered, a naïve evocation of sunlit meadows, wrought in gentle colours.

Sidonie was beside him again, seeming to consider the painting with as much concentration as he. "It is a shame that disposing of anything valuable or significant means that all you have left are things like this," he said, after an awkward silence.

"It is not very good," she said, her voice oddly guilty, as if confessing to some crime of taste. "Is it accurate?"

"Accurate?"

"Is that what a meadow in sunlight would look like?"

"In simple terms, I suppose. The colours are too muted, I think, and clumsily used. See the contrast between the leaves of that tree and this one." He gestured to the centre of the canvas. "The shadings on real trees would be much more subtle. Of course, you cannot see the tones truly in lamplight anyway. In natural light, you would be able to see the colours as they were intended. Light is a quality as much as pigment. The light here in the North is grey at its heart. I have heard that in the far South, in the desert, the light is golden. Not just what it touches, or the sky, but the light itself. I have always wanted to see if the tales are true." He stopped, remembering suddenly that if she had her way, he would never have the chance.

"I do not remember it," she said softly. "For two thousand years, *this* has been my natural light."

It was true, Matthew thought, in surprise. She could see in the dark far better than a mortal, but even she could not change the essential nature of light. All the colours that revealed themselves only under the sun, all the pale pearly tones of dawn and the ruby splendour of sunset, everything that he took for granted—she had lost them forever. She had kept the painted landscape for the same reason she struggled with her herb garden; because no matter how poor a substitute it was, it was all she had left of the day.

The magnitude of her loss, the price that she had paid for eternity, stunned him. Merely to imagine losing the light, to be imprisoned in a chiaroscuro world with so much of its life drained away, was like a blow that bruised his heart.

Their eyes met and she flinched away suddenly, as if struck. "If you dislike the painting so much," she said, "you should create me another one. Of course, it will have to be a winterscape. Unless you would care to imagine the way the sunlight will fall on the flowers on your grave."

She left him standing there, staring after her, stunned by the crude viciousness of the words, wondering what he had done to provoke them. Then he realized what she might have read in his eyes and understood. He knew that Sidonie must be accustomed to being feared and desired. He did not suppose that she had often been pitied.

He took a step towards the doorway and then stopped, knowing that there was nothing he could say, certainly nothing that he should wish to say. If he had hurt her, it should not trouble him.

He heard the distant howl of the wolves and went to the window, grateful for the distraction. It was not the first time their eerie song had echoed through the valley. Despite the memories it stirred of the terrifying moonlit hunt through the woods, he had become almost accustomed to hearing the strange symphony as he worked. Once or twice he thought he had seen their tracks in the snow on the terrace outside the ballroom.

Yet now it seemed that the song had a different sound.

There was an urgency and anger in it that he had never heard before. Curious, he cupped his hands around his eyes to peer out into the darkness.

The moon was a bright crescent above the far mountains. By its light, he thought he saw something moving on the far shore. He blinked and blurred motion formed itself into the grey shapes of wolves running across the snow towards the lake. He heard another chorus of howls, this one sounding breathless and weary. The wolves moved in several groups, clustered together. At first, he thought that they were being pursued by the dark forms dimly visible behind them, then he realized what he saw.

They could not be wolves, he thought. They must be dogs, though closer kin to their wild brethren than those in the city. Irrational hope swept through him. Was it possible that his family had not been deceived by the forced reassurances in his letters? Could they have notified whatever authorities existed in this wilderness?

He was at the door before he paused to consider what the arrival of his chance for escape might mean. He could hardly accuse Sidonie of being a vampire. They would think he was mad. If they did not, what would that mean for Sidonie? Would they kill her?

It would not come to that. He would say merely that he wanted to leave and they would take him. Sidonie would not dare to try to stop him. His flight would leave his father vulnerable...but surely disgrace was better than the loss of another son. His mind slid away from the thought. He would deal with that problem when it arose.

The howling was louder now, audible even in the hall. They must have reached the island. Sidonie emerged from the door of the darkened library. Her face was expressionless but he could see tension in the set of her shoulders. "Come into the library," she said as he stepped towards the foyer.

"But…"

"Now." The word was as sharp as the crack of a whip. His feet moved him automatically towards her, without his conscious ordering. He was at the door before he knew it. As she reached to take his hand and draw him into the darkness, he stared at her with dawning horror. She had *compelled* him. She had that power. She had possessed it all along. Fear shaded into bewilderment. She had more weapons against him than he had ever imagined…and she had used none of them.

The call of the wolves rang in his ears as she pulled him towards the window. Before they reached it, she paused, then eased forward, carefully positioning herself where she could see the terrace yet remain concealed from those out-side. Over her shoulder, Matthew saw the animals sliding to a halt in the snow. A second pack appeared. Though seemingly exhausted, they did not collapse onto the ground but paced and twisted in their bonds. A desolate howl echoed off the eaves. They did not look like any dogs he had ever seen, he acknowledged. They looked like wolves.

A figure moved into view, cloaked but bareheaded. The moonlight touched a wind-blown banner of silver hair. Sidonie drew a harsh breath. Her fingers tightened on his arm, so hard that he winced. She turned and looked at him. "Stay here."

"Who—" he began. She shook her head.

"You do not know what is at stake here. Stay here, out of sight. No matter what."

She did not wait for his assent but slipped past him towards the door. He turned back to look out the window. He could see figures moving among the animals, releasing them from their traces. Freed, they bounded into the darkness. Wolfsong filled the night.

Someone knocked on the great front door.

Matthew moved towards the doorway of the library, careful to stay in the shadow. Sidonie vanished for a moment then reappeared, backing away from the foyer. He heard voices and the snarls of the wolves.

Someone stepped into his range of vision. Shimmering hair flowed over the black fur collar of a long coat. The profile was etched in the fire's glow. The arch of the cheekbones and the sharp, narrow jaw were achingly familiar.

"Hello Sidonie," a male voice said softly. She did not move. Matthew saw that her fingers were knotted together, as if she feared what they might do if let loose. "Is that any way to greet your old friend?" When she did not reply, the vampire held out his hand. They stood like that for a long moment, as if posed for a staged tableau in a mysterious drama. Then Sidonie sighed and stepped forward. Her hand slipped into his and he drew her into his arms.

Matthew saw white fingers tangle in the dark silk of her hair. Their kiss seemed sensual and greedy, a ravenous feeding. When it ended, she put her head against the vampire's shoulder. His hands slid along her back. Matthew felt a strange tightness in his chest and was suddenly aware he had been holding his breath. He let it out in a careful sigh. The tightness did not go with it.

At last, Sidonie lifted her head and started to step back. The other vampire held her still, his arm around her waist. "That is better. Now I might believe that you are happy to see me."

"What are you doing here, Tal?"

"We were travelling across the country and thought that we would come and visit you in your northern exile. It has been so long since we have been together, after all." Matthew saw her glance beyond Tal's shoulder to the entrance hall.

"How did you get here?"

"Ysabel happened on a mortal who knows this country and provided the sleds. We provided the wolves. They make somewhat reluctant servants, I admit, but are certainly much more interesting than dogs." He lifted one hand and drew his finger along the arch of her brow. "If you frown, my dear, I will think that you do not want us here."

"You are my blood," she said, so quietly Matthew almost did not catch the words. She stepped away and this time Tal let her go. "Come in." Matthew saw figures pass the doorway. In the quick glimpses he dared, he could see that several looked human while three others bore the unmistakable aura of vampirism. "I was not expecting guests," Sidonie said. "You are welcome to stay, of course, but I fear you might find it rather boring."

"Nonsense," a feminine voice replied, husky and edged with an unidentifiable accent. "Tal has been dragging us all across this continent. A rest will suit me nicely."

They moved into the Hall and the conversation shifted to practical matters: where would they sleep? could their mortals be accommodated? It was decided that the rooms on the second floor above the dining room would be acceptable. Matthew thought about sharing the house with more vampires and felt an icy touch of fear. He shifted uneasily, uncertain whether to move or not. Surely Sidonie could not expect that he could remain hidden from them for the length of their stay, however long that might be.

As the vampires and their servants vanished up the stairs, Sidonie appeared at the door. When he went to her, he could see the concern in her eyes. "I have no choice but to let them see you," she said quickly. "When I do, stay for a few moments, then go to the ballroom. It might be best if you did not go to sleep until dawn."

"Are they dangerous?"

"*We* are dangerous," she corrected. "But there are rules. You are mine. Remember that."

Voices from the hall drew her gaze away. "Wait here," she said and hurried back into the hall. With a stab of bitter humour, Matthew remembered his wild hopes of rescue and escape. Instead of salvation, he found himself in greater danger than ever. He did not want to have anything to do with creatures even Sidonie did not seem to trust. Though there had seemed to be nothing of distrust in her welcome of Tal, he thought, remembering the way she had yielded her mouth to his.

He took a deep breath, straightened his jacket and walked towards the doorway. He was tired of skulking in the darkness. Whatever trial Sidonie envisaged, he might as well get it over and done. At the edge of the doorway he paused and looked around. Two men were carrying a chest up the stairs to his right. Tal had shrugged off his coat and settled himself into one of the chairs by the fire. A woman, wanly beautiful and very young, stood behind him, brushing the snow from his silver hair. He was looking at the centre of the room, where Sidonie stood with three others. Two were vampires, Matthew knew, though the man must be much younger than Sidonie and Tal for his face was far more human. He was very dark, his skin the colour of oak, his hair as black as Sidonie's. As he spoke to Sidonie, his hand absently caressed the back of the mortal woman who stood beside him, her face bent. The female vampire was as pale as the male was dark. Against her white skin and hair, her mouth was very red, as were the pupils of her large eyes.

There was a movement in the obscuring shadows at the end of the Hall. A woman turned from the bank of windows and stepped into the firelight. In a moment of wild fancy, Matthew thought that she was covered in blood, then he realized that her clothing and her hair were the same shade of crimson. Her eyes met his. She stopped and then a slow smile curved on her lush, ruby lips. "I thought that you said that we would be bored here, Sidonie."

Matthew saw Sidonie start then turn to follow the woman's gaze. Her face went still and for a moment he regretted that he had disobeyed her. He was distantly aware of Tal rising from his chair. "And I thought you said that you were not expecting visitors."

"I did. I did not say I did not have any already. Have you been thinking that I spend all my time out here alone?" Her voice had taken on a faint, mocking edge. She moved across the room towards him. "No wonder you persuaded the others to come, Tal. You have made them feel sorry for me." Matthew met her eyes and saw that some of the anger in them had faded. "You may go on about your business."

This time he decided it would be prudent to follow her instructions. The distance to the door of the gallery at the other end of the hall suddenly seemed immeasurable. He decided to cross to the music room instead and reach the ballroom by that less direct fashion. "Wait." Tal's voice was startlingly close and he turned to see the vampire standing only a few feet from him. Sidonie took a step, as if to move between them. Matthew found his gaze held by a pair of grey eyes that seemed bottomless. "You have not introduced us."

"Is it the custom now to introduce servants?" Sidonie asked.

"I think we might make an exception in this case. For a guest." Matthew caught Sidonie's shrug from the corner of his eye then she was beside him.

"This is Matthew. Matthew, this is Tal." The vampire smiled and inclined his head. Matthew echoed the gesture, knowing that he should make the acknowledgement more servile but unable to force himself to do it. Sidonie continued the introductions. "Rodrigo and Theodora." The dark man lifted an eyebrow. The white woman smiled with only vague interest. "And Ysabel." The red-haired vampire had joined the others. She licked her lips. "Now he has things to do and he will leave us."

Matthew stepped towards the door of the music room, reaching for the knob, turning his back uneasily on four pairs of curious, hungry eyes.

"Things more important than waiting on you?" Tal asked. "Than providing for you?"

"I am adequately provided for, Tal. I apologize if my arrangements do not suit your taste but they are *my* arrangements. If this distresses you then perhaps you had best not stay." Sidonie's voice was sharp but Tal only laughed.

"Nonsense, my dear. You always were eccentric. Amuse yourself however you choose."

Matthew found the doorknob and turned it, sliding through the opening into the darkness. He shut the door and leaned against it, aware for the first time how hard his heart was pounding. He could still hear the murmur of voices beyond the door and strained to hear.

"What is in there?"

"Nothing that concerns you." After a moment of silence, she spoke again, her voice lighter. "Humour me, Tal. You are right, I am eccentric. That is why I live here, after all. The mortal is simply one of my eccentricities."

The sound died away, and though he put his ear against the door, he could hear nothing else. Sidonie's advice came back to him. He would have no trouble at all staying awake until dawn.

Filling the hours proved harder, as he had not stocked the ballroom with books or food. He would have to do that tomorrow, he decided. He was too distracted by the rise and fall of sound from the Hall—voices, laughter, noises less identifiable—to concentrate on painting. He did practical work instead: preparing a new canvas and thoroughly cleaning his brushes. The chilly air helped to keep him awake, though as the night wore on he found himself longing for the warmth of his fire and the heap of blankets on his bed.

He leaned against the window, watching the night. He thought perhaps there was some definition now between the blackness of the sky and the dark bulk of the mountains surrounding him. He had no way to track the passing hours but guessed that dawn must be near. He closed his eyes and let his thoughts drift for a moment. The rattle of the door shocked him back into wakefulness and he spun around to see Sidonie stepping into the room. The door closed behind her.

"I am sorry to come in but I had no choice," she said as he crossed to her. "I must ask you a favour."

"Where are they?"

"In their rooms, making sure they are secure against the dawn. You must listen to me. I need you to go to the village during the daylight hours. You must tell Joseph that there are other vampires here. He is to make sure that none of his people wander at night. He should keep watch, as well."

"Would they harm the village?"

"I do not think so. I hope not. But I would have the villagers take no chances. As well, you should gather whatever you need to be comfortable here during the night. Stay out of their way."

"Would it not be better to let me go?" he asked, almost by reflex and saw her forehead crease in distress.

"If it comes to that..." she began, then shook her head. "I refuse to let them interfere." There was an odd distance in her eyes and voice, as if she spoke to herself and not to him. She reached out and put her hand on his chest, sliding

it upward until her cool palm lay against his throat, possessive and intimate. "I will not let them touch you. You
are mine." He could not speak, the words unable to shape
themselves beneath the weight of the caress. Her lids lowered and her lips parted. She could feel the pulse in his
throat, he thought, but the terror that recognition stirred
seemed very far away. His blood throbbed beneath her
touch. His hand lifted to cover hers but he was not sure
whether he meant to pull her fingers away or press them
closer.

She seemed to come back to herself suddenly. Her
hand dropped away beneath his and the gilded gaze
became calm and unreadable. "Trust me," she said softly
and disappeared back through the doorway.

Matthew stared blankly after her. He put his hand to
his throat again and felt the beat of his blood. It seemed as
if he could hear it, its passage through his veins, whispering in a voice that he knew from his dreams. *Mine. Mine.
Mine.*

Chapter 29

Joseph took the news of the arrival of the other vampires with his customary show of unconcern. Matthew could tell he was worried, however, reading the faint lines that formed around his mouth and the speculative distance in his eyes. "Thank her for the warning," he said, rising from his seat beside the iron stove. Matthew stood up and took the hand extended to him.

The morning sunlight on the snow made him squint as he emerged from the dark cabin onto the porch. He suspected that it was a mark of trust that he had been allowed inside, though perhaps it was only because of the cold. The cabin was warm, at least near the stove, though he thought he could feel the draught from some unprotected chink in the wall. The furnishings were simple: a table, two chairs, a bed covered in furs. If Joseph had a wife, she was nowhere in evidence.

Matthew pulled on his gloves and the fur hat he had acquired from one of the abandoned rooms. As he stepped off the porch, he heard Joseph clear his throat. When he looked around, the man was staring off at the mountains. "You need to be around ordinary folk, you

226

come down here."

"Thank you," Matthew managed after a moment's surprised silence. Joseph nodded and vanished back into his cabin. As he turned to begin the walk back to the house, Matthew considered what the unexpected offer might mean. Was it sanctuary that Joseph was offering? Or simply a way to avoid the vampires for a brief time? If he accepted, what price might be exacted from the village?

He was so distracted by the question that it took a moment for him to realize that the voice that called his name was not merely the echoes of his dreams. He looked up and saw Rebeke leaning against the porch pole of the cabin to his left. The loose fall of her hair held the same rich brown hue as the furs wrapped around her shoulders. A cup of coffee steamed in one hand. "You haven't been back to see us," she said. He stepped off the path and followed the footsteps in the snow to the edge of the porch. She held out the cup and he took it, taking a sip and holding the hot liquid in his mouth for a moment before swallowing.

"I've been busy." She laughed, tilting her face into the sunlight with unconscious pleasure. He noticed the crinkle of lines around her eyes and mouth deepening with her smile. Her sun-browned skin was tinted pink with the cold. How long had it been since he had seen sunlight on mortal skin? he wondered suddenly. He had forgotten how beautiful it was.

"You coming to the festival?" He shrugged. "You should. Lots of music, dancing. Some of Mother Norit's home-brewed hooch. Be a change for you."

"It certainly would," he admitted and handed back the cup.

"So you'll come."

"If I can."

"You just come." She looked at him again and flicked back an errant lock of her hair. "You'll have a good time."

The smile creased her face again. "Believe me."

"I will do my best," he conceded and headed back to the path. When he glanced back, she was still leaning on the pole, her face lifted up to the sun as if she were a wild plant, absorbing life from each ray.

After the bright briskness of the morning, the house seemed dreary and confining. The presence of the sleeping vampires hung in the air, charging it with a chill more bitter than usual. Matthew could not help hurrying through all his actions, as if dusk was ever on the verge of arriving and trapping him unprepared. He moved clothing and blankets into the ballroom, along with a selection of books. He made certain to eat dinner early, before the sun set. He expected to see the mortal servants but they seemed to keep the same hours as their masters.

He began the preliminary work on a new painting and it kept him busy long past the time he should have slept. He caught a fitful, uneasy nap just before dusk then returned to the ballroom, regretfully acknowledging that he was condemned to another night awake. Far away, he heard the slam of a door and suppressed a shiver. Another night awake in a house full of monsters.

He began to work again, determined to ignore the sounds that he heard. The sun vanished behind the mountains. Voices drifted from the Hall. He was so accustomed to the silence that they sounded unnatural, like the indecipherable whispers of ghosts. He waited for a knock on the door, or for Sidonie to appear, but no one disturbed him.

Sometime after midnight, he knew that he could not stay awake without coffee or some other stimulant. He went to the door of the gallery and stood there for a moment, straining to catch any sound from the Hall. It was silent. He lingered there, caught by indecision, then risked opening the door. He could hear voices then, but they were muffled and unclear. Moving as quietly as he could, he eased out of the door, closed it behind him and made his way across the Hall. A fire burned in the hearth but the room was empty. They were upstairs, he thought, catching the echo of laughter.

The kitchen seemed safe, if cold and dark. He lit a lamp and stoked the stove then filled the kettle. Resigning himself to lingering until it had boiled, he passed the time by considering the stores on the shelves. It would be good when the intruders were gone and Sidonie could cook again. She was much better at it than he was. He closed the cupboard door.

"Hello, Matthew," said a voice at his shoulder. His body jerked in surprise and he turned, his heart hammering. Ysabel stood behind him, an amused smile on her lips. "Did I frighten you?"

"You startled me," he said, seeing no advantage in denying it. Her heavy auburn hair was coiled on the top of her head, with a tendril or two left to snake across the white skin of her throat and shoulders. She wore a red silk dress as fashionable as any Allegra might own, though he suspected Allegra would catch a severe chill if she attempted anything so bare in such a place. Lamplight caught the rubies in her ears and around one thin wrist. She was much younger than Sidonie and Tal, possessing none of their undeniable otherness. She could pass for mortal without any glamour at all. Not that she was without glamour, he admitted, automatically considering the planes of her face, the voluptuous mouth, the shape of her body beneath the thin silk.

"What are you doing?"

"Making some coffee. I assume you would not care for any." She wrinkled her nose and shifted to lean against the counter.

"No, thank you. I prefer other...sustenance." Matthew felt himself step back automatically and changed it into a movement towards the stove to check the kettle. "Where did Sidonie find you?"

"The city."

"And are there any more like you there?"

"I would imagine there is whatever might interest you there." He heard the dark music of her laugh and busied himself with finding a cup, an action that did not take nearly as long as he had hoped.

"Have you been here, with her, for very long?"

"A while."

"Do you like it here in such a barren place as this?"

"What has my liking it to do with anything?"

"How sad. If you were mine, I would take you back where you belong. I would give you fine clothes instead of these ancient rags." He felt the brush of her fingers against the sleeve of his jacket. "I would see that you had everything you desired."

"Until you finished with me and dumped my body in the river." She drew a breath at his bluntness, but he could see the wicked amusement in her eyes.

"One river is very much like another. Though perhaps you think that she will make you last till spring, until the ice melts." Her hand slid up his arm and across his shoulder. The memory of Sidonie doing the same thing flared. His heartbeat seemed to stagger and then race. It was so loud he was certain she could hear it. He looked down at her. The lamplight sculpted her face into exquisite lines. Beneath the shining vermilion silk, he could see the lift of her breasts as she drew a slow breath. Her eyes were the pale blue of the winter sky.

Her fingers touched the base of his throat, so cold they seemed to burn. He saw an expression of surprise flicker across her face, then she caught his chin in her hand and tilted his head to one side then the other. As he opened his mouth to protest, she let go and caught his hand in hers.

She pushed the cuff of his shirt back and ran her fingers across the underside of his wrist. She repeated the action on the other arm and then her face lifted again. She smiled, teeth very white against the ruby lips. "A virgin...and we never suspected. No wonder you are so unhappy here."

"I am not..." he began, then wondered which statement he was planning to deny. Behind him, he heard the kettle begin to whistle. It sounded like a cry for help.

"She is like this place, ancient and cold," Ysabel whispered. "You need heat..."

"Ysabel!" The voice shocked his gaze away from Ysabel's arctic eyes and burning mouth. Sidonie stood in the doorway. Her hand dropped from the door and the bracelets on her bare arms clattered. "Leave him alone, Ysabel. You know the rules." Tal's narrow, sardonic face appeared over her shoulder.

"Yes, Ysabel. You know the rules. Never play with someone else's food."

Ysabel grimaced and stepped away from Matthew with a shrug. She glided past Sidonie and accepted the arm Tal held out for her. As the door swung closed behind them, Matthew heard her plaintive voice: "You can hardly blame me, love. If she is not going to use him, she should give him to someone who will."

The shrill cry of the kettle became unbearable. Matthew turned and snatched it from the stove. "I told you to stay away from them," Sidonie said. He looked back at her, startled by the harshness in her voice.

"I had very little choice in the matter."

"Of course not."

He slammed down the kettle. Boiling water spilled on his hand but he barely noticed.

"No doubt if I had asked her politely to leave she would have gone. That always worked with you, after all." He heard her sharp breath but did not glance her way, concentrating on retrieving the kettle and pouring the coffee.

"Stay away from her, Matthew," she said. "She is one of my kind...no matter what she looks like. You would die as surely from her kiss as from mine."

He looked up but she was already gone. The kitchen door closed with a sharp sound. It occurred to him that if she were mortal, he would think that she was jealous. The absurd thought made him smile, at least until the pain from his scalded hand finally reached his brain.

Chapter 30

It was simple to plan to avoid the vampires but much harder to manage it, Matthew discovered. He could not spend all of his time in the ballroom. Even if he could have, he feared that his retreat there would only stir their curiosity and encourage them to invade his one sanctuary. If an hour or two in their presence would satisfy them for the night, he told himself that it was a small price to pay for safety.

They had taken to congregating in the Hall, sprawled on chairs and couches dragged in from the other rooms. Even in that, he could sense their subtle hierarchy. Tal took the chair with the grandest curves, set closest to the fire. He insisted that Sidonie sit beside him. Theodora claimed the seat across from him, leaving Rodrigo the stiff-backed loveseat positioned at the edge of the fire's glow. Ysabel claimed the last couch, set to Sidonie's right, almost out of Tal's range of vision. If she felt exiled, she did not show it, lolling languidly on the cushions like an oriental queen in a costume drama.

The mortals were expected to find what comfort they could on the fringes of the constellation of vampires. The only requirement was that it be within easy reach of their master. It took Matthew some time to discover their names, for the vampires rarely used them unless it was to distinguish one mortal from another. Tal's thin, childlike beauty, Joelle, normally huddled on the hearth beside his chair. Theodora's Lawton sat on an ottoman next to the albino vampire. Matthew could not tell whether Lawton was his first name or his last, nor could he guess at how old the man might be. His hands looked young but his ascetic face had the drained, haggard look they all shared. Elisa, the blonde woman who served Rodrigo, sat on the floor at his feet. Ross, who he decided must be Ysabel's local conquest, did the same by her couch, unless he was allowed to share it with her. He seemed the healthiest of them, but his eyes had the glazed, broken look that Matthew imagined one would find in the eyes of animals in an abattoir.

When Tal insisted that he join them, Matthew knew that it was a test. His place should have been beside Sidonie, trapped between her and Tal or Ysabel. Instead, he retrieved a hard-backed chair from the dining room and set it ten feet behind Theodora's, close to the wall. There, the shadows kept the firelight at bay but he could clearly see both Tal and Sidonie. It was an instinctive move—to keep his back to the wall and his enemy in clear view. Tal's slow smile told him that the vampire had recognized the gesture for what it was. "Surely he should sit over here, by you," he said to Sidonie.

"He can sit wherever he likes," she replied into the sudden, eager silence. From the corner of his eye, Matthew saw the glitter of Rodrigo's lazily curious glance and Theodora's white face as she glanced back at him.

"Be patient, Tal," Ysabel put in, shifting to stroke Ross's uncombed hair. "After all, virgins are shy. Perhaps she's saving him for their wedding night."

Their laughter sounded like glass chimes, brittle and on the verge of breaking into something sharp and dangerous. Sidonie's face showed nothing but perfect, immortal stillness. Matthew kept his in the shadows. From then on, though the barbs continued, pointed and vicious, they never tried to drag him from that shelter.

The purpose of the gathering, as far as he could tell, was to amuse themselves with reminiscences and debate. The remembrances seemed to consist of atrocities committed, either alone or together. All ended with the death of whatever mortal had attracted their attention. The debate was equally horrible, centring on methods of seduction and murder or the superiority of one type of mortal blood or another. The tales alternately bored and disgusted him and yet he forced himself to pay attention, in hopes that there might be clues that would give him a weapon against them.

There was only one thing that made it bearable—Sidonie rarely spoke. If she had, if she had joined in the litany of torture and degradation and death, he knew that he would have been unable to listen. There were tales that involved her though, mostly told by Tal with gleeful elaboration. She never disputed them.

If the stories passed the time, they seemed to serve another purpose for the vampires as well. For them, the recollections of conquests past seemed to enhance the present ones. Often they would pause in their recitations to take blood from the wrist or throat of their mortal slave, much as a guest at a dinner party might indulge in a sip of wine. As the night wore on, the breaks became more common and the act of drinking more dramatic. The stories were their pornography, he realized in revulsion, and they a group of jaded decadents unable to take the smallest pleasure in the act without greater and greater stimulation.

The first night, he endured an hour before he slipped

away, blocking out their mockery behind the ballroom door. Inside, he flung open the French doors and breathed the cold, clean air for a long time, welcoming the chill after the heated atmosphere of the Hall. The vampires' rituals had a perverse power, an evil eroticism that even his revulsion could not entirely deny. He rubbed his wrist, the skin there suddenly tender with the memory of Sidonie's teeth against it.

Was it a spectacle devised for his benefit? he wondered, then dismissed the thought. It seemed too automatic, too natural to them for that. He stared up at the moon, shivering a little. If what he had seen was mere prelude, he did not want to know what the climax of the entertainment was to be. Even more disturbing to contemplate was Sidonie's role. Would they offer her a taste of the blood of their servants? Would she accept it? He could not guess what that might mean to him. Replete with other blood, would she value his less? Would she let him go? Or having regained the taste for mortal blood, would she decide that his consent made no difference to her?

His shiver turned into a shudder and he closed the door. Speculating on it made no difference and led inexorably to questions he did not want to consider. Such as whether the sight of Sidonie bent over another throat would make him feel revulsion, relief or jealousy.

As it neared dawn, he heard a knock on the window and saw Sidonie standing on the snow-covered terrace. He pulled on his coat and opened the door again. She would not come in but stood in the doorway. "I am sorry you were subjected to that."

"Did they do it for me?" he asked and she shook her head.

"That is what they do. What we do. I have never lied to you about that."

"No," he admitted. Tal's stories of her had not horrified

him as much as he had expected—or Tal had no doubt intended—perhaps because she had never hidden what she was. Yet her unvarnished inhumanity was very different from their gleeful malevolence. He could not imagine Tal asking for his consent or Ysabel offering him absolution.

"Will you give me your blood to drink, even though you die of it?" The words were no more than a whisper and he caught her nervous glance at the closed door to the gallery.

"No." She nodded and turned to walk away across the terrace. He saw that the feet that dented the snow were bare.

The next two nights followed the same pattern. Tal would insist that he join them, he would bear what he could until it seemed safe to slip away, and Sidonie would appear at the ballroom door in the early hours of the morning to ask him the question. Tal and Ysabel continued their relentless needling of him, or Sidonie. Theodora and Rodrigo ignored him. Once in a while he would meet the dull eyes of the mortal slaves and see something like sympathy there.

The next night, Matthew resigned himself to the playing out of the same vile, dangerous farce. As the rites began, he sensed a shift in the atmosphere. Ysabel was sulkier than usual and Tal's banter with Sidonie more vicious. Theodora seemed bored. Rodrigo did not even bother to appear. From his place in the shadows, Matthew watched them, aware for the first time of the change in Sidonie. To a casual glance, she appeared as composed as ever and responded to Tal's barbs with either wit or bored nonchalance, but there was a brittleness in her he had never seen. She moved with careful precision and her smile was a tight crescent that seemed intended to imprison emotion rather than express it.

He glanced from Sidonie to Tal and saw with a cold

shock that Tal was watching him. The narrow mouth curved in a smile and one eyebrow lifted. He sees it too, Matthew thought, and felt the chill return. Whatever was changing in her, Tal had seen it. Sidonie and Tal had a long history, that much was clear from the stories he had heard. They had been lovers, of a sort. Beneath the caresses he gave and she accepted, beneath the mockery disguised as wit, Matthew sensed the dark currents that moved between them. Whatever Tal wanted from her, she was not surrendering it to him. At least, not yet. He wondered how long the old vampire would wait.

Tal smiled, as if he could read the flow of Matthew's thoughts. He turned to Joelle, who sat on the hearth beside his chair, and lifted her hand, turning it to bare the thin wrist. Even in the firelight, Matthew could see the bruises tracing her veins. Tal bent his head. Joelle's eyelids fluttered and she moaned softly, her breast rising quickly as she drew a shaky breath. Tal dropped her hand suddenly and leaned over to bestow a lingering kiss on Sidonie. When he sat back, Matthew could see the blood on her mouth. There was a terrible look on her face, longing and loathing mixed. Her tongue slid across her lips. Tal's smile was triumphant.

She was on her feet in a quick, jerky motion, pushing past Lawton on her way to the kitchen. Matthew saw Tal begin to rise and stood up hastily. He met the grey gaze, amused and speculative, then turned to follow Sidonie.

The kitchen was dark, except for a gleam of moonlight from the far window. He heard the gush of water then the sound of choking. "Sidonie?" A shadow at the sink resolved into her shape. She lifted a glass of water to her mouth and then spat into the sink, washing the blood from her tongue. He stepped towards her and said her name again.

The glass shattered on the counter. As he opened his

mouth, he felt her fingers cover it. Her hiss sealed the words in his throat. He could not see her face, for it was turned away from him, bent so that her hair curtained it. She was very close to him, close enough that he could have taken her in his arms. He clenched his fists and kept them by his sides. Her fingers slipped away from his lips, but not before he felt the tremor in them.

"Why do you endure this?" he whispered. "Why don't you send him away?"

"I cannot." Her voice sounded as broken as the glass. "He is my blood."

"You are his blood," Matthew corrected gently, half-hoping she would deny it. "He is the one who made you, isn't he?"

He heard a soft sound and thought that he could see her nod. "Yes." There were two thousand years of anguish in the word.

She wants to kill you, he reminded himself. You can see the process of that death out there in the eyes of the ones her murderous kin have chosen. It is not rational to ache for your executioner's pain.

He closed his eyes and put his arms around her. She drew a short breath and he felt her fingers grip the fabric of his jacket. "It will be over soon," he said to the darkness behind his closed lids. "They will go away." She shivered and her body shifted, settling against his. Something quite unlike sympathy stirred inside him. He felt her head move against his shoulder, then the brush of her breath on his throat.

She thrust him away with such force it staggered him back against the edge of the counter. She stepped away and he saw the moonlight slip across one cheek, gleam in the white of one eye. "I warned you to stay away from them," she said unsteadily. "Now I must warn you to stay away from me."

He remembered the taut look on her face, the sharpened angles of her bones beneath skin that seemed to have
lost some of its lustre. He remembered the rigid control in
her movements, as if she feared any spontaneous action
might split her apart. She had not left the house since the
others had arrived. She had not fed in five nights. Instead,
she had sat through her kin's orgies, breathing the heat of
their satiation, the sweet vapours of the blood they spilled.
He caught his breath, chilled at the thought of what his
blind compassion for her had almost cost him.

He heard the door opening a moment before Tal's
voice. "Whatever are you doing in here, Sidonie? Dining
in private? Did I interrupt the defloration?" As the edge of
the light touched her, Matthew saw her turn her face back
into the shadows, as if afraid what might be read on it. It
was Tal's eyes she feared, he knew. Any weakness shown
before him was a weapon the old vampire would not hesi-
tate to use. He felt the sudden boil of bitter rage and
stepped into the light so that his shadow would shelter her.

"Perhaps if you would leave us alone," he said sharply,
the first thing that came into his head. Tal's eyebrows
lifted and he took a step forward. Sidonie slipped into the
space between them.

"Really, children. Stop posturing. It's tedious." Her
voice had regained its sharp, armoured edges, taking on
the arch tone he had only ever heard her use with the
other vampires. "Matthew, clean up the glass. Tal, you can
hardly begrudge me my own remedies when you make me
ill on the thin blood of your half-dead doxy."

"You mustn't let me keep you from them then, my dear.
But you might let us watch."

"You never change. Always the voyeur." She took his
arm and pressed herself against him, turning him back
towards the dining room. The door swung shut behind
them. Matthew stood in the darkness, swamped in impotent

anger, shocked at the depth of his hatred for the silver-haired vampire, even more shaken by the sympathy he felt for Sidonie, for the pain she must be enduring. She could have slaked her hunger any time she chose but instead she had warned him, had struggled with her need for his sake. She is what he is, he reminded himself savagely. Everything you despise in him is part of her. You cannot change that by holding her in your arms. When they are gone, she will still be here and she will kill you. If she does not do so now, it only means that she has not yet obtained whatever it is she wants.

He took a deep breath. He would have to stay here for a while now. He could not bear to walk across the Hall, beneath their greedy, calculating eyes. If one of them, any of them, spoke to him in their cruel, casual voices he did not know what he might do. Whatever else had happened, he supposed that he should thank Sidonie for sensing that and giving him a few moments of safety.

He fumbled for the lamp and then began to clean up the shattered glass.

Chapter 31

❧✦❧

The dreams returned, haunting the few hours of restless sleep he managed during the daylight hours. If they were not quite the old nightmares of drowning, they were unpleasant enough. He did his best not to remember them.

Finally, he abandoned the pretence of rest and rose. When he pulled back the heavy curtains, he discovered that the mid-afternoon sun was bright and warm, glittering on the snow and ice. Looking at it, it was almost possible to believe that the night, with its madness and danger, would never come.

He went to the ballroom and spent a restless and unsatisfactory hour working on preliminary sketches for a new painting. The images held no lasting allure and he flipped through the sketchbook seeking new inspiration. He was careful not to consider the drawings he had done of Sidonie but found his attention unwillingly arrested by a series of furtive sketches of Tal and the others. He had found that his fingers were unnervingly skilled at recreating the shapes and structure of their inhumanity. Each line seemed to recall how much like them Sidonie was, no matter how much he might wish otherwise.

242

He contemplated the drawings with dissatisfaction.
They were accurate, technically accomplished and somehow utterly unsatisfying. He added a line or two thoughtfully, then set down his pencil. He had no desire to
elaborate further, he realized suddenly, or to ever sketch
them again. For all the vampires' terrible power, drawing
them was unchallenging, even boring. Beyond the alien
alteration of their features and their strange beauty, their
faces were blank and unchanging. They had none of the
lines of life that gave human faces their complexity and
interest. Even Sidonie's face, stripped of its otherness and
the weight of his own emotions, had that immutable
emptiness. He had forgotten that as he had grown to know
her and learned to read the subtle shiftings of her features
that signalled her emotions.

He snapped the sketchbook shut with an obscure feeling of triumph. That he could find them uninteresting and
uninspiring seemed a singularly fitting victory. As empty as
it might be, he resolved to savour it. The first step in that
celebration seemed to be to get beyond the cold walls that
sheltered them.

A few minutes later, he left the house and stood on the
terrace. The sunlight was as warm as it had looked and he
found himself lifting his face to it as Rebeke had done. The
heat seemed to tingle as it soaked into his skin, as if awak-
ening nerves gone dormant in lamplight and darkness.

He noticed there were fresh footprints in the snow of
the narrow path that led around to the terrace outside the
ballroom. They could not be Sidonie's as it had snowed
since her visit in the early hours of the morning. He had
noticed no one passing while he worked. Curious, he
turned and followed them up the pathway.

As he emerged onto the terrace, he saw the man sitting
on the balustrade. Sunlight gleamed on his pale hair and for
a moment he thought that it was Tal. Then the man looked

back over his shoulder and he recognized him. "Lawton."

"Matthew." The acknowledgement had a sardonic edge. Matthew went to lean against the stone barrier beside him. Lawton was looking up at the mountains. In the bright light, Matthew could see the tiny brushstrokes of lines around his eyes and mouth. His skin had a sallow pallor. Beneath the signs of weariness and illness, there were fine bones and the shadow of aristocratic confidence. The man was no more than a few years older than he was, Matthew guessed.

A coil of smoke rose from Lawton's hand. When he lifted it to his mouth, Matthew saw the slender cylinder of a cigarette. The breeze shifted and he caught a hint of sweetness. It was not the scent of tobacco. "It's very beautiful here," Lawton said after a moment. His voice had a familiar cadence. Matthew struggled for a moment to place it, then remembered. Allegra's rich, titled friends had voices like that. Allegra had a voice like that. "It looks so pure and untouched. I forget that such things still exist in the world. I forget what the sun feels like."

"So do I."

Lawton looked at him then extended the cigarette. "Care to join me?"

Matthew stared at the bright tip for a moment, thinking of nethys and wine and oblivion. At last, he took it into his fingers and drew a slow suck of smoke. A sweet heat filled his mouth. He held it there and then exhaled. Lawton accepted the cigarette back and dangled it lazily between two fingers.

"Nightbloom," Matthew guessed, tasting the smoke on his tongue. Lawton smiled.

"I thought that you looked like a man who knows his narcotics."

"Oh?"

"It was that subtle perfume of turpentine and the paint

on your cuffs. You're an artist. Artists always know where to get the best drugs." He laughed, a slow, thick sound. "Though this is not exactly a place I would have expected as a source. Have you any to spare?"

"No. There is wine, of course. I had a little nethys but it is long gone."

"Nethys?" Lawton's eyebrows lifted. "Very brave of you, taking that in such a place as this."

"It was not an experience I am in any hurry to repeat," Matthew admitted. He opened his coat and climbed onto the balustrade to settle beside Lawton. They sat in silence for a few moments, contemplating the mountains and the slow swirls of smoke as the cigarette passed between them. The warmth of the sun and the heat of the nightbloom seemed to merge, loosening the knot of muscles at the back of his neck.

"Why are you here?" Lawton asked at last. When Matthew did not answer, he continued. "Rude of me to be blunt, I know, but recent circumstances have made me forget my manners."

"It is a long story. I came to pay off a family debt. I did not know what I was getting into—and now I cannot leave." He caught the man's sideways glance.

"Cannot or do not want to?"

"Cannot. Believe me, I have tried. It is two days on horseback to the railway line and the train only runs once every three days. It cannot be done."

"There might be something to be said for freezing to death."

"I have thought of that as well. But there would be other prices for my…failure to co-operate. Others would suffer."

"How altruistic of you."

"I am not dead yet," Matthew pointed out, stung by the amusement in the man's voice. "I have not even been harmed."

"Yet." Lawton said the word, even if Matthew had not. "If Tal has his way, you will be soon. Tal doesn't care for you."

"The feeling is mutual." He looked more closely at Lawton, but the man was contemplating the dark mass of trees below them. "Do you mean that he is planning to kill me?"

"I think he would prefer that Sidonie do it."

"Sidonie is not required to oblige Tal." His voice sounded stiff and formal, as if that could make the words truer.

"You think not? He made her."

"I know. Why should that matter?"

"That is how it works among them. The oldest of the bloodline has the most power. That is why they do what Tal wants. He made them all. She is the only one who has ever left him without his permission." Matthew remembered Sidonie stepping slowly into the other vampire's arms, turning her face into the darkness so he could not read her eyes. He thought of her furtive visits to his door at dawn and her warning to the village. Could Tal compel her as she had compelled him the night the other vampires arrived? He did not want to think about it.

"How did you end up here?" he asked quickly and Lawton's mouth twisted.

"Like this, you mean?" He looked towards the horizon and drew another long drag on the cigarette. "I was young, rich and stupid. I thought that I wanted to learn about the dark side of life. My own heart was the blackest thing I knew, after all. I thought that it would be possible to dabble in horror and remain untouched. I was wrong."

"What happened?"

"Theodora happened. They are like black flames who can sense when some foolish moth is toying with oblivion. I came too near the fire and was consumed. Now

Theodora has all my money and I die a little more every night. I might be somewhat wiser than I was, I suppose, but it is hardly a fair exchange."

"Why do you stay? Why don't you, any of you, escape?"

"Where would I go that she could not find me? They do not care to be crossed. Believe me, no hole would be deep enough to hide me. Joelle and Elisa have their own reasons for remaining, I would suppose. Ross," Lawton sucked on the cigarette again and let the smoke slide from his lips. "Now Ross may manage it. I would not be surprised to wake up one evening and discover he had cut his own throat."

"Why not kill them? There are four of you. They are helpless during the day."

"Why have you not killed *her*?" Lawton countered. "Could you do it? Put a stake against that beautiful breast and take an axe to that exquisite throat?" When Matthew did not answer, he gave one of his short, jagged laughs. "You know nothing about them, about what they can do. No matter what you think that you understand, you know nothing so long as you remain a virgin to them."

"Tell me then. If there is something that I don't understand, tell me what it is." Lawton met the challenge with a long look. The distracted amusement faded from his face. After a moment, he shrugged and returned his gaze to the far mountains.

"I think that you are a man with some experience with addictions. Am I right?"

"Yes."

"They...what they do...is an addiction worse than any you can imagine. With most drugs, every time you take them, the experience is the same. You know what you will find at the peak. You know the path by which it will be reached. You even know what you will feel when you fall from the other side. But with the feeding...the variety is infinite. It can be the most intense pleasure or the most terrible pain. More erotic than your wildest dream of sex or as impersonal as if you were no more than a bottle of their favourite vintage. And you never know which it will be. Eventually, it does not matter. Pain or pleasure, passionate or distant, you must have her kiss. No matter what price you have to pay." The glowing tip of the cigarette scattered ash as his fingers shook. "You will find out for yourself."

"No." Matthew felt the stone rough and hard beneath his fingers. He gripped the edge of the balustrade. "I will never consent to it. Never."

"Does that matter?" Lawton asked. For a moment, Matthew thought about telling him everything, yet some instinct kept him silent. If there was one lesson he had learned during his rebellious youth, it was that it was dangerous to trust an addict.

"It has to be my choice. That is what she promised," he said carefully.

"If your mistress—"

"She is not my mistress. Not in any sense of the word."

"With them, there is only one sense of the word. If your mistress has given you a choice, she can take it away. Could you stop her?" Matthew said nothing. "The bonds of her humanity, whatever humanity she possesses, are very thin. They grow thinner every night we stay, every time she looks at you. They are addicts as well, in their own way. They are slaves to the hunger as surely as we. She is desperate. Everyone can see it. How long will it be before, like any opium-ravaged whore in the gutter, she breaks every promise she has ever made to you or herself?" He gave him a death's head smile. "But don't worry. They usually give you the pleasure first."

Lawton shifted to slide back to the terrace. "It has grown cold," he said and, without another word, turned towards the path. Matthew watched him disappear into the trees, then looked back out over the frozen lake. The petty triumph of his artistic disdain for the vampires and the distanced contentment the nightbloom provided had both been wiped away by the seriousness of the conversation. He heard the wind move through the pines and thought of Sidonie's voice warning him to stay away from her. The chilly touch of the breeze felt like her breath on his throat.

Lawton was right. She was an addict, fighting her need. Sooner or later, she would lose, especially with Tal and the others surrounding her with the explicit evidence of everything that she was denying herself. He was astonished by how much the thought distressed him. He had known all along that she would kill him. He had said so aloud countless times. Yet, while it had only been the two of them, while the ritual of question and refusal could be counted on to contain her, he had clung to the belief that he might survive. Some part of him believed that if he could only refuse her for long enough, until the winter ended, she would tire of the game and let him leave.

As long as it had only been between the two of them, even the thought that he might one day surrender was almost bearable. When he died, at least he would do it privately. To be taken in front of the other vampires, under Tal's gloating eyes, to be reduced to one of their abject bloodslaves…that was unendurable.

His eye caught the gap in the trees that signalled the path to the village. Lawton's voice echoed in his ears: there is something to be said for freezing to death.

He swung back over the balustrade and went to the doors of the ballroom. If Tal and the others did not leave, he could always go down to the village and steal a horse. He could head for the railway.

At least if he froze to death, he would do it with all his blood still in his body.

Chapter 32

When Matthew eased open the door of the gallery at midnight, the Hall was empty. The fire had burned low in the hearth and the chairs and couches in front of it were, for once, unoccupied. He leaned out of the doorway carefully. He could hear the murmur of voices, from the library he guessed, and the far-off slam of a door. Perhaps the unrest he had sensed in the vampires the previous night had finally come to a head. Part of him was relieved that they had become bored with their evening ritual and another part feared what kind of entertainment they might seek to replace it.

He stepped out into the Hall and walked to the kitchen to make a cup of coffee. He found a pile of dishes in the sink and crumbs scattered about the counter. He had never seen the vampires' mortal servants eat, but had only found the evidence of it afterward. The vampires themselves paid no attention at all to their slaves' human needs. He could not imagine Theodora cooking dinner for Lawton.

He managed to acquire the coffee without being cornered and, cradling the hot cup, stepped back into the

Hall. At the entrance to the gallery, he froze. The door to the ballroom was open. He had closed it. He always closed it. A rush of dread and outrage propelled him across the room. In the doorway, he stopped.

All of his paintings had been turned to face outwards. The three fantastical ones were in the centre, a triptych composed of pigment and nightmares. Tal stood in front of them, contemplating them with the exaggerated air of a pompous art critic.

Matthew stepped into the room, pulling the door closed behind him automatically. Tal turned at the sound. A thin shark's smile curved on his lips. "I am impressed, I must admit. You are quite talented."

"Thank you." The words meant nothing but gave him something to say. He crossed to his easel and set down the cup of coffee. He picked up his palette and added a dab of red to the small landscape on which he had been working. When he looked up, Tal was still there, standing in front of the nightmare paintings.

"I especially like these. I am quite modern in my tastes, for a vampire. I do not expect strict realism. Though that may have been because you had no model." Tal turned to look at him. "Perhaps I should sit for you. I would make a splendid Lucifer, don't you think?" He struck a theatrical pose.

"I am not in my angel period at the moment," Matthew said shortly and stared hard at his painting. The colours ran together, blurring until he saw nothing but black and red.

"I have never thought of Sidonie as a patron of the arts. Is that why she is keeping you alive? So that you can do more flattering portraits of her? But she hasn't seen these, has she?" Matthew did not reply. It did not matter what he said—Tal already knew the answer. From the corner of his eye, he saw the vampire prowl closer. "Or maybe she is performing an experiment. Sidonie is very fond of experiments."

"What type of experiment?" Matthew could not stop himself from asking.

"There has never been a great vampire artist. We have no poets, no painters, no musicians. I do not know why. Perhaps because we need not leave anything for posterity—after all, we are our own posterity. Perhaps she is trying to create one. Or perhaps she is only interested in what blood tastes like when it is mixed with paint."

"You will have to ask her what her motives are. I do not know." Matthew ground his brush into the palette, crushing the colours beneath the fragile bristles. Tal leaned against the dresser's model, his arm around its bare shoulders.

"I don't have to ask. I know what she is doing." He laughed when Matthew looked up. "That intrigues you, does it? Shall I tell you?" He rolled his eyes up at the ceiling as if thinking very hard about the question. "That would ruin the experiment, of course. She would be very unhappy about that."

"Then I suppose that it depends on whether you want to make her unhappy or not."

"What about you? What would make *you* happy?"

Matthew abandoned the pretence of painting, putting down the palette and leaning back against the table behind him. "Surely you do not expect me to believe that you have any interest in my happiness."

Tal laughed and crooked his finger at him, as if acknowledging a point scored. "No, you are right about that. It is only Sidonie who matters to me. I am concerned about her. She isn't looking at all well these nights. So the question becomes: what is best for her?" He paced across the room, hands clasped behind his back. Matthew thought absurdly of Simon, lecturing. "The problem is that she does not always know what is best for her. She never has."

"When she disagrees with you, you mean."

"No." For the first time, the vampire's voice held a thread of anger. "Sidonie never disagrees with me. At least, not for long."

"Have you considered that it might be best for her if you just left her...us...alone?"

"I don't think that would be right at all. I really think that it is up to me, as her creator, to protect her from herself. There is only one way to do that." Matthew saw the vampire draw himself up and turn to face him. The grey gaze held his and he felt the subtle pull of the vampire's power. "Will you give me your blood to drink, though you die of it?"

"No." The answer came instinctively, even as his mind spun to consider this new ploy. He had never heard any of the other vampires ask their victims for blood and he had begun to believe that they did not. Perhaps it only had to be asked once, so that one act of consent would deprive you of the choice ever after.

Tal shook his head ruefully and started to turn away. Matthew almost sighed in relief.

In the next heartbeat, he found himself borne back across the table, the vampire's hands wrapped around his throat. He clawed at the fingers pressing into his flesh then struck out at the silver-haloed head fading in and out of focus above his. "Too bad that it does not matter to me whether you agree or not." The voice sounded distant and distorted, as if through water. Darkness began to creep into his vision, swallowing up the sight of the face bent over his. Soon all that he could see were the sharp teeth in the wide mouth, gleaming like lamps hung in the darkness.

His outflung hand caught something slender and pointed. His palette knife, he thought dimly and swung it up with his last strength, aiming for the vampire's face.

The blow dissolved into air as the weight left his chest. He slid to the floor, clutching his throat. Several raw, choking breaths later, the black fog across his eyes began to fade. He heard voices shouting and saw blurred forms moving above his head. He blinked and the sounds became words, the shapes melted back into their real forms.

"Ysabel I might have expected this from, but you? Tal, are you mad?" Sidonie demanded. She stood very close to Tal, hands closed over his upper arms. The older vampire pulled away from her and smoothed his disordered hair.

"Really, Sidonie. You might have torn my jacket. You had no need to assault me like that."

"No? I find you about to feed from my mortal—mine, Tal—and you wonder that I do not stop to ask you what you are doing."

"If it is any consolation to you, he refused me."

Matthew saw the fury in her face shade into something closer to dread. "What do you mean?"

"I asked him the question. You know which one I mean. I suppose it might have been upsetting to you if he had said yes to me after denying you for so long."

She lunged forward again, seizing the lapels of his jacket. "What did you do?" His body jerked as she shook him. "What did you do?"

"Did I tell him? Isn't that what you want to know?"

"Tal!" It was almost a wail of pain.

"Let me go and I'll answer." Her hands fell away and he stepped back, brushing at his lapels with fastidious precision. "I should have. For your own good. It will only hurt you when you fail. You know that, my dear. Then I thought it might be cruel to require you to dispose of him, after things were spoiled, so I decided to solve the problem. I only did it to spare you."

"You did it to punish me," she flung back at him. "You decided to kill him because you thought that would hurt me the most."

"Kill him? Oh no, my love, I wasn't going to kill him." Tal's smile was pure malice. "I was going to turn him."

For a moment, her face went blank. "Tal..." She caught a hard, ragged breath. "I want you to go. Take your menagerie and go."

"Sidonie," he began but she put up her hands as if to ward off the words.

"No. You may wait until tomorrow at dusk to leave but that is all the grace I can offer you. I want you out of my house."

"Or? What will you do if I refuse?"

"If you do not leave, if you say one more word to this mortal or come near him, then I swear to you that I will rise in the daylight and burn this house to the ground."

"You will die," he pointed out and she nodded.

"Most likely. But that does not matter to me. If your life matters to you, then I suggest you do as I say."

"I made you."

"I don't care."

"I can compel you."

"Try."

He took a step towards her. "Sidonie, my sweet, my child..."

A shudder ran through her and for a moment it seemed that the set of her shoulders softened. Tal extended his hand and her own half-rose to meet it. Then she shivered and shook her head. "No. No more." Her voice was raw but resolute. "Get out of here, Tal, or I will burn it all down." They stood there for a long moment then Tal shrugged and brushed back his hair.

"I could still tell him, you know. I could still kill him. Do not delude yourself that your threats have prevented that. But now I see that winning this battle and losing the war will hurt you more than I could ever hope to do. Play out your pathetic delusion, if you wish, but do not hope to come back to me when it fails yet again." He turned and walked towards the door. As he opened it, he looked back over his shoulder. "You might have a look at your beloved mortal's work while you are here. He really is quite talented. Have you seen his portraits of you?"

As the door closed behind him, Matthew groped for the top of the table and pulled himself to his feet. Tal's last words echoed in his ears. His gaze was drawn to the paintings and he saw them as if for the first time, bright, naked and undeniable. The black angel with her hungry eyes, the seductive sepulchral wraith bleeding gold, the siren wreathed in blue and black. Each one with Sidonie's face refracted through the horror of his nightmares and fear, embodied with his old guilt and grieving.

Sidonie stared at the door for a moment then turned slowly. Matthew tried to catch her eye, to stop her before she looked around. Her name came out as a croak. She took a step towards the revealed canvases and then stood still.

He could not see her face, only the stiff lines of her shoulders beneath her blue dress. "Sidonie." He managed the word and then a step forward.

"So that is what I look like," she said. Her voice was steady and interested, as if commenting casually on a work of art in a gallery. "I had wondered."

"Sidonie—"

"Tal was right. You are very talented."

"Sidonie, they are not—"

"To think that you did not even have to risk going blind by staring at the sun."

"Let me—"

Her hand came up, signalling him to silence, but she did not look at him.

"Will you give me your blood to drink, though you die of it?"

"Sidonie, don't make me do this." He could not say yes, could never say yes, but to say no to her tonight would be twisting the knife already thrust into her inhuman heart.

"Will you give me—"

"I won't answer that." Her head turned slowly and he saw her face clearly for the first time. It looked like the skull of his paintings, skin stretched tight over the altered bones. Her eyes were darker than any colour he had ever imagined, a black that was not composed of all other hues but was pure unto itself. The blue had been swallowed, the gold extinguished. Her gaze burned with pain and hunger and a cold, ancient sorrow.

"If you do not answer me," she said clearly, "I will kill you." He felt a wave of sickness and gripped the edge of the table to keep from falling. He closed his eyes so that he would not have to see the betraying paintings and the terrible, broken look on her face.

"No."

When he opened his eyes, she was gone.

Chapter 33

"Well, my dear, I believe that this is farewell." Tal stood in the snow on the front terrace. The reluctant wolves he and the others had summoned snapped and snarled in their traces. The farewells of the other vampires had been perfunctory. Theodora kissed her cheek, Rodrigo the air beside it and Ysabel had only managed a desultory wave from her fur-covered bower on the sled.

"Goodbye, Tal," Sidonie said from the doorway. She mistrusted his smile, his good humour, his willingness to go. She mistrusted herself to allow him to leave, knowing that it was the severing of her oldest tie to the world. It seemed as if whatever soul she might possess had been stretched taut, pulled in all directions by a thousand needs and hungers, and that at any moment it might break beyond repair.

He took her face in his hands. "So you will know what you have thrown away," he whispered and kissed her, a caress intimate with two thousand years of knowledge, with the cruelty of a destroyer and the tenderness of a creator. He had planned that she could not resist it and knew her too well. When he lifted his mouth, her arms were around him. "I hope that it is worth it."

She looked into the ashen eyes and thought she saw a flicker of compassion somewhere in their depths, behind the triumphant malice. Then his mouth curved in a sly smile and she decided that she must have imagined it.

He stepped back and moved lithely onto the back of one of the sleds. "Ha!" he shouted and the wolves surged forward. Sidonie watched the last sled vanish around the corner then snatched her coat from its hook by the door. If he thought to check, Tal would know that she followed them, but it was a risk that she would have to take. She did not know where they were going and did not care, but there was always the chance that, denied his opportunity to hurt her through Matthew, Tal would decide to strike at the village. She dared not take anything for granted.

The snow crunched beneath her feet as she followed the marks of the sleds. The moon was veiled by clouds but that did not matter—she could see well enough. She had to admit that she had grown to love this part of her isolated life. Running through the snow-shrouded forest, breathing the sharp-edged air, it felt as if every sense was awake to lives that moved around her. Their blood called to her, but the winter night seemed to have cooled even that agonizing need. She could wait until she knew that Tal and the others were truly on their way. She could run the woods until dawn if she wished.

But would she be running…or running away?

An image flashed through her mind. She saw a white face floating amid blue-black waves: predatory, fiendish, utterly inhuman. There was a sudden pain beneath her heart and she slowed her pace, as if that could ease it. She heard Tal's voice in the wind: *Have you seen his portraits of you?* I wanted to know, she thought bitterly. I wanted to know what he painted all those nights. I wanted to know what he saw when he looked at me. I was foolish enough to have begun to believe it was something other than fear and revulsion.

I hope that it is worth it, the wind sighed in Tal's voice. She wondered if it was. She had known that this gamble came with a high price, for she had paid it before. Yet this time, it seemed that the stakes had become higher than she had anticipated. No matter what happened, she had broken the oldest bond of her life, had turned her back on the only kin she had known for two thousand years. She had done all this for the chance of the impossible, held in the blood of a man who saw only horror when he looked at her.

The brush to her left crackled and then a dark shape plunged across the path ahead of her. A musky, animal scent filled her nostrils. The smell of blood was so strong that she could taste it. She swerved without thinking, the deer's heat like a magnet drawing her. Usually she lured them, seduced them to her with the power of her mind and then drank in delicate sips from the offered throats. This time, she chased her prey to ground, forgetting Tal, forgetting Matthew, forgetting everything that bound her to the world of humanity. To the world of pain.

The doe went down in a small hollow, borne to earth as Sidonie's weight caught her haunches. Sidonie saw the red rim of the animal's dark eyes as they rolled in terror. A hoof caught her shoulder but she barely felt it, as she surged up the length of the beast's body. Hot, sweaty hide filled her mouth, then she found the vein. The shock of the blood on her starved system was so great that she almost lost consciousness. The doe heaved beneath her, dragging her back to awareness. She could never take enough this way, not with the animal struggling so hard. Her hand caught the knife at her belt. She did not take her mouth away as she slit the creature's throat, simply transferred it to the new fountain she had created.

When at last she drew back, the doe was dead. Sidonie knelt in the bloodstained snow and wiped her face. Her hand came away dark with the animal's life. It was smeared across her coat and matted into her hair. She stared at her mottled fingers, seeing the tremor in them but unable to still it. At last, with a shudder, she plunged them into the snow. They emerged from its whiteness as black as before.

Monster, she thought. She was a monster. How could she have thought she could ever be anything else? She had prided herself on being honest. She had believed that she was showing Matthew the truth, but her truth was just a façade. The velvet dresses, the cultured manners, the civilized restraint—they were nothing but lies. Every kindness, every comfort she had offered him was a lie.

She felt the deer's blood burning on her skin like a brand. With a strangled cry, she tore the stained coat from her body. The rest of her clothes followed. She seized handfuls of snow, sharp with icy crust, and scrubbed them through her hair and across her skin. Her perfect, immortal, monstrous skin. She scraped herself so raw that she bled, but the wounds closed almost immediately. Finally, eyes scalded by shadow-tears, she threw the last handfuls of snow away and looked at the dead doe. Its round, brown eye was open. Bloody froth foamed at its mouth.

She put her hand out to stroke its still side tentatively. "I am sorry," she said, to more than the creature that had died to preserve her. "I cannot help it." Wearily, she climbed to her feet and drew her torn clothing back over her unmarked body.

She reached the house an hour before dawn. As the door closed behind her, she saw Matthew rising from a chair beside the hearth, an expression of curiosity and concern on his face. She saw the eye of the dead doe and looked away from him. She did not want to deal with him. Dealing with him would only bring back the raw ache she thought that she had driven from her heart through exhaustion and cold.

Shrugging off her coat, she stepped into the hall. "Are they gone?" he asked.

"Yes."

"Thank God for that. I think we must agree to no more visits from your relatives." It was an awkward jest and must have been hard for him, implying as it did some more permanent connection between them. She recognized the effort but could not make herself smile. His gaze dropped and she saw his eyes widen as he stared at her shirt. She looked down and saw the pattern of blood across her breast. She touched the stiff dappling with one finger. "Are you hurt?"

"No," she said slowly. "This is not mine." She caught the flash of horror in his eyes. To dispel it, at least for the moment, would only take a word. He had said that he did not care for deer, after all. She turned away towards the darkness of the library and said nothing.

"Sidonie." She stopped. "You have to let me explain about the paintings."

"It is not necessary," she said, staring into the library. The light from the Hall caught the curving glass of a lamp on a table there and made it look as if it were aglow. "You have an artist's eye and you must paint what it sees. It is as simple as that."

"No, it's not. It wasn't you in the paintings."

"Wasn't it?"

"No. It was…" He paused, groping for the words. She wondered if he believed them or was only trying to assuage the emotion she had not been able to hide. "It was what I saw in my dreams."

"Would you have had those dreams in the city? Would you have seen those things if you had not come here?" There was a long silence.

"You are right," he said at last. "But an artist can only paint what he sees—and sometimes he does not see very clearly. Sometimes he does not see everything." Sidonie forced herself to turn, to look at him, to shape her lips into what she remembered must be a smile. If she did not, then she knew that he would go on talking. If he continued, then she might find herself believing what he said.

"It does not matter. There is nothing to be gained from discussing it. I am very tired and I need to be alone. Good night."

"Aren't you going to ask me the question?" There was an undercurrent of astonishment in his tone, as if he were as surprised as she to find himself speaking.

She did not want to do it. The words would taste like bile. They would burn her tongue like acid. But if she did not say them, then she had lost; Tal had won and all that she had endured was wasted. Besides, a secret shameful part of her mind whispered, perhaps this time he will say yes.

He said no.

Chapter 34

❧❦❧

Several days later, Matthew remembered the midwinter festival. He had dismissed any idea of attending, for it seemed far too normal and pleasant a thing to be possible in his strange prison. Yet why shouldn't he go? he asked himself, moving to the window to stare across the lake at the gap in the trees that signalled the trail.

Surely after the madness and tension of the last week he was entitled to some small measure of pleasure, some semblance of escape. It could hardly matter to Sidonie what he did, as long as he came back before dawn. The truth was that she might prefer his absence. They had returned to the pattern established before the arrival of the other vampires. She once again cooked dinner and sat across from him as he ate it. Yet some essential thread in the fragile weave of peace between them had been broken. She said little and responded to any comment that he dared with formal economy. When he finished eating, she asked him the question quickly and then retreated into her sitting room. It had no door to close but the message was clear, her desire for solitude unmistakable.

If the situation had been different, he might have found

some amusement in the reversal of their roles. Now it was she who retreated into sullen sorrow while he struggled to maintain a façade of normalcy in their interaction. He knew that Tal and the other vampires had stirred that unhappiness in her, along with whatever had happened the night they left and she returned to the house covered in blood. He also knew that those causes were minor compared with his own responsibility. While she had been prepared for whatever wounds Tal chose to deal her, the ones he had inflicted seemed to have caught her unguarded.

His own guilt had caught him by surprise as well, he acknowledged. She was his death. It should hardly matter to either of them that he had put that death on canvas. She should not be surprised that he saw her as monstrous. It should not concern him that she found that depiction painful. Yet his halting apology had been honest; what he painted was true but it was not the whole truth. She was the inhuman, perversely compelling instrument of his doom…but that was not all she was. That was the most frightening truth of all.

He turned from the window and finished cleaning his brushes. He was tired of thinking. What he needed was the noise and heat of humanity, the smell of smoke and sweat, the taste of food made by mortal hands and liquor brewed in home-made stills. If he could never again have the late-night haze of a café, the jumbled, noisy darkness of a bar, then he could at least have one last night of celebration in the village. It was almost dusk. If he left now, he could be there before all the promised "home-made hooch" was gone.

Darkness caught him halfway there and in the wind in the trees, the crackle of brush, he heard all the promised terrors of the North. He brandished his lantern like a weapon and kept moving, pausing once or twice when he thought that he heard a following footstep echoing in the crunch of his own in the snow. At last, he saw a faint gleam of light through the trees and rounded the bend to the village. A great bonfire had been built in the centre of the town and dark figures moved back and forth in front of it. Pine branches garlanded the porches of the darkened cabins he passed. He saw a lazy curl of smoke, a white wisp against the night, emerge from Rebeke's cabin and paused. There was no other sign of life or light, however, so he went on into the heart of the village.

A child of indeterminate gender ran past him, shot him one wide-eyed glance over its shoulder, then dashed away. He heard laughter and lively music and his pace quickened. At last, the firelight rendered faces visible and he saw Helen in the curve of a young man's arm and Mother Rachel rocking at the edge of a porch. A silhouetted shape detached itself from the fiery backdrop and approached him.

"So you came," Joseph said. Matthew nodded. "She know?"

"I left her a note." Joseph's eyebrow lifted and Matthew laughed. "I am certain she is just as happy to be rid of me for the night. Now, Rebeke promised Mother Norit ran an excellent still. And no, I have no intention of turning back into a drunk."

Joseph snorted but led him to a table bearing an assortment of mugs, bottles and pitchers. "Help yourself." Matthew selected a mug that looked clean and filled it from one of the unlabelled bottles. He knew enough to keep the first sip exploratory. The liquor seared his throat.

"They gone?" Joseph asked, refilling his mug.

"Yes. Now that is something to drink to, believe me." They touched mugs and Matthew swore he saw something that resembled a smile on the other man's face. He decided that Joseph must be drunk. He also decided that, promises about becoming a drunk aside, he was going to do the same thing.

Halfway through the first mug of liquor, the curious stares of the children no longer bothered him. At the end of it, the careful glances of their elders did not either. The night air had lost the bitterness that had edged it most of the winter and the fire took away the rest of the chill. The food—deer and rabbit, bread and a smattering of vegetables—was hot and satisfying. After a while, the music drew him to the doorway of the large cabin closest to the fire. He could barely see the musicians through the whirl of dancers, but he could hear the beat of a drum and the scratchy tones of a fiddle. He found a place against the wall and unfastened his coat. Smoke wreathed the ceiling and the room smelt of sweat and tobacco.

After a moment, as the music died and the dancers stilled for a heartbeat or two, he saw Mother Norit enthroned in a shabbily upholstered chair across the room. Easing through the throng of bodies, he made his way to her side. Her face creased in a yellow-toothed smile when she saw him. As the music began again and the room reverberated with the stamping of feet, he crouched down beside her chair to shout a greeting. She grinned and put out her hand, grinned wider when he kissed it. She said something he could not understand and so settled for smiling and nodding.

"She says she is glad you are not a ghost," a voice said into his ear, and he glanced up to see Rebeke bent over him.

"Tell her that I'm glad about that as well."

She put her hand on his shoulder as she leaned over him to translate. The rough veil of her hair brushed his cheek. "She says that she is also glad you are not a drunk."

He laughed and lifted his half-full mug. It was his third. "Perhaps not, but her brew is very good."

Rebeke spoke and Mother Norit smiled to acknowledge the accolade. Another burst of speech and Rebeke leaned back. Her hand left Matthew's shoulder. He rose and looked at her. There was a flush of heat across her cheeks. He noticed the earrings of bone and feather dangling against her throat.

"She says thank you but says you had better stop paying her so much attention. People will think you are courting her and the old one might get jealous."

The words slipped beneath the fog of euphoria in his mind like a draught beneath a door. "If you would do me a favour, I would appreciate it," he said, leaning closer so that she could hear him.

"Of course."

"Do not mention her again." He met her gaze and saw the trace of pity there. Then she smiled and put her hand on his arm.

"Dance with me, city boy." Before he could respond, her touch had turned into a grip and she was pulling him out into the crowd of dancers.

"I don't know how," he tried to protest, but she just shook her head, caught his hand in hers and whirled him into the dance. The liquor spilled from his mug but no one seemed to care. A moment later, he did not either. The music throbbed in his ears, in his bones. With it filling him, with the rhythm driving him, there was no room for fear or doubt or regret. He banished the future to the darkness behind the alcohol haze and surrendered his mind to his body.

He lost count of the times his mug was refilled, though he felt no more inebriated. Perhaps he, like the rest of them, simply sweated it out in the dancing. His coat was long abandoned, the old white shirt pulled free. He danced with women other than Rebeke, women he did not even know, but it seemed that Rebeke was always there, her hair and skirt swirling as she moved. The musicians were magicians, sensing when the crowd tired and changing the tempo to allow couples to move in slow circles, arms entwined. Then, when heartbeats had steadied, the drum would pound faster, the fiddle wail and the entire cabin would shake with the rhythm of the dance.

When the musicians at last took a break, the room emptied as the weary, sweat-soaked celebrants sought the sweet chill of the night air. Matthew noted distantly that the fire had burned down to glowing ashes. Children no longer streaked across its glow or chased each other through the crowd.

"Come on," Rebeke said at his side, and before he knew it they were walking down the road, his arm around her waist.

"Where are we going?" he asked, even though he knew.

"We're going to find out what city boys are made of."

"I would like to qualify one point. I am not a boy." He felt her body shake with laughter.

"I am old enough to be your mother, city boy. Or at least your older sister. So I'll call you what I choose till it's proven otherwise."

He stopped, some semblance of sense slipping into the dizzy arousal he felt. "What about Sidonie?" he managed and she turned into the curve of his arm to look at him.

"What about her?" When he did not answer, she went on. "I got no use for what she wants and she's got no use for what I want." She sounded very sure, so sure that he pushed aside the dim, dream-memory of Sidonie's mouth against his and let Rebeke pull him forward.

Her cabin was cool, the fire he had seen hours ago having long since died. She lit a lamp and stoked it back to life again. Her home was much like Joseph's but not nearly as spartan. A thick fur covered the broad bed. Woven rugs warmed the floor and decorated the walls. Rebeke straightened and smiled. The cabin was very small. It only took him two steps to reach her.

They fell over the end of the bed, laughing between kisses as they struggled with each other's clothes. He submerged himself in her; the taste of tobacco and liquor in her mouth, the scent of her skin and its musky, salt taste, the sheen of sweat across the arch of her collar-bone, the weight of her breasts and the pale, sweet lines of childbirth on her belly. In everything, all the pleasure and the imperfection, that was real and solid and mortal.

In the end, it was not enough.

He rolled onto his back and stared up at the rough wooden beams of the ceiling. For the first time, he felt the chill in the air. His stomach twisted and a wave of despair surfaced through his drunken detachment. After a moment, he saw her hand lift and push away a strand of hair that lay across her lips. "I'm sorry." He hated the words, their weakness a mocking echo of his impotence.

"No need. It don't matter."

"It does. I wanted to make you happy." She laughed and shifted onto her side, propping herself on her elbow. He risked a glance at her and saw her smile with amused resignation.

"Don't you worry about me. I saw a star or two. If they didn't all go shooting through the sky, it don't matter to me."

"I wanted..." To make myself happy, he thought, but could not say the words.

"I know you did." She leaned over to brush her lips against his. "But not with me."

"Rebeke—"

"Hush, city boy." She sat up and leaned over the side of the bed to retrieve her shirt. He saw the firelight slip across her back, muscled with work and hardship. "Don't think about it. I'm going to go and have a dance or two more. If you're here when I come back, we'll give it another try. If not..." She shrugged on her shirt and buttoned it over her full breasts. Her teeth flashed in a grin and she flicked back her hair. "No hard feelings."

He left soon after she did, heading towards the path back to the house. He had left the lantern behind but the moon was full, reflecting on the snow. The journey was not easy, the darkness forcing him to concentrate on his steps, and he was grateful for the challenge. It kept him from thinking.

No light came from the house on the island. He hoped that meant that she was hunting. He did not want to see her, did not trust what he might say. Rebeke had been wrong about one thing: Sidonie might have use only for his blood, but she was taking everything else from him as well.

He trudged resignedly up the path and pulled open the heavy front door. It closed behind him with a betraying thump, very loud in the silence. He lingered in the foyer, removing his coat and pulling off his boots. As he straightened, Sidonie appeared in the doorway. "You are back," she said, and he could not help his brief, sharp laugh as she stepped back to let him pass.

"So I am. Were you waiting up? No one has done that for me since I was seventeen."

"Did you have a good time?"

"It was...educational, in its own way." The long walk home and the icy air seemed to have banished his inebriation but he found that he was suddenly very tired. He had to enunciate carefully to manage the words. He started to walk towards the stairs but was caught by Sidonie's voice.

"You could go more often, if you wished. I would not object."

"I don't think so."

"Why not? Were they impolite to you?" He turned to look at her. The firelight gleamed golden across her skin, now seeming to glow again with a light of its own. He no longer felt the old shock of dislocation when he looked at her. The unnatural bones of her face had become as familiar to him as his own. The indigo-black fall of her hair was silk over the velvet of her dress. A delicate necklace of gold filigree lay like a cobweb across her collar-bones. You wanted to…but not with me, Rebeke had told him. Who else then? That was the question he had avoided asking himself during the cold walk to the house. He would not ask it now.

"Why? If someone was, would you kill them?" The accusation was unfair, he knew. Nothing she had done or Joseph had said suggested that she had ever done them any harm. But once he had released them, he found he could not damn the flow of words. "No need to worry, they were kindness itself to me. Just like the people of a civilization my father once told me of, who chose one man among them to live like a god for a year and then tore out his beating heart when that year was done. The villagers did their best to make me happy. Give Matthew his last drink, give Matthew his last dance, give Matthew his last…" He caught the betraying word before it left his lips and turned away from her, heading for the stairs.

She asked the question as his foot touched the third step. He refused her on the fourth. He climbed the rest carefully and did not look back.

Chapter 35

She suspected that Matthew had been with one of the village women. It had been a long time since she had needed to recognize the cues, for her lovers usually were blind to any but her, but she knew them. They were there in the averted eyes, the odd air, half-guilty, half-angry, with which he spoke, the words he had left unsaid.

She was certain of it when Joseph arrived near dawn, bleary-eyed and hung over, bearing a selection of barely edible remnants of the previous night's feast. "Thought these would be of use," he said as they stood in the dark foyer.

He thinks I will be angry, Sidonie realized. That I will wreak some unexpected vengeance on the village for the crime of touching my chosen prey. She was saddened by the thought that he believed her capable of such irrational cruelty and disturbed to discover that she was angry. There was a part of her that wanted nothing more than to seize the man and shake from his taciturnity the who, and where, and how and how many times…

She found a smile somewhere but saw by the almost imperceptible narrowing of his eyes that it was edged in all the emotions she could not hide. "Thank you, Joseph. Now, you look somewhat the worse for wear. You should be home sleeping off the festival."

"Men can't help being men," he said after a moment, "any more than wolves can help being wolves." The odd, unnervingly sympathetic words shocked an uneasy laugh from her.

"That, my friend, is the oldest line in the world. As I should certainly know." The words did not take the wariness from his eyes and she put her hand on his arm in the lightest of touches. "You might be right. Now go on home. Everything is fine."

He shrugged, seeming to accept the assurance, and vanished down the path. Sidonie stood for a moment on the doorstep. She could not see the eastern horizon beyond the trees that surrounded the terrace but she could feel the dawn there, waiting.

She could hardly blame them, she supposed. Not Matthew for seeking mortal comfort, not Joseph for fearing for the safety of his people. She was a monster, a thing to be kissed only when seeking oblivion, a creature to be trusted only lightly. Sidonie stepped back into the house and closed the door. After two thousand years she knew herself very well. This was not the first time she had felt such a morbid self-pity. There were cures for it: the rest of a day or a century, a change of locale, the caress of a new lover. As there was only one of which she could avail herself, she went to the hidden entrance to her secret rooms. She would have to hope that rest would be enough.

In the end, the day's sleep restored some semblance of her humour. She thought, at least, that it would be possible to face the night. For once, Matthew was still asleep when she ventured downstairs. When he rose some time later, they met in the dining room as had become their custom. He was silent and distracted, saying little as he ate. In his shrugs and monosyllabic replies, his half-concealed unease, he reminded her of Joseph.

At last, with a sigh, she said: "Matthew, I know." The look of guilty surprise on his face at least seemed better than the expressionless façade that had preceded it. "I know that you were with someone last night. It does not matter."

"How did you know?" he asked carefully.

"No one told me, if that is what you mean. I know, that is all. It is nothing. It is only to be expected." She kept her voice light and casual.

"It does not bother you?"

"Why should it?" She had not meant to ask the question. It hung in the air between them, a sword that could turn to cut either way. Matthew set down his fork with careful precision.

"And if I went back?"

"Will you?" His gaze dropped from hers and his mouth bent in a brief grimace.

"No. I suspect it will be easier for everyone if I do not."

Sidonie bent her head to hide the foolish smile she could feel on her lips. "There, that is said. We do not have to discuss it again." She rose and crossed to the door, pausing to look back for a moment. "I am going to read for a while. You are welcome to join me, if you wish." As the door swung closed, she saw him nod.

Several hours later, he appeared at the doorway of her sitting room. She caught the fresh scent of turpentine and paint as she gestured for him to enter. He sat down in the chair opposite her and, after a moment, put his feet on the ottoman. He stared at the fire for so long that she returned her attention to the book in her lap. "Did you mean it when you told Tal that you would burn down the house?"

"Yes," she answered after a moment and closed the book, setting it on the end-table beside her chair.

"I thought that vampires could not rise in the day."

"It would be very difficult. A younger vampire could not do it at all. But with age comes some small immunity to the things that endanger us."

"Would it have killed you?"

"Most likely. If the fire did not, then the sun surely would. I could rise in the day—I could not necessarily survive it."

"So your life truly doesn't matter to you?"

"No," Sidonie said slowly, wondering how much of the truth she would tell him, how much of it she even knew. "And yes."

"That is not an answer."

"Cannot mortals hold two contradictory views at the same time? Cannot mortals value their lives yet be willing to throw them away in battle or in despair? Have you never longed for death, all the while knowing you could not bear to leave life?"

"Yes. You know that I have."

"That is your answer then." A faint, sad smile acknowledged her point.

"I cannot imagine living for two thousand years," he said after a moment.

"Every century is only years and every year is only days and nights. We live, those of us that survive, always in the present. Those the past claims soon lose their ability to function in the world. Those who think too much on the future go mad. Sometimes, when we grow too weary of our existence, we sleep for decades. Sometimes we forget things, as if our minds can hold only so many memories. I slept for much of the eighth century, for example, and remember little of the fourteenth. That is why I need my talismans, my books." She paused and looked down at her hands, her fingers pale gold against the dark leather of the book. She thought of Tirzah and the villa, high in the dusty hills above the rivers at the beginning of the world. "And some of us do not stand it at all."

"What do they do then?"

"What mortals do. Kill themselves. I knew one once." She turned her hands over and considered the lines on her palm, barely aware that she was still speaking. "She was older than I am now, older even than Tal. We shared a villa for a time. I saw her grow thinner, more remote with each night but thought it was no more than the melancholy that seizes us all at times. Then one day, my sleep was troubled with terrible dreams filled with horrifying screams. They were cries of unbearable anguish, as if not only a body was being tormented but a soul was being torn apart. When I rose at twilight, Tirzah was gone. Standing in the moonlit courtyard, I could hear her screams, as if the bricks held their echoes. I knew what she had done. She had sat in her favourite place by the fountain and let the sun come up around her for the first time in thousands of years."

"How did you know—"

"That she was dead? I knew, though her body had long since turned to ash and blown away in the desert wind." Sidonie blinked, shook herself and felt the wails fade away into the back of her mind. She looked up and saw Matthew watching her with uneasy fascination. "You must forgive me. There are things we cannot forget, even if we wish to."

"Have you ever been tempted to end it?"

The question dragged her back to the present and anchored her there. She knew that if he had not stepped from the dock he never would have had the nerve to ask her that and she never would have answered him truthfully. "Of course. More times than I could ever count."

"What stopped you?"

"Small things. Each time that I think *now it will be done*, some other thought will whisper *not tonight*. Not tonight because the moon on the ice is beautiful. Not tonight because a nightingale is singing. Not tonight because the breeze smells of jasmine. Not tonight because I have not finished that book. Not tonight because someone in a café just smiled at me. So I put it off for a tomorrow night that never quite seems to come."

The silence that followed her words was so long she almost reached for her book again, as distraction from the uncomfortable quiet. Matthew watched the fire from over his steepled fingers. At last, he looked at her again. "Tal said that he was not going to kill me but turn me." Though he did not ask it, she could hear the question in his voice.

"Turn you into a vampire."

"And he thought that would hurt you?"

"It would not have been a gift, it would have been rape. Just as it was with me. It would eventually have meant the death of your art." It was not precisely an answer but she knew she could not tell him the truth, could not explain the subtle cruelty of forcing her to see him as a vampire, an eternal mockery of her dreams.

"It would have meant that my blood was of no use to you."

"That too," she admitted. "But the price for immortality should never be paid without consent."

"Consent," he repeated. "By all means, let us be sure that Matthew consents to his damnation—one way or the other."

"I ask," Sidonie said sharply, stung by his tone. "Tal never would."

He turned away to contemplate the fire again, pulling his feet from the ottoman, drawing himself away from her. "I know," he said. "I also know that things are much different between us than between the other vampires and mortals. Whatever reasons you have, I thank you for that."

She accepted the grudging apology, sensing the thing that he had not said. Between all the carefully selected words was the reluctant admission that, if she had chosen, she could have enslaved him as the other vampires had their mortals. Though she had known that all along, had struggled against the urge to do so, it gave her an ambiguous pleasure to hear him acknowledge it. If he recognized her power—and her refusal to wield it against him—perhaps she dared to hope that he would not always see her as the demon of his nightmares.

His movement as he stood drew her attention back to the conversation. "I still have to say no."

"I know," she said, generous in her sudden optimism, and smiled.

Joseph brought the letter two days later. He left it in the drawer of her desk as always and she did not find it until after dinner, when Matthew had retreated to the library to read. Sidonie stared at the handwriting and postmark for a long moment before moving to the farthest angle of the window, the very edge of the light, to read it.

When she finished, she folded the letter carefully and tucked it into the pocket of the trousers she wore. Then she stared at the night for a long time. When at last she turned away and resumed her comfortable seat by the fire, she found herself struggling with the book she had begun, the text turning to incomprehensible scratches on the page. Frustrated, she flung it aside. It hit the hearth and fell to the floor with a thud. Matthew appeared in the doorway. "What happened?"

She gripped the arms of the chair and closed her eyes. "Will you give me your blood, even though you die of it?" After a surprised silence, he gave her the same answer as always. "Then I am going hunting."

She ran the hills for hours. She caught nothing, did not

even truly try. She heard the howls of the wolves rising
from the pine-scented darkness and stood still, listening to
them wail the desolation in her heart. At last, the itch of
the coming dawn between her shoulder-blades, she stumbled wearily back into the house.

The Hall was dark, the fire in the hearth dead. No light
came from the library or beneath the closed door of the
ballroom. She climbed the stairs, feeling as if they led to
an executioner's platform, knowing that the axe was in her
own hands.

Matthew's door was unlocked. She slipped noiselessly
into the room and lit the lamp on the dresser. Standing
over the bed, she looked at him for a long moment.
Asleep, he looked younger than his years, the lines of life
and strain smoothed away. Beneath the heavy blankets, she
could see the rise and fall of his chest. There was a sudden
pain beneath her breast, as if her heart were burning to ash
inside her. She said his name.

He came awake in a start, moving away instinctively
when he saw her. "Do not be afraid," she said and took the
letter from her pocket. "I brought you this." He took it
from her extended hand and then climbed warily from the
bed, wrapping himself in a brocade robe. With a pang of
painful humour, she realized that it had once belonged to
Christian. Matthew moved closer to the lamp and examined the open flap of the letter.

"It is from Gabriel," he said unnecessarily, turning the
envelope in his hands as if he feared to open it. She had
made no secret of the fact that she read all the correspondence from his family before she gave it to him. She said
nothing, simply moved to sit in the chair by the cold fire.
He unfolded the letter and began to read. She saw him
swallow hard. "I have to go."

"It is not possible."

"You know what the letter says. My father is dying. He

might already be dead."

"Then it makes no difference whether you go or not."

"You cannot mean that."

"Why not? Why should you expect any human senti-
ment from me?" She knew the bitter words were aimed at
herself, trapped as she was between choices that all seemed
destined to end in failure. He came to kneel beside the
chair.

"Sidonie, please. I have to go. I'll come back, I swear it.
I'll leave all my paintings here, so you'll know. I will not
say anything about you to anyone. I will make you any
promise you ask, if you will only let me go."

"Any promise?" she asked softly and looked down into
his face, shadowed by fear and resolution.

"Any price you name," he repeated and she knew that
he meant it. For a moment, she was tempted but she knew
that such a demand would be a coercion certain to render
his sacrifice meaningless. She would have his blood and his
life, but nothing else.

She should never have shown him the letter. She knew
that as well as she knew that she should refuse him permission to leave. He would have discovered the truth eventually, of course, and would have hated her for her deception
but by that time it would likely no longer matter. She
should have burned the letter and drowned the ashes.

From the moment she had not, her course had been
decided.

"You must return within the month. Write to me with
the date of your arrival and I will send Joseph to fetch you.
Do you promise me this?" The calm sound of her voice
astonished her. She could not have told from it how deeply
each of the words cut her.

"Yes."

"If you are lying, I will come to the city and find you. It
does not matter what I promised. I take it back. If you defy

me, I will kill your family, turn your friends into monsters and, in the end, I will have what I want. Do you understand?"

"Yes."

"Joseph will be back during the day. I will leave him instructions. He will wait with you for the train, if necessary. Take anything from the house or kitchen you think you will need."

"Thank you."

Sidonie looked at him for a moment. She felt the sudden urge to reach out, to touch him. She clenched her fist to keep her fingers still. He caught the motion and she saw him tense in automatic wariness. The embers in her heart flared in pain. "Come back to me," she whispered.

"I promise."

On the way down the hall, she could hear the rustle of clothes as he began to pack. It was nearly dawn. When she woke up at dusk, he would be gone.

What had been the use of her icy reserve, her noble self-control? All the times she had kept her smile remote, denied the hunger of her hands to touch him, dampened the seductive allure that was the power of her kind—all for nothing. It would have been better to be like Tal and Ysabel, to have taken what she wanted. Then at least she would have had *something*.

Tal had been right after all. He knew the world better than she, knew its bitterness and blind, uncaring cruelty. She had torn herself to pieces for the sake of a delusion.

She remembered her thoughts as she had knelt beside Matthew's bed the first night he had spent in the house. You will watch him ride away with your dreams turning to ashes and dust in your mouth. And now he was going, just as she had predicted.

Despite his promises, despite her threats, she could not quite make herself believe that he would ever come back.

Chapter 36

As the train moved on, Matthew felt the North begin to vanish behind him. Mountains melted into forest and then fields, and it was as if the mountains had never existed. The lines of the frozen valley and grey stone house grew hazy, transforming into an imaginary landscape of strange and perilous beauty observed from the safe distance of pen or paint.

He knew that it was still there behind him, waiting, but he let the alchemy of travel do its work. He allowed himself the luxury of celebrating the escape in which he had never been able to stop believing. In the five days of the journey from the house to the city's great rail terminal, he let the North fade away behind him, along with the echoes of the promises he had made in return for his release.

When he reached the city, he used the last of his money and took a cab to his father's house. There was time enough to go to his cold garret room, paid for these months with Gabriel's money, after he made certain that Simon was safe. Once that was done, he would deal with rest.

He climbed the stairs to the front door, carrying the

one bag he had brought back with him. Everything looked as he remembered it. As he reached for the knocker, he noticed a strand of black ribbon caught in its hinge. The end was ragged, as if it had been torn away from some greater decoration to which it had once belonged. Matthew felt the first cold fingering of dread. It was just Mrs. O'Brien, he thought, decorating the house for the holidays now past. She must have used the ribbon to bind a wreath to the door. It was black only because there had been no more festive colour available.

He let the lion's head knocker fall and heard the metallic thud echo inside the house. He was reaching to knock again when the door opened. Mrs. O'Brien stood there, unmistakably real and familiar, her hair tucked up in its customary circle of grey braids, an apron over her simple, sober dress. "Mr. Matthew," she said in disbelief.

"Hello. I came as soon as I could. Is Father here?" He stepped into the hallway and dropped his bag, looking automatically up the stairs towards the study. "Did he have to go back to the sanatorium? Gabriel was not very specific in his letter, he just said come as soon as possible because Father was ill. Did he have another attack?"

"Mr. Matthew—"

"If he's at the sanatorium, I suppose I will have to ask Peter to drive out. Or maybe Gabriel will be going soon."

His vision narrowed suddenly until he saw nothing but the stairs vanishing up into the darkness. A voice was babbling annoyingly and it took him a moment to identify it as his own.

"Mr. Matthew, I am so sorry. Dr. Donovan passed away last week." He heard the words and behind them the rush and groan of the great black wave bearing down on him. For a moment, it filled his ears, deafening him. The force of it carried him up the stairs, into the shadows. A voice buzzed somewhere below him but he paid no attention.

His father was dead. He knew what he should be feeling. Filial bereavement, decorously expressed, was what was required of him. He recognized the terrible weight of loss on his chest, the cold hand of grief around his heart. He knew the symptoms well, from their visits after the deaths of Raphael and his mother. He also knew that below them in the dark tide of emotion lurked the other feelings. Guilt twisted its knife, for he should have been here and was not. Rage sputtered and steamed, laying blame for his abandonment. Surfacing like a stubborn current was the worst of all: relief. If Simon was gone, then he did not need to die to save him.

I absolve you. He heard her voice, unexpected and unrelentingly compassionate. It was not blind forgiveness, he realized, but acknowledgement that very little in life was pure. If loss was shaded by guilt or rage or relief, that did not mean that the loss was not real. To give a colour depth required darkness. It did not negate red to add black, it only made it a different kind of red.

With that thought, the midnight wave receded. He was standing in the centre of his father's study, drained and shaking. He took a step towards the door, felt his knees give way and sat down abruptly on the worn sofa. He breathed the air full of the memory of his father; the dusty scent of old books, the faint tang of ink. He felt the first tears trace down his cheek. He closed his eyes.

Much later, he heard the sound of footsteps on the stairs and looked towards the open doorway. Gabriel appeared, still wearing his coat and carrying his silver-headed walking cane. "Matthew!" He opened his arms and Matthew rose and went into them. His brother's body felt warm and solid. After a moment, Gabriel drew back and looked at him. "Mrs. O'Brien called us—" Matthew became aware of Peter standing in the doorway. "And a good thing she did too. You look wretched."

"What happened to Father?"

"Another attack," Peter said, extending his hand. Matthew took it, held it while his brother patted his shoulder awkwardly. "He seemed well enough one day and then the next... The decline was very quick."

"I'm sorry I wasn't here. It took two weeks for your letter to reach me and another for me to get home."

"We waited as long as we could before holding the funeral. We were beginning to be worried. I was in favour of a search party." The careful lightness in Gabriel's voice did not dispel the sudden chill Matthew felt as he remembered Sidonie's veiled threats.

"It is just as well you did not. It takes two days on horseback to reach the house from the railway. You would hate it."

"It is good that you are back," Peter said. "There are a number of decisions that must be made—"

"Not now, Peter," Gabriel interrupted. "Mrs. O'Brien has generously made dinner, no doubt on the theory that a hot meal will solve all ills. I think that we should at least allow Matthew to eat before he is forced to think about those things."

"I agree," Matthew said, quite certain that he did not want to think about anything at all. Whatever decisions Peter had in mind, considering them would lead inevitably to the private ones he had been avoiding.

They talked of the funeral and of the tribute that had been held at the university. Peter told him of his latest business concerns and the health of his family. Gabriel added the most recent gossip from the theatre and art circles. Matthew said very little.

"So," Peter began, a spoonful of Mrs. O'Brien's cake halfway to his mouth, "I assume that this business with... that woman...has been settled."

"Not yet."

"Not yet? Did she change her mind and ask for money after all?"

"She never wanted money," Matthew said carefully. Peter snorted in disbelief.

"Very strange. I cannot imagine why on earth she would want you to stay there for so long. Still, here you are. So it must be over." Peter looked up sharply. "You did discuss this before you left, I hope. You did not simply run off and make her angry."

"One can hardly 'run off' up there. If one could, I would have done it long ago."

"Just as well you couldn't then. If you had done that she would have exposed Father."

"Father is dead," Matthew pointed out.

"His reputation isn't. The university is naming the chair for him. There are to be scholarships in his name. It would be a terrible scandal if those unfortunate facts came out now."

"We should tell the university ourselves then, before they do all these things in Father's name. They would keep it secret, if only to protect their own reputation."

"Everything has been announced. It is too late to change it. We cannot allow a scandal. Father would be disgraced."

"He's dead!" Matthew found himself halfway from his chair before he could stop himself. He sat back down slowly, aware of Peter's annoyance and Gabriel's unconcealed curiosity.

"We are not," Peter replied and returned his attention to his cake in a manner that suggested he considered the matter finished. Matthew gripped the arms of his chair.

"So that is what this is really about. Not Father's reputation at all, but yours. To have a parent who cheated his way into society would hardly be a good reflection on you. Well, I might have been willing to die for Father's sake but

I am damned if I am going to do it for yours."

"What on earth are you talking about?" Peter demanded. "No one is expecting you to die. Good God, give me that woman's address and I'll settle this myself."

Matthew fought the hysterical laughter bubbling in his throat. "You do that, brother. You go and offer her money or honours. I will be fascinated to hear what she says." He heard her voice so clearly that it seemed she was in the room with him, asking the question he dreaded. He imagined Peter trapped in the cold prison of the house, sitting across the table from Sidonie, forced to confront the inevitability of his death again and again. His malicious amusement died suddenly, falling away into something that felt perilously like longing.

"If money and recognition aren't enough, what *does* she want?"

"Everything," Matthew said wearily. "She wants everything." His grip on the chair loosened and he stood up. "I'm very tired. I want to go home. Can we discuss this some other time?"

"Of course." Gabriel rose, forestalling any comment from Peter. "But you cannot go back to that appalling room tonight. I am certain that the landlord has been storing ice in it. You must come and stay with me."

Matthew shrugged, too tired to resist. When Gabriel wanted something, he generally got his way. That he had some motive beyond kindness was certain but Matthew did not care. He allowed himself to be collected and steered from door to cab to door to bed. He fell asleep as soon as he pulled the silk-smooth sheets of Gabriel's guest bed over his body.

In the morning, he donned the robe that Gabriel had left him and ventured out into the apartment. His brother had redecorated the living room in the months he had been gone. The walls were now brick red and there was new furniture of rich wood, carved in lush, swooping shapes. The door to Gabriel's bedroom was closed but Matthew could hear a clatter from the kitchen. His hand was on the doorknob when he heard a voice behind him.

"Don't go in there. You'll scare the maid to death." He turned to see Gabriel leaning in the doorway of the dining room. His silk robe was even more extravagantly patterned than the one he had lent Matthew. "There's tea in here. Breakfast will be ready in a few minutes."

"What time is it?"

"Almost noon." Matthew settled into one of the comfortably padded chairs set around the circular table and accepted the offered tea. Gabriel might feign disgust at the late hour but he knew that his brother rarely rose before noon himself. The maid arrived a few moments later, bearing a tray laden with pastries, fruit and two omelettes.

When the food had been consumed and the dishes consigned to the kitchen, Matthew leaned back in the chair and took another sip of fresh tea. "You shouldn't mind Peter. You know how he is," Gabriel said. "Father's death hurt him a great deal but he has to bluster and order everyone else around in order to prove that it didn't."

"I know. It is only that this time, he has no idea at all what he is talking about." He managed a smile and saw Gabriel return it. The speculative gleam in his brother's eye made it clear that the discussion would not end there. Matthew took another sip of tea and contemplated the painting on the opposite wall. With a sense of dislocation, he recognized it as one of his own.

"Are you going to tell me what happened to you up there?" Gabriel asked.

"What makes you think anything happened?"

"Let me see. You write three letters, quite lovely examples of grammar-school construction I might add, that say exactly nothing. You look terrible, if you don't mind me saying so. I can't imagine the last time you had your hair cut—"

"I apologize that I do not meet your sartorial standards. The North is a somewhat less formal place than the city," Matthew interrupted.

"That is not the point. You look as if you have been awake all night for months and had not one moment of pleasure to show for it. You look...haunted." Gabriel pounced on the word with triumph.

"I am perfectly healthy, as far as I know. I have been eating. I have even been getting exercise. What else could you want?"

"The truth," Gabriel said, refusing to be diverted. "Come now, this is Gabriel, not Peter. I don't imagine that he heard a single thing between the lines of what you said last night but I did. You did not stay there of your own will, did you?"

"It was the price of protecting Father," Matthew admitted carefully. "And it is not an easy place to leave."

"What did she want? No, I suppose you do not need to tell me that. I can guess."

"You can?"

"Of course. You are not completely without the Donovan good looks, little brother." Matthew realized that Gabriel had assumed that he was Sidonie's lover. He started to laugh, heard the embarrassment in the sound, and stopped. "Don't look so shocked. She can't be any older than her early forties. I know for a fact that you have had your share of experience with women of a certain age, as the phrase goes."

"She is somewhat older than you might expect," Matthew managed, then remembered Sidonie saying the same thing during the time her true self was still hidden. The thought sobered him somewhat. "That sort of arrangement was never discussed." That might be true, but the visit of Tal and the others had made it vividly apparent that the tie between mortal and vampire was almost as erotic as it was bloody. He had managed to avoid wondering whether surrender to Sidonie would carry that price—or reward—as well.

"Good heavens, you look like a scandalized priest," Gabriel said, and to his mortified surprise, Matthew felt the heat in his face. He stared down at his teacup and heard Gabriel's laugh die away. "Then what did she want?"

For a moment he wanted to tell the truth, as if he were a child again and his older brother could somehow protect him. He sighed and set down his cup. "She was lonely, I suppose," he said. "She was tired of being by herself in her palace of ice."

"What is she like, this secret lover of Father's?"

Matthew ran his finger through a streak of spilled tea on the polished table. He had never thought about what she was like—what she *was* seemed the only thing that mattered. The standards by which one judged others' personalities did not seem to apply to her. "She is an excellent cook. She has an exquisite, if unusual, collection of jewellery," he began hesitantly. "She is intelligent and learned. She is honest even when it is not in her interest to be so. She is ruthless and sad and, when you least expect it, kind." He caught himself, aware that he had said more than he had intended.

"I gather that she wants you to go back."

"I promised that I would. I left my paintings there as surety. That was the price I had to pay to come home."

"If you refuse, will she expose Father's secret?"

"She might. She is certainly capable of it. She is capable of almost anything in pursuit of what she wants." Her threats against his friends and family tolled in his ears like a funeral bell. Despite that, he could not quite rid himself of the vision of her face as she asked him to come back, the resignation and sadness there.

"What will happen if you go back?" Gabriel's voice seemed very far away.

"If I go, then I think it is likely that I'll never come home."

"Will you go?" Matthew looked over at his brother.

"What do you think I should do?"

"To start, I think you should ignore Peter. Father cared about his reputation but not nearly as much as he cared about you. He would hardly ask you to give up your future for his good name. Peter will survive a scandal. It might even be good for him. As for me, well, you know what they say: any publicity is better than no publicity. There are only two questions you have to answer to know what to do." When Matthew looked at him curiously, he continued. "Do you consider a promise given under duress a promise that you have to keep?"

"I don't know," Matthew admitted. Gabriel pushed back his chair and stood up, collecting his cup of tea as he started towards the door.

"Well, I do have appointments to keep today. If you want to be off to that miserable garret of yours, you had best get ready." Matthew nodded and rose. As Gabriel held the door for him, he paused.

"What was the other question?"

His brother gave him a sad, knowing smile.

"I thought that was rather obvious," he said. "Do you want to go back?"

Chapter 37

The month that Sidonie allowed passed.

Peter, as executor of Simon's estate, made arrangements to sell the house. The proceeds of the sale, along with the rest of his assets, were divided evenly among the brothers. There was more money than Matthew had expected, certainly enough for him to afford better lodgings and a separate studio. He deposited his portion in the bank and forgot it.

His rooms proved as cold as Gabriel had promised but he was used to the chill. He bought painting supplies to replace those he had left behind and began to work with an energy that surprised him. The second night of his return, he went to the nearby café and found Paul, Andre and Jack sitting at their usual table. For a moment, he had the mad fantasy that they had been there since his departure, like automatic puppets in a play that needed an audience to proceed. Then Paul saw him and stood up, shouting his name, and the thought vanished in a celebratory round of embraces and a long night of carousing.

He fitted himself back into his old life, and if there were parts of him that no longer seemed shaped to the pattern he had known, he ignored them. If his friends noticed that the space they had left for him in their lives was not quite filled, they said nothing.

He did not keep track of the days but when the deadline passed, he knew it. He was not defying her, for that suggested that his inaction was a matter of will. He did nothing because it was simpler than deciding what to do. Peter badgered him periodically but in the end gave up, declaring that Matthew was no more reasonable as an adult than he had been as an adolescent. Gabriel avoided the subject with a delicacy that made it clear he desperately wished to discuss it.

Matthew worked, made the rounds of the bars and cafés, and slept. To do anything else would break the spell of inertia that he had spun about himself, would breach the wall of thorns that kept him safe from the competing, contradictory urges circling beyond it.

Late one morning, three weeks after the deadline, someone knocked on his door. For a moment, he froze, his brush poised an inch from the canvas on the easel before him. He had heard that knock before, more than once. It shattered his sleep, sending him staggering to the door to lean there waiting for it to sound again. It never had.

It is daylight, he thought and felt the twisted coil of fear and anticipation in his stomach unwind. He set down the brush and went to open the door.

Allegra stood on the tiny landing. "Good morning," she said. "May I come in?"

"Of course." He stood back to let her slip by him into the room. He had seen her several times since his return but always in the company of others. She had hinted, quite unsubtly, that alternative arrangements could be made, but he had always found a reason why accepting her invitation would be impossible. He should have known that eventually she would confront him about that. She was as accustomed as Sidonie to getting her own way.

"I have luncheon reservations at La Noiresse. I thought that you might care to join me."

"You came to take me to lunch?"

"Don't look so shocked, love. I assume that you still eat once in a while," she answered with a laugh, pulling her hands from the wolf-fur muff that sheltered them against the cold. Her black coat was trimmed in the same fur: it matched the extravagant hat perched on her head. She had cut her hair in his absence and the soft, golden waves ended at her jaw. Her porcelain skin was blushed with chill, dimming the contrast of the absurdly dark glow of her red-painted lips.

"I would be delighted," Matthew replied with pleasure tinged with relief. La Noiresse was very expensive and very good. More importantly, this invitation seemed to suggest that Allegra was not angry at him for refusing the others. He had the sudden, startling realization that losing Allegra's friendship was something he would regret a great deal. "Let me clean up here first."

She nodded and wandered over to settle on the bed as he began to clean his brushes and tools. "I like that," she said, and he glanced back to see her considering his work-in-progress as she removed the ridiculous hat. Matthew smiled, pleased, and let his eyes linger on the painting for a moment. Centred on the canvas was a glass of wine set on a table. The crimson liquid seemed to glitter, as if throwing back the light like faceted glass. Scattered at the base of the goblet were red gems, forming a necklace that glowed with its own light. At the extreme left of the painting, a hand resting on the table had been sketched, its whiteness now just the faint wash covering the canvas. "It is a shame that you did not bring any of your paintings back from the North. I think that the experience must have been good for you."

"My sketchbook is on the window ledge. You can look at it, if you like." It was a peace offering, the only thing that he could think to give her as a token of apology for the distance he had kept from her. He was rewarded with a brilliant smile that hung in his vision as he retreated behind the wooden screen to wash the paint and turpentine from his hands. If La Noiresse was the goal, then shaving was in order as well. It was several minutes before he emerged to hunt in his wardrobe for an ensemble that would minimize the maître d's inevitable disdain.

He glanced at Allegra, who was standing by the window, his sketchbook in her hands. "Well? Do you think that I improved, my muse?" he asked lightly, uneasy at her stillness and the unexpected vulnerability that he felt at the thought of his sketches exposed to her eyes.

"Oh yes," she said slowly. "I would say that the creator of these sketches had improved a great deal. Come here and I will show you." When he moved to her side, she flipped through the pages for a moment then held the book up to the sunlight. Matthew felt his stomach knot as the first of his sketches of the false Sidonie appeared. "You see the tentativeness, the lack of focus, in this sketch. It looks competent enough, of course, but none of the lines seem quite true. Then here—" The pale paper moved beneath her paler fingers. He knew what came next but it was still a painful surprise to see the stark, exaggerated lines of his study for the evil angel. "It is the same woman, now distorted beyond humanity. As if the artist wanted this face to bear the weight of all the evils men have ever ascribed to women and all the beauty that they cannot seem to resist."

"Allegra—"

"No. You asked me to play critic so now you must hear my judgement. Last of all, we have this." It was the last sketch before the white stretch of untouched pages began.

He had done it after Tal and the others had left, after Sidonie had seen his nightmare visions of her. "This is the same woman again, of course. That strange, inhuman look is still there. How odd it is that the lines here, in this fantasy, seem true while the ones in the realistic sketch do not. Yet there is no horror here. The artist has seen beyond fantasies of evil and dreams of beauty. There is a human soul in these eyes, a human sadness in the curve of the mouth." Allegra's finger touched the lines as she spoke. She set the sketchbook back on the window ledge. "Speaking as a critic, I would say that the artist has learned to see beyond the illusion of appearance, to see the true heart that lies behind the most grotesque imagining." She paused for a moment. "Of course, speaking as a woman, I would say that the artist has fallen in love."

"That is ridiculous."

"Is it? Then why do you spend every night in the cafés with your eyes on the door, as if at any moment you expect your most secret dream to walk through it? Why does your heart always seem to be somewhere else while your body laughs with us as if nothing is wrong? Why haven't you come home?"

"It is not love I'm expecting to see," Matthew said reluctantly. He had thought that he had concealed his fits of nervous vigilance from them. At odd moments, the memory of Sidonie would resurface and he would be unable to keep his gaze away from the door, expecting at any moment to see her framed there, exquisite and deadly.

"Isn't it?" Allegra asked, a faint frown of disbelief folding her forehead. "Very well. Then prove it."

"What are you talking about?"

"If it is your art that is lying and not your words, then prove it. Make love to me. Here and now." There was no flirtatious frivolity about her, not even seductive challenge. She watched him with serious, sober eyes.

"Allegra—" He looked away. His eyes clung to the absurd hat sitting on his bed, like a round, eyeless creature curled there. "The restaurant, the reservations..."

"They will wait." Matthew looked at her again. Images of Rebeke and his failure rose unbidden in his mind. If it happened again, it would be a sign that he did not want to acknowledge. Yet now he was not drunk and among strangers. He was in his own world again, with a beautiful, sensuous woman who had shared his bed without complaint dozens of times before. She was wrong about him, about the sketches. If she wanted proof of that, then he would provide it.

She made a soft sound as he caught her in his arms, pressed her back against the wall and kissed her. It felt like the culmination of a thousand nights of longing. A wild sense of relief swept him, desire rushing in its wake. It would work, he thought triumphantly. It would be as it had always been between them, as it had been in his dreams.

Her mouth slipped from beneath his and he pressed his lips to her throat. He could feel the wild beat of her pulse. She drew a long, ragged breath. When she spoke, her voice sounded thick. "Very nice. But you have to tell me..."

"Anything."

"Who are you really kissing?" With the words, something flared through his mind, a door opening into the darkness. It had never been Allegra in those dreams he did not allow himself to remember. It had been hair of midnight that slipped across his skin, blue eyes starred in gold that closed in ecstasy, a wide, hungry mouth that devoured his...

Matthew released her, stepping back so abruptly that she sagged against the wall. His hip struck the easel behind him and sent the canvas tumbling to the floor, tipping over his paint stand as it fell. He turned away, stumbling through the wreckage of his work until the wooden screen stopped him. He gripped the frame hard, to keep himself from flinging it across the room. He pressed his forehead against the wood and the pain was sweet and simple.

After a moment, the roar of blood in his ears faded. He could hear the floor creak beneath Allegra's step. "I was right," she said softly, at his shoulder. "I always am about these things." She stood there for a moment, as if waiting for him to reply. There was nothing he could say. The words would not shape themselves in his mouth. He could not deny it, could not accept it, could do nothing but cling to his flimsy wooden support as the flood swallowed him. "I said that I wanted to be your friend. I meant that. So as your friend, I tell you that you left more than your paintings behind. The only way to reclaim either is to go back." The silence that followed her words seemed to stretch painfully. "Goodbye, Matthew."

He heard the words, then the quiet click of the door closing. After a long moment, he loosened his grip on the screen and straightened up, turning around slowly. His painting was face down on the floor. In his frantic escape, he had stepped on the tube of red paint and it had spurted, bright as arterial blood, across the back of the canvas. He bent and stretched out his hand to the thick slash of colour. When he touched it, the paint clung to his fingers, as persistent as memory.

Chapter 38

❧

The next day, he wrote the letter and, after walking past the post office a dozen times, mailed it. It vanished into the vast metal postal chute without a sound. Once that was done, he felt a strange sense of relief. He could not change his mind now.

The rest of the arrangements were complicated by his family and friends' desire for explanations and his inability to provide them. Gabriel reluctantly agreed to store his belongings and did not ask why Matthew was giving up his room this time, even though his longing to know was clear in every line of his face. Peter promised him funds—a reasonable sum, of course—if the "bothersome woman" changed her mind and required money after all.

Paul, Andre and Jack badgered him, then gave up and settled for another drunken farewell. When Paul mentioned a second gift of nethys, Matthew politely declined. Allegra merely watched him with sympathetic eyes. He knew that even if he came back, his place in her bed was gone. Oddly this did not bother him—a place as one of her friends would be more than enough for him.

He paid for his own train ticket this time.

When the train stopped at Bitter Creek, he stepped out onto the snow-covered ground beside the tracks. As the train began to pull away, he had one moment of panic and almost flung himself after it to snatch at the rail of the final car and pull himself back into the world. He clenched his fingers on the handle of his satchel and watched the end of the train disappear into the woods like the black tail of a serpent.

Matthew clambered through the snow to the sheltered spot where he and Joseph had camped, waiting for the train headed south. There was no trace of their fire. The snow had melted somewhat during the weeks he had been in the city. White no longer outlined the pine branches and he could see patches of dark ground on the far side of the track. With the sun warming his shoulders, he could almost believe that winter had loosened its grip on the mountains. The valley and the island must be beautiful in the summer. There would be a thousand places to set up an easel and... He thrust the thought aside. For one reason or another, he would not see the valley in summer.

He paced beside the tracks for two hours, his feet growing cold in the snow. Joseph was late. Matthew hunched his shoulders and pulled the collar of his coat tighter. Was it possible that Sidonie had not received his letter? Or had received it and decided not to acknowledge it, to leave him shivering by the side of the tracks until the cold claimed him or the train reappeared?

He stamped down the track towards the trailhead. He recognized it well enough, even imagined he could see the path trampled in the snow by their horses. There was no other way to the railway line from the valley. If he set off along the trail, sooner or later he would meet Joseph. It seemed a reasonable assumption but he knew that the forest and mountains were deceptive. It would be very easy for him to become lost. It would be very easy to freeze, waiting here, the other part of his mind argued. At the very least, walking would keep him warm.

With a sigh, he shouldered his satchel and started down the path. Following it proved easier than he had expected, though at each fork or turn he had to stop and consider his direction. At last, he emerged into a meadow he recognized from his other journeys. Above the far mountain, the sun had the dull red glow that signalled its descent. There was no sign of Joseph. Wearily, he trudged on until he reached the river. In the fall it had been little more than a creek. Now, fed by the beginnings of the spring melt, it rushed across the rocks in a wide band.

Matthew crouched on the bank and scooped a handful of icy water to his lips. He allowed himself to consider what he would do if Joseph did not appear. He had a little food in his satchel. He was certain there was a box of matches in its depths as well. Remembering the cold, uncomfortable journey out to the railway, he had bought a pair of good gloves and warm boots. None of these things would help him if he encountered wolves or catamounts or bears, of course, but there was little he could do about that. He had committed himself now; he had no choice but to keep on and hope that he did not become lost.

He found a semblance of shelter in a copse of trees and managed to light a weak, temperamental fire that seemed ever on the verge of extinction. He ate a little, donned his extra clothing under his coat, and found what comfort he could leaning against a fallen log. Catching sleep in the brief moments when the fire seemed strong and he forgot his fear of freezing to death, he passed the night.

At dawn the next day, he began to walk again. It was harder to keep his mind on the path, his brain fogged with weariness and cold. Once or twice he caught himself on the edge of a wrong turn and walked carefully for a while, until the exhaustion began to drain away his attention.

More than once he sat on a log or rock to rest and each time it took longer to rouse himself to motion again.

He survived the second night in the woods, sucking water from snow and consuming the last of his food. He could not keep himself awake to feed the fire and it was nothing but cold ash when he awoke. For a long time, he sat in the snow staring at it, thinking with a dry sob of Lawton's words: there is something to be said for freezing to death. Finally, he staggered to his feet and went on, telling himself that he refused to consent to that fate. To perish that way would render his hard-won decision meaningless.

The day drifted by in a haze of numb pain. He walked until his feet would betray him and he would slip or stumble to lie in the snow. Several times he closed his eyes, thinking that a moment's rest was all he needed, but each time a voice in his mind goaded him to his feet again.

He did not even see the plume of smoke rising from the patch of trees ahead of him until he had almost passed it. When he noticed it, white against the darkening sky, he stopped and stood swaying on the path. "Hello." The hail came out as a croak. He stepped forward, stumbling through the brush. "Hello."

A dark shape loomed in front of him and he stopped, blinking. "What the hell are you doing here?" a voice demanded.

"Joseph," Matthew said with a giddy laugh, staggering into the sheltered clearing. "You're late." Then he dropped to his knees beside the fire and closed his eyes. Someone shook his shoulder, thrust a flask under his nose. He took it and tossed down a gulp, welcoming the fiery liquid. He rubbed at his face with icy gloves for a moment and then looked at Joseph.

"You came back," the man said after a moment, his voice expressionless.

"Yes."

Joseph shook his head in astonishment and then gestured to the fire. "Rabbit be ready soon. You hungry?"

As they ate, Matthew discovered that Joseph had deliv-
ered his letter but had never received any instruction from
Sidonie about meeting him at the train. "Ain't seen her in
weeks," the man admitted slowly. "Left a note saying
Helen didn't need to come no more."

"Could she have gone away?"

"Usually says if she is but..." The man shrugged. Had
he missed her, Matthew wondered. Was she even now in
the city searching for him, carrying out her threats to
destroy all those around him? "Guess you'll see when you
get there."

"Yes. I suppose that I will," he said slowly, considering
what he would do if she was not there. He could, of
course, turn around and go home, but the thought of
another journey through the mountains did not appeal.
Perhaps he would spend a night or two with a roof over
his head and a warm bed to sleep in before he asked
Joseph to escort him to the track or the town. This time,
he would find a way to take his paintings.

In the morning, they rode on, Matthew on Joseph's
unhappy pack horse. The snow forced them to keep to the
lower passes, lengthening the journey by another night.
Mid-afternoon of the next day, they emerged from the
trees and Matthew saw the grey bulk of the house on the
island. At the edge of the lake, he dismounted and collected his satchel. Joseph handed him a rabbit, one of
those he had collected from his snares as they travelled.
Matthew took it carefully, aware equally of the absurdity
of accepting it and the depth of Joseph's optimism in offering it. "Be by in a day or so with whatever else I catch.
Don't figure there's much food left there."

"Thank you," Matthew managed, resisting the impulse

to say that he was hardly likely to require ongoing provisions. He put the rabbit, remarkably bloodless, in his bag and set out across the lake.

Some of the snow on the path and the terrace had melted. He saw no fresh footprints, no clue that Sidonie had passed this way on her hunting expeditions. The front door was unlocked. He pushed it open and stepped slowly inside. It fell closed behind him, sealing him in the cold, shadowy interior of the house.

He walked into the Hall, looking about carefully. Nothing had changed but there was a different air about the place. It seemed as it had that first night, empty and haunted by memories of old happiness long lost. The kitchen was barren, devoid of any sign of use, not a cup or forgotten plate left to betray a human presence. He put the rabbit in the pantry and saw that the shelves of food were dusty. A cobweb spread from a bag of flour to the wall. With a shudder, he abandoned the thought of a cup of tea and went upstairs to his room.

The room was dark, the curtains drawn. He lit the lamp on the dresser and then the fire. Dropping his bag to the floor, he surveyed the room. It smelt of dust and abandonment. The bed was unmade, just as he had left it. He remembered his strange fancy that life in the city had frozen, awaiting his return. He had been right about the image, perhaps, but wrong about the place. The house felt frozen, suspended in ice and silence, waiting. Waiting for dusk, he thought tiredly. Waiting for its ghosts to wake. He lay down on the bed. The pillow was cold beneath his cheek. Dust seemed to swirl above his head in the flickering firelight. He watched it with drooping eyes, the quiet cold encasing him like a fly in amber.

When he woke, the fire had burned out. Shivering, he climbed to his feet and went to the window, pulling back the curtains to see the moon floating over the mountains.

He tugged on his jacket and left the room, aware that the house seemed as quiet as before. It was well past dusk. Sidonie should have risen hours ago. Was it possible that she did not know that he was there?

The Hall was as empty as before. No light came from the sitting room. Matthew stood in the silence for a moment. "Sidonie?" he said softly. "Sidonie?" There was no reply. She is out hunting, he told himself. She will be back soon.

There was plenty to do, a stream of practical actions that kept him occupied. He lit the fire in the hearth, found the makings of a meal in the kitchen, made tea to drive the stiffness from his fingers. He ventured a glance into the ballroom and discovered it undisturbed, though as desolate as the rest of the house. The circle of tables and chairs remained, as well as the dressmaker's dummy in its funerary shrouds. Dust lay like a translucent film across the face of the canvases he had abandoned.

At last, he wandered from the Hall to the library to Sidonie's sitting room. He lit another fire there, eager to recapture some of the warmth the room had once held. As the blaze flared up and he rose, he noticed for the first time that the collection of ornaments had disappeared from the mantel. In their place stood the haunted triptych of paintings. Matthew felt his heart twist. Had she sat here, in the room that had once been her sanctuary, staring up at those fearful images of herself?

He looked at the paintings. He could remember their creation, the battle fought between perfecting his vision and denying it. Yet though he knew each brushstroke, each subtle colouring, it seemed that he saw them clearly for the first time. He wondered whether Sidonie had seen them as he did now, had seen the ambiguity betrayed at their heart. Or had both of them failed to recognize the true source of his fear of her? Not her ancient inhumanity, not even her terrible beauty...but what he sensed beneath both those things. The heart, the soul and the self that something in his own heart, his own soul yearned towards with reluctant longing.

He sank down into her chair. The small table beside it bore a book and a wine glass, all brushed with dust. She must have gone away. If she were still here, the house would not be so full of desolation and despair. He rose and paced across the room. The garden of herbs and night-blooming flowers was withered and brown. He saw her fingers moving among the green leaves, coaxing life and scent from them in their frozen exile from the sunlit South. He did not believe that she had left, despite the evidence of it, despite the sense it made, despite the sad, heart-rending look in her eyes when she had let him go.

"Sidonie." It was a whisper, growing to a shout. The walls echoed with it for a moment. In the painful silence that followed, he thought he heard a sound. He did not know what it was or where it originated. Part of his mind insisted it was the creak of the old house settling or the beat of the blood deep in his body. The rest, the greater part, insisted that it meant that she was there, if only he could find her.

Months ago, he had given up trying to find where she slept, having hunted more than once through rooms that held nothing but cobwebs and darkness. He had abandoned the search for fear of what he might have to do if he was successful. But he had no stake in his hand now...

He crossed the room again, considering the problem. There was a secret room somewhere, one with more than one entrance. He thought about the house, visualizing the architecture and floor plan in his mind. He thought of a madman building his castle, haunted all the while by secret hunger for his vampire lover.

It came to him with sudden clarity, so simple that he

realized he must have always known it. He started at the inner wall by the door, searching the bookcases, knocking on wood and plaster. Halfway around the room, he began to doubt, fearing his conviction was born of too many colourful gothic novels. All his prodding and poking, his knocking and twisting accomplished nothing. Finally, at the corner of the inner wall, he pressed his fingers over one of the carved roses that climbed the edges of the bookcase and heard a soft click. He stepped back and the bookcase swung outward.

He slid his fingers into the gap and pulled. It opened only a foot but it was enough. Snatching up a lamp, he eased into the dark hollow now revealed. A narrow hallway ran the width of the sitting room. There was likely an entrance from the stairwell on the other side of the wall as well. At the end of the corridor, he saw the dim shape of a twisted metal staircase.

The steps had been carpeted for silence and the joints were well oiled. The staircase led to a second hallway. He found the secret door and opened it into the dusty, funereal gloom of Christian's bedroom. He closed the door and climbed on. At the top, where the floor of the third storey would be, he discovered a trapdoor set in the roof above him. It opened without a creak. He took the last few steps carefully, easing the trapdoor back as he went. When he released it, there was no sound. Curious, he reached out and felt the softness of the thick carpet that covered the floor. He lifted the lamp and looked around.

Christian had built a suite for his lover, concealed above his own. Tapestries draped the walls and Matthew could see the dark shapes of furniture about the room. A fireplace was set along one wall. It must be connected to the one below, he thought, so that the smoke would mingle and no one in the house need ever know that a secret life was lived above their heads.

He moved carefully through the room. There was no sign of Sidonie. Beyond the fireplace was a closed door. For a moment, he paused there, his eye drawn by the curving patterns carved into the wood. Roses climbed the sides and vines coiled in serpentine patterns across the width of the door. Set in the centre of them he could make out the faintest outline of a face. Its serene, remote features were not Sidonie's but he knew that it was a portrait of her just the same, a portrait as mistaken as the ones that now stared out from the mantel of the sitting room. He put his hand on the knob, rough with the shape of a rose, and opened the door.

The first thing that he saw was the great, canopied bed. It filled the room, seemingly shaped of darkness, curtained in shadows. From where he stood, he could not see if it was empty. Lamp lifted, he moved forward. The light slipped between the translucent, fraying draperies and touched the bed. Thin fingers materialized from the shadows, then an arm, a shoulder. He saw her face and the lamp shook in his hand. Her head was turned towards him, the closed eyes lost in the dark sockets, her cheekbones turned to blades beneath her brittle skin.

Crouching beside the bed, he set the lamp on the bedside table and put his hand out to touch her wrist. "Sidonie?" His voice sounded thick, as if choked by cobwebs and dust. "Sidonie, can you hear me?" He slid his fingers beneath her still ones and gripped her hand.

In the flickering light, he thought he saw her eyelids flutter. He said her name again. The hand in his moved, fingers clenching weakly. Her eyes opened. A frown creased her forehead. "Matthew?"

"Yes." She blinked, as if testing her vision. Her hand lifted his and she stared at their entwined fingers for a moment.

"You came back."

"I promised that I would." He reached out hesitantly and touched her cheek. Her skin felt dry and smooth, like bone. "What has happened to you?"

"Nothing." Her voice sounded a little stronger and she moved to sit. He leaned over to push the pillows up behind her and she let him help her settle herself against them. The blankets covering her slipped away and he saw her collar-bone standing in sharp relief at the base of her throat. A thin white gown hung from her shoulders. Her face was a death's head, flesh stripped from alien bones until only the wide mouth held any hint of life.

"You look…" The words died in his throat. She smiled weakly.

"These things happen to us, sometimes. It is nothing."

"I was afraid the house had been abandoned."

"I have not been downstairs, out, in a few weeks, that is all. If I had known you were coming back," her voice shook and he felt her fingers trembling in his, "I would have taken more care."

"I wrote to you. Didn't you read my letter?"

"No. I gave up looking for it, you see."

"You didn't believe I would come back?"

"Did you?" she asked, a flash of her old self that made him smile despite the seriousness of the question.

"No. That is why it took me so long. But here I am. Joseph even gave me a rabbit to celebrate my return." She gave a thin laugh. "Now, no matter what you say, you are not well. Is there anything that I can do for you?"

The laugh was raw and painful this time. "Only what I have always wanted you to do." Her voice sounded bitter, as if she hated herself for saying the words but could not stop them. Brutally fair, he thought, just as she had always been. She would not exploit her weakness any more than she had used his. He looked at the ancient, inhuman face, half-turned from his.

"Yes," he said softly. For a moment, her face remained averted, the spasm of her fingers the only betrayal of emotion.

"What did you say?"

"I said yes." He saw her breasts lift with her swift breath. She turned her face into the light and her gaze met his.

"I can survive without it. Have Joseph bring me a live beast or two and I will be fine. This is not necessary to save me."

"I know."

"Then why?"

"I have done a great deal of thinking about this. I know that whatever you are doing, it is not what vampires usually do. I know that it has some purpose, though I cannot imagine what it might be. I know that it is possible that I will not die."

"It is most likely that you will. Do not delude yourself about that."

"I know. It doesn't matter. The truth is," he gripped her fingers and looked at her squarely, "I love you." Her eyes widened but he could not read whatever lay in the blue-gold gaze.

"Enough to die for me?" she said at last, her voice harsh.

"Yes."

She drew a long, slow breath. "Will you give me your blood to drink, even though you die of it?"

"Yes."

Sidonie reached out to slide her fingers into his hair. She leaned close and he saw her smile, voluptuous and tender and sorrowful at the same time. "Then kiss me."

"Yes," he whispered and gave himself up to the one magic that was older than even she, to the one siren song that he had never had any hope of resisting.

Chapter 39

At first, Sidonie was certain that she was dreaming. This dream had surfaced in her delirium more than once. It was not possible that this was real, that Matthew was here in her bed, kissing her with a desperation that tasted utterly new and painfully familiar. She feared that any move, any thought, might break the spell and spill her back into the cold world of loneliness and failure.

Yet her dreams had never been this sweet. In her dreams, the word love was never spoken. So they must be real: this touch, this whisper, this embrace that was so much more intoxicating than anything she had imagined. With that realization came the hunger, throbbing in time to the beat of his blood. It was a craving stronger than anything she had ever experienced, an ache that seemed to go right to the core of her. It entwined itself with her passion, feeding, for the time, from the same feast, satisfied, for the time, to taste only the same pleasure.

The moment came when desire was no longer enough. She sat back and looked at Matthew lying beneath her. He opened his eyes, then closed them slowly. She leaned down, her hand against his chest, feeling the heat of his heart beneath the skin. She found the vein in his throat. He groaned and wrapped his arms around her, holding her hard against him. The blood filled her mouth. Thought scattered and fled, swept away on the tide of ecstasy that filled her. Dimly, she heard her whimper of satisfaction, his moan of pleasure, of pain.

After a few moments, she felt his arms loosen and fall away from her. The heartbeat beneath her hand seemed to stutter. His blood tasted richer, sweeter than ever—the last of it always did. In another moment or two, his life would be gone. Yet she felt nothing, no change, no moment of epiphany. It was too soon, it must be. To know if it had worked, she would have to finish what she had begun. She would have to kill him.

Articulated, the thought burned like black fire through her mind. She felt her throat stop working, her mouth instinctively pull back from his flesh. Her body shaking, she crouched there, her mouth an inch from Matthew's throat, his heart beating weakly beneath her palm. Go on, her mind screamed. This is everything you have dreamed of, everything for which you have suffered and sacrificed. Take his life and take back your own! A terrible pain ripped through her, as if she were being torn in two.

She flung herself from the bed and collapsed on the floor, her hands over her mouth, her body racked with tears she could not shed. She could not do it, she realized in despair. She could not bear the thought of taking his life.

She could not do it because he was not the only one who loved.

She sat shivering on the floor for a long time, rocking slowly, holding herself against the pain that seemed to be clawing its way through her. At last, she crawled to the door and pulled herself to her feet. Stumbling to the stairs, she almost fell and had to cling to the iron railing as she descended.

The sitting room was dark. It seemed like a stranger's room, a place that offered no shelter, no comfort. Her head was aching, her body shaking from the shock of the blood and the pain of its loss. She found the chair and sank into it, pulling her shawl around her. She closed her eyes and let the sweet darkness of oblivion drag her down.

When she woke, she did not know where she was. Then memory flooded back, searing her as if the hours of her sleep had never happened. She gripped the arms of the chair and clenched her jaw, holding in the despairing scream she could feel buried in her throat. When it faded, she took a slow, shivering breath. She let go of the chair and wrapped the shawl tighter about her body. After a moment, she looked up at the sinister, seductive visions of herself staring out from the mantel.

Monster, she thought. Forever and always a monster. She put her hands to her mouth and held in a moan. She had thought that she was so clever this time. She would not frighten him, would not seduce him, would only exert inexorable, subtle pressure until he at last, of his own will and without madness, gave himself up to her. Yet she knew now that it would not have been enough.

Matthew had found the answer she had never even suspected. If she had continued what she had begun, had drained his body of its last life's blood, her oldest dream would have come true. She knew it in her bones, in the wild part of her that still cried out for that salvation. Simple surrender was not, had never been, enough. The secret that had eluded her during all the other attempts was love. The blood must be given from love: not from fear, or lust, or madness, or even reason. Such a love could not be wooed and seduced or given to an illusion. The giver must know everything she was and love her anyway.

No more than a handful of mortals in two thousand years had been capable of that. None of them had been among the few of whom she had asked the question. It might be centuries before she found another mortal who had the courage to love her. That thought was terrible enough. Worse, far worse, was the knowledge that she would no doubt love them back, as she loved Matthew. She would no more be able to murder them than she had been able to take his life.

She would have to give up the quest and admit that Tal was right. The dream that had haunted her for two millennia was nothing but a curse, a perverse trick as dark and cruel as the one Tal had played on her in the ruins the night he had transformed her. She understood with sudden, frightening clarity how important her belief in it had been to her. Though she had lived generations without actively pursuing it, it had always been there in the back of her mind, a promise that she could make good when she wished. She had wasted years and lives on a sad fantasy and now she must acknowledge the truth. She was a vampire and would be a vampire until the end of time.

Sidonie leaned her head back against the chair and closed her eyes. It was not so hard a thing to be, after all, she told herself. She was quite accomplished at it. She had survived for two thousand years; no doubt she could live two thousand more.

Damn him, she thought bitterly. Why hadn't he defied her and stayed in the city, forgetting her except in dreams? Her pain at his loss had been dull and cold, a slow, reptilian basking in despair, all sensation numbed. It had been misery but it had been bearable. It was nothing at all to the anguish she now felt. Better for her that he had died on the jagged back of the mountains, dragged down by wolves, buried beyond recovery by an avalanche. Then he could not have awakened her, brought her back to the world with a kiss, opening the thorns inside her, leaving her helpless as they tore her apart.

There was an itch behind her eyes. At first she thought that it was shadow-tears, the old memory of pain that she could no longer express, but then she knew that it was the coming of the dawn. It was time to seek the shelter of her room. She shivered. If Matthew was still alive, she would have to remove him. If he were not (her mouth crumpled in pain at the thought), well, it would not matter if he shared her bed or not.

She put her hands on the edge of the chair and pushed herself to her feet. She had taken three steps before she realized that she was not heading for the staircase but for the Great Hall. In her dull surprise, she kept walking.

At the foyer, she paused for a moment. Her nerves were burning, symptom of the sympathetic magic that bound her to the rising sun. *Are you certain of what you are doing?* a voice inside her head asked, and for a moment she was afraid. She wanted to run back to the safe darkness of her rooms, pull the covers over her head and lie there forever, sealed in the shadows.

But she knew that, for her kind, forever was not a metaphor. Forever was a curse. There was another voice whispering in her head now. It was older than her fear, as old as her empty dream. She knew it well, though it had never been so clear.

Now, it said clearly, *it is now.*

Always before, it had also taken back those words. But she knew that it would not do so this time. There was no reason to do so. She had nothing left but the wreckage of the old dream that had sustained her and the raw ache of the new love that would end in loss, just as all her loves had.

"Yes," she said and opened the door.

She stepped out onto the terrace to greet the dawn.

Chapter 40

Matthew opened his eyes to utter darkness. For a moment, he thought that this featureless black, unshaded by any tone of grey, must be the colour of death. Yet if he had died, why was he cold? Why did his throat hurt? He swallowed and reached up to touch the right side of his neck. His flesh stung beneath his fingers.

He was alive. He closed his eyes again, lost in the sudden rush of emotion. When he reached out, he discovered that the bed was empty. "Sidonie," he said softly and sat up. His head spun, sparks whirling in the black before his eyes, and he had to remain still for a moment. He moved carefully then, searching for his clothes. His shirt he found in the tangle of sheets, his jacket and shoes on the floor. Dressed, he risked standing and fought another rush of groggy nausea.

He could see nothing at all. There was no light for his eyes to use. He groped blindly to the door of the bedroom and then through the other chamber, dropping to his knees to crawl when he feared that he was close to the open trapdoor. At last his outstretched hand met nothing but air.

He rested there for a moment, before risking the stairs.

His head throbbed and his limbs felt filled with lead. She had almost drained him. He fought a shudder, a reflex of horror stirred by the memory. At the time, he had felt no fear at all, only dizzying pleasure. He knew how close he had been to death. His drug-driven plunge into the lake had been nothing but a foot upon the stairs, he knew now. Last night, he had stood on the threshold and would have let her take him across it.

But she had not.

He stirred and started down the stairs, wondering how long he had lain unconscious. He felt as if he had slept for hours, though that could not be. If it were true, it would be nearly dawn and Sidonie would surely have been sleeping safely beside him.

At the base of the stairs, he noticed for the first time that there was a wide column of light emerging from the entrance to the sitting room. As he stumbled towards it, he felt the first stirrings of dread. He was certain that he had closed the door behind him. He was equally certain that Sidonie would never leave it open.

The light was weak but steady, not flickering as would a fire's glow. He knew light, had spent years learning to use it. Even before he pushed his way into the sitting room, he knew that it was daylight that he saw.

Matthew caught his breath to call her name. The scream took it away. It was a cry of heart-rending anguish, the voicing of a pain that was beyond his imagining.

He ran to the Hall and saw the square of light that lay across the carpet, the betraying sunlight turning it to crimson and gold. He froze for a moment then turned to look out the open door. The terrace was empty except for the last lines of snow. He forced himself to move, to step to the edge of the doorway. A thousand terrifying images ran through his mind as he looked out across the terrace. He imagined Sidonie's body burning in the sun, her flesh melting from her bones, a scatter of charred ash blowing away in the wind.

She was on her knees, her back bent until her face seemed pressed to the stone. Shudders ran along the line of her spine and he could hear her broken sobbing. He rushed forward, ready to snatch her up and drag her back into the sheltering darkness. Four feet from where she huddled, he stopped uneasily. None of the things he had feared were happening. No flames consumed her, her body did not look as if it might crumble to ash at a touch. Only the racking sobs that shook her gave any clue to her pain.

He crouched down carefully, trying to see the face that was shielded by her hair and hands. He was about to say her name when she sat up slowly. Her hair still veiled her face but he saw her hands slip away. She extended them, turning them in the sunlight. He heard her ragged breathing, a soft "oh" of amazement. She lifted her face, her fingers moving back as if to protect it. She looked at the sun, just visible above the mountains. "Oh."

"Sidonie?" For a moment, he thought that she had not heard him, enraptured by her contemplation of the sky. Her head turned slowly and she looked at him. Her hands fell from her face. Matthew caught his breath in disbelief.

The gold in her eyes was gone, replaced by the bright silver of tears. Her mouth was still wide but the jaw around it was no longer unnaturally narrow. The sharp angles of her cheekbones had softened. The honey-toned skin was flushed with cold and sheened with tears. She looked like, and yet profoundly unlike, the Sidonie who had opened the door to him the night of his arrival. "It worked," she said, her voice shaking and bewildered. "I don't understand...I didn't kill you...but it worked."

"What worked? What happened?" She did not seem to hear him but looked distractedly back at her hands. She stretched her arms out into the light and then gazed around her.

"It is so beautiful. I had forgotten that the daylight was so beautiful. Look how green the trees are...and the sky...oh, the sky..." Her voice trailed off into a sob. She stared upward, tears falling from her open eyes. She was shivering in her thin gown. Matthew could see the pattern of goosebumps along her bare arms.

He moved forward and reached out, half-afraid that if he touched her it might shatter her or the spell that protected her from the sun. He could not take his eyes from her face, awed by the transformation. When his fingers brushed her arm, she looked at him. Her eyes were red-rimmed with weeping. He saw that there were delicate lines at their edges now and the corners of her mouth. There was a thin streak of grey in her heavy black hair. "It's cold," he said very gently. "Come inside and tell me what happened."

Her gaze dropped to the place that he had touched her. She rubbed her palm across her skin in fascination. "Cold. It feels so strange to be cold."

"Come inside—"

"No!" The refusal was vehement, as if she too feared that whatever magic held them might vanish if she left the sunlight.

"Very well. I'll get your coat. Stay here." He retreated to the hallway and retrieved both their coats. Donning his own, he returned to her side and draped hers over her shoulders. She pulled it close and he noticed for the first time that her feet were bare. He crouched and touched her arm carefully. "You must stand up. You will catch your death on these cold stones."

"Catch my death," she repeated then began to laugh giddily. Matthew tightened his grip a little, pulling her to her feet. She did not resist when he led her to the old stone bench beneath the library window. As he sat down beside her, she shivered and looked at him, as if truly seeing him for the first time. "How are you?"

"I feel as if I almost died," he said honestly. "I thought that I would."

"I could not do it. That is what I do not understand. I was so certain that if I took your life then the prophecy would finally come true. When I could not kill you, I thought that I had lost any chance of ever succeeding."

"I think that you will have to start at the beginning," he said, stilling the thousand questions that he knew would only lead to more if he asked them. She nodded and looked out at the mountains. For a moment he thought she was caught in the spell of the daylight again, then she began to speak.

"I told you how I came to be a vampire and of the madness that followed my transformation. I only returned to sanity through the kindness of a hermit that I met in the barren hills. He was mad himself, I suppose, mad with the love of his god and his hunger to be scoured clean of anything but that love. He had lived alone in a cave for decades when I met him. I was ready to take his life as I had so many others, but when he saw me he made the sign of his god and wept for me. Not from fear or to plead for his own life but for the pain he saw in me. Some remnant of my humanity must have reawakened then for I could not kill him. Instead, I left him and found a place to dwell not far from his shelter. I would have let him be, but he would not do the same for me." She raised her hand to wipe away the tears on her cheeks then stared at her damp fingers for a moment with distracted curiosity.

"He knew what I was though he had no more knowledge than I about what being a vampire meant. He believed that I had been cursed, by his god or some other. He prayed for my salvation. He tried to exorcise me, in case some demon had taken possession of my soul. He begged me to give up my evil nature but I had no other nature left. He even suggested suicide, as the lesser of two sins, but I could not surrender my existence. I think that he came to see my redemption as the test he had been set to prove his devotion to his god. At last, he went into the desert below the hills to fast and pray.

"After a month, despite the danger, I went after him. I found him dying beneath a twisted juniper. I carried him back to his cave and sat beside him while he raved, calling for his god in his fever dreams. Then one night, I saw his eyes clear. I know that he saw me, knew me. He said my name and took my hand. 'My god has given me a vision,' he whispered. 'There is a way to cleanse your soul and find your lost humanity. For you to be whole again, you must first purify yourself of the blood of men. Then you must take what you desire from a mortal who gives it to you in perfect freedom and perfect slavery, who is prepared to die for you. You cannot take it without consent—you must ask for it each night, no matter how often you are refused. You must follow the instructions of my god, my lost angel, and believe.' After these words, the glaze of delirium fell over his eyes again and, when I rose the next night, he was dead.

"For many centuries, I did not believe him. He was a mad, dying man and I...I revelled in my new life. My humanity had been taken from me and I did not want it back. When I foolishly told Tal what the old man had said, he dismissed it and mocked me for even remembering such a thing." She fell silent for a moment. The distant expression that he had come to recognize from her reminiscences settled on her features.

"But you did believe it," Matthew prompted gently and Sidonie nodded.

"There came a time that I hated what I was. I thought

that I would try to fulfil the conditions of the old man's vision. What had I to lose, after all? I found a young man, a priest, and took him captive. After a week, he consented from fear, desire and a secret hunger for martyrdom. I drained away his life and nothing changed. I tried again and again over the centuries, always failing yet always clinging to the hope that it might be possible."

"Why did you want my father to come here?"

"I knew that he had loved me once, in a fashion. He owed me. He was a rational, sensible man. Consent won by coercion, fear and desire had never worked. I thought if I gave him the choice and did not harm him, eventually he would see the inevitable logic of submission."

"No wonder you were unhappy when I arrived instead."

"I almost let you go but I could not bear to lose the chance. I had gambled so much on this. So I did what I had to do."

"Until you let me leave." She sighed and glanced away.

"Yes. Even though I knew that you would not come back. I would not have come after you, you know. I could not bring myself to be so cruel, though I knew that I should. I was so wretchedly unhappy when you left. It was unbearable to be awake, all alone with the knowledge of my failure. Eventually it seemed easier to sleep than to live." He saw her take a deep breath and push her hair back from her face with both hands. "But you came back and willingly gave me what I wanted," she said, her voice shaking. "You did it out of the most perfect freedom and perfect slavery imaginable. I could feel the change waiting inside me as I drank your blood. I knew the secret dream I had held onto for two thousand years would finally come true—and I let it slip away. I realized that, even if such a chance should ever come again, I would only fail once more. There did not seem to be any reason to go on, knowing that I was doomed to be a vampire for all eternity."

"So you walked into the sunlight, thinking you were going to die," Matthew finished and she nodded. "But you lived."

"I know. I do not understand why." He looked at her for a moment. Her face looked familiar to him now, though it was neither the one he had first known nor the one he had feared and then loved. It had none of the false Sidonie's youth or strange, undefinable blankness. Traces of the vampire Sidonie remained in the too-wide mouth and sharp, elegant bone structure but the otherworldliness was gone. It was no longer the face of an alien sphinx untouched by time but that of a woman, blessed with the texture and tracery of experience, the weight of wisdom and sorrow and life. It was the face of her soul, he thought suddenly. He felt the sudden urge to retrieve his sketchbook and set his fingers to work at capturing this new, infinitely more complex beauty.

"Why did you let me live?"

"Because," her hands knotted in her lap and her gaze dropped as if she were contemplating them, "I loved you too much to take your life."

He looked at his own hands. He swallowed once. She had not said the words before, not even to whisper them while they lay in the dark bower of her bed. He had not expected them of her. He had known quite clearly what she was—and that what she was did not feel love for mortals.

"Did the old man say that you *had* to kill the one who consented?" he asked after a moment, when the leap of his heart had settled somewhat. She shook her head.

"No. He said that I had to take what I most desired…" Her voice faded and he saw her face go suddenly still. "I see," she whispered. "I understand now. How could I have been so blind?"

"Sidonie?"

"How simple it all was...and how unlikely. Not only did I have to find a mortal who loved me enough to die for me, I had to love him enough that what I wanted most was for him to live. I had to be prepared to sacrifice my life for his." She stopped and he thought that she would weep again, then she took a slow breath and straightened. The silence lingered for a moment. His hands itched to touch her, to trace the curves of her new face, to warm the chill from her vulnerable new flesh. He kept them at his side, aware of how brittle her composure seemed. Some of the joy seemed to have seeped from her face and he wondered if she already regretted what she lost, finding the prize not worth the price she had paid for it after all.

"How does it feel to be mortal?" he asked carefully.

"It feels...strange," she admitted. "It changes everything."

"Does it?"

"I think it must." She glanced at him, her gaze guarded. "I am not what I was. All of that is gone forever." There was a question buried in the words but he could not quite determine what it was she feared so to ask. "I am not the vampire with which you fell in love."

"It is not the vampire that I love. It is you. It is the soul, your soul, that I finally learned how to see underneath the vampire's skin."

"I do not look the same," she said, frowning slightly. "I can tell. I will grow old, just as mortal women do."

"And I will not, I suppose?" He took her face in his hands. Beneath the chill left by the winter air, he could feel the heat of her mortal flesh. "You are," he said softly and kissed her mouth, "the most beautiful woman I have ever seen." She put her arms around him and he felt the warmth of her breath against his throat.

"I am afraid," she confessed in a whisper.

"So am I." He closed his eyes and leaned his cheek

against her hair. The sunlight was warm on his eyelids.

"My hands are cold," she said with interest. Matthew laughed and stood. He held out his hand.

"You are most definitely human now. Come inside."

"Will you warm them for me then?"

"Forever," he promised. She smiled and took his hand.